To Marcy, with Love

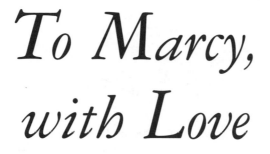

To Marcy, with Love

A NOVEL

Henry Denker

WILLIAM MORROW AND COMPANY, INC.
New York

It is the policy of William Morrow and Company, Inc., and its imprints and affiliates, recognizing the importance of preserving what has been written, to print the books we publish on acid-free paper, and we exert our best efforts to that end.

Library of Congress Cataloging-in-Publication Data

Denker, Henry.
    To Marcy, with love : a novel / Henry Denker.
       p.   cm.
    ISBN 0-688-14612-0
    I. Title.
  PS3507.E5475T6   1996
  813'.54—dc20   95-37577
                                                  CIP

Printed in the United States of America

First Edition

1 2 3 4 5 6 7 8 9 10

BOOK DESIGN BY SUSAN HOOD

TO EDITH, MY WIFE

I wish to express my deep gratitude to those who have so generously shared their expertise, their experience, and their time with me to make this book as authentic and dramatic as it is:

Dr. Jeffrey H. Wisoff, Assistant Professor, Division of Pediatric Neurosurgery, New York University Medical Center.

Sharon Luckenbaugh, Director of Speech Pathology, Glens Falls Hospital, Glens Falls, New York.

Joyce Sadewicz, Director of Physical Therapy, Glens Falls Hospital, Glens Falls, New York.

Willard Young was not aware on that New Year's Day that some of the most momentous events in a man's life often occur in the most ordinary of ways.

Forty-one years old, tall, still athletic in build if slightly over-weight, Willard Young stood in the foyer of his large home and summoned his son, "Bud . . . you coming? We've got miles to go, as your mother's favorite poet once said."

The phone rang. Before he could reach the living-room extension someone had answered. Probably another of Gwen's friends calling, he thought. What in the world thirteen-year-old girls have to talk about for hours Willard would never know or want to know.

But instead, his wife, Lily, called to him from the doorway to the kitchen.

"Pep . . . for you."

Since his early years in high school, part in admiration, part in jest, he had been called Pepper, evoking memories of a long time ago radio serial called *Pepper Young's Family.*

The name had stuck because of his effervescent personality,

which made him the business success he had become. So that now the only person who called him by his proper Christian name was his mother. And then only when, by way of reprimand, she spoke it with a rising inflection on the second syllable as if he were still her overactive mischievous little boy.

Pep Young turned to the kitchen to call, "Whoever it is, I've gone. Left. Won't be back till maybe four or five o'clock."

"Pep, it's Lester Cory," Lily said in a manner that indicated she knew he would take this particular call.

"Les? Sure." Pep started into the living room to pick up there.

"Hi, Les! Happy New Year! How's Ellen? Great. Wouldn't it be terrific if he was born on New Year's Day! Wouldn't have any trouble remembering his birthday then."

Pep's laughter was interrupted by a more serious attitude as he said, "Les, no need. Now, please. Look, kid, let's say I did it as much for my own selfish reasons as to help you. After all, I've got a record to maintain. I've never lost a salesman in my division except to have him move up in the organization. And I was going to make damn sure I didn't lose you. So you and Ellen just have a great New Year and I hope she does have that little one today. And if she does, you and I will go out and have a drink on it Tuesday. Les, Les, I said no need. You did it. I only helped you a little. Kiss your bride for me."

As he hung up, he heard Lily from the archway to the living room.

"You should have given him a chance to thank you. He feels so indebted. You saved his job. You practically saved his life."

Pep Young reached out to pull his wife close and embrace her.

"Hon, one thing I will never forget. *Our* first New Year together. When I was in the same spot as Les. First job out of engineering college. A kid really. Trying to sell expensive machinery that you needed to have an engineering degree to even explain. And I wasn't cutting it. Nowhere near cutting it.

"I'll never forget that winter. The toughest, coldest time of my life. The barest Christmas we ever had. I was terrified to face the New Year because I was sure Beecham was going to fire me. Only Christmas kept him from doing it. But when I came in to work the Monday after New Year's, instead of firing me, Beecham took me out in the field, made some calls with me. Watched me make a few presentations. Told me what I was doing wrong. But, more important, told me what I was doing right. I made a sale that very day. Not a big one. But to me the biggest sale I ever made.

"When we got back to the office, Beecham said to me, 'Kid, I didn't do this for you. I did it for the company. One day you're going to be a hell of a salesman.' That's all it took. If a tough man like Beecham thought I could do it, by God, I could do it!

"I made up my mind that day, if ever I had the chance I'd do the same for other men. And of course, these days, other women."

"Whatever the reason, darling, you did a terrific thing for that young man, and his wife." Lily kissed him, saying softly, "I am very proud of you."

"Never mind me. Where's that boy?" Pepper called in the direction of the stairs, "Bud Young! You are holding up progress."

By that time Bud Young, sixteen, already an inch taller than his dad, came down the stairs three at a time. One look and Pep pretended to be disappointed. "Bud? We can't go empty-handed."

"You never said we have to bring gifts on New Year's Day," Bud replied. "It's just to say Happy New Year and maybe have a cup of eggnog."

"Exactly, boy," Pep responded. "A cup of New Year's cheer. But where's the cup?"

"The hostess supplies . . ." Bud started to protest, then realized, "Dad, you're not going to make me bring that cup again, are you?"

"Bud, when you're a father, and your son wins a silver cup as the Most Valuable Player in the All County Football League, you'll know how I feel."

"But, Dad . . ."

"Son, when I was your age I was a pretty damn good quarterback myself. But I didn't have time to play. I had to bag groceries in the supermarket on Saturdays and Sundays. Well, now that I do have a chance to be proud, you are not going to deprive me of that. Get the cup!"

As Bud started back up, the doorbell rang. Pep opened the door to find a delivery man presenting a large wicker basket and asking, "Mr. Pepper Young?"

"Yes,"

"Sign here."

Pep signed, tipped the messenger, and sent him on his way with a "Happy New Year." He started for the kitchen, the large, heavy basket resting on his outstretched hands. At the same time he called, "Bud! I'm waiting."

Lily stood aside to give her husband entry into the kitchen, asking, "What in the world . . . ? Must be from someone who forgot to send a Christmas present."

"I hope it's not from one of my salespeople. I have a strict rule against that."

By that time he had set down the basket. He flipped open the wicker catches, lifted the lid. There was a holiday envelope in red and silver. He opened it to read aloud, "To Pep, the best district executive in the entire United States. And Canada. And now Mexico, too." It was signed "Hugh Beecham."

Nestled under layers of white protective plastic popcorn lay four black bottles of champagne.

"Holy . . . wow! Dom Pérignon! This stuff is eighty, ninety dollars a bottle! We'll take two of them over to Mother's. It'll make New Year's dinner even more special."

"Don't forget, darling, we're due there promptly at six," Lily pointed out.

Because he resented the implication lurking behind her reminder, he replied, "You think by the time we get to my mother's I'll be looped. Has that ever happened before?"

"I wasn't even thinking of that," Lily denied.

He embraced her, held her closely, spoke softly into her ear, "Look, doll, about last night . . . sorry . . . very sorry. But a man is entitled to a few drinks to see the New Year in."

"I wasn't going to mention that. But since you have, I must remind you that you didn't see the New Year in. By that time you weren't able to see anything in . . . or out."

"I know. Sorry. Won't happen again." He kissed her. While

he held her he asked, "Gwen . . . she . . . she didn't see you bring me home, did she?"

"She was asleep by then."

"Good."

But Lily could not resist reminding, "Pep, this afternoon . . . making your New Year's calls . . . all that eggnog . . ."

He laughed, "Hon, a little cup of eggnog? I know, it's really the cholesterol you're worried about. All that rich cream."

When she did not respond to his joke, he felt forced to assume a more serious attitude.

"Hon, your husband is not an alcoholic. Sure, sometimes when I have a struggling salesman whose productivity is way off, he's losing his morale, like Les was, I'll visit him. Take him out to dinner, find out if he has any personal problems or has lost his nerve. It takes a few drinks to loosen him up. Sometimes more than a few," Pep hastened to admit before she could point that out.

"But, hon, that's business. It's the way I keep my organization on top. And it does not happen very often. You have to admit that. I can go days without a drink. Days!"

Before she could say, "Make this one of those days," Bud came bounding down the stairs once more, self-consciously holding the silver loving cup his father had insisted on.

"Okay, boy, let's go!" Pretending to be a wide receiver Pep started for the front door, looking back for the pass. "Let 'er fly, kid!"

Bud threw the silver cup, which did not exactly describe the spiral he was used to throwing as a quarterback. But Pep caught it at the door and called, "Touchdown!"

As they started out, Lily called after them, "Just remember . . . we're due at your mother's at six!"

As Lily Young watched her husband and her son start down the freshly cleared walk toward the station wagon, she thought, *He's anxious to have Bud along so he can tell everyone how he won that Most Valuable cup for throwing the pass that won the Thanksgiving Day game. Pep gets a bigger kick out of that than Bud does. Not that it's a crime for a man to feel so proud of his son. Especially when he has a son like Bud to be proud of.*

If only Pep had had the chance to make one such play when he

was Bud's age it would have made a . . . a different . . . I don't mean
better . . . I mean just a different man out of him.

No, I'm being too judgmental. Not many men in our set have done
as well as Pep. This large house, our way of life, the security for the
kids' future, everything a woman could want.

Of which the best is two terrific kids. With, thank God, none of the
problems some parents have with kids these days.

Especially Bud. He's deeper than anyone knows. Even Pepper. To his
Dad he's a star quarterback, but Bud's got more than a football schol-
arship in mind. He's a real student. And if the time ever comes when
he has to choose between football and science, I know . . . because he
knows . . . which one he'll choose . . .

Lily had just seen the wagon cut through the pile of snow to
make it onto the open street when Gwen Young came rushing
down the stairs, calling, "Dad, wait for me!" The manner in
which her last "me" trailed off like a dying rocket told Lily how
disappointed her daughter was.

"Gwen, honey, when you're about twice as old as you are now
you'll learn there are certain things men like to do together. I
used to think that if I got into football so I could discuss it
intelligently, it would bring your dad and me closer. But it's
not the same as men talking football. They like to watch together. Drink beer together. And go places where they can talk
without women around. My father did that. His father did that.
And now your father is doing that. And when you get married
eight or ten years from now, your husband will do that."

"Yes, but . . ." Gwen started to protest.

"Yes, but," her mother anticipated "since that Thanksgiving
Day game and Bud winning the Most Valuable cup, Dad's been
closer to him than he has to you. It isn't that he loves Bud more.
Believe me, darling, no father has ever loved a daughter more
than Dad loves you. It's just that . . ."

This time Gwen did the anticipating, "It's just that Bud was
able to do everything Dad wanted to do and never got the
chance."

"My baby has learned a great deal in only thirteen years."

"I am no longer your baby," the red-haired freckle-faced
young woman protested.

"Dad may not be as open with his feelings about you. That's because he's really a shy man when it comes to personal feelings. But a very nice human being. Aside from being my husband and your father. So don't ever worry about being second best. You are your father's first and best daughter and always will be."

As Lily had a habit of doing, she wound strands of Gwen's soft red hair into a silky coil.

"Now let's go decorate that cake we're taking to Gramma's."

Pepper Young was backing the wagon out of the Hansons' driveway when Bud reminded, "Dad, it's almost four o'clock."

"So?" Pep demanded, his irritation sparked by the eggnogs he had drunk from Bud's silver cup during their last four New Year's drop-ins.

"So we're due at Gramma's at six," Bud reminded.

"Which gives us just enough time to make one more call. The Jerrolds. Can't slight the Jerrolds. We'll just drop in. Show 'em the cup, wish 'em a Happy New Year, have another cup of kindness as the old song goes and be on our way with time to spare."

"Dad . . ." Bud began, about to point out that Dad had already had more than a few cups of kindness in which the frothy, creamy, nutmeg-spiced eggnog was only an excuse for the bourbon. Rather than confront his father, even in a diplomatic way, Bud changed his mind. "Dad, please don't make me tell the story of that touchdown again. It'll be the fifth time today."

"Why not? You turned a busted play into a touchdown that won the Thanksgiving Day game. You know, son, when you've been in business as long as I have, you'll learn that instead of a virtue, modesty can be a fault. I wouldn't be where I am today, with the president of the company sending me the best champagne in the world, if I depended on modesty. That isn't what fires up my sales staff. It's the good old Pep that does that.

"Bud, you've got to tell that story. Especially to Herb Jerrold. Just so's I can enjoy the look on his face. How he wishes his Craig could have thrown a pass like that. Fifty-one yards through the air. Not many high school quarterbacks coulda done that."

"Dad, many of them have. And more will. It was not so unusual," Bud protested.

"On the last play?" Pep demanded, a bit impatient now. "And to win the game? If it was such an everyday thing I wouldn't have had calls from four different universities about your future plans. Two of them in the Big Ten. I call that damned unusual. You make it in the Big Ten and who knows? The NFL. Do you know what quarterbacks get these days just for signing a contract? A million dollars. Sometimes more!"

Pepper realized, as did his son, that his protest and his dreams were, in part, the bourbon in those sweet easy-to-go-down cups of kindness.

They drove on. To reopen the dialogue, Bud said softly, "You know, Dad, that pass . . . it was a Hail Mary . . . I had no idea what would happen when I let it go."

"All I know . . . all anybody knows, you threw it. Jody Hines caught it just over the goal line. Touchdown! Game! Best season for our team in nine years."

Bud did not reply. He stared ahead at the two-lane blacktop wet with slushy melting snow from the banks that lined both sides of the road.

Good thing the sun's still out, Bud thought. *Else this stuff'd freeze in a minute.*

They had stayed at the Jerrolds' longer than Bud had expected. Once he had acted out his famous touchdown pass and thought he was free, the Hinkles arrived. So Pepper, under the influence of several more cups of New Year's cheer, insisted Bud refill the cup with eggnog and relive that historic football moment yet again.

Because it was the only way to placate his father, who was now obviously drunk, Bud told of his exploit in as hasty a version as possible, despite his father's insisting on every detail.

Only the phone call from Lily Young asking if Pepper and Bud had left prevented the telling of the longer version and cut short more toasting from the silver trophy.

As they started down the Jerrolds' walk between the snow-covered lawns, with Pep clutching the silver cup, Bud cast a glance at his father, then asked in what he thought was a casual way, "Dad, whatdya say I drive home?"

"No!"

"Why not? I've had driver's ed and passed it," Bud protested.

"It takes a hell of a lot more experience than driver's ed to manage on these icy roads," Pep replied. "So just watch your old dad and learn a few tricks about driving."

"But, Dad . . ."

"No 'But, Dads'!" Pepper insisted. "You do not have a license yet, young man. And until you do, you do not drive any car in the Young family. Understand?" Pepper declared with the self-righteousness of the inebriated. "Would be against the law. And no matter what other people do, we Youngs do not break the law!"

As they climbed into the station wagon, Pepper continued to hold forth in a way that convinced Bud how drunk his father really was.

"Trouble these days, people got no respect for the law," Pepper declared as he turned the starter on the running motor for the second time, causing it to grind. "Fault of the courts. And those lenient judges."

They were on the road now.

"Watch it!" Bud cautioned suddenly.

"Why? What's wrong?" Pepper demanded indignantly.

"That guy in the red sports car—you cut him off, almost forced him into that snowbank."

"Sonofabitch ought to learn the rules of the road," Pepper replied. "Crowding me like that."

Their rear tire caught a patch of ice, forcing the wagon to swing to the left, barely missing an oncoming car.

"Dad, please, pull over. Let me . . ."

"Damn it, Bud! Stop distracting me with all your nagging! Let me concentrate on my driving!"

They were nearing the ramp onto the Interstate. Not the shortest way home but the quickest. In his confused state, debating his alternatives, Pepper Young overshot the turnoff. He slammed on his brakes. The wagon spun into a sharp erratic skid.

The last thing Pepper Young remembered was Bud's terrified, "Dad!!" followed by the wrenching shock and grinding sound of metal and shattering glass.

At the same instant his air bag exploded. The force of it knocked Pepper Young unconscious.

It took the sound of approaching sirens to bring Pepper Young back to consciousness. He reached up to his face, felt the slight warm ooze of blood from his nose. Aside from that, he felt only the residual bruises from his impact with the air bag.

At once he reached across. "Bud? Son? You all right? Bud?"

"Yeah . . . I . . . yeah . . . okay . . ." Bud replied, breathy and in obvious pain.

The sirens pulled up alongside. Two state highway patrol cars. Four officers jumped out to surround the crumpled wagon.

"S'okay, Officer," Pepper tried to assure them. "I got a little nosebleed. But Bud's fine. We're okay. Little shook up, but okay. Right, Bud?"

Pepper reached out to his son, but one of the officers interdicted him with a sharp "Don't touch him!"

"He's my son," Pepper started to argue. "Tell him, Bud."

"Yeah . . . he's . . . he's my Dad . . ." Bud managed in slurred fashion.

But having observed the bulge in the windshield, the officer repeated his warning, "Don't touch him. Don't try to move him!" He called back to his partner, "Radio medevac!"

"We're okay," Pepper protested. "Bud, tell the officer we're okay."

Bud opened his eyes, blinked, then tried to smile, but his pain was too strong, so he whispered, "Okay . . . we're, okay."

"See, he's okay."

The highway patrol had set up flaming red flares back down the road to detour cars into the left lane. The drivers all slowed to a crawl to stare at the wreckage, which was leaking different kinds of fluid while emitting a cloud of steam from the motor whose twisted hood hung suspended precariously in midair. The smell of spilled gasoline cut through the cold, clear winter air.

Against the advice of the troopers, Pepper Young had eased his way out of the driver's seat to stand alongside Bud, who was imprisoned by the crumpled passenger-side door.

Pepper was strongly tempted to hold Bud's hand to reassure him and warm him, but the troopers forbade it. So Pepper watched and spoke encouragingly to his son, who breathed shallowly in gasps as if it were too painful to inhale more deeply.

"It's okay, son. Just keep calm. Keep . . . keep breathing. The medevac'll be here any minute," Pepper assured, all the while thinking, *Lily, Lily, what'll I tell Lily?* At the same time he scanned the dark sky for the medevac helicopter but saw no sign of it.

Growing fearfully impatient, he started toward two of the troopers who were conferring grimly. He intended to insist they send a second distress call to make sure that copter was on its way.

He caught only a fragment of their discussion, the end, when one of them said, "It's obvious. We got to test him now."

"Look, Officers," Pepper intruded, "I hate to pull rank. But I've got some pretty important friends in this city. H. W. Beecham for one. So I want you to get on that radio and call medevac again. Insist they get that chopper here at once! After all, this is my son!"

"Cool it, mister. Help is on the way," the senior officer said in an attitude that Pepper Young, in his half-frightened, half-intoxicated mood, resented.

He returned to the crashed wagon, leaned in through the twisted door to plead, "Just hold on, Bud. They're on their way. Be here any second. You hear me, boy? You hear me?"

"Yeah . . . Dad . . . hear you . . ." Bud managed in a voice less than a whisper now.

In desperation at his son's deteriorating condition, Pepper insisted, "Bud . . . Bud . . . just keep breathing . . . keep breathing. If only for your mother's sake . . ."

Since he had become hysterical, both troopers pulled him away. At that moment the sound of the helicopter came within earshot.

"There, you see?" one trooper said, pointing to the blinking red and white lights approaching. "He's going to be okay."

The copter circled until the pilot determined a safe landing place, close enough to the wreckage. It touched down. Before the blades even stopped whirling, Dr. Janice Crowell, a young woman in uniform, leaped from the open cockpit. She turned back only long enough to catch the black medical bag the copilot dropped to her. She started toward the wrecked car.

She could identify Pepper Young at once as one of the victims. But she also recognized that he was in no need of immediate attention. She signaled the officers to pull Pepper away from the twisted door to give her access to the other passenger.

"He's my son," Pepper announced to her as the troopers dragged him out of the way. "You take good care of him. You hear? I'll make it worth your while!"

She didn't even bother to reward him with an impatient glance to register her resentment at his assumption that she could be influenced to deliver her most meticulous care only by such a promise. She dismissed it as the terrified pleading of a distraught father.

How much reason he had to be distraught, Dr. Janice Crowell was about to discover. Twenty-seven years old, she had far more experience dealing with trauma victims than one would suspect.

One glance at that windshield which, though it had not shattered, bore the deep indentation of a human head, told her how grave this case could be.

At once she checked for vital signs. She found Bud's carotid artery. Pulse forty-one. It was obvious his respiration was slow and shallow. Very slow. Very shallow. She applied her electronic thermometer: 95.2.

Well, she consoled herself, *at least he's still conscious. If we can get him to the hospital that way, he's got a chance.*

Automatically she instituted the ABCs of dealing with such victims.

Very carefully she raised Bud's head slightly, opened his mouth to clear out any debris such as glass or metal fragments. Fortunately, there were none. He had a clear Airway.

She could assess very quickly that he had no external Bleeding.

She proceeded now to the C part of the trilogy of trauma treatment, Circulatory support. She reached into her kit, drew out intravenous apparatus and a plastic bottle of medicated fluid to provide him both fluid and protection. Once the IV was inserted and she had secured a protective brace around his neck, she called, "Need a hand here!"

The co-pilot raced to her side. Together, they lifted Bud out through the battered door, with the doctor supporting his head very, very carefully. Once he was on the ground, she knelt beside him to perform a more specific examination to determine the type and extent of his injuries.

Pepper stood over them, staring down at this young woman whose abilities he had begun to doubt. While she examined Bud's arms and legs for signs of fractures, Pepper insisted, "He doesn't have any broken bones. Anybody can see that. And no wounds. His head is fine."

To make the doctor's job less difficult, the troopers dragged Pepper away, saying, "Mister, we got some business to attend to."

"Business? What kind of business?" Pepper demanded, still trying to break loose and reach his son's side.

"It won't take long. Just breathe into this tube, that's all," the troopers said, holding out a small black box. Except for the short white tube that extended from it, it appeared to be a tape recorder.

"You want a statement from me?" Pep asked.

"No, just breathe into this white tube."

"What for?" Pepper demanded.

"This is an Alcosensor."

"Alcosensor . . . hey, you guys think I'm drunk? You're outa your minds!" Pepper protested.

But they pulled him away and to the side of one of the patrol cars to administer the test.

Meanwhile, Dr. Crowell took Bud's blood pressure, listened to his heart. She did not like his vital signs. While what his father had said was true—the young man had no gross bleeding head wound—the doctor could not dismiss that bulging windshield. She had the grim sense that she was dealing with a CHI, a closed head injury.

Fortunately, he was still conscious. She could at least communicate with him.

"Son, open your eyes."

Bud complied, although keeping them open appeared to take great effort. Dr. Crowell shone a small flashlight into them to study his pupillary responses. Not very encouraging.

Carefully she felt along his neck. She could not detect any broken bones. At least that was to the good.

"Board!" she summoned.

Both pilot and co-pilot responded by bringing over a long flat board about twenty inches wide with a broad tape secured to one end. Under her guidance the pilots very carefully lifted

Bud onto the board, placing him flat on his back. She was affixing the wide tape across Bud's head to assure he could not move and injure his spinal column during transit to the hospital. She became aware that Pepper was hovering over her again.

Her look of resentment caused him to assert his right to be at Bud's side. "He's my son!"

"Then how come you had him riding in a seat without an air bag?" she demanded impatiently. She had worked at her profession long enough, had seen too many such accidents, lost too many victims, to be indulgent about such matters.

"We're waiting for our new wagon. It'll have double air bags," Pepper tried to explain.

But the doctor ignored that to ask, "What's his name?"

"Name? What the hell difference does that make?" Pepper demanded in his anguish.

"His name!" the doctor insisted.

"Willard Young, Junior."

"What do you *call* him?" she asked impatiently.

"Bud. Everybody calls him Bud."

The doctor leaned close to Bud, spoke directly into his ear, and loudly, "Bud! Bud, can you hear me? If it hurts to talk, just blink your eyes. Understand? If you can hear me, blink your eyes. Good. That's it. Good, good boy."

She took his blood pressure once more, checked his pulse. To make sure he continued to have a clear airway she carefully inserted a tube into his mouth and partway down his throat, making sure all the while not to bend his head and put pressure on his spinal cord. She also carefully avoided traumatizing his larynx. Should he recover his voice would not be affected.

"We'd better move him," she said.

Before the pilots could lift him, Pepper Young demanded, "Where are you taking him? I have a right to know!"

"Mercy Hospital," Dr. Crowell informed. "So get on a phone. Call his mother. Tell her to get there. In a hurry. A big hurry!"

Pepper Young insisted on following the trauma board to the copter. But one of the troopers interceded. Finally he had to seize Pepper in a powerful bear hug to hold him back.

While Pepper strained and called, "Bud . . . Bud!" the trooper kept saying, "He'll be okay. He'll get the best treatment. . . . "

But Pepper continued to cry out, "Bud . . . Bud . . ." until the copter's blades started to spin, then whip the frosty air. Finally it lifted off, banking and speeding away to the left. Only then did Pepper relent, going limp in the arms of the officer.

Distraught, still in shock from the accident itself, Pepper Young began to ramble, "He's uh . . . that's my son . . . Bud . . . threw a pass . . . fifty-one yards . . . for a touchdown . . . that's the kind of kid he is . . . now . . . they took him away . . . they can't do that . . . can they? Take a man's son away like that . . . he needs me now . . . needs his ma, too . . . got to find a phone . . . yeah, a phone . . ."

"Before we do that, Mr. Young, we got that little business to take care of," the senior trooper said.

"We already did that," Pepper protested. "I've got to call Lily!"

"Sure. But first . . ."

"We already did that!" Pepper protested.

"Damn right. And, mister, you have tested point-o-three on the Alcosensor. Well over the legal limit for conviction of driving under the influence. If it wasn't for your son's condition I'd run you in right now. Instead, take this citation. Answer it on the return date. And bring a very, very good lawyer. You'll need one!"

In Pepper's mind the trooper's advice was of little consequence compared to his son's condition. He continued to babble on, "Needs me . . . should be there . . . I should be there . . ."

The troopers exchanged glances that asked, "Do you drive him to the hospital or do I?"

"Okay, Mr. Young, let's go."

Pepper started toward the patrol car, then stopped, turned back toward the wrecked wagon.

"Mr. Young!" the trooper ordered.

But Pepper waved him away with a vague gesture and stumbled toward the wreckage. He reached in, groped in the darkness. Found something. He started back toward the trooper hugging a badly bent silver loving cup in his arm.

"Okay. Let's go," he said to the astonished trooper.

In the copter on its way through the winter night to a landing on the roof of Emergency at Mercy Hospital, Dr. Janice Crowell was in radio communication with the Trauma Unit. She briefed them on every detail of her patient's condition so they would be prepared with all the personnel, equipment, and facilities necessary to keep him alive once he arrived.

As she worked on Bud, she reported as well.

"Pulse thirty-eight. Respiration very slow, very shallow. Temp eighty-five point four. But conscious. Still conscious. Giving him a shot of mannitol to inhibit edema of the brain. Will insert Foley catheter to assist urinary function.

"Just keep breathing, Bud . . . just keep breathing. . . ."

When she received no response, she shifted her area of concern to his face, his eyes.

"Bud . . . Bud, if you can hear me, open your eyes. Open, Bud!"

There was no response.

She spoke into the microphone once more to report, "Lost consciousness. Will get back to you."

She affixed a second IV to prevent his going into shock. Then she started him on a respirator. Breathing thus assured, she began to perform what would be the first of many formal Glascow Coma Scale tests. If he survived.

Though she held out little hope she proceeded meticulously with each step. "Bud, open your eyes. Open your eyes!" No response.

She reached for his arm, pinched it hard. No response. Unable to respond to pain, the patient must be listed as *nil* on the Glascow Scale and graded E-1, lowest on the eye-opening test.

She proceeded to test his motor responses.

"Bud, move your arm. Lift your arm. Lift your left arm, Bud. Just . . . just raise your hand if you can hear me."

As she had expected, no response. She pinched him hard on the cheek. He did not flinch. Though his head was fixed in place he should have at least evidenced a grimace or some other sign. Instead he remained totally unresponsive.

Discouraged, she continued nevertheless to apply sharp and painful pinches to his arms and legs. She used a hypodermic needle to deliver sharp stabs to his left arm and leg. And then to his right.

Finally she evoked a response, a primitive reflex. A sudden and awkward extension of his right arm and leg in a bizarre and unnatural movement.

Obvious abnormal flexion and, on the Glascow Scale, worthy of an M-2 for deficient motor response.

Her attempts to evoke any verbal response failed completely. Not a confused response. Not even inappropriate words. Only a few incomprehensible sounds. She had to note in his chart V-2 for bare verbal response.

The total result was quite obvious. A Glascow Coma Scale of E-1 and M-2 plus a V-2 equaled a total of only 5. This patient was now far below the minimum score of 8, the dividing line between unconscious and comatose.

She relayed the information to the Trauma Unit at Mercy Hospital.

A patient comatose at this stage had only a 50 percent prognosis of survival. The battle now was to stabilize him and keep him alive on oxygen and a respirator so all other indicated steps could be taken. The first of which, on arrival at the hospital, would be an X ray of his entire body to detect any hidden fractures or internal injuries.

The highway patrol car pulled up in the circular driveway of Mercy Hospital. Pepper Young reached for the door handle only to find it locked. Before the trooper would release him, he warned, "Don't forget that citation. And your lawyer!"

Citations, court dates, lawyers were the furthest things from Willard Young's mind as he stumbled into Mercy Hospital still clutching the damaged silver cup. He found the Trauma Service and demanded to see his son.

Dr. Crowell used the opportunity to check out Pepper for any possible injuries. Aside from his nose, which had long stopped bleeding, and the chest and facial bruises from his impact with the air bag, he exhibited no aftereffects of the disastrous crash.

Throughout the examination he continued to protest, "My son . . . Bud, where is he? What happened to him? I have a right to know."

"Bud's in X-ray. He'll be down shortly. Meantime, I strongly urge you to call his mother. Tell her to get here at once."

Her meaning, though unstated, was quite clear in her tone of voice and in her sharp blue eyes.

"He's . . . he's . . . that bad?" Pepper dared to ask.

"Just call her. Tell her to get here!" Dr. Crowell ordered, pointing to the phone on the wall of the examining room.

Pepper Young approached the phone hesitantly. He lifted it. It slipped from his trembling hand. Dr. Crowell caught it before it hit the floor.

"What's the number?" she asked. Pep told her. She punched it in. She held on until she received a response. She handed him the phone.

"Lil . . . yeah, yeah, I know, we're late. . . . Where are we? We're . . . we're . . ."

He could not continue. Dr. Crowell took the phone from his hand. "Mrs. Young. This is Dr. Crowell."

Pepper seized the phone from her. "I got to do this. . . . Lily . . . Lily . . . we are at Mercy Hospital. There's been an accident. . . . "

"Bud! What about Bud?" Lily Young demanded frantically.

"Lil . . . the doctor said to get here as soon as you can."

Dr. Janice Crowell swiftly mounted the fresh X-ray films on the backlit viewing wall. A hurried but accurate reading of each film indicated there were no fractures of legs, arms, or pelvic area. And no visible internal injuries. Most important, no fracture of the spine or neck bones, making it possible to extend the patient's neck to safely insert an endotrachial tube for breathing.

But first she made another examination of his pupillary responses to determine if any changes had occurred in the brief time that had elapsed. In these cases things happened fast. The more dangerous the developments, the swifter they seemed to occur.

Her examination of Bud Young's pupils revealed that his left pupil was considerably dilated, indicating a possible mass or other damage on the left side of his brain. Only one thing was mandated now. A CAT scan of his brain.

The gurney bearing Bud Young, accompanied by appropriate intravenous poles, was being wheeled out of Trauma toward the elevators when Lily Young entered at the far end of the corridor. A mother's instinct told her it was her son on that stretcher. She raced after it, desperately calling, "Bud . . . Son!"

Before she could reach him, Dr. Crowell intercepted her.

"Mrs. Young?"

Lily tried to avoid her to reach her son. But Crowell blocked her way, saying, "Right now, time is everything. We've got to get him up for a CAT scan." At the same time she gestured the orderly to rush the gurney to the elevator.

Straining to escape Crowell, Lily Young peered around her as the stretcher disappeared into the elevator. Once the door had closed, Lily relented and appeared resigned to dealing with the doctor.

"My husband?"

"The waiting room down the corridor." Crowell pointed the way.

Lily nodded, then asked, hesitant and fearful of the response, "CAT scan . . . that's for serious things, isn't it?"

"Can be *very* serious," Crowell informed, in her own way preparing this mother for the most likely outcome in such a case.

"What will . . . I mean . . . how do they . . . is there anything they can do? I mean really do?" Lily asked, a woman terrified as much as confused. "Only this morning he was . . . I mean, when he left the house he was . . ." She could not complete the thought in any comprehensive fashion. Suddenly she asked, "Pepper?"

Crowell was puzzled.

"My husband . . . is he . . . he's okay, isn't he?"

"I checked him out. Shaken up. But otherwise okay," Crowell replied. "And as I said, in the waiting room."

She beckoned Lily to follow her. With both parents together, this was a good time to introduce them to the awesome realities of their son's condition.

Pepper Young sat in the far corner of the waiting room, his head slumped forward, his fingers pressed against his forehead, his hands covering his eyes. At her first sight of him, Lily Young stopped. She felt a stab of pain in her belly. It was the first time in the eighteen years of their marriage that she was seeing her husband cry. He had always been the strong one. Her main support emotionally and in all other ways. Suddenly her entire sense of security collapsed. Until this moment she had not realized how totally she had depended on him.

"Pep . . ." she was able to say.

He looked up at her through damp eyes which blinked at being exposed to the light suddenly. He rose to embrace her. They sought strength in each other.

Dr. Crowell watched, thinking, *And they are going to need strength, a great deal of strength, to face what's coming. Even the best of what's coming. If I'm any judge of that young man's condition.*

"Pep . . . what happened . . . how did it . . ." Lily Young started to ask.

"It was the road . . . the ice . . . I was just deciding to take the Interstate . . . had to hit the brake. . . . We . . . I . . . Lil, if anything happens to my son . . . our son . . . I'll . . . I'll . . . I don't know what I'll do . . ."

At that moment an orderly came into the room carrying some official forms. He whispered to the doctor. She nodded as if she had expected this.

"Mr. Young, you're going to have to sign this."

"Sign? Why? We've got plenty of coverage. My company has the best medical plan . . ."

"Mr. Young! This is an informed consent."

"Informed . . ." He was puzzled.

"We have to operate on your son. We need to have this signed."

"What do you mean, you have to operate?"

"The scan revealed a hematoma. A large blood clot on the left side of his brain. We have no time to lose. So will you sign this?" When he hesitated, Crowell added, "Whether you do or not we have to operate if we're to save his life."

Stunned by the news, in shock, Pepper Young reached for the form, for the pen Crowell held out to him.

Meantime Lily asked in a painful whisper, "Brain surgery? Oh, my God."

"I'll let you know immediately what we find," Crowell said as she folded the form.

"Is there any chance . . . can we see him before the surgery?" Lily Young asked.

"There's no time. Anyhow, he wouldn't know. He's been unconscious."

"Unconscious," his mother echoed. "Dear God."

Left alone, Pepper and Lily Young stared at each other, not
knowing what to say. He, out of guilt. She, out of stunned shock.

He reached for her hand. She did not so much offer it as let
him take it.

"You're right. Blame me. I deserve it," he said.

"Shut up, Willard," Lily Young replied. "Don't say anything.
Words don't count. Not now. So just . . . just be quiet. If you
have to do anything or say anything, just pray."

"Pray? I wouldn't know how," he admitted. "I'm used to
having someone else pray for me. Reverend Butler. Or something in the Book of Common Prayer. But to pray in my own
words, I'm no good at that. No good at all. Especially not now.
What could I say that God would listen to after this?"

"We'll just ask in Bud's name. He's such a fine . . . such a
good person . . . he deserves better than to . . . to . . ." She could
not say the word. She added, "Not at his young age, not with
so much of his life still ahead of him."

They fell silent, forced only to hold hands. Cold hands, damp
and sweaty hands.

Lily and Pepper Young, silent and grim, sat in a corner of the
waiting room. Neither of them dared to speak their fears. Nor
did either dare to cry for fear of the other losing all control.

They were disturbed by a loud voice from the outer entrance.
"Bud Young . . . We're here for Bud Young!"

Pepper thought he recognized the voice. He started for the
door calling, "Jody? Jody Hines?"

"Yeah, Mr. Young, it's me. We're here!"

By that time Dr. Janice Crowell came out of E.R. to discover
the cause of the disturbance, a group of between fifteen and
twenty burly teenagers.

"Young man! I don't know who you are and what this gang
of yours wants here, but keep it down! This is a hospital."

"You Bud Young's doctor?" Jody Hines asked as Pepper came

into view. "Oh, Mr. Young. We heard on the television news about Bud. We're here to give blood."

"Young man, keep it down!" Dr. Crowell ordered.

"But we're here to give blood. . . . "

"Your friend does not need blood," Crowell informed. "And what he does need none of you can give him. So please leave here. At once!"

Pepper Young nodded to support Doctor Crowell's command.

In a whisper, Jody Hines asked, "You'll let us know, huh, Mr. Young? We're all worried. What a shock. You hear these things on television all the time but you never think it's someone you've known all your life."

"I understand, Jody. Just leave quietly. I'll keep you informed."

"Thanks, Mr. Young. And when you see Bud, tell him we were here. The whole squad. It'll make him feel better to know."

"Yes. Sure. Of course."

"Just tell him he'll always be our quarterback."

"I know. Just go . . . please."

Up in Operating Theater 4H, neurosurgeon Albert Newman was scrubbing at the stainless-steel sink while at the same time studying CAT scan results posted on the wall before him. They revealed slit ventricles, with the subarachnoid cisterns almost absent. Diffuse brain swelling. And that very obvious subdural hematoma at the left rear of the brain.

While one nurse drew a sample of Bud's blood for a complete blood count and typing in the remote event a transfusion became necessary, another technician was shaving Bud's head. The nurse stood by ready to paint it with antiseptic Betadine solution. The patient was ready for Dr. Newman.

Very precisely Newman drew a purple line down the center of the exposed scalp. The nurse slapped a sterile scalpel into his hand. He made an incision that followed the purple line from the front to back of the scalp.

He carefully folded the left half of the scalp to one side, exposing the skull and affording him access to the back left area where the dangerous hematoma had formed. It might even now be enlarging, exerting pressure on Bud's already injured and swelling brain.

Using a shiny stainless-steel electric saw Newman cut out a section of the skull. Once inside, he discovered a branch of the middle cerebral artery had ruptured, causing the massive clot to form. There were also contusions in the Broca's area, not uncommon in closed head injury cases.

Such a large compression on the left side of the brain would account for the neurological deficits Dr. Crowell had already discovered. How long those deficits would persist or if they would become permanent it was too soon to tell.

In fact, almost all the residuals of this type of accident were beyond the scope of doctors and surgeons to predict so early.

Well aware of his responsibility, his capabilities, and his limitations at this stage, he knew the primary responsibility of the entire trauma team was to keep the patient alive. Keep him free of infection and other preventable aftereffects. Healing would, in the main, be a matter of chance and the patient's ability and will to regain his faculties.

Having removed the hematoma and returned the excised portion of the skull, Newman replaced the scalp and sutured it into place.

Now, using a high-speed electric drill, he bored a tiny hole on the right side of the skull. Very gently he inserted a thin colorless plastic tube which held an equally thin but sensitive instrument that would measure the buildup of pressure within the brain.

Whenever that revealed a dangerous buildup, the valve of the transducer would be opened by the doctor or a nurse to allow the excess accumulation of fluid to drain off.

That device, plus injections of manitol every four hours, might contain any further dangerous brain swelling and buildup of pressure.

But Newman was well aware that in cases such as the patient under his hands at this moment, no surgeon could venture an accurate prediction or prognosis.

With closed head injuries when the patient was comatose, as Bud Young was now, that 50 percent mortality rate defied every neurosurgeon.

So for now, keep the patient alive, free from any excessive movement which might cause further damage.

Newman completed his surgery. He consigned his patient to postsurgical Neuro-Intensive Care with orders to administer muscle relaxers and keep him mechanically hyperventilated in an effort to control intracranial pressure.

He also noted on the chart that the patient was to have another CAT scan in fifteen hours.

Having performed the surgery, Newman was now in charge of this patient until either of two things happened. The patient improved sufficiently to be passed on to Rehabilitation.

Or died.

His next duty, much as he disliked it, was to confer with the family to inform them of the dire facts in cases like this.

Before he could face the Youngs, still another emergency arrived requiring him to scrub once more. Meantime, he gave orders that the Youngs be permitted to view their son through the glass walls that surrounded each cubicle in Intensive Care.

5

"Is he down from surgery yet?" Lily Young asked the nurse at the desk.

"He's just being brought down now," she informed.

"Can we at least see him? I haven't seen him since . . ." She stopped. Determined not to cry.

"Dr. Newman left orders. As soon as they have the patient comfortable you can see him."

"He's okay? I mean as . . . as okay as is possible under the circumstances?" Lily begged for reassurance.

"Doctor Newman is still up in the OR. When he comes down he'll explain," the nurse replied.

Lily Young and her husband realized that the nurse was being as kind and informative as she could under very trying circumstances. They must wait for the surgeon.

The phone on the nurse's desk rang. She answered, then said, pointing, "It's down the corridor to the end and make a right turn. The arrows will point you to ICU."

Pepper and Lily Young stared though the glass at their son, who lay with eyes closed, head wrapped in white bandages, mask over his nose, two IV lines taped into place in his arms. Alongside, a mechanical device rose and fell with every breath their son took.

Aside from his mechanically assisted breathing he exhibited no sign of activity, no sign of consciousness. Immediately, with a terrifying rush, both Lily and her husband recalled all the images they had seen on television, in the news and in melodramatic films, of patients lying there in the same condition. Always the question seemed to be, Shall the equipment be turned off and let the patient die?

"No," Lily determined. "No."

She turned to her husband for courage and strength. He embraced her. But as he drew her head close to his shoulder to comfort her and she grazed his lips she pulled back. With a strong pang of guilt he knew why. She smelled the whiskey on his breath. There was little he could say that would help now. All he could do was hold her close. Pat her on the shoulder while he stared through the glass at his only son, his dear son, of whom he was so proud, lying there unconscious, motionless. This young, strong, active athlete and scholar now reduced to a patient kept alive by lines connected to inverted bottles of clear liquid and a mask that made it possible for him to breathe. Pepper Young, and now his wife, knew the fault was his.

After some minutes, the ICU nurse suggested gently, "There isn't much to see. He's doing as well as could be expected. So why don't you both wait for Dr. Newman? He'll be in charge of your son from now on."

They were seated in a corner of the waiting room, removed from the few other late-night visitors. They needed privacy to confess their fears.

"The nurse said, 'as well as could be expected,' didn't she?" Lily asked.

"Yes, darling. That's a good sign," Pepper encouraged.

Lily nodded, her thoughts no different from his. They knew only one thing. Their son was still alive. Unless one knew what was "expected," the phrase was meaningless. But neither of them dared admit that.

They had been silent a long time. Lily became aware that the other visitors were staring at her.

She tried to hold back her tears but could not.

Pepper moved to shield her from the intrusive stares.

She looked up at him in gratitude. That was Pepper, always trying to shield her from all harm, all stress, any embarrassment. He was, from the first day of their marriage, protective, loving, kind. And even more so of Bud and Gwen.

In her effort to comfort him, and reassure herself, she said, "It can't be too bad. There's not a mark on him. No bandages except for the operation. And without all that equipment he doesn't look much different than if he was sleeping."

"Yeah," Pepper agreed, more for her comfort than his own. Having witnessed his son's treatment and condition from the very beginning, he felt a terrible threat hanging over Bud which neither of the doctors had yet identified. Trying to raise his wife's spirits he recalled, "Remember the time he got that concussion . . . last season . . . and they took him to the hospital just to make sure. He didn't look any different then. Did he?"

"No, no, he didn't," she was quick to agree.

But their little charade broke down. Lily started to weep once more.

"Lil . . . darling . . . people are staring . . ."

"The hell with them. Let 'em stare!" she replied.

At that moment, a nurse appeared in the entryway.

"Mr. Young . . . Mrs. Young . . . Dr. Newman can see you now."

Dr. Alfred Newman was thin almost to the point of being ascetically gaunt. His fierce black eyes gave him the appearance of a prophet of old. While the first sight of him might have created the impression of a pessimistic judgmental man, he was known among his colleagues and the hospital staff to be most compassionate. Sometimes, too compassionate. He fought to keep patients alive whom other surgeons would have let go. Sometimes he blamed himself for it, considering it, in the long run, a professional weakness.

He tried to be realistic with the families of his patients, while at the same time careful not to alarm them about the unavoidable consequences many of his patients were doomed to suffer.

He had tortured nights when he himself questioned the wisdom of his decisions. Families who early on were cheered and tearfully grateful at the news he gave them, later turned grim in face of their own conflicted feelings about a patient whom Newman had struggled to keep alive and who lived on for months, even years, without regaining consciousness.

People didn't know. They had no way of knowing, not really. They heard an announcement on the TV of just another automobile accident on some familiar highway. With the inevitable "Film at ten."

And if they happened to be awake at that hour they saw what has become an all too familiar scene of our time. The wrecked car. The rotating red and blue lights of the highway patrol cars. The stunned driver. The ambulance or helicopter arriving at the scene. An unconscious passenger or two or three being stretchered away.

No one showed the TV viewer the aftereffects that doctors like Albert Newman had to deal with. The weeks after, the months after, the years after, often the lifetimes after.

All this came with almost every case that passed across the operating table of Dr. Albert Newman in his daily practice.

"If only people knew . . ." he often said.

But he had learned that, whether they knew or not, people continued to act with the abandon they always had. It was enough to make a caring man quit.

If there weren't always another patient who needed his skills and his knowledge.

So he overcame his strong temptation to desert his area of neurosurgery and devote himself to infants and children born with congenital but correctable deficits. There lay hope and a sense of accomplishment. Setting an infant or a young child on the road to a good life, or at least a better life, that was something a man could be proud of. Saving the wreckage of human error, such as the victims of carelessness or drunkenness, was not nearly so heartening.

Yet he went on saving lives where he could, even damaged lives. And explaining as truthfully and mercifully as he could to the families.

This time, having to confront the parents of Patient Willard Young, Jr., was even more difficult. For Newman himself had a son only a year older than Bud Young. He knew only too well how he would feel if some surgeon were to say to him the things he now had to say to the Youngs.

Pepper Young had left his wife's side only long enough to intercept Dr. Newman as he was entering his office.

"Doctor . . . I know things are bad. Very bad. So, if you don't mind, just tell me. The whole truth. No matter how bad. Leave it to me to tell her. I can . . . somehow, I will find a way to make it easier on her. Doctor?"

"Mr. Young, I know how you feel. But I have found that the best way in the long run is the truth. Told as gently as possible. Trust me," Newman said. "I'll see you both in about ten minutes."

As he sat across the desk from Willard and Lily Young, Newman could see the ravages that the last half dozen hours had inflicted on them. He had to ask himself, *No matter what Young had said, are they prepared for the difficult weeks, months, years that might be in store for them? If they knew, would they be praying that their son live, as they undoubtedly are doing now?*

Compassionate or not, Newman knew he must be direct but soft-spoken.

"Mrs. Young . . . Mr. Young . . . I don't know how your son became involved in this accident . . ."

With a glance of guilt at his wife, Pepper Young managed to say, "The wagon skidded on the ice . . ."

"A boy his age shouldn't have been driving on these roads, not on a day like today," Newman remarked.

"I . . . I was driving," Pepper admitted.

"Oh." Newman had confined his judgment to a single syllable. He then proceeded, "Of course, from a neurosurgical point of view, a medical point of view, it doesn't matter how the trauma occurred. The fact that it did is what we have to deal with. A classic case of CHI."

"CHI?" At once Lily assumed, "You found something during the operation. A tumor. Brain cancer."

"No, Mrs. Young. CHI is the shorthand medical term for closed head injury."

"You mean," Pepper asked, "even if there's no head wound, there can still be an injury?"

He looked to his wife with renewed concern and guilt.

"To understand CHI, you have to realize that the brain is an organ of soft tissue. Floating in a sea of fluid, cerebral spinal fluid. The skull, that rock-hard bony structure around it, is just the container Nature has developed to protect the soft brain, which, along with the brain stem, keeps us alive and breathing."

At Newman's use of the word "alive" a single tear started down Lily Young's cheek.

Softly, Pepper entreated, "Lily . . . not now . . . please?"

Newman continued, "In an accident, when the hard skull crashes up against another hard object, like a windshield, the skull stops with sudden impact. But the soft, floating brain plunges forward against that hard skull with tremendous force.

"We call that acceleration. Now, as you probably remember from your science classes in high school, every action has an equal and opposite reaction. So it is with the brain. That acceleration is followed immediately by what we call deceleration. The immediate backward impact of the brain against the rear of the skull.

"So that in a split second the brain is battered not once but twice. The damage inflicted by that double injury we cannot undo. All we can try to do is keep the patient alive and deal with the consequences."

"And you're doing that," Pepper said, seeking reassurance.

Newman corrected, "We are *trying* to do that. We won't know for several days if we will succeed. And even then we can't promise you that he will be out of danger."

The surgeon hesitated for a moment. Lily noticed that the muscles in his very lean jaw tensed, then relaxed as if he had considered and come to a conclusion.

"I want to be frank with you. When a patient arrives at a trauma center unconscious, the odds are fifty-fifty that he will not survive."

Pepper reached for his wife's hand to ward off any outcry. Lily grasped his hand, but began to weep softly nevertheless.

"Of course," Newman added quickly, "that means that fifty percent *do* survive. Let's hope that your son is in that fifty percent."

But he pretended to be no more optimistic than that.

"Doctor . . ." Pepper began, "what are the . . . I mean, when the brain hits like that, what can happen?"

"In most cases tearing of arteries in the brain . . . intracranial bleeding . . . swelling of the brain . . ." Newman proceeded to enumerate.

But Lily Young interrupted, "Never mind most cases. Bud . . . I want to know what happened to Bud . . . to *his* brain."

"Lil, please," her husband intervened. "Give the doctor a chance to explain."

"I don't know about *you,* but *I* am only interested in *my* son!" she declared in a manner that even Newman found troubling for reasons he would rather not even consider at such a crucial time. The patient's survival should be the only consideration.

To her husband, Lily's outburst conveyed a different message. For the first time, he thought, Lily was blaming him. Which made his guilt even greater than it was. For he had no defense against that.

Even Lily herself was surprised at her outburst. She had promised herself, and silently promised God as well, that if Bud survived she would hold no grudges, make no accusations.

In a more moderate tone of voice, and with more control over her feelings, she asked, "Doctor, about Bud . . . that's the only important thing. Bud. His condition."

"Right now we have him in ICU. As far as we know, he's reacting as well as we can expect at this time. His vital signs are . . . are, well, adequate. He seems to have a good strong body, which can only help."

Pepper could not resist explaining, "He's an athlete. Always in training. Football. He's a quarterback. Maybe you read about him in the local paper. That Thanksgiving Day game. That fifty-one-yard pass on the last play that won the game."

"Oh, I do remember," Newman said, considering, *Maybe I should tell them the whole truth now. The chances of that young man ever throwing a football again are slim. Very slim.* What convinced him to be at least a little more explicit was Pepper Young's next words.

"He gets over this, there are four big universities waiting for him. Two in the Big Ten."

Newman decided it was time, if not for a complete revelation of the possibilities, at least for enough to temper any unrealistic ambitions.

He began by sounding somewhat optimistic. "Mr. Young, it is possible that your son, Bud, could have a complete recovery." Then, without changing tone or attitude, Newman continued, "But the facts are that of that fifty percent who survive, thirty percent are left with certain deficits."

"Deficits?" Pepper echoed, puzzled and troubled besides.

"Physical limitations. And cognitive limitations," Newman explained. "Fortunately, the remaining twenty percent come away practically intact."

"That'll be Bud!" Pepper declared. "He's tough. A fighter. Doesn't give up. Right down to the last play. If it can be done, believe me, Dr. Newman, Bud'll do it!"

"Let's hope so," Newman said, reserving his own more realistic opinion to himself. "Right now, our goal is to get him past the first seventy-two hours."

Which was Newman's gentle and oblique way of avoiding, for the moment, the fact that the longer Bud remained unconscious, the less his chance of surviving or recovering any of his physical or mental abilities. Albert Newman had seen too many young patients end up in wheelchairs. And worse.

No reason to explain all those realities to the Youngs now.

If their son did not survive, there would be no need.

If he did survive, there would be much time to confront all the medical and psychological results of his trauma.

It was just past eleven o'clock at night. Neuro-Intensive Care had been fairly calm for some hours. There had been one quiet episode. The patient several cubicles down from where Bud Young lay in his comatose condition, a young woman of twenty-four, had slipped from coma into death, which was noted only by the change in the sound of the oscilloscope that had monitored her failing heart. Despite all the attention, medication, stimulation, and other therapy the most advanced medical science had to offer, she was beyond help.

Quietly, efficiently, the matter was handled with dispatch so as not to alarm other patients in ICU or relatives who, because of the serious condition of the patient, had been allowed to stay past normal visiting hours.

Lily and Willard Young witnessed the covered body being silently wheeled out of ICU to the elevator to be taken down to the hospital morgue.

For reassurance they went to stand outside the glass wall behind which Bud lay. They watched his monitor in its slow but seemingly steady march across the screen. They found great comfort in that green light as it persisted. To them it was the light that kept Bud alive, not Bud whose heart action activated the bouncing light.

Reassured, Pep whispered, "Lily, we can't be of any help here. And there's Gwen."

"I left her with the Dolingers. She'll stay over. She'll be all right."

Two nurses, one female, one male, entered Bud's cubicle.

"What are they . . ." Lily started to ask in a voice too loud for her surroundings.

"Shh, Lil . . . easy. I'll go and ask."

He slipped into the cubicle just as the male nurse was releasing the locks under the wheels of Bud's bed.

"Look . . . I'm the boy's father. Where are you taking him at this hour? And why?"

The female nurse, who seemed in charge, replied, "To Radiology. His second CAT scan."

"Why? He's doing all right. I mean, at least he's holding his own, seems like."

The nurse did not reply at once but checked the cranial monitor that Dr. Newman had inserted after he had completed surgery to remove the hematoma.

"What's it say?" Pep asked.

"Twelve point five," she informed.

"Is that good or bad?"

"If we can keep him under fifteen for the next forty-eight hours, he has a good chance."

From behind Pep he heard Lily ask, "Good chance of what?"

The nurse would rather have avoided responding, but she did not hesitate to inform, "Ma'am, if we can keep your son's cranial pressure under fifteen for the next seventy-two hours he has a good chance of surviving."

The response, simple, factual, brought a rush of tears to Lily's eyes but she managed to contain them.

The two nurses very carefully wheeled Bud's bed out of the cubicle. One directing the bed, the other alongside to make sure that the IVs continued to function.

Minutes had slowly dragged by. To both Lily and Pep Young the length of time that elapsed seemed to be a measure of their son's condition. As if the longer it took, the worse the results of the scan.

"They must have found something terribly wrong if it's taking so much time," Lily said.

Though he agreed with her, Pep tried to deny it. "These things take time, hon. Who knows? Maybe there were two or three patients ahead of him. This is a big hospital."

"How many patients could be getting scans at twelve-thirty at night?" she disputed.

"I don't know. Maybe new patients just brought in. S'what they did with Bud. First thing. Brain scan. So with a holiday and the icy driving conditions . . ." His voice and his intentions trailed off vaguely. Any mention of such accidents could only focus attention on the cause of Bud's tragic condition.

Sensitive to his self-reproach Lily said nothing. This was not a time for rebuke or recrimination. This was a time for a family to stick together, to find strength and solace within themselves and from each other.

They sat on the hard wooden bench outside ICU awaiting the return of their son. Twice Lily started to say something, twice she became abruptly silent.

"Hon?" he asked.

"Nothing," she said.

"Can't be nothing. Something you started to say and didn't. What?" he insisted.

She refused to answer.

"Lil?" he asked again. "God, if we can't talk at a time like this . . ."

"All right. You want to know. I'm thinking . . . thinking maybe something happened up there in Radiology. Maybe they . . . they just covered him up and moved him to wherever they move people who . . . like that young woman. There. That's what I was thinking," she admitted, determined not to cry.

"And if it did happen . . . it was all my fault . . ." he added.

"I didn't say . . ." she was about to deny when the elevator doors opened. The nurse wheeled Bud back onto the floor again. Lily and Pep hurried to their son's side.

"What did they say? What did they find?" Pep demanded.

"Dr. Newman will be here in a little while. He'll tell you."

The nurse wheeled the bed back into the cubicle. She attached Bud to the machine once more and the green light started its slow but fairly rhythmic trail across the screen.

The Youngs stood outside the glass watching, studying the screen, studying their son, seeking some sign of movement. Behind them they heard footsteps approach. They turned to discover Dr. Newman.

"Doctor . . ." Lily began, in a beseeching tone he was quite accustomed to hearing.

"Mrs. Young, you can come in."

She followed Newman into the cubicle. While he proceeded to administer the usual neurological tests to Bud, he explained.

"The second scan did reveal some petechial hemorrhages in the deep white matter of his brain."

"Oh, God . . ."

"However, there is no sign of sufficient traumatic force to rupture any axons or small capillaries. Which is to the good. Best of all, the mannitol seems to be controlling the cranial pressure, which is what I worry about most in the first few days."

Meantime, Newman was applying pressure to Bud's fingernails to evoke some response. He took a needle out of the alcohol jar on the night table. He delivered sharp stabs to Bud's arms and legs. He drew no response but covered his concern by saying, "Well, it's a little early for him to react."

Actually Newman thought, *All that work, all that effort, and he's slipping away, slipping away. Well, we'll wait it out. Another twenty-four hours, another forty-eight hours . . . Who knows? And the joke of it is, ironic joke, this poor mother is pinning all her hopes on me. She thinks that I have anything to do with it. That I have some magic. We've done all we can. If this boy is to survive, it will depend not on what we do but on what his body, his brain do.*

To sustain her, Newman said, "Mother, all things considered, he's doing as well as we can expect at this time. Why don't you and your husband go home? Get some rest. So you'll have the energy you need for tomorrow. We'll see him through the night. These are good people on ICU. Trust them. Okay?"

It took a long moment before Lily Young was able to say, "Okay, Dr. Newman, if you say so. Because we trust you."

Damn, but I wish they didn't, Newman thought, *I can't do miracles. But it makes them feel better to think I can.*

As they pulled up to the house in Lily's car, they were surprised to discover the lights on in all the downstairs rooms.

"What's going on?" Pep demanded. "I thought you left Gwen with the Dolingers."

"I did."

They pulled into the garage. Went quickly through the door into the kitchen, Lily calling, "Anybody home?"

"Mom" was the terrified cry from Gwen as she came racing into the kitchen, throwing herself into her mother's arms and starting to cry.

"Gwen . . . darling . . . please . . ." her mother consoled.

"Bud? How's Bud?"

"He's fine . . . he's doing . . ." Lily was at a loss for reassuring words, so she fell back on Newman's words. "He's doing as well as can be expected at this stage. Now why aren't you still at the Dolingers?"

"I couldn't wait . . . I had to be here. I had to find out . . . is Bud going to die?"

Sobered by the events of the last harrowing hours, Pep took over. Releasing Gwen from her mother's arms, he dropped to one knee beside her, held her close, and spoke very softly, "Darling, nobody in the hospital said anything about Bud dying. He's been injured. But they have everything under control. The pressure inside his head. His heartbeat. Everything. It's just a matter of waiting it out. Time. A few days and everything . . . everything'll straighten itself out."

"Is he in pain?"

"He doesn't seem to be in pain," Pep improvised, casting a glance in Lily's direction, seeking her help.

Before she could come to his aid, Gwen asked, "Well, what did *he* say? *Is* he in pain?"

Lily decided to put an end to any further evasions.

"Gwen, dear, Bud didn't say anything. Because he can't say anything. He's unconscious."

"Unconscious . . ." The child repeated the word slowly. "Just out of it?"

"Yes, dear, out of it."

Gwen did not reveal the extent to which the news shocked her. She shook her head almost imperceptibly and said only, "Bud . . . poor Bud . . ."

"Now," Lily took command, "I think we all better try to get some sleep. It's going to be a long day tomorrow."

"Yeah," Pep agreed. "Sleep. We could all do with some sleep."

It was just past two o'clock. Pep woke from a troubled sleep which had been dominated by fitful dreams that all ended up with the wagon going out of control. Each time he woke short of crashing. As if part of his mind were trying to rewrite what had happened.

He eased himself out of bed under the delusion that Lily was still asleep. He went into their bathroom to find one of the antacids he usually took after overindulging in food or drink. He found only an empty carton.

Damn it, why keep empty cartons around? Throw them out. So a person will know when to replace them, he fumed silently until he realized that he was the one who had used the last envelope in that carton and never tossed it out.

I must get over this tendency to blame Lily for everything that is my fault. Belatedly he added, *Especially now. Especially after what happened yesterday.*

He went down to the kitchen, hoping to find an antacid there. He found none. So he contented himself with some club soda on ice, thinking that if he could force a few burps it would relieve the pressure and the burning. It didn't help.

He went into the living room. He thought for an instant to turn on the television. Decided not to. He slipped into his regular easy chair, from which he watched all the football games, the baseball games, always with Bud.

Good God, I must have been out of my mind, driving that wagon in the condition I was in. Bud . . . Bud . . . you've got to get well. You've got to! No matter what it takes, we'll do it. If Dr. Newman can't do it, we'll find some doctor who can. And I promise you, son, if you get well I'll never take another drink as long as I live!

He heard steps on the stairs. Bare feet.

"Lil?"

No response. Then into the room came Gwen.

"Daddy . . ."

She went to him, climbed onto his lap as she used to when she was a child of five, six, seven. After which she considered herself too grown-up for such childish conduct. She was always an independent one, Gwen was.

Not on this night.

After some minutes in which she lay there pressing against her father's chest for comfort and reassurance, she spoke in a soft voice, "I . . . I'm sorry . . ."

"Sorry, baby? About what?"

"Bud . . ."

"We're all sorry about that."

"No, I mean, I'm specially sorry. Like in some way I'm partly to blame. . . ."

"You? You weren't even there. You had nothing to do with it," Pep pointed out.

"What I mean, the last few years, I didn't like always being introduced as 'You know, she's Bud Young's kid sister.' "

"I know, sweetie, you don't like being called a kid anymore."

"It isn't that. I don't like being someone's sister. I'm me. I'm Gwen Young. I'm a person. Not somebody's something."

"Well, baby, soon people will accept you for what you are. Yourself. Don't worry about it."

He kissed her on the head.

"What I . . . Daddy . . . what I mean, maybe my resenting Bud . . . and stuff . . . maybe it had something to do with what happened. Maybe I put some sort of hex or something . . ."

"Of course not!" Pep insisted. "You had nothing to do with what happened to Bud. Only one person was to blame. Only one person."

After a long silence Gwen asked, "Dad . . . can I go to the hospital . . . can I see him?"

"I think it'll be all right . . . at least I'll ask."

Lily entered, surprised to find Gwen still awake.

"Darling, tomorrow is a school day again. You need your sleep."

"I can't sleep."

"None of us can, I suppose," Lily replied.

Which Pepper took to be a rebuke.

"Gwen, honey," he said, "you go up to bed. Try to get some sleep. We'll talk more in the morning."

She kissed him on the cheek, untangled herself from him, and started for the stairs. She lingered just outside the living room in case they said anything not intended for her ears.

Pepper Young and his wife faced each other in the unlit living room. Only the faint light from a streetlamp diffused the darkness.

Neither of them could speak a word. Lily sighed softly.

"I know what you're thinking," he anticipated. "You don't even have to say it. I'll do something about my drinking. I swear! So you don't even have to say it. That's what you were thinking. Right?"

"Yes . . . That. And more." She was silent for a moment before she said, "I never thought . . . during all the years . . . How many has it been between junior high school and high school . . . how many years has he been playing football?"

"Five . . . six . . ." Pepper tried to recall.

"Five years, three months, counting last Thanksgiving," Lily counted back. "I remember every month. Every game. I really didn't like to go. Not that I wasn't proud of him. The way people cheered him. The way his teammates loved him. But each time I saw him get hit, something inside me got hit as well. I could never forget the stories I used to read in the newspapers . . . usually tucked away in some part of the sports page . . . about some college or professional player getting hit, suffering a spinal-cord injury, ending up paralyzed. Or worse. Each time Bud was hit, I would pray that he would get up, shake it off, go on playing. Or better still, that the coach would take him out of the game. But it seems they could never spare him. So he went on playing. And I went on feeling the pain inside. But never . . . never did I think it would end up like this . . . never."

"This isn't the end, Lily. That doctor said he'll make it . . . make it."

"No, Pep, that is not what he said," Lily corrected with a

precision that expressed her fears more eloquently than her words. "He talked percentages. He talked figures. He never did say that Bud would make it."

Pepper Young leaned forward in his easy chair, hands clasped before him, staring into the darkness to find her eyes.

"All right, Lil, say it."

"Say what?" she asked, truly confused.

"I know what's kept us both awake all night."

"What?"

"*I* did this. *I* did this to our son . . . my son!" Pepper accused.

Lily did not reply. For he had touched the very nerve, the pain she had been trying to ignore for hours.

"That damn patch of ice. It just happened to be in the wrong place. And it was covered with snow. I couldn't see it. Nobody could. If I knew it was there, would I have slammed on the brakes? Would I? You know me, I'm a very careful driver. I haven't had an accident in years. Years. It just happened . . . it just . . . oh, God, if I could only have that minute back . . . if only I . . . Lil . . . Lil . . ."

He broke down and wept. Lil moved to kneel beside him. She put her arms around him.

"He'll be all right. Somehow I know it," she consoled and reassured.

"No, Lil, go on. Say it."

"Say what?"

"All the things you've been thinking. Accuse me. God knows, I deserve it."

She released him, said no more, stood up, and started for the hallway. She stopped at the archway.

"Pep, if it would make me feel better I would say it. But then what would we have to hold on to between us?"

She lay in bed, alone. She was reminded of the many nights she had spent alone in the eighteen years of their marriage. When they were first married, she was a secretary and Pepper was still a new salesman on the field staff of what was then Beecham Products. He was out on the road half the time. Always he would be loving and warm when he returned. Always promising,

"Hon, I'm getting closer . . . closer. One day soon Beecham is going to know how good I really am. He's going to take me off the road and give me a spot in the home office. I promise you. Then we'll start to live. Really live. Have kids. Be a real family."

Even after he was called in from the field, promoted to assistant group manager, he put off their having a child until he was earning enough so that she no longer had to work.

It had to do with his own childhood. When his father was shipped to Nam. Living on a corporal's pay, even with allowances, wasn't enough. His mother had to work to make sure Pep and his two sisters had all the things kids are entitled to have.

Pep never forgot the days when he and his sisters came home from school to an empty house with only a note on the table telling them what was in the fridge for a snack. Sometimes, what was in the fridge for supper, if she had to work late. Days when he was sent home from school because he had a sore throat and the school nurse thought he would be better off at home in a warm bed with some hot soup. But Mom wasn't there and she was afraid to be called at work because it might jeopardize her job.

Pepper Young had promised himself in those days that when he married his kids would have a full-time mom Who would be there when they needed her. Since the fifth month of her pregnancy with Bud, Lily Young had been a full-time mother. Other women might try to balance a career with mothering, but not Pep Young's wife.

His kids were not going to be denied what was their right.

Pepper Young took great satisfaction from the fact that his success in business made it possible for him to afford his children that luxury. It meant more to him than success itself.

Lily lay there thinking, *And now it's over. All the years spent being Bud's mother, all the love, and care, and worry, it's come down to this.*

God, how I wish I had faith. Believed. That Bud will make it. But somehow deep down inside . . . in my belly . . . where all my feelings seem to be; I have this terrible fear . . . this terrible fear . . .

Her pillow damp with tears, Lily Young lay on her side, facing away from Pep, who had finally fallen into a troubled sleep. The events of this day and night had finally overcome him. She eased out of bed so as not to disturb him.

Needing to be close to her son during the hours when he was alone as his life hung in the balance, she slipped into his dark room. It had been daylight when he left this afternoon, so the blinds were not drawn. The light from the streetlamp was enough to make visible all things in the dark room.

His bed, neatly made. After his summers away at Scout camp he was always good about that. . . . Bed with corners squarely tucked in.

Lily looked around the dimly lit room at the honors and trophies Bud had won. Football, baseball. His baseball coach once said Bud must have been born running. There were pictures on the wall, some of Bud in uniform. Many of his sports heroes. There was one of Joe Montana. Inscribed *To my pal, Bud,* written the time Pepper had won the trip to San Francisco after his division racked up the best sales record in the country. And he had taken young Bud along.

Mixed in with sports heroes were trophies. Including Best All-Around Athlete in his junior year. And also other awards Bud had won.

Bud the athlete could be quite surprising at times. Deeper than people thought. That's how he won the Student Humanitarian Award. It was his idea for his rock group to give that concert to raise money for the starving children in Somalia whom he had seen on television. Originally they had planned to play in the gymnasium, but the outpouring was so great they were forced to move into the football stadium.

Next to that award was a photograph of Bud turning over the proceeds and being congratulated by their senior United States senator. About whom there was now talk that he might be a candidate for the presidency. A potential president smiling and shaking hands with our Bud.

Lily sat down at the desk. Bud's desk. With the computer Pep had bought for him. Bud loved to work at that. Writing reports, compositions, term papers, letters to camp friends who lived a long distance away.

Sometimes, though he was shy about it, and showed very little of it at first, he liked to try his hand at poetry.

Some of it very good, Lily insisted silently. *Or am I the loyal mother speaking? No. His poetry was good. Very good. His English teacher in his sophomore year said so. To prove it she submitted one of his poems to the school annual. And it was accepted. One of only two sophomores to be accorded that honor.*

Lily sat down at the desk. Her fingers played along the computer keys, not attempting to punch in any message. But it reminded her of when she was a novice secretary at the old Beecham Products. Considered one of the fastest, most accurate typists in the secretarial pool, she acquired a reputation for being a good speller too. That was before machines corrected one's spelling. Once she even dared to correct Mr. Beecham. Which everyone thought was a terrible mistake.

Beecham himself was amused and said, "Should be more people in this organization willing to speak up."

Shortly after that episode she had been picked out of the pool and assigned to an ambitious salesman named Pepper Young.

Trying to recapture old times, she flipped on the computer. The screen lit up, an eerie faint green presence in the dark room. She allowed her fingers to wander over the keys. How easy it was compared to her old electric machine back at Beecham Products. Now the slightest touch created only a hushed sound and the letters appeared silently on the screen without the sharp staccato noise of her old machine, even though it had been labeled a Silentspeed.

She was about to flip off the machine when she became aware of what she had imprinted on that screen. She drew her hands back swiftly as if burned.

For on the screen there appeared words that she had no conscious intent to write.

My fault . . . all this is my fault. . . .

She protested at once, *No, no, not me . . . if it had been up to me this would never have happened. Not my fault,* she continued to protest.

But the longer she stared at the words, the more she was forced to admit, *Yes, my fault . . . because it was up to me. Pep is the nicest, most considerate man in the world . . . sober. But I also know what happens to Pep when he's had one drink, then two or three. And I know what those New Year's Day visits are like. I never should have let them go. Never let Bud go. I should have found some reason. Or else just insisted—outright, "No! Bud is not going! If you want to take that silver trophy and show it around, do that. But Bud is not going!"*

That's what I should have done.

Because if I had, by this time tonight Bud would be asleep in this bed, surrounded by all his heroes, trophies, and awards. Not lying there in Intensive Care surrounded not by trophies and awards but by all those machines and tubes that are supposed to keep him alive.

But there were no promises, no real promises from that doctor, considerate as he tried to be.

Lily Young stared at the screen and at the words printed there.

My fault . . . all this is my fault. . . .

The irony of the situation struck her. *The day that Bud was born . . . that very night Pep went out to celebrate with the boys. That euphemism that men employ when they want to avoid being judged as men. And he tied one on. That was the phrase they always used when they talked about Pep Young's big celebration binge. They all thought it was funny. Very funny some of the things he did that night.*

Even I thought, if it wasn't funny it was at least understandable. A man's first child. And a son. Who has better reason to celebrate?

But there are ways to celebrate besides getting so drunk they had to escort him out of the hospital late that night.

Whoever would have thought that what started that night would end up like this? I should have thought . . . I should have known. If what Pep has done to Bud is some sort of crime, then I am an accessory.

Because in a way I gave him permission. The excuses I made for him. He's such a kind and loving husband, such a good father. No one is perfect. This was just one of Pep's little faults. Somehow in my mind, unconsciously, I always accepted the fact that from time to time, Pep would get drunk. The next day he would be unusually loving and attentive. And I would forgive him. Each time I forgave him I was adding to the time when this would happen. Looking back, I was giving him permission.

My fault . . . all this is my fault. . . .

Does it all end here? she was forced to ask herself.

This fine young life . . . all the promise for such a bright future . . . does it all end here . . . ?

Dr. Albert Newman was making his early morning rounds. His first stop this morning was in Neurosurgical ICU. His first patient, *Young, Willard, Jr.*

Newman checked the chart for temperature, blood pressure, and heart action. Temperature and blood pressure as close to normal as one could expect under the circumstances.

He took a reading of the ventricular catheter gauge. Pressure was beginning to build. He made a note on the chart to increase the dosage of mannitol every four hours.

Meantime he opened the valve of the catheter to draw off the excess brain fluid. It came out pinkish in color. A sign of some minor vestigial bleeding.

He checked the bottles of the intravenous lines. Everything as ordered.

Sixteen hours post trauma, thirteen hours post surgery, breathing with assistance, but all other signs within the limits of expectations; the patient was not doing too badly. Not that one could draw any comfort from such signs in the first twenty-four hours. Or even the first forty-eight.

To satisfy his own curiosity, despite the nurses' notes on the chart as to the patient's Glascow Coma score, Newman repeated the test: eye response, motor reflexes, verbal response. Very low on the coma scale.

He left orders that if the patient's mother or father wanted to visit and stay on, they be permitted to do so. Except they were to have no physical contact with the patient. A patient in this precarious condition must be physically disturbed as little as possible. Movement could result in further damage.

Newman came out of ICU to make his rounds of patients who had progressed beyond the point of requiring intensive care. As he should have expected, the Youngs were already there and waiting.

"Doctor?" Lily Young asked.

Newman knew that particular reading of that particular word, that manner of address that was timid, self-conscious at daring to trouble the doctor, and yet, at the same time, desperate to know how the patient was doing.

Newman promised himself that one day in such circumstances he was going to let loose and say, "What do you people expect? You subject your own flesh and blood to all kinds of preventable accidents, automobile crashes, bicycle smashups, Rollerblade disasters without helmets, and then come crying to us. Begging us to just keep them alive. And if we do, then the next thing you'll ask is make them whole again, bring them back to what they used to be. Well, that isn't up to us. Sometimes I don't think it's even up to God. It's something that happens, or it doesn't. And most times nobody, especially the doctor, knows why."

All these things he was strongly tempted to say. Someday. But that day never seemed to arrive.

So he responded to Mrs. Young's plea as comfortingly as he could.

"There's been a little change. All of it to the good. He's pretty well stabilized. There has been a buildup of pressure in his brain but we have it under control."

"Is there anything else that can be done?" Pep Young asked. "Any treatment, any tests . . . no matter what it costs."

"Mr. Young, your son is getting everything he needs. Right now what he needs most is time. Time to recover."

"Has he . . . has he said anything . . . done anything . . . ?" Lily asked.

"No" was all Newman replied, for to say any more would give words to his fears and add even more to the Youngs' torment. That could wait until later.

He turned to start on his way when Pep Young stopped him with an apologetic "Doctor . . ."

"Yes?" Newman asked briskly. He had no desire to engage in any discussion with the father who, in his judgment, being the cause of it all, was not entitled to consideration.

"Bud . . . my son . . . has a sister. Thirteen years old. She's very much attached to him. She'd like to come . . . see him. She's a very grown-up thirteen. She won't be any problem, I promise."

Newman hesitated, then replied, "Yes, of course. But only for a short stay."

He had added that qualification because of his experience in the past. Children were always anxious to visit parents or siblings on his service. Yet they were often so shaken by the sight of the patient lying in a coma, surrounded by, and invaded by, all the medical apparatuses, that many of them fled in tears. Having found not the assurance they sought but the fear of confronting death for the first time in their young lives.

Lily and Pep Young stood at the foot of their son's bed, watching the monitor that reflected his heart action. They studied his face for some sign, some flicker of consciousness. There was none.

They had to be content with the fact that he was at least breathing, even if that required assistance. Every so often the ICU nurse came to check his IVs or replenish them. To measure the output of his Foley catheter. To check his cranial pressure. She was efficient, pleasant with the Youngs, but not nearly as informative as they would have liked.

She never said less than "Ah, good, good." But neither did she say more.

Once Lily asked, "Is there any change, any improvement?"

The nurse smiled, as pleasantly as she could in the circumstances, and said, "It takes time, time." But that was all.

On the afternoon of that second day, Pep Young was summoned from his son's bedside by an urgent phone call. It was

Mr. Beecham, president of BCI, which was a merger of Beecham Products and Chandler Corporation.

"Pep, what's this I hear?" Beecham began.

"There's been . . . I had an accident. My son, Bud . . ."

"That boy of yours, the football hero?"

"Yes, sir. Hurt. Pretty bad. He's still unconscious," Pepper Young explained.

"Oh, I'm terribly sorry to hear that; we're all terribly sorry to hear it. Pep, look, anything we can do . . . you know, he's covered by our health plan, of course."

"Yes, sir. And a good thing. Because this looks like it could take time."

"Well, take all the time you need. And tell that lovely Lily of yours we all sympathize and wish for the best. Our prayers are with you both, Pep. So, keep in touch. Let me know."

"Yes, sir, I will do that."

"Oh, by the way," Beecham seemed to remind himself, "do you have any idea when you'll be back? What I mean is, you've got that sales staff tuned up like a Stradivarius violin. I wouldn't want them to let down because you're not here."

"No, sir, of course not. Give me a day or two and let's see how things go. Okay?"

"Okay, Pep. You're the boss," Beecham said.

As he hung up, Pep Young knew that in their highly competitive business, in this highly motivated company, there was always some man, or woman, eager to move up and take over. Beecham's call, affable and sympathetic as it was meant to sound, was also a subtle hint.

It was almost midafternoon when Pep was able to convince Lily to come down to the hospital cafeteria to have some lunch. He could swear just by looking at her that she had lost pounds in just the last forty-eight hours.

As they started out of Bud's ICU cubicle, a woman they could not recall seeing before was waiting to enter.

She was a small dark-haired woman, who appeared to be in her mid-thirties, or even a touch younger. She wore a white lab coat over her slacks and shirt. There was a plastic badge on her upper left pocket, but they had no chance to read it.

The Youngs stopped to watch through the glass wall as the woman picked up the chart at the foot of Bud's bed, scanned it, then leaned over him to study his pale, expressionless face.

She took a slender metal cylinder out of her pocket. She forced open Bud's right eye and directed the cylinder toward it. It turned out to be a flashlight. She tested one eye, then the other. It was impossible to tell from her reaction whether she was encouraged by what she found.

She pulled back the light blanket and sheet to test his arms and legs. She pinched his arms. He did not respond. She pinched his legs. There was still no response. She took a needle from the glass of antiseptic solution on the table. She made a number of quick stabs at his arms, then his legs. There was a reaction as his left leg jerked to the side slightly. Aside from that she could elicit no reaction from him.

Once she had covered him and made a note in the small red leather book she produced from her pocket, she turned to leave. She came out to be confronted by the Youngs.

"Miss . . . uh . . . ma'am . . ." Lily began, "we're Bud's parents. What were you looking for? What did you find? Is he doing all right?"

"Mrs. Young, Mr. Young, I'm Dr. Curtis. It's a little early for me to become involved in your son's case. But I like to pick up on a case the first moment possible. We'll be talking one day soon." This was all Dr. Curtis would say.

Because what she had discovered in this first exploratory session was not particularly encouraging.

On the first day of school after the holiday, Tuesday, January 3, 1995, Jody Hines, supported by the entire football squad, appeared in the office of their coach.

"Mr. Dugan, what Mr. Young told me the other night, it's pretty bad for Bud. He's in a coma. So what we thought, the team and the whole school should hold some kind of prayer service or something for Bud. I mean, just the fact that we are thinking about him, praying for him, it might help in some way."

"That's a very nice thought, Jody," the coach agreed. "Let's go talk to Mr. Goodale right now. A general assembly . . . the whole school . . . it's a wonderful idea."

"Assembly . . . the whole school?" Principal Alex Goodale pondered, his reservations obvious in his attitude.

"Yes, sir," Jody insisted. "Everybody praying in his or her own way. I know every student in the school would want to be there, would want to join in."

"Oh, I have no doubt. Bud's the most popular student in the school," Goodale agreed.

"Then we can do it," Jody assumed.

"I'm afraid not, Jody," Goodale said.

"Why not?"

"Prayer . . . in our school . . . that's illegal. Unconstitutional."

"But this is for Bud Young!" Jody protested.

"Sorry, boys, I wish I could. But I have no choice."

"It's not like the school is doing something religious," Jody tried to argue. "It's just for Bud."

"Sorry, son, my hands are tied."

By the lunch break hand-drawn signs had appeared in the school cafeteria and on the corridor walls.

THREE O'CLOCK MEETING. STADIUM.
BUD YOUNG NEEDS YOU

There was a light snow falling on the football field. Through the entrances from under the grandstand, students of all grades, male and female, drifted onto the field.

Some of the young women began to hold hands. Soon the entire student body had joined hands. They ringed the field, forming a continuous chain.

Jody spoke first, loud enough to be heard by all as his voice carried through the snow-filled air.

"Bud isn't just a terrific quarterback, he is a terrific guy. A great friend. There isn't anybody better. And if there's any justice in this world, he's going to make it. He's got to make it!"

Others spoke up as the spirit moved them, lauding Bud for all his good qualities, of which he had many. They saluted his athletic ability, his modesty, his willingness to help any student who needed help.

Finally, Mr. Venable, the balding, most senior member of the faculty, and considered a tyrant by most students, spoke up. Chilled as he was, standing there bareheaded in the snow, his collar pulled up to protect his skinny wattled neck, he spoke in a thin nasal voice. But there was no mistaking his genuine concern and love for Bud Young.

"Yes, Bud Young is all those things you have said about him. But I hope in your admiration of his athletic ability and his personality you will also remember what a fine student he is. One of the finest and most eager to learn that it has been my good fortune to have taught in my years in this school.

"More than once he has confided in me his ambition for a career in the sciences. So his scholarship, too, should be honored here today. I have always considered him one of the finest student-athletes this school has produced in my time here. I was looking forward to seeing him go on to one of our better universities and there reflect great credit on this school.

"If that will ever be true rests now in the hands of God, to whom I pray, in my own way, that Bud recovers and comes back to us. If you don't mind I would like to . . ."

To the surprise of the entire student body, and in a voice more powerful than any of them expected, Mr. Venable began to sing.

"Rock of Ages, cleft for me . . ."

By the time he had sung a dozen words, others started to join in. Soon the entire stadium was filled with their voices.

Principal Goodale and his secretary looked down on the snowy scene from his office window.

"What a fine tribute," his secretary remarked. "And no one deserves it more than Bud Young."

"Yes," the principal agreed. "I just hope no one reports this. After all, the stadium is school grounds. And these days we could have all kinds of protests."

On the morning of the third day, when Lily arrived at ICU, she found Dr. Newman, assisted by a nurse, implanting yet another line into Bud's body. This one not in either arm or leg but into his side.

At once she felt a grip of terror in her stomach. Something had gone wrong. Terribly wrong. She could hardly contain herself until the procedure was completed.

As Newman came out, at his first sight of her and even before she could ask, he assured, "It's just a gastrostomy tube. For nutrition. Our way of keeping him fed and starting his digestive system working again."

"Keeping him fed . . ." Lily absorbed that fact, then asked, "How long will he have to be fed that way . . . before he can eat on his own?"

"We don't know at this time," Newman said, avoiding discussing the worst of the possibilities.

"One thing, though," he added, in a more hopeful tone, "I'm moving him out of ICU today."

"Oh? Good!" Lily exclaimed. "I wish Pep were here to see that."

"Not coming today?" Newman asked.

Embarrassed, Lily Young explained, "He has to appear in court today."

"Oh, yes, I seem to recall . . ." the doctor said, not wishing to dwell on the subject since he knew the tension and the pain the cause of this accident must inflict on the entire Young family.

Within the hour the nurse and an orderly, both exercising extreme care, rolled Bud Young's bed out of ICU and into Room 302, a slightly larger private room.

Once they had hooked him up properly, made sure all IVs were working efficiently, they left Lily alone with her comatose son. She sat by his bedside, studying his face anxiously, seeking any sign of change, even a flicker of consciousness.

Several times she thought she detected something. She rose to lean over him for closer scrutiny. Each time she realized that it was not her actual perception but her desperate hope that had excited her.

On orders from his attorney, Lawrence Meade, Pepper Young appeared at the courthouse earlier than the time specified in the citation.

"You wait here," Meade said. "Let me handle this. Maybe we can avoid your appearance altogether."

Presuming on a casual relationship—they both belonged to the same country club—Meade went directly to Judge Bruce's chambers. Since the judge had a golf handicap of only four and Meade's was nineteen, they had never played in the same foursome. But they had a passing, nodding awareness of each other, which gave color to the attorney's claim to the judge's secretary that they were friends.

Judge Bruce was just slipping out of his suit coat and about to don his black robe when he was alerted by the knock on his door.

"Yes, Eleanor?"

"Judge, there's an attorney here to see you. Lawrence Meade." When she did not receive the expected reaction, she explained, "Said he's a friend of yours."

"That means he wants a favor. Okay. Show him in."

As soon as Meade appeared in the doorway, Bruce recognized him. "Oh. Of course. Just that I didn't know your name was Meade. Come in, come in. What can I do for you?"

"Your Honor, I've got this case before you . . . very unfortunate situation . . ."

"Has your client appeared?"

"Yes, of course. But I thought in view of the circumstances you might want to hear this in chambers."

"Why? Is he physically disabled?" Judge Bruce asked.

"No, Your Honor. It's just that the situation is so delicate, this might better be disposed of without any publicity," Meade suggested.

"What's the charge?" Bruce demanded a bit brusquely.

Meade hesitated, "This man . . . he's a reputable member of the community. Good position. Good references. It would be a shame to expose him to public . . ."

Impatient, the judge interrupted. "What's the charge?"

"DWI," Meade admitted.

"I see. Is he sober right now?" Judge Bruce asked, a tinge of sarcasm in his voice.

"Yes. Of course," Meade replied.

"Then have him wait out in the courtroom like all the others!"

With that Judge Bruce denied Attorney Meade's plea for special consideration.

"And next time, Counselor, don't say 'friend' when even acquaintance overstates the case."

An hour and a half of routine violations had been heard by Judge Bruce. He had meted out fines and sentences that were stiff enough to indicate he was not in an affable mood this morning. Finally the case of *People* v. *Young* was called.

Willard Young and his attorney stepped before the bench.

Judge Bruce studied the copy of the citation and the follow-up report on the case.

"Mr. Young, do you have anything to say?" the judge asked.

"Your Honor, if I may," Attorney Meade intervened.

Judge Bruce turned his attention to Meade, "Yes, Counselor?"

"This situation is more involved than would appear on its face. This is not merely another case of driving under the influence. It is a case deserving of special consideration. If this man is indeed guilty of these charges, he has surely suffered enough, been punished enough. So that in all fairness he should be entitled to leniency. Therefore, I urge that the charge of DWI, Section 104B, be dismissed. Of course, I think a proper fine for a lesser charge would be in order. That, and an appropriate apology from this defendant. Which he stands quite prepared to offer to this court."

"Counselor, you are hinting at special circumstances. Exactly *what* circumstances?"

Having hoped the judge would ask just that question, Meade launched into his prepared dramatic plea.

"Your Honor, at this moment, lying in Mercy Hospital is Mr. Young's sixteen-year-old son. A fine young man. A star athlete. A good scholar. A young man with a wonderful life ahead of him. A life which, his doctor tells me, may tragically be cut short at any moment. What a burden for a father to bear. But even more, this defendant is the emotional support of his wife, who has been shattered by this calamity. In view of these tragic circumstances, Your Honor, I suggest this man has been punished enough. Especially since this is the defendant's first offense. So I urgently recommend that this charge be satisfied by any fine the bench considers appropriate and this unfortunate matter be laid to rest. I suggest that in a case such as this, not legalities but leniency would better serve the cause of justice."

Judge Bruce had listened expressionless. Now he asked, "Counselor, do I infer correctly that this young man you refer to finds himself in that tragic condition as a result of his father's driving while under the influence? Didn't I see something about this on the TV news?"

"Your Honor, if I may recall to you the weather and conditions on New Year's Day. It had snowed the night before. And it was quite cold the next day. The roads were icy and . . ."

"Counselor," the judge interrupted, "I remember New Year's Day very well! It was cold. The roads were icy. And if you are pleading that by way of mitigation, forget it! When roads are icy, even sober drivers can't be too careful. And surely a driver who is impaired should not drive at all. Now I am ready to respond to your plea for leniency.

"Everything you told me about this unfortunate young boy is very sad. I am sorry for him. But for you to come into court and plead for leniency for the man who inflicted this fate on him is like a man who kills his parents and then begs for mercy on the grounds that he is an orphan. Next you'll tell me this defendant's name isn't Young but Menendez. So for you to suggest that this defendant has been punished enough is not quite true. His *son* has been punished enough.

"*Because* of what happened to his son, it is the feeling of this court that rather than receiving leniency, this defendant should suffer an even greater penalty. Since the results of his crime are terrible indeed."

"Your Honor . . ." Meade tried to intervene.

"Counselor, I'm not finished. Now, I am not unaware of the problems confronting this defendant's wife and his son. So I will impose a sentence of only ninety days in the city jail."

"Your Honor . . ." Meade tried to interpose a second time.

"*Suspended*," the judge modified. "So long as he joins Alcoholics Anonymous, and every day of that ninety days attends an A.A. group. Should he fail to attend even a single session I will revoke the suspension and force him to serve the rest of that ninety days."

"Your Honor, if I may point out . . ." Meade waited for permission.

"Yes, Counselor?" the judge demanded brusquely.

"Your Honor, my client is a man with a very responsible position," Meade began.

"Which is no excuse for drunk driving," the judge responded.

"What I wish to point out is that his work, of a highly executive nature, demands that he travel out of town frequently . . ."

Judge Bruce interrupted to declare, "Mr. Meade, there are A.A. groups in every city and town where your client may find it necessary to be. He will find no shortage of opportunities to attend. Now, in addition, I will assess the maximum fine the law allows in such cases. Plus two hundred hours of public service. We must have an end to drunk driving on the roads of this state!"

He then turned to Willard Young.

"Mr. Young, do *you* have anything to say?"

"No, Your Honor."

"Counselor?"

"No. I think Your Honor has been extremely . . . uh . . . fair. Yes. Fair." Meade was anxious to agree.

"One further word, Mr. Young. Your attorney has pleaded on your behalf that this is your first offense."

"It is, Your Honor," Pepper confirmed.

"Mr. Young, don't try to kid this court," Bruce replied angrily. "If I know anything about drunk drivers, this isn't your first offense. It's the first time you've been *caught*. Now, Mr. Meade mentioned that you are a very important executive. Your presence is demanded in all sorts of places away from this city. Exactly what line of work are you in?"

"Sales executive for this entire region for BCI Corporation," Pepper informed.

"Sales executive for this entire region," the judge considered. "Tell you what, Mr. Young. Since you have the ability to inspire people, I hereby sentence you to two hundred hours of service working with high school boys and girls on the South Side of town. Teaching them about business, what's required to get into business and succeed. The opportunities. Instilling in them the idea and the ambition to go out and make something of themselves in the world of business. Right now, most of them don't think they can."

"Your Honor, I give you my word I will try to find the time to do that."

"Mr. Young, people who want to do something don't 'find' the time. They 'make' the time. And I can give you a head start. The principal at the Martin Luther King High School is Gerald Francis. We play squash together once a week. So I will be keeping tabs on you, mister. Now, give your wife my sympathy. And I hope to God your son recovers. Next case!"

A wind-whipped snow had begun to fall when Pepper Young came out of Mercy Hospital. He had left his son in the same condition he had been in for the last week, lying in bed, in a coma, a prisoner of the thin transparent plastic lines that kept him alive. Lily had insisted on remaining by his bedside. Pep could not coax her away even by reminding her of her duty to Gwen, who also had needs.

But Lily insisted, "What if he wakes . . . what if no one is here . . . and he thinks he's been deserted?"

It did no good to remind her that Dr. Newman had said that from all he could tell, such an immediate event was most unlikely. But Lily persisted.

Women, Pep thought. *They can be most arbitrary and unreasonable when they are wrong. The damndest thing—when a woman is right you can sometimes convince her to change her mind. But when she's wrong, oh boy!*

He turned up his collar against the cold and the damp snow to start toward the parking lot. On the way he thought, *Not that it's wrong to hope. And that's all Lily is doing. Hoping. The only reason I'm leaving now is not because I want to. I have to. Judge Bruce is waiting for my first report.*

He pulled up at the church whose address he had been given by the answering machine of the local chapter of Alcoholics Anonymous. He turned off the ignition but did not move. His automatic headlights eventually turned themselves off. Still Pepper Young could not move.

He watched several people enter. A man, a woman, then two women together, another man. Several men, a man and a woman together.

God. How many of them are there? Do I know any of them? Would any of them know me? What if one of my men or women is in the group? How the hell am I expected to stand up and say the things those people say, if you believe what you read and what you see in the movies and on TV?

He studied his car clock. In the darkness it read 8:12. The meeting was scheduled to start at quarter after. He'd better move if he wanted to report to the judge's secretary in the morning. *Time to join them,* he decided.

Until he realized, *I am one of them. If I weren't I wouldn't have just left my wife sitting by my son's bedside with that look on her face. And those red eyes. She hasn't cried in front of me the last few days. But she cries. She cries alone. To spare my feelings. I'd better get in there and face it.*

He climbed out of the car. Trudged through the snow that was beginning to accumulate now. He made his way into the building. Studied the slip on which he had written the information. He found the room more by the buzz of conversation than by its number.

His first hasty embarrassed glance revealed no familiar faces. He felt considerably relieved. Seeking anonymity he took one of the folding chairs in the third and back row.

Moments later, promptly at eight-fifteen, a very slender man, about fifty or so, Pepper judged, with the neat appearance of a modest college professor, mounted the low platform at the front of the room. He adjusted his glasses, tugged a bit nervously at his neat bow tie and simply announced, "I am Hector. And I am alcoholic."

There was a response from the group that indicated to Pepper that the man was well known to them and accepted as their chairman for the evening.

"Before we hear from our regular members of the group, are there any newcomers who would like to be heard?"

Pepper knew from the manner of his address that the chairman had identified him as a novice. Two people in the front row strained to look back.

Pep's first compulsion was to get up and leave. But he forced himself to raise his right hand slightly, his forefinger protruding tentatively.

"And your name?" the chairman coaxed.

His legs trembling under him, Pepper Young forced himself to rise. He studied the faces of those who had turned to look at him, expecting to find judgment in their eyes. They were curious. They were concerned. Mainly they appeared to be understanding, eager to help, waiting to hear how . . .

Pepper Young had addressed many sales conventions, many groups much larger than this one. But tonight he found he had no way to begin. This was not an occasion for starting with some joke that he could somehow use to lighten his admission. This was a time for being forthright. Which he felt certain was more difficult for him than it had ever been for any previous member of this group.

He must make a start, must do it now. Because they were beginning to stare. He would do it as he had heard the chairman do it.

"My name is . . ." he paused to choose between Willard and Pepper. He settled for "Willard . . . my name is Willard," he repeated.

Now for the hard part, he realized. "I am alcoholic. This is my first time here. And I am scared."

"Hi, Willard," several of the group welcomed.

But he could not let it rest at that. He felt compelled to explain, "I'm not really . . . what I mean is . . . I don't drink all the time. But there are times . . . not too often . . ."

From the second row on his left, a woman turned back to smile, shake her head sadly and point out, "Denial, Willard. The easy way out. Willard, what are you trying to say? That you are only drunk *some* of the time? Not *all* of the time? And therefore you are not really an alcoholic?? Is that it?"

"No, I didn't mean . . ."

"What *did* you mean?" one of the men asked.

"I meant . . ." Pepper started to explain, "I meant I'm here because the judge said . . ."

"Oh, so you didn't come here on your own?" a third man asked. "Then maybe you're not ready to join this group."

"You don't understand," Pepper protested.

"I think we understand," the first woman said. "You are here because drinking got you into trouble with the law. So the judge laid this down as one of the conditions for your release. So here you are. But you do not wish to be called an alcoholic like the rest of us. Who, to you, are merely a group of drunks. Well, Willard, to belong to this group, the first thing you have to do is face the truth. A good place to start is to tell us what you did that brought you before the judge."

Pepper appealed to the chairman with a glance that asked, *Do I have to?* And the chairman in return nodded, *Yes you do.*

"I . . . I was given a citation for driving under the influence," he confessed.

"And?" the woman coaxed.

"And what?" Pep countered.

"Was that it? DWI? Nothing more?"

What right do these people have to cross examine me? What the hell am I doing here in the first place? I ought to get out now while I can.

The chairman coaxed, "Willard . . . one of our basic steps to recovery . . . declare to the group the harm our drinking has done and then declare it to those we've harmed. It's the only way to start."

Pepper stared down at his hands, which seemed like strangers to him, and fidgeted nervously. All he could think was *I could probably do this if . . . if only I had a drink.*

That thought more than any other convinced him how much he needed help.

"Okay," he conceded. "It wasn't only that I was driving while under the influence of too many eggnogs. It was that my driving led to an accident. I totaled my station wagon. And in the process I . . . I think I may have . . . may have totaled my son as well.

"I've just come from the hospital where I left him lying there . . . in a coma . . . with all kinds of tubes in him . . . and . . ."

He couldn't go on. He found himself in tears. He shook his head, turned away from them to find refuge by facing the wall behind him.

There was not a sound from the group. Just a long silence interrupted only by his sobbing.

Finally the chairman said gently, "It's okay, Willard, we understand. We've all committed our sins while under the influence."

Pepper considered that permission to slip back into his seat. He spent the rest of the evening listening to the admissions of other members, about events in their lives since the last meeting, or earlier in their lives, of temptations avoided and also some to which they had yielded. Of members helping other members surmount the desperate need to have that one drink that would only lead to more drinks and even more after that.

Some were in constant danger. Others were, like Pepper, the binging type, who could go dry for days, even weeks. Until one time when one drink wiped away all control, all resistance. Then terrible things happened to them or to those they loved.

When the meeting ended he was comforted that he was not alone. But felt no less guilty for what he had done.

He knew he would have less of a struggle attending the next meeting.

As he turned to leave, Hector caught up with him and drew him aside.

"Whenever you feel the need for help . . . for reinforcement . . . when that feeling gets too overpowering to handle alone, give me a call."

He passed a slip of paper to Pepper.

"Any hour of day or night," Hector said, with the compassionate attitude of one who himself had battled the craving and the pangs.

Taken aback, Pep said, "Thanks . . . thanks a lot, Hector." Though he was sure he would never have need to make such a call for help. He read the slip hastily. It consisted only of the name Hector and a phone number. He slipped it into his pocket and headed for the door.

A woman seemed to be lingering there. As it turned out, she was waiting to speak to him.

"I work at the hospital. I know your son's case. Don't give up. I've seen cases like his that get better, much better."

As he drove home he relished those words. Until it struck him, *What did the woman mean, "that get better, much better"?*

Why not just "that get better"? Meaning, all better, perfect, good as new. Why that "much better"? Which means not nearly perfect, or totally well.

It troubled him all the way home. And through the night. Troubled him so much that Lily, half asleep, asked, "Pep . . . what's wrong with you tonight?"

He decided not to mention that to her. Dr. Newman. He would ask Dr. Newman.

But about the rest of the events of this night, at least I made a start. Tomorrow night should be easier. And the people there, Hector, and that nice woman who helped me through the worst parts of it, they're good people, all good people.

10

Now that Bud had been moved from ICU, Lily and Pep agreed that it was time to take Gwen to see her brother. Since they decided it had better happen when they were both present, they selected the early evening, just before Pep went off to attend his now regular A.A. meeting.

The reason they felt it necessary for both of them to be there was that Gwen was in those years of her life when even minor experiences became cataclysmic. The end of summer camp, when she had to say good-bye to her bunkmates, was followed by hours of weeping and depression.

So Lily felt compelled to prepare her daughter for what she would face at the hospital.

"Darling, just remember, all that equipment Bud is surrounded by makes his condition look far worse than it is. It's just to keep him going in good condition until he comes out of his coma."

With the impatience of youth, Gwen replied, "Mother! I'm not an idiot. I read. I watch television. Give me credit for having some brains!"

"Sorry, sweetheart. I know. I always keep thinking of you as being nine instead of a grown-up thirteen."

"Do you realize that I am now able to conceive a child?" Gwen demanded, asserting her right to be considered an adult.

"Yes, dear, I realize. Which is why I pray it doesn't happen," Lily replied. "Now, if you're ready, let's go. Dad'll be waiting."

Despite her self-assured declarations, as they started down the hospital corridor toward Room 302, Gwen began to lag a little. Lily noticed but said nothing.

They passed rooms where the doors were partially open, heard the forced encouraging chatter of nervous visitors. Heard an occasional laugh that betrayed itself by being too shrill to be genuine. Each room had its own share and kind of trouble.

Lily could sense the effect it was having on her daughter, who became paler and more grave as they approached 302.

They were at the door. Before either of them could reach for the knob, the door opened and a nurse came out carrying an empty IV bottle.

She greeted Lily, "Ah, Mrs. Young. Your husband's been waiting for you. And is this Bud's sister? Your dad was telling me all about you. He's very proud of you, young woman."

With that she was on her way to other duties.

The door open, Gwen peeked in.

"Dad?"

"Come in, honey. Come in."

Gwen looked back at her mother. Lily urged her on. She entered. Her first sight of her brother caused her to stop, stare, and look at her father. He gestured her forward.

"Go on, dear," he whispered.

She approached the bed. She studied her brother's face.

"He's like . . . like sleeping . . . like if you shook him he'd wake up," Gwen said. "Can I . . . you know . . . touch him?"

"Very, very gently, dear," her father said.

She ran her fingers lightly over Bud's face. Then did it once more. There was no reaction.

"He's really ticklish, Mom. Nobody knows that. It's a secret just between Bud and me. We have lots of secrets. Things we'd talk about that nobody else knew. I bet if I talked to him now . . . told him some of those things, he'd hear me. He would," she insisted.

Lily looked to Pepper, Pepper glanced back, both trying to decide whether to encourage her or not. She made the decision on her own.

She leaned close to Bud so she could speak directly and secretly into his ear.

Lily and Pepper watched, tried to catch a word or a phrase that might give them some inkling as to what Gwen was saying but could make no sense of any of it.

In her growing anxiety to elicit some reaction from her brother, Gwen grew more animated. She began to laugh at jokes they had shared, things they had known together. The more frustrated she became, the more intense became her whispers and her forced laughter until finally she was laughing but crying at the same time.

Lily embraced her to ease her away from the bedside, while Gwen protested, in tears, "He doesn't remember. Doesn't know me at all . . ."

Pepper drew his daughter close to wipe her damp eyes.

"Honey, they say it'll take time. Time," he repeated, for he could think of nothing else to say.

"What if he . . ." Gwen started to ask.

But Lily interposed, "We don't think that way, darling. We never think that way."

On the morning of the ninth day, Lily Young appeared at the hospital promptly at seven o'clock as had now become habit for her. In just a matter of days, her daily routine had been completely adapted to the needs of her son.

While the nursing staff might have resented her intrusion on their busy early morning routine—waking patients, bathing them, feeding them—still they had sufficient sympathy for mothers in her predicament to accept her. As they had many mothers and fathers before her.

This morning was also the first time that Pepper Young had found the will and the ability to drive to the office and fully resume his duties by delivering his annual start-of-the-new-year speech to the entire sales force. On the way he rehearsed.

1996 is a new year. But not just another new year. True, our economy as a whole is growing. But times have changed. 1995 is the start of the new era in business. Competition has made everyone lean and mean. BCI wants not only its former market share but more than its share. And it is there for the taking. But a man or a woman has to go out there and take it. You're going to tell me that's not easy. Well, let me tell you it has never been easy. I didn't get where I am for nothing. I started like all of you did. Making those calls. Cultivating those clients. Keeping at them . . . why when I started out . . .

His thinking began to falter. Clichés. He was mouthing clichés. Ordinarily, he might have been able to sell his speech to his sales staff by his sheer enthusiasm, his reputation for past exploits. But this morning all he could think was *They'll be sitting there saying, who the hell is he to tell us what to do, after what he did to his own son?*

For the first time in his career he found he could not make it to the office. He pulled off to the side of the road at a gas station and diner that announced itself to be a truck stop. He went in for a cup of coffee. Once inside he realized coffee wouldn't answer his needs. He wanted a shot of whiskey. Not wanted, needed. He determined to beat it. He ordered a cup of coffee, added lots of sugar to make it more palatable. But could not drink it.

At the same time he reached into his pocket for his wallet. He fumbled through the assorted cards and slips of paper he had assembled there, searching for a particular one. He found it, unfolded it to reveal an unfamiliar handwriting. Just one name. *Hector.* And the phone number.

He sat there stirring his now tepid coffee, debating with himself. This must be one of those times they talked about at the A.A. meetings, when a man needed a friend, some support. A phone call would do it. By now he had heard a number of such stories. Men, and women, who had been saved from a disastrous relapse by a phone call to a friendly mentor. But still he wanted, needed, that drink. Just one. Just enough to see him to the office and through that damned speech.

He turned from the coffee counter to search for a telephone. There was a bank of two phones on the far wall. Both were in use by truck drivers reporting to the home office. Pepper stood behind one of them waiting his turn, at the same time staring across the dining area at the bar, which was lit up by half a dozen neon signs advertising different brands of beer.

Determined to resist, Pepper turned away, forcing himself to listen to the truck driver, who was now arguing with his dispatcher. Eventually, after minutes that to Pepper Young seemed like hours, the man shouted into the phone, "Screw you, too!" and hung up.

Pepper seized the phone as if it were a lifeline. Holding the paper in one hand and pressing in the number with the other while cradling the phone between his shoulder and his ear, he managed to place the call.

He listened for the ring. It rang once, twice, three times. Then on the fourth ring he heard Hector's voice. But not Hector. This was his answering machine.

"This is Hector. I'm sorry I can't come to the phone right now. But please, please, leave your name and number and I promise I will call back at the very first moment. Hold fast. Just hold on till I call back."

Pepper Young hung up the phone but clung to it for a long moment. Then, with all the excuse that any alcoholic ever needed, he said, *I tried. God knows, I tried. It's not my fault he wasn't there. Besides, all I need is one drink. Just one to see me to the office and through that goddamned speech. Just one.*

He approached the bar. He ordered a bourbon. As the bartender was pouring, Pepper amended, "Make it a double." The bartender's eyes flicked up from the bottle to glance at Pepper. He knew the kind of customer he had before him.

Pepper downed the double shot, took a deep breath, and felt, *There, that's it, done! Now I can get going.* But he found himself unable to turn away. This time, instead of ordering, he motioned to the bartender, who knew that gesture very well. He poured a second shot, making it a double on his own this time. And he left the half-full bottle there.

It was the sound of his automobile horn that woke him. That and the hard knocking on his side window. He pushed back from the steering wheel to glance at the angry face of a man who was shouting at him through the closed door.

"What the hell's the matter with you?"

Pepper tried to shake himself awake. He sat there trying to recollect what had happened. He could vaguely recall having had a drink . . . one . . . or was it two . . . and something about a bottle . . . then he could remember nothing more. He must have staggered out to his car, somehow got in, and fallen asleep. Eventually he'd slumped against the wheel, starting the horn blasting.

Time . . . what time is it . . . ? He glanced at his digital clock. *Four-forty-two. And it's dark out. Have I been here all day? What about the office? Did they call? Were they looking for me? And the hospital? Lily? Bud?*

He managed to get out of the car and make his way back to the bar. A necessary trip to the men's room and he was ready to make those calls.

Maybe if he had just one more shot of bourbon . . . no, he decided, better make those calls first. He called the office. Spoke to Sheila, his secretary.

"Tell the gang I'm sorry, but an emergency came up at the hospital and I just had to be there."

"Bud . . . he's . . . he's not any worse, is he?" his secretary asked in great alarm.

"No . . . no . . . it worked out finally. What seemed like a serious emergency passed, thank God."

"Good, good, I'm so glad. I'll tell the group. I'm sure they understand."

So far, so good, but what a low miserable thing, to use Bud that way, and to thank God for saving him from an emergency that never happened. But now the hospital. The hospital. And Lily.

He fumbled with that call, had to try it three times and lost two quarters in the process. But finally he placed it, asked for Bud's room, and heard Lily's voice.

"Lil . . . hon . . . I'm sorry I couldn't get there, couldn't call. What with my being away so much it's been a madhouse at the office. . . ."

She interrupted with a single word which told him more than he wanted to know.

"Pepper!" Once he fell silent, she continued in a low but firm voice as if she wanted to avoid being overheard. "You weren't in the office."

"Did you call my secretary?" he asked, fearful she had betrayed his entire charade.

"You know I wouldn't do that," Lily said, "though I should stop protecting you. It's what you need. To shake you up."

"Look, I'll come get you, we'll go down and have some dinner. . . ."

"No, we won't. You will go to your A.A. meeting. You'll tell them what happened. Tell them how you used your son to cover your drinking, and used your job to try to fool me. Yes, tell them! Tell them everything!"

She hung up.

She had done her best to sound angry, but once she hung up she could not resist weeping silently, then had to wipe her cheeks dry with her hands when one of the nurses came in unannounced.

Pepper Young went back into the men's room to wash up. He stared at himself in the mirror. At his rumpled shirt collar, his tie askew, his watery eyes. They all rebuked him. But mainly his eyes. He kept staring at them in the mirror. They looked back, accusing him, in Bud's name, in Lily's name, and everyone else he had used in this disgraceful episode.

All the way to his meeting Pep kept repeating, *I've never done anything this low before, making up such cheap transparent excuses. This can't happen again, mustn't happen again. Won't happen again.*

From the moment he entered the meeting, something in the eyes of the others told him that they knew. They had some special sense about each other. They knew when one of them had failed. Their looks rebuked him, but yet, in a strange way, made it slightly less painful to stand before them and admit, in all the details he could remember, what he had done and how ashamed he felt.

At the end of the meeting, Hector apologized to him for not being immediately available when he had called. But he had spent the night before and all that day supporting another member of the group who was facing a serious professional crisis and was strongly driven to resume drinking.

"I was able to see him through it. He's fine now. But as for you, Willard, I feel in view of your special problem, which unfortunately will persist for weeks . . . months . . . God knows how long . . . a little acceleration of our process might be called for. So, here, take this."

Hector handed him a slim two-page document. Pep opened it, glanced at the title, *Twelve Steps, Twelve Traditions.*

"This is the bible of A.A. I know about this," Pep replied.

"Because of your special problem, study Steps Eight and Nine. Try to put them into practice. It should help."

Pepper Young left that meeting stronger in his resolve that this disgraceful episode would never be repeated. But then he reminded himself, he always felt such resolve after his unfortunate lapses.

When he arrived home he was relieved that both Gwen and Lily had gone up to bed. He could not bring himself to face them, even if Lily did not rebuke him. His own guilt was enough.

He slipped into the den, dropped into his easy chair, and under the desk lamp close by he studied Steps 8 and 9 as Hector had urged.

8. Make a list of all persons we have harmed, and be willing to make amends to them all.

9. Make direct amends to such people wherever possible except when to do so would injure them or others.

Pep sat holding that slender but powerful document that had helped so many through the hell of alcoholism. He started to take score. People he had harmed . . . not a short list . . . and make amends . . . to Lily? To Gwen? To Bud?

Whatever he might do or say to Lily or Gwen, how could he possibly make amends to Bud?

Is this Hector's cruel punishment for my having gone off the wagon in such a disgraceful way? Doesn't the man realize that I'm tormenting myself enough without his prodding?

There I go again, putting the blame on Hector instead of on myself where it belongs.

He reread Steps 8 and 9.

11

On the morning of the tenth day Lily Young again appeared at the hospital promptly. She went at once to room 302.

She had made it a rule, each time she entered that room, to call out a cheery "Good morning, Bud!" Or "Hi, Bud. This is Mom!" If he hadn't heard her yesterday, he might today. If not this morning, then this afternoon. And if not this afternoon, then tomorrow. One day, one day, she promised herself, he would wake and hear her.

He would smile at her as he always used to. And she would know the world was all right again. So, as she reached Room 302 she forced herself to take on a cheerful tone of voice as she called, "Good morning, Bud. Mom's here!"

She failed to enunciate that last word. For the space Bud's bed had occupied for these last days was now a gaping empty place. The ventilator stood by unattached, silent and motionless.

He died . . . during the night he died was her first chilling thought. *They should have called me . . . they should have . . . they had no right to just . . .* her thoughts became feverish accusations.

When she was able to utter a sound, she called out, "Dr. Newman! I want to see Dr. Newman! I insist! Where is he?"

Nurses, therapists, orderlies came racing out of rooms along the corridor to see the cause of the woman's hysterical outburst.

Newman himself was in a room at the far end of the floor testing another patient for neurological reactions. He turned away from the bed, raced into the corridor to see for himself.

At once he recognized Lily Young. As he started toward her the elevator doors opened and Pep Young emerged.

Lily greeted him with a cry of pain and anger, "Pep . . . Pep . . . he's gone . . . gone. . . . "

He hurried to her side, took her in his arms. Had to stifle his own pain in order to comfort her.

"Now, honey . . . please . . . cry if you want . . . go on . . ."

By that time Newman had reached them.

"Mrs. Young . . . Mrs. Young . . . no need to cry."

"Bud's dead and there's no need to cry? What kind of human being are you?"

Easing her from Pep's embrace, Newman said, "My God, didn't they call you? Bud's had a slight reverse. A touch of pneumonia. Not unusual in cases like this. As a precaution we moved him back into ICU. That's all. I left orders for you to be notified. Now, let's go have a look."

Gently Newman took Lily's hand. He led her down the hall toward Intensive Care. From outside the glass-enclosed cubicle, he pointed out, "There he is. And as you can see from the monitor, a fairly stable heartbeat. I have him on a regimen of antibiotics. In forty-eight hours I think his temp will be down and his chest X rays will be clear."

Gasping, brushing back her tears, she looked up at Newman for permission.

"Sure. Go on in."

She went to her son's bedside. Aware of Newman's warning about unnecessary movement, she touched Bud's hand very lightly. That his skin was soft and somewhat warm reassured her.

Outside, Newman said to Pep Young, "When I get done with my rounds, we must have a talk. You, Mrs. Young, and I."

They stood by the side of their son's bed staring down at him, almost breathing with him. Comforted again, they could talk of other things.

"You were going into the office, you said."

"Couldn't. It all just seems so unimportant compared to being here," he explained.

"What about Beecham . . . BCI?"

"They owe me time . . . lots of time . . . for all those days and weekends when I had to leave you, leave the kids, to fly to some place where some salesman was on the verge of cracking up. Well, now it's my turn to need help. Before I crack up."

"You said that to Beecham?" Lily asked.

"No. But I will," Pepper determined. "Nothing in this world is more important now than my son."

A tall young black woman carrying what looked like a doctor's bag entered the ICU cubicle. She smiled pleasantly.

With a soft "Do you mind?" she slipped between them and Bud's bed. Without a word she began to perform some tests.

Both Lily and Pep watched closely. Having seen those same tests done several times now, they were accustomed to the routine. The flashlights in the eyes. The pinches. The slight needle stabs. The words spoken closely into the patient's ear.

This time, as at all previous times, Bud's responses were negative. Except that Lily remembered very distinctly one time when that woman doctor had stuck a needle into Bud's left thigh and there had been a slight kick in response. Today that response was missing.

Something has gone wrong. He's deteriorating, she concluded. *I must ask Dr. Newman about this!*

They had been shown into the doctor's office. Even before they were seated, Lily said, "You don't have to go easy with us. I know he's worse. I saw it myself."

"Mrs. Young, I don't know what you think you saw."

"I didn't 'think' I saw. I saw it. And if you don't believe me, ask that doctor who did the first test."

"Exactly what *did* you see?" Newman asked.

"The other day when she stuck him with that needle his leg reacted. Today? Nothing. No sign, no hint of movement."

"Of course not," Newman confirmed. "The pneumonia, the medication, have dulled his senses even more. I didn't expect he would react. That's precisely why I asked that therapist to stop in."

"There, you see, Lily, it's not so bad after all," Pep tried to encourage.

"Now," Newman resumed, "I think it's time we had a very frank talk about the entire situation. I will tell you what we know, what we expect, and also what we fear. You can ask any questions you wish."

Pep leaned closer in his chair to be at Lily's side.

"We have stabilized Bud. This pneumonia is not an unexpected reverse. We have it under control. And I think he will overcome it.

"I must warn you, however, that there are other possible reverses that could be worse. For one, thromboembolism. Because of his comatose condition, a clot can form in an artery. And if it gets to his heart there is nothing we can do. Also, since he has several tubes in him, there is always the possibility of infection. We take all reasonable precautions. But there can be no guarantees. Nor is there any guarantee against hydrocephalus— buildup of fluid in the brain that we can't always relieve. These are all dangers we must be conscious of and try to guard against. Any questions thus far?"

Pepper Young asked very directly, "Doctor, the odds . . . what are the odds of any of these things happening?"

"There aren't any odds," Newman replied. "Each case stands on its own. What failed to happen in a hundred cases might happen in the hundred and first. Even though we do everything in exactly the same way. What happens in these secondary effects of closed head injuries is in the main a mystery to us as well as to the patient's family.

"Now there are some things we do know. Where we can quote odds, as you call them. If we get a patient safely past the first seventy-two hours, we have a good chance of keeping him alive. And we've more than done that with Bud. His most recent brain scan looks good.

"So we come now to the matter of his coma. As a general rule, the patient who comes out of a coma within a week or so has a good chance of not only recovering but recovering most of his faculties as well."

"Then do whatever you can to bring him out!" Lily insisted.

"Mrs. Young, we have no way of bringing a patient out of a coma. We can talk to him to evoke a response. We can apply what we call noxious stimuli—pressure, slight pain, needle stabs—which can sometimes result in involuntary reactions. But only the patient can bring the patient out of his coma," Newman was forced to admit.

"Doctor," Pep asked, "what you said before, about coming out of it in a week or so, what if he doesn't?"

"The rule we must go by, the longer the coma persists, the worse the patient's chances," Newman said simply.

"So what *do* we do?" Pepper asked.

"Wait and see," Newman said grimly. "Wait and see."

Lily's chin began to quiver. Pep feared she would start to cry. But she straightened up slightly, determined not to.

"At this stage of things, Mr. Young, Mrs. Young, I think you should become better acquainted with Dr. Curtis. Since she'll be overseeing Bud's care from now on."

"You're giving up on him," Lily accused.

"No, of course not. But as a neurosurgeon I've done all I can for your son. What he needs now are the specialized skills of another kind of doctor."

"What 'other kind' of doctor?" Pep asked, sharing his wife's uneasiness about any change, since they had both formed a deep respect for Newman, especially for his frankness with them.

"Dr. Curtis is what we call a physiatrist. A relatively new specialty."

"Physiatrist . . . sounds almost like a foot doctor," Pep repeated.

"A physiatrist is a physician who takes over the treatment of a trauma patient once the neurosurgeons have done their part," Newman explained. "She is responsible for all aspects of the patient's care and recovery. His physical health, his rehabilitation . . ."

"Rehabilitation?" Lily reacted, alarmed once more.

"I think she might better explain that," Newman said. "Let me set up an appointment for you." He lifted his phone, punched in an extension number. "Phyllis . . . Al Newman. I have sitting in my office the Youngs. Yes, yes, that boy you saw after we discussed him at grand rounds. If you could see them soon . . . now? Now would be the best time. I'll send them right along."

Newman penciled a room number on his pad, ripped off the sheet, and handed it to Pep.

"Doctor," Pep asked, "if sometime along the way . . . we would like to talk to you."

"Anytime. I'll be following Bud's progress all the way."

When they were shown into Dr. Curtis's office, Pepper realized that she was the woman who had examined Bud while he was in ICU. Now that he took a good look at her he thought, *Too young. She's too young to be very experienced. Still, Newman said this was a relatively new specialty. So maybe they have to be young. But I would feel better with an older doctor, and a man, like Newman. Yet he recommended her. Let's see how it goes.*

"Mrs. Young, Mr. Young." Dr. Curtis gestured them to be seated on the other side of her desk.

Since she was a slender woman, and only slightly over five feet two, of trim figure, she appeared younger than thirty-four. Though that added to Pep's qualms about her experience, she had the air of a very confident person when she spoke.

"First, I know that you are going to hear all kinds of rumors from friends and relatives about similar cases they've heard about. How someone's third cousin had an uncle who had a similar injury and some doctor used some magic drug or treatment and achieved a miraculous cure. I urge you to avoid all rumors, gossip, and volunteered information.

"Rehabilitation is not amenable to sudden cures or miracles. That happens only on television or in films. What we do here is a long, slow, sometimes tedious process. Recovery is slow. Rehabilitation of body and mind is oftimes even slower.

"So the key word is patience . . . patience," Curtis emphasized.

"I'd have all the patience in the world if only he'd open his eyes . . . say a word . . . even just smile. . . . " Lily said.

"Mrs. Young, patience doesn't start *after* he opens his eyes, but *before*. We have techniques we bring to bear to try to facilitate his coming out of coma. But they can only facilitate. It's the patient who really does the recovering."

"Surely there must be something a mother can do, a father can do. . . . " Lily insisted.

"There is. Do what you're doing. Come to the hospital. Spend time at his bedside. Cooperate with us. Give us helpful bits of information about him—his likes, his dislikes. What he responded to before, so we can try to see if he will respond now. Such things. And also one other . . ."

Curtis paused to give her words added importance, then said, "The one thing you should *not* do . . . is blame us for any failures. This is not surgery—where we can operate, correct the offending condition and the patient is cured. Or internal medicine, where we prescribe a drug, the patient takes it and eventually recovers. We deal in uncharted areas. Damage to the brain, an organ we still don't fully understand. So give us time. Give us your cooperation. Most of all, your understanding that everything we do we do with the best of intentions within the limits of our present knowledge. Meantime I give you a promise. We will do everything we possibly can to keep your son in good stable condition, promote the recovery of his physical and mental abilities to the fullest extent possible."

They thought she had finished when she reminded herself, "Oh, yes, one thing more. I've assigned Marcia Ethridge to your son's case. She's as good as they come. Like myself, she will always be completely honest with you."

By the time she had finished, Pepper Young had a quite different and much higher regard for a doctor named Phyllis Curtis.

It was several days since Bud had been moved from Intensive Care back to room 302.

Lily Young arrived at the hospital early in the morning. She had sent Pepper off to his office, had made sure Gwen was to be picked up for school. Now she greeted those of the nursing staff who had come to know her well. She entered Bud's room calling out, as cheerily as she could, "Good morning, Bud. Mom's . . ."

She never did complete her greeting for she was surprised by the presence of the young black woman of light color who had examined Bud once before. She was leaning over Bud, lifting his right arm and rotating it in a slow, wide circling movement. The young woman was attractive, had a strong compact body that bespoke considerable physical strength and ability.

Her unexpected presence and her unusual activity caused Lily to adopt a rather cautious attitude.

"Who are you? And what are you doing to my son?"

The young woman rotated Bud's arm one more cycle, gently set it down before she turned to respond to Lily.

"I'm Marcia Ethridge. Didn't Dr. Curtis tell you?"

"Well, she . . . mentioned a Ms. Ethridge . . . but I didn't expect . . ."

"A black woman?"

Flustered at being confronted so directly with the truth, Lily denied it, "Oh, no, not that . . . not that at all. Just someone so young. You can't be more than twenty-three, twenty-four. . . ."

"Twenty-seven," Marcia Ethridge corrected.

"You look so much younger," Lily commented. "So you're the therapist who's going to bring my Bud out of his coma."

"Mrs. Young, we therapists make no promise except one: We are going to do our *damnedest* to bring your son out of coma. Until then we are going to keep his muscles active and his body in as good physical shape as we can for the time when he might come out of coma."

"And that's what you were doing now," Lily realized.

"Yes," Marcia replied as she resumed working with Bud. This time she lifted aside the sheet. She began to flex his leg, bending his knee, bringing into play all the muscles of his thigh and his leg. She then applied herself to his other leg.

"This is just the beginning," she explained to Lily. "His activity must be increased bit by bit, day by day. Several times a day."

She had expected that Lily would take the hint and observe more closely. But since she did no more than react with a slight nod, Marcia Ethridge realized that more explicit instructions were necessary.

"You might learn by watching," the young woman said.

The look on Lily's face revealed her puzzlement.

"Mrs. Young, it might be necessary for you to do this. Especially once Bud is released from the hospital."

"Once he is released . . ." Lily started to ask, then realized, "You mean they could . . . would release Bud while he is still in coma?"

"That can happen," Marcia confirmed. "Or when we therapists are overloaded with patients and don't have enough time, it would help if you could pitch in. At the rate people are destroying themselves and each other, we can't train therapists fast enough to care for all of them."

For half an hour Marcia Ethridge exercised Bud Young's arms and legs, lifting them, putting them through all the motions he would normally do. Lily watched closely, making mental notes of the manner in which the young woman worked.

When Marcia had covered Bud once more, made sure his IVs were all in place and functioning normally, Lily assumed that the exercise was over.

"You do this for the patient every morning?" she asked.

"Twice each day. More if the nurses are too busy to do their share the other two times. Very important. Not only keeps his muscles from becoming tight but will help ward off another bout with hypostatic pneumonia. Patients in coma who are allowed to lie motionless are prone to pneumonia."

"I've already learned that," Lily said. Assuming the young woman's work was completed, Lily added, "Thank you very much. Not only for what you did for Bud but for the information as well. I promise you I'll learn how to do this. What time will you be coming back today?"

"I'm not leaving. Not yet," the young woman said. She turned to lift a black physician's bag to the bedside table.

Curious, Lily watched as the therapist laid out a dozen surgical swabs and several small bottles of various colored fluids. When she opened the first bottle, Lily was immediately assaulted by the strong odor of garlic, so penetrating it seemed to fill the room.

Marcia soaked the cotton swab in the garlic compound. She brought it close to Bud's nose. She wafted it back and forth, back and forth, slowly, affording Bud ample time to react to the strong odor if indeed he was aware of it.

He did not react. Not by movement or grimace. Not by any attempt to avoid the stench.

Lily could not resist asking, "You mean he doesn't . . . you would think that a smell so strong . . ." In her effort to hide her disappointment she could not express herself too fluently.

Marcia Ethridge realized that whatever Lily had been told by Dr. Newman and by physiatrist Curtis, it had not been explicit enough. Or else, having heard, Lily was unable to accept what she had been told

So while she continued to try out different scents to evoke a reaction from Bud, Marcia Ethridge used the opportunity to prepare this patient's mother for all the usual and expected eventualities in these cases.

"You see, Mrs. Young, the first aim in speech and physical therapy is to make the comatose patient aware, alert, and attentive to instructions. The only way we have of even attempting to accomplish that is by employing his own senses."

"Smell . . ." Lily realized.

"Plus touch, taste, and hearing. We try all four, hoping that one of them will work."

"Hoping," Lily commented grimly.

To encourage her, Marcia said, "Sometimes it just happens. I mean we can fail at all our efforts . . ."

"Such as right now," Lily said pointedly, as Marcia capped that last vial that had smelled strongly of a noxious chemical odor.

"Yes," Marcia had to admit, "such as right now. But we've only failed with his sense of smell. We've lots further to go. Lots."

With that she left the room with a quick " 'Scuse me."

She returned a few minutes later with a small bucket of ice cubes and a stainless-steel pan which held an object Lily had never seen before. It resembled a narrow life belt of tan canvas. Except that the steam that rose from it betrayed it was intensely hot. If Lily had any doubt, it was dispelled by the manner in which Marcia handled it. Using a forceps she lifted it and proceeded to wrap it in not one but three heavy towels.

She laid the towels across Bud and lifted his arm onto it.

Lily protested, "He's very sensitive to heat. You'll burn him."

But too soon she realized that, far from burning him, the intense heat evoked no reaction at all. He made no attempt to pull his arm away.

Twice more Marcia repeated the exercise. Twice more Bud failed to respond. She abandoned that in favor of applying the ice cubes to various areas of his arms, legs, even his groin where he should be most sensitive.

She had elicited no response. No hostile or rebellious movement, no rejection, no evasion.

"Nothing . . ." Lily whispered. "Nothing . . ."

Undeterred, Marcia Ethridge proceeded to apply physical stimuli. She pinched him, stabbed him with needles, exerted what would normally be unbearable pressure to his fingernails. All without any sign of success.

Aware that with each failure the patient's mother was becoming more and more unnerved, Marcia had to decide how to treat the mother as well as the patient. Either banish the woman from the room or else enlist her cooperation. From experience, she had learned that relatives who feel they have an active part in assisting the therapist generally handle disappointment better than those who only stand and watch.

"Mrs. Young, would you do me a big favor?"

"Sure. If I can. Anything," Lily offered immediately.

"Would you stand right here? As close to Bud as you can. Place your mouth against his ear and say in a loud voice, 'Bud, dinner's ready!' "

" 'Dinner's ready'?" Lily asked to make sure.

" '*Bud*, dinner's ready,' " Marcia corrected.

Lily proceeded to do as instructed. She pressed her cheek against her son's face so that her lips were up against his ear.

"Bud, dinner's ready!"

"Louder," Marcia instructed.

"Bud, dinner's ready!"

"Louder still," Marcia insisted.

"Bud, dinner's ready!!!" Lily shouted, then drew back saying, "I hope I didn't disturb any of the other patients."

"They're the least of my worries," Marcia said, to conceal her own disappointment. This could prove to be one of those intractable cases that resisted all her efforts to rouse the patient from coma, with the most morbid of results.

She stood over the patient and, aiming directly at his ears, she clapped her hands as hard as she could. She repeated that six times. The explosive sounds had no effect on him.

She reached into her bag once more and brought out what Lily recognized as a plain, everyday farm cowbell. She swung it over Bud's head. Still no reaction.

Lily watched with fading hopes and growing despair. But Marcia Ethridge seemed anything but despairing. Each failure seemed to challenge her. She delved into her bag and brought out a grinding noisemaker of the kind Lily had seen and heard making such a distracting racket on New Year's Eve. Marcia held it over Bud's head and spun it swiftly, producing as much noise as possible for what seemed minutes.

Surely, Lily thought, that will do it. But still Bud remained unmoving, unreactive, responding only to the respirator which kept him breathing at a slow steady rate.

The therapist finally seemed to admit defeat, momentary defeat at least, for she asked, "Mrs. Young, what is Bud's favorite food?"

"His favorite food?" Lily asked, confused by the suddenness and the seeming irrelevance of the question.

"Some special food you prepare, that, when he comes into the kitchen his face lights up and he says something like "Wow, are we having that for dinner tonight?"

"There're several things I do . . . some of the simplest things that he thinks I make better than any other mother in the world," Lily replied.

"Like?" Marcia pressed.

"My chocolate chip cookies for one. When I'm baking those he can smell them even before he comes downstairs."

"Then, do that!"

"What?" Lily asked.

"Before you come in tomorrow, bake some chocolate chip cookies. But double all the fragrant ingredients. The chocolate. The vanilla extract. The things that give them that special fragrance he reacts to. Then bring a few in tomorrow."

"You think something like chocolate chip cookies can do it?" Lily asked.

"Mrs. Young, if we knew what 'can do it' we'd do it. We don't. So we have to try every familiar thing we can think of to reach your son. Familiar smells, familiar sounds, familiar words, familiar songs. Anything that will get through to him."

"Familiar . . ." Lily echoed the word. "There's his school song. And a rock group he plays with and . . ."

Marcia interrupted, "Rock group? Bud plays with a rock group?"

"Oh, nothing professional. I wouldn't want you to think that. Just a bunch of the guys in his class," Lily explained.

"Good enough. Can you round them up? Would they come here?"

"They'd do anything for Bud," Lily said proudly.

"Then get them together. Have them come in. With all their equipment. Electric guitars. Synthesizers if they use them. Amplifiers. The works," Marcia Ethridge said with considerable enthusiasm and expectation.

"I'm sure I can get them all together in a day or two."

"And anything else familiar that you can think of that might affect his senses of smell, touch, hearing."

"I'll get working on it as soon as I leave," Lily promised.

"Mrs. Young . . . if I may . . . and please don't misunderstand. But there is very little you can do here all day. Exercising him when you're here, yes. But sitting by Bud's side all day and into the evening isn't going to make the difference. And surely you have other family duties."

"But if he wakes and there's no one here he knows . . ." Lily protested.

"Mrs. Young, if he wakes, if he does come out of this, I promise you, you'll know it minutes after it happens," Marcia assured, at the same time, as gently as possible, informing Lily of the unlikelihood of such an event in the immediate future.

There was a look between them. Lily's blue eyes and Marcia Ethridge's soft brown eyes exchanged a moment between women that only women would understand. The one trying to say, *This won't be easy, or quick, but I'm doing my very best.* And the other that said, *I understand. Much as I hate to admit it, I understand. And I know you'll be doing your best.*

Softly Lily said, "I'll just . . ." She leaned over and kissed her son on his cool cheek. "I'll be back this afternoon."

"Good," Marcia Ethridge said.

She watched Lily Young cross to the door, stop, turn back, and almost change her mind. But a nod from Marcia sent her on her way.

Marcia Ethridge turned back to her patient. Without the presence of his mother she could indulge her own feelings.

This handsome young boy, just verging on manhood—what a shame. What a waste. She knew the odds. And they were not good. In her years of practice, few by some standards but four long rigorous years at her profession, she had seen patients as young and some younger who lingered and never came out of coma. Whose families finally begged to have all the machines turned off. Some who even had to go to court to get permission.

Sometimes after such a case Marcia Ethridge would go home at night and face herself in the mirror and ask, *Why do I do this? Why not go into some other form of therapy?*

Instead of working this hard as part of a hospital staff, why not become a school therapist? I'd be paid more and have to work only nine months a year instead of twelve.

Or why not start up a business like a weight-reduction clinic for overindulged women. It wouldn't call for any different ability or training than I already have. And it would be so much less taxing on my emotions and so much more rewarding financially.

It seems in our society the less necessary a commodity is, the more profitable to provide it.

But to Marcy, each new patient was a new challenge. And she brought just enough of them through to a reasonable state of health to make her feel her efforts were worthwhile.

She would be back again to work with Bud Young this afternoon. And tomorrow. And tomorrow. And all the tomorrows until . . . She preferred not to think of all the possibilities. Just one.

She was determined to bring this young man out of his coma.

13

Marcia Ethridge returned to room 302 and patient Willard Young, Jr., after she had applied her skills to six other patients during the rest of the morning and the early afternoon.

One patient was a sixty-seven-year-old man who had suffered a stroke. The second was a twenty-six-year-old cyclist whose motorbike had skidded on the icy road and slammed into a utility pole. Two other patients were the results of a single automobile crash that had taken place three weeks ago. The fifth patient was a young woman who had suffered an embolism and partial paralysis during childbirth. The sixth was a four-year-old boy who had fallen from a fifth-floor window which, through negligence, failed to have the required window guard in place.

The little boy was still in a coma. As was one of the crash victims. But the others were in various stages of recovery. All with a long way to go to attain self-sufficient functioning.

When she opened the door of 302, her first glimpse told her that Mrs. Young was back. She was seated alongside Bud's bed, her physical attitude one of tense defiance. In her lap was a transparent plastic bag full of cookies, which even from a distance Marcia could identify as of the chocolate chip variety.

The aroma that drifted toward the door informed Marcia that far more than normal amounts of vanilla extract and chocolate had gone into these cookies.

"Good afternoon, Mrs. Young," Marcia began pleasantly to defuse the tension that was obvious.

Lily Young did not return the greeting but announced accusingly, "Didn't work."

"What didn't work?" Marcia asked.

"Did exactly what you said. Extra vanilla. Double extra chocolate bits. Didn't work."

"How do you know?"

"Tried them. Held them under his nose for minutes at a time. Then broke them to let more of the aroma escape. Didn't work."

"Let me have a go at it," Marcia said, fully aware that her chances were not much better.

She held a piece of cookie under Bud's nose. For an instant she thought she detected a slight twinge of movement. But she soon realized she was mistaken.

"I'm afraid you're right, Mrs. Young. It does not work." *But, she thought, this is as good a time as any to set the ground rules.* "Mrs. Young, you must not fall into the habit of thinking that every suggestion I make is a promise. We're not in a position to make any promises. We try and fail and try and fail until one day, we hope, we will try and succeed. Now, what did you do about the rock band?"

"They're supposed to be here at four, soon as their classes are over."

"Good!" Marcia commented. She proceeded to put Bud through the physical part of her therapy. Lily watched closely, hoping to detect some response, even if it was only a move to reject the manipulation intended to keep his muscles from wasting away during his present state.

Marcia was engaged in applying pressure to Bud's fingernails when they heard the knock on the door. A young man's voice asked timidly, "Mrs. Young?"

Lily opened the door to a group of four students, each of whom was carrying several pieces of sound equipment plus a guitar. The leader was carrying a keyboard as well. All four were dressed in jeans ragged and worn open at the knees. The leader had a scraggly ponytail tied back with a red rubber band. All four wore T-shirts with slogans on them, some memorable, some better instantly forgotten.

They entered in silence and on tiptoe. None could avoid glancing at Bud, then turning away. As if to stare would be an intrusion.

The leader asked, "Ma'am, is it okay to set up?"

"By all means," Marcia said. "That's why you're here."

When they had set up their instruments and plugged in all the electronic equipment so that the cables on the floor seemed to be a nest of black snakes, the leader asked, "What do you want us to do, miss?"

"What are Bud's favorite songs?"

"He's got a dozen favorites. Long as they got the beat."

"Then let's start with any of them. But loud. Real loud," Marcia instructed.

"Miss, you sure? After all, this is a hospital," the leader replied.

"Loud. Real loud!" she insisted.

"Okay, lady," the leader replied. He gave his little band the downbeat and they started to play.

Even Lily, who had heard them before when she and Pepper acted as chaperons at school dances and knew what to expect, felt blasted out of the room. But Marcia nodded, urging them on. At the same time she studied her patient, hoping to see some reaction to this sound which caused the entire room to vibrate.

They had played a set of four numbers to no effect. As they paused to ask further instructions, there was a severe knock on the door.

Marcia answered to admit Dr. Phyllis Curtis.

"Ms. Ethridge, would you please step outside?" the physiatrist asked in a tone more compelling than a request.

Once in the corridor, Dr. Curtis asked, "May I ask what in the world is going on in there? There've been complaints from all over the third floor."

"An exercise in patient awareness by stimulating his sense of hearing," Marcia informed in technical language.

"I appreciate the effort, though personally I am not a devotee of rock music," Dr. Curtis said in her severe mode, so that nurses and visitors who had come out of other rooms could overhear. Then she lowered her voice to ask, "Marcy, is it having any effect?"

"No detectable effect, I'm afraid."

"Give it another shot. After which I will have to pretend to rebuke you for insubordination. But this is a hell of a good idea and worth pursuing," Curtis said.

The band had played through another song, as loud as before. Each of the four kept his eyes glued on Bud, rooting for him to respond. But by the time of the expected reprimanding knock on the door, they all knew, as did Marcia and Lily, that this, too, had failed.

As the young musicians disconnected their gear and gathered it up, they each apologized.

"Sorry, Mrs. Young. But if Bud didn't react to that last number he's just never going . . ." one said.

Realizing he had blundered, the young man turned red as the slogan on his T-shirt. He tried to amend his statement but ended up lamely, "just . . . never going to react today, I guess."

"Thanks, guys, thanks a lot. You did a terrific job," Lily said to send them on their way feeling a little less guilty. Though she herself had been badly unnerved by this failure.

Once alone, Marcia said, "Mrs. Young, we have to be realistic about this. Another trial, another failure. Tomorrow we try again."

"How long . . ." Lily started to ask but felt the need to repress her anxiety.

"There's no answer to that question, unfortunately," Marcia replied. "We just go from day to day."

It was the beginning of the second week of Pepper's attendance at his A.A. group. Most of those in attendance were the same as on all his other nights. But several who had been there were not present on this night. And there were two members who were making their first appearance. The proceedings followed the same format as always.

Members introduced themselves, acknowledged their inability to manage their addiction to alcohol by themselves. They recounted the tragic and sometimes sordid events which had brought them to seek the aid of their fellow alcoholics. One reported having relapsed but felt that she had recovered sufficiently to have earned their continued support.

Just about the time Pepper assumed the meeting was over and was feeling relieved to have escaped the need for further self-revelation, Hector stood up to ask, "Anybody here who'd like to report on taking their next step?" He was looking directly at Pepper Young.

Resentful that he was singled out, even more resentful because he felt that Hector was trying to make up for his own deficiency in having failed to be home when Pep called for help, he responded, "Unfortunately, that wouldn't be possible in my case."

"You can't do it? Or you think the party you wronged would refuse to listen to your apology? We hear that one quite often. But we've yet to see a case of anyone who refused to hear an honest, heartfelt confession and apology."

Several of the group joined in supporting him based on their own experiences.

Much against his will Pepper felt called on to justify himself.

"Mine is not like any case any of you have ever faced before. So just take my word for it. It is not possible for me to explain and admit my guilt in this particular instance."

"Why not?" demanded one member, who seemed particularly disturbed by Pepper's reluctance.

The woman who had tried to befriend Pepper at the end of the first meeting rose in his defense. "There is something to what Willard is saying. This *is* unlike any case we've had before."

One member declared, "I had to make the damnedest confession and apology to a son I hadn't seen in six years. Had to track him down. Make him listen. Even though he didn't want to ever see me again because of things I'd done to him and his mother when I was a drunk. Willard's situation can't be any worse than that."

"Take my word for it . . ." Pepper's defender began to say.

But Pepper stood up and declared, "There's only one way to

handle this. The truth. My son, to whom I would go on bended knee to apologize, can't hear me. Not *won't*. *Can't*. He's in coma because of what I did while under the influence. So it wouldn't do any good to apologize to him. He can't hear, he certainly can't forgive."

The chairman considered Pepper's explanation for a long silent moment.

"The question is," he responded, "which is more therapeutic? To make the confession? Or to hear the words of forgiveness? I think we should leave that to Willard to decide for himself."

With that the meeting came to an end.

But Pepper Young's struggle was just beginning.

Several days had passed since that evening session of A.A. The challenge raised by the chairman continued to pursue Pepper, coming back with increasing frequency. During days at the office, he thought of it. During speeches he made to his sales staff. During lunches with Beecham, who had to ask, from time to time, "Pep, you listening to me?"

"Oh, sure, of course, B.C." he would reply.

Mainly it troubled him in the evening when after a tough day of meetings, training sessions, new product sales development, he was able to free himself and race to the hospital.

As always, Lil would be sitting alongside Bud's bed. It seemed to Pepper that she never took her eyes off their son. Watching, peering, studying his face for any sign that he might be returning to consciousness.

Much as his son's condition devastated him, what it was doing to Lil was worse. Times when he entered that room he could swear she was about to accuse him.

But she never had.

Each evening he tried to convince her to go down to the coffee shop. Just to get away from this room. But she never would. She just sat there, watching, knitting mechanically at times, but always watching.

On this particular evening when they had followed their ritual, he suggesting she take a break, she refusing, he became aware for the first time that when she remained so steadfast, he actually felt relieved.

It troubled him that evening. It woke him in the middle of the night. Despite his insistence to Lily, was he actually relieved when she refused to leave, because it prevented him from being alone with Bud?

As long as Lil was present he could always delude himself with the excuse that he was not free to talk to Bud, could not say the things he felt obligated to confess.

Finally he determined to face it. He recalled what Judge Bruce had said in another context: You don't *find* the time, you *make* the time.

That evening when he arrived at the hospital he followed his usual routine. He kissed Bud on his cool pale cheek. He kissed Lil and while he held her he whispered, "Lily! I insist you go down to the coffee shop."

"But I'm not hungry," she protested.

"Go down, anyway!" he insisted in a stern attitude he rarely used with her. And she was aware of it.

"Pep?" she demanded an explanation.

"I have to be alone with my son."

"Oh, no," she refused. "I know exactly what you have in mind."

"You do?" Pepper was astonished. How could she know?

"Like me, you've gotten all kinds of telephone calls. Friends, people, some we don't even know, keep calling. Our answering machine is full of them. They know of some treatment, some trick, that can get Bud out of his coma. And you want to try one of them on him now. I won't allow it! I'll call Marcy Ethridge. I'll call Dr. Curtis if I have to. But I won't allow you to experiment on my son!"

"Lily . . . Lily . . . believe me. I had no such thing in mind."

"Then why do you want to be alone with him?" she demanded.

"I . . . uh . . ." He found it difficult to say because it would sound too strange, even to his own wife. But he knew he had to say it.

"I want to talk to Bud," he said simply.

"Talk to Bud? That's all I've been doing, all Marcy has been doing for days now. It doesn't help. It just doesn't help."

Out of consideration for the tears that were forming in her

eyes, he said very slowly, very softly, "Lil . . . it is part of my treatment."

"A.A.?"

"It is something I have to do, which is just between my son and me. So, Lil . . . please?"

Without a word, Lily Young slipped out of his arms and started for the door.

Alone with his son for the first time, Pepper Young approached the bed. He stood beside him, watching him breathe.

He reached to touch his face, to trace his profile with his forefinger. *Handsome,* he thought, *but better than handsome, good. A fine young man. A good person. Well liked. No, well loved by everyone who knew him. Yet now . . .*

It was difficult to begin. Pepper Young had never had to make such a declaration before. How to start . . . what to say . . .

"Bud . . . this is Dad. I know you can't hear me now. But somehow I have a feeling that, like a computer, these words are being imprinted on your brain. So that one day when you're"— he had to fumble to find the correct word—"when you're . . . yourself again . . . and you will be—I'll move heaven and earth to make sure that you are. And when you are, you will know how sorry I am that all this ever happened.

"My fault, Bud, mine alone. I would have given anything to prevent this from happening. Anything. Except I couldn't give you those damn keys to let you drive. What foolish stubborn pride takes hold of a man when he's in that condition? Is it the need to prove that he's right and the whole world is wrong? Or is it the need to conceal his sense of shame that he is drunk and everyone knows it?

"I don't know those answers, son, but I am trying to find them. I go to A.A. now. It's doing me a world of good. I feel better now, stronger. I haven't had a drink since . . . well, since . . . that one day. And I teach a class two times a week. For the kids in the high school on the South Side. Some good kids there. Very good. And they look up to me. Which hurts.

"That they look up to a man who could do this to his own son. Bud, I give you my word I'll do everything to make you right again. I'll see this through until you wake, until you're able to talk to Mom and to Gwen. She was here, you know.

"And able to talk to me again. I live for the day when I hear you say, 'I forgive you, Dad.' That will be the greatest day of my life."

He had not been aware that during his confession he had taken Bud's cold hand. Gently, carefully, he laid it down atop the clean crisp white hospital bedsheet.

He turned away, brushed the tears from his eyes. He was relieved to hear the door be eased open, and hear Lily ask, "Pepper?"

"It's okay, Lil, it's okay."

On days when he knew his out-of-town schedule might prevent him from returning in time for evening visiting hours at the hospital, Pepper Young would take advantage of a special dispensation he had been granted to make a very early morning visit to his son's room.

This morning, though he was going out of town for the day to bolster a salesman who was having difficulty, Pepper Young did not go directly to Mercy Hospital. Instead, carrying a large object wrapped in a blanket, he went to a jeweler's shop on Broad Street. He arrived there as Mr. Eisenstadt, the proprietor, was just unlocking the metal gates that secured his shop windows from nighttime intruders.

Carrying his bundle, Pepper stepped out of his car as Eisenstadt turned off several alarms before being able to unlock his door.

Almost self-conscious, the old man apologized, "When I first started in business we didn't need iron gates on the windows. Or three alarm systems. But these days . . ."

Like all such conversations it concluded in mid-thought since it was expected the listener could supply the unfortunate conclusion himself.

"Well, what can I do for you this morning?" the old jeweler asked once they were inside the shop.

Pepper opened the blanket to reveal a silver loving cup that was so badly dented as to be misshapen.

"Aha," Eisenstadt commented, "I see we have been very careless."

"Yes. Yes, you could say that."

"You don't mean someone deliberately did this to such a lovely trophy?"

"Look, the question now is not *how* this happened. It's what can be *done* about it? I want this fixed up like new."

"Well," the old man equivocated as he took the cup in hand to examine it from all angles. "Like new, I don't think so. I could send it back to the company who made it. Maybe they can do it. But I doubt it. No matter what they do, this will never be like new."

"You're absolutely sure?" Pepper persisted.

"Absolutely sure?" the jeweler scoffed. "There is no such thing as absolutely sure. But in my forty-six years in this business I have never seen a cup damaged like this come out even *near* perfect. How a cup could sustain such bad damage . . . beats me."

"Never mind that!" Pepper replied with considerable irritation. "The only question is what can be done."

"I know. We could duplicate it," Eisenstadt suggested. "I could call the manufacturer, give them the description. Then I engrave it so no one would know the difference."

"How long would that take?" Pepper asked.

"If they have one in stock, a week or two," Eisenstadt said. "If not, maybe a month. Even on special order. Which would cost . . ."

"I don't have a month!" Pepper replied angrily.

"I'm sorry," Eisenstadt replied. "But that's the best I can do." He examined the bent and twisted cup once more, saying, "How this could have happened . . . even if a man lost his temper and . . ."

"It doesn't matter how it happened!" Pepper protested.

"Easy, mister, easy. I didn't mean any harm," the old man apologized. "If you want my advice, and if no one is supposed to know what happened to this cup, get the new one. They'll never know the difference."

"But everyone does know . . ." Pepper was forced to admit.

"In that case . . ." the old jeweler expressed his inability to be of service.

Pepper Young wrapped the damaged cup in the blanket and with a disappointed "Thank you very much" left the shop.

It was early enough to stop by the hospital briefly and still make it to the office in time. When he reached Bud's room, he found the morning nurse bathing him. She was taken by surprise when he entered but recovered at once.

"Oh, Mr. Young! I was expecting Marcy." Assuming he wanted a report on his son's condition, she continued, "About the same, I'm afraid. But his vital signs are good. That means there's a"—she was forced to reach for a less discouraging word—"a . . . uh . . . good chance. Good chance." To cover for her unfortunate choice, she said, "I've seen cases go this long, even longer, then suddenly they come out of it. I say, as long as his signs are good, there's always . . . always hope."

She was relieved to complete the bathing routine and escape.

Pepper looked around the room, seeking some place, some piece of furniture or equipment, on which to install the cup he still carried wrapped in the blanket.

In a room this spare, with only a bed, a now-unused respirator, a night table crowded with medical supplies, only two visitor's chairs, there was no place to set down a damaged silver trophy.

He considered just placing it on the floor in the corner of the room nearest the window. But from such an obscure location it could not work the purpose he intended.

He was forced, finally, to go out to the desk to ask that a small table be sent in. Busy as they were with their morning routines, the nurses referred him to one of the porters. A ten-dollar bill produced a table on casters that was rolled into the room in minutes.

Wheeling the table from corner to corner, from wall to wall, to find the spot to which Bud might look the first time he opened his eyes, Pepper finally settled for the wall directly opposite the bed. Wherever Bud's eyes might wander when they finally opened, they were sure to focus finally on that wall.

Having decided that, he used the blanket to polish the cup. He placed it on the center of the small table. He stood beside his comatose son trying to see it from his eventual perspective.

Perfect, he decided. Now, all the cup had to do was work its spell. Pepper Young was sure that its very presence would reach into Bud's mind as none of that therapist's attempts had been able to do.

Feeling a sense of accomplishment and hope, he left for the office. He would take care of calls and the most urgent business details, then pick up that faltering salesman, go out and make a few calls with him to show him what he was doing wrong and how to do it right. Especially how to close a sale, a talent for which Pepper Young was noted.

Perhaps he might yet make it back to town in time for evening visiting hours at the hospital.

However, as things developed, the very last call he and his salesman made late that afternoon was challenging but also promising. So Pepper persisted until it was past seven in the evening, when he finally convinced the president of that company to sign the contract.

It was a triumph of skill and persistence. A great demonstration to his fledgling salesman of what could be accomplished with a seemingly intransigent prospect. That salesman would retell the story many times, adding to the legend of Pepper Young.

It was far too late to get to the hospital that night. By the time he arrived home, Lily and Gwen were both asleep. There was a note on the kitchen table about the supper Lily had left for him.

Strange, he thought, no mention of the silver cup in Bud's room. Lily must have been too tired to write details, even important details.

He went to bed, determined to get to the hospital first thing in the morning to make up for his lapse of the night before.

He rose earlier than usual after a restless night. He showered, shaved, dressed, all very quietly so as not to wake Lily, who was beginning to show the fatigue of almost four weeks of daylong stints at the hospital while at the same time trying to run a

household, see to all of Gwen's needs, and maintain some semblance of a normal family life.

It was just past eight when he arrived at the hospital. He
went at once to Bud's room. The nurse had already completed
her early morning duties. The IV bottles were all full and freshly
installed. The bed was neatly made up. From his appearance
Bud had been bathed and his hair, long, combed.

Must get a barber in here to cut his hair, Pepper decided. *Must
be some provision for barbers in cases like . . . The cup! Bud's cup! What
the hell happened to Bud's cup? Good God, is nothing sacred? Who
the hell would steal a cup from a young boy in a coma?*

He raced out into the corridor on his way to the nurses' station
to complain but collided with Marcia Ethridge with such force
that it tore her black bag out of her hand. While she scrambled
to pick it up, and all the implements and utensils it contained,
she demanded, "What is the matter with you this morning, Mr.
Young? Or . . ."

She rose swiftly, asking hopefully, "Something happened?
Bud finally responded!"

"No, he did not. But some damn thief stole his cup! I want
him found. I want him punished!"

"Mr. Young, no one stole that cup," Marcia started to say.

"I know, you have to protect the reputation of Mercy Hospital. But I want that miserable sonofabitch found and punished.
Most of all, I want that cup back where it belongs. In Bud's
room!"

"Mr. Young," Marcy replied, "that cup was not stolen. It was
removed."

"What the hell do you mean, removed?" Pepper demanded.

"Removed," she affirmed, then added, "by me."

"By you?" he repeated in a voice so loud that Marcia took
him by the arm to usher him into Bud's room.

"Now," she said very quietly, "we can discuss this in a reasonable and intelligent manner."

"You had no right . . ." he began to accuse.

"Mr. Young, that patient is in my care. I have every right,"
Marcia Ethridge said. "Now, first, what did you intend to do
with that cup?"

"I want it there. It might have some . . . some power, some influence . . . because of what it means to him . . . he might somehow become aware . . . it might bring him out." Then finally he admitted, "I don't know. I thought if it was the first thing he saw when he did open his eyes . . . I guess I feel that Lily is becoming desperate. She doesn't say anything . . . but I can tell . . . she's reaching the end of her hope. . . ."

"She? Or you, Mr. Young?" Marcia demanded.

"What difference does it make? I want that cup in here. I want it where he can see it when he opens his eyes."

"And I do *not* want it in here," she contradicted.

"Why not?"

"Because, first, I do not believe in amulets or other magical artifacts. But mainly because I do not want him to see that damaged cup if he does open his eyes."

"You said 'if,' " he seized on the word.

"Yes, until he opens his eyes that's the only correct word I know. But *if*, and *when*, he does open his eyes I do not want him dwelling on something from his past that is as damaged as that cup. I do not think that would be in his best interests."

"But he won that cup . . . Most Valuable Player," Pepper protested.

"He doesn't need that to remind him," Marcia remained steadfast.

"If that cup is not returned to this room by the time I return this evening, there is going to be hell to pay, young woman!"

"If you really want to help, there is something," Marcia said.

"What?"

"A football."

"Just a football?" Pepper demanded.

"Yes. Just a football." Marcia replied.

"No football could be as important to Bud as that cup!" Pepper protested.

"Just a football, Mr. Young. And as for there being hell to pay, I've been through hell before, Mr. Young. You don't scare me."

Because he took her at her word, he stopped on his way out of the hospital to drop in on Marcia's boss, Physiatrist Phyllis Curtis.

Summoning all his talents at being persuasive while sounding reasonable, Pepper explained the situation, including his unfortunate confrontation with the therapist.

Whereupon, Dr. Curtis explained, "Mr. Young, as between an anxious parent who is becoming desperate and a therapist who has dealt with hundreds of such cases, I'm afraid I must trust the judgment of the therapist."

"Damn it, what harm can there be in a silver cup just sitting there?" Pepper demanded, impatient once more.

"If Ms. Ethridge thinks it might adversely affect the patient on regaining consciousness, I must take her word," Curtis replied with a gentle firmness that indicated the issue was closed.

As Pep Young left her office, Dr. Curtis could not help but feel sorry for him. She knew it was his guilt that added to his desperation and made him appear stubborn to the point of sounding almost irrational.

Most other men would have allowed the matter to rest there. But not Pepper Young, not the man reputed to have a special talent for reversing implacable and unfavorable decisions. He knew one intelligent person in this large hospital who had always proved to be a reasonable and cooperative individual. Always understanding, always with time to discuss a patient's problems with the family.

He sought out the neurosurgeon who had played such an important role in keeping Bud alive and minimizing the damage to his brain in the early stages of his condition.

"Dr. Newman, I know you're a busy man. And I don't like to impose on your time. But I am up against a stone wall. Against two of the most obstinate women I have ever had the misfortune to deal with."

"Oh?" Newman replied, prepared to listen to yet another of the complaints that families make when confronted by less than the miraculous cures they had expected.

Briefly Pepper told Newman the frustrating experience he had just suffered. Newman nodded attentively, even sympathetically.

"Now, that young woman . . . that Ms. Ethridge . . . I don't want you to think I'm against women in the professions. Or in business, for that matter. Two of the best producers on my sales staff are women. But this Ms. Ethridge, she is just not getting anywhere with Bud. His condition is the same today as it was four weeks ago when she first started with him."

"I wouldn't say that," Newman demurred. "Physically she has brought him along. He hasn't had a recurrence of his pneumonia. His muscle tone is good."

"But he hasn't opened his eyes! Hasn't responded. Hasn't come out of it. She has failed. Now, I'm not one to complain. And you know I'm not a bigot."

Aware that most of the bigoted statements he had ever heard began with that same preamble, Newman was prepared for the inevitable. So he replied, "Of course, Mr. Young."

"But I was wondering . . . mind you, it's only a suggestion . . . but I think that young woman should be replaced by some other therapist."

"A white woman, perhaps?" Newman suggested.

"It's not a matter of white or black. But someone who is not an affirmative action type. If you know what I mean. Now don't get me wrong. I'm not against giving people a chance. But, after all, I don't want her practicing on my son. I want someone who is already experienced, who is there because of ability. Not special treatment."

"I see."

"Believe me, this is not a matter of race or religion. I can tell you now I was relieved, greatly encouraged when Bud was put into your hands. I've always said that Jewish doctors are the best in the world. Our own family doctor is a man named Solomon. Terrific internist. Do you happen to know him?"

"Yes, yes, I do," Newman replied.

"Then you know I'm not prejudiced."

Newman smiled in such a provocative and amused manner that Pepper Young was forced to ask, "Dr. Newman?"

"Mr. Young, I'm afraid there's been a little mistake."

"Mistake?"

"I think you may have made an incorrect assumption," Newman replied. He took a moment to phrase his remarks diplomatically. "Dr. Solomon and I do not worship in the same place."

"You mean one of you is Reformed and the other is Ortho-
dox," Pepper assumed. "So what?"

"No. I mean we do not practice the same religion."

"You can't mean . . . after all, your name, Newman . . . all the
Newmans I ever met are . . . I mean . . ."

"Mr. Young, when you were in high school, didn't any of
your friends belong to the Newman Society?"

"Yes. But they were all . . . oh, my God, you're one of *those*
Newmans. You're a . . . a . . ."

"I'm afraid so, Mr. Young. I'm one of *those* Newmans. Cath-
olic."

Pepper Young wished that he were anywhere in the world
except across the desk from Dr. Albert Newman.

"So much for bigotry, Mr. Young. Now, let's get down to
cases. Forget anything you ever heard about affirmative action.
Do you know what it takes for a person to be accepted on the
staff of our Rehab Service here at Mercy Hospital? Four years of
college, with a major in science. Two years for a master's degree
in rehab specialties. Then one year of clinical training under an
experienced rehab therapist. And only after she passes a strict
written examination is she certified by the Department of Health
of this state. It so happens that Marcy has not only done all that,
but she graduated with honors for both her bachelor's and master's degrees.

"We're damn lucky to have her here. I'm sure what decided
her to come to Mercy is our day-care program. These days, if a
hospital wants to attract and keep the best therapists and nurses,
you have to assure them that their own children will be taken
care of while they are taking care of others.

"And since Marcy has a child, a little boy of six. And his
father is . . ."

The look on Pepper Young's face made Newman hasten to
add, "No, Mr. Young, not what you're thinking. She was married. It didn't last. I was never nosy enough to find out why.
But she's been on her own ever since. And the dearest thing in
this world to Marcy is that boy. What's best for him is best for
her. Fortunately for us, and for Bud, what's best for her son is
our day care.

"I personally asked Dr. Curtis to assign Marcy to your son's case. If anybody can help bring him out of his coma, she can. Always bearing in mind that there are no guarantees, Mr. Young. No guarantees. Wishing won't make it so. It will either happen or it won't. But it is my opinion that with Marcy he has his best shot."

Pepper could not resist one last attempt to justify his position. "But what harm could that silver cup do just sitting there?"

"Mr. Young, I have to go with Marcy's judgment," Newman said to conclude the interview, which had not been easy on either of them.

15

Five weeks and five days had elapsed since Bud Young had been helicoptered to Mercy Hospital.

Life in the Young household had settled into a grim routine. Pepper rose especially early every morning to make his stop at the hospital before driving to the office. Lily began her mornings by making sure that Gwen was ready for school. Books, homework, fresh clothes, arrangements for after school activities.

Once Gwen was off to school Lily did only the work necessary to maintain a clean, comfortable home. She prepared meals ahead of time so that they would be ready for whoever came home in the evening. Simple meals. Meals that could be heated up with little trouble. The joy of cooking food or eating it had disappeared from the Young household. The custom of the family dinner was no longer observed.

The three Youngs were never at home at the same time. Lily spent much of her day at the hospital. Making up for lost time, Pepper was at the office longer than usual, then spent the evening with his A.A. group. Gwen Young spent her days at school, her afternoons at the homes of friends whose mothers doted on her, eager to console "poor Gwen," as they had begun to refer to her because of Bud's prolonged coma. Having once inadvertently overheard that term used, Gwen had become less eager to spend time with friends. She had become more reclusive. Though she termed it self-sufficient. She did not wish to be an object of anyone's pity.

None of this did she ever complain about to her mother. And Lily, so consumed with determination to see her son awake and alive again, was too busy to notice.

There were others willing to share Lily's burdens. Her mother. Pepper's mother. Her Aunt Harriet. Friends, women with whom she served on the PTA, and other groups.

By the end of the third week they had all begun to call, "Lil, darling, if you need anything . . ." Or "Lily, what you need is a day off. Let me sit in for you tomorrow." Or "Lily Young, you're not doing yourself or Bud any favor by wearing yourself out. Let me spell you for a day or two."

Lily rejected them all with the appropriate thanks. She did not doubt that all offers were well intentioned. But she felt sure that no one could care for Lily Young's son as well as Lily Young.

"Somehow he knows I'm there," she insisted.

Twice each day Marcy Ethridge arrived in Room 302 with her bag of therapy equipment. Each day she worked Bud's arm and leg muscles. She massaged them with great care. She flexed them with her strong hands. Always gently but firmly, for she did not wish to induce any muscle contracture which would require a splint to correct. Each day she worked at stimulating his senses to evoke some response. Each day, unfortunately, she failed.

All this Lily watched with lessening expectation and growing fear. She said nothing. Marcy said nothing. They both shared the same sense of disappointment.

They had to be content with the fact that he was alive. Was breathing on his own. Though fed by that gastrostomy tube in his side. Their only consolation was that his condition did not grow worse.

Marcy's fear, which she shared only with Dr. Curtis, was that if the patient continued in this condition for very much longer, he might never come out of coma. Or if, at some much later date, he did, there would be little by way of speech or other cognitive abilities remaining to salvage.

Each week at the staff meeting, the condition of the patient in 302 was discussed. The decision was always the same. Continue with therapy to maintain muscle tone and avoid pneumonia. Increase the level of stimuli. Although Marcy explained they were at almost too intense a level now.

Though no one expressed it in those words, the inevitable conclusion was *What else can we do?*

So each day, aside from trying to bring into that room some moment of cheer with her bright, "Good morning, Mrs. Young," Marcy went about her business in her usual professional manner. She did not avoid conversation, neither did she encourage it. For she had run out of optimistic things to say as well as little anecdotes from her past experience in which seemingly hopeless cases had resulted in remarkable recoveries.

Marcy had been told by the nurse in charge of floor care that if she wished, they would enforce the usual visiting hours, which would keep Mrs. Young away during Marcy's sessions with the patient.

But the therapist replied, "I can stand her presence much better than she could bear being banned from her son's room. Let her come. Let her stay."

"That's up to you, Marcy. But personally I wouldn't like an anxious mother breathing down my neck while I work."

On the sixth day of that same fifth week, with still no change in Bud's condition, Marcy opened the door to Room 302 in her usual manner, about to bid Mrs. Young good morning. She stopped abruptly. Her hand still gripped the metal door handle so as not to make any unnecessary sound. For what she discovered was Lily Young on her knees at Bud's bedside, teary eyes closed, speaking very softly.

". . . and dear God, he is such a fine young man, good human being . . . so loving, so loved. He's never done anything to deserve this . . . never. So please, dear God, for his sake, and for the sake of his father, make this happen. Only You can. You must, for after all this time, and all they have tried to do for him, nothing else seems to help."

Silently, Marcy Ethridge eased out, permitting the door to close so slowly that it did not make the usual slight, almost imperceptible sigh that well-constructed doors tend to make.

She waited in the corridor for several minutes, then with a brisker attitude she swung the door open and greeted warmly, "Good morning, Mrs. Young."

Just powdering away the signs of her tears, Lily Young responded as brightly as she could, "Ah, Marcy, good morning."

Marcy went about her usual routine. Physical exercises, exerting even more force into the way she rotated Bud's arms and flexed his legs. She was even brisker with his massage. She accompanied her activity with little sounds and words, like "There! Good!" Or "Let's try again." Or "There we are!" when she achieved a good result.

All the while Lily stood at the foot of Bud's bed watching, watching, watching. Every move of Marcy's. Every unfortunate lack of reaction from her son, who had grown paler and paler during the past five weeks.

When Marcy had finished, Lily did not ask, but the pleading look on her face did.

"No change, I'm afraid," Marcy said.

"No change," Lily accepted.

Marcy began her neurological procedures. Flashlight into the pupils. Pressure on nails. Needle to legs and arms. During those steps she began to talk in a manner that seemed extremely private, as if talking to herself as one oftimes does when engaged in routine activity that is not mentally taxing.

"Do I wish he was here now . . ." Marcy said, then heaved a weighty sigh. "He'd know . . . oh, yes, he'd know . . ." Always in the tone and attitude of a woman speaking her concerns aloud for her own solace.

Lily could not resist.

"Who?" she asked.

As if suddenly made conscious of another person who might have overheard, Marcy denied, "Oh, nothing . . . you wouldn't be interested . . . he was just an old man. Happened to be my great-grandfather. But aside from his little congregation, didn't matter much in this world."

"He was a minister?" Lily asked.

"Preacher," Marcy corrected. "Minister is more likely a title for a man who's been to divinity school. Grampa Ezra was one of those who *declared* himself a preacher. Studied the Bible though. Knew it possibly word for word. Both testaments. And that man could preach. Why . . ."

Marcy turned from her duties to give her full attention to Lily.

"Why, when he preached about Noah 'n' the ark 'n' that flood you could almost feel the waters lapping at the church floor. And when he was in the lion's den with Daniel, he made it so real you could feel the hot breath of those angry lions. That man could make that Good Book live.

"One time . . . I was no more than five or six . . . long before I had any idea of going to college or studying rehab therapy . . . but I'll never forget that Sunday morning.

"It was Palm Sunday. Grampa was telling of the way of the cross. How the Lord Jesus was struggling under his heavy burden. Grampa, he made it so real that three men from the congregation jumped up out of their pews and rushed forward to help poor Jesus lift that cross. Yes, my old grampa, he could preach up a storm," Marcy said.

Then, as she returned to her neurological procedures, she added, "Of course . . . with his powers of preaching, people were always asking him to pray with them. To beseech the Lord for all kinds of favors."

"Favors?" Lily asked.

"Things they would ask that were outside their own powers to attain. And Grampa would say, 'I be most willin.' That was his favorite response. 'I be most willin.' Except when someone asked to have some natural process reversed.

"Then Grampa Ezra would say, 'Child' . . . Person could have been forty, fifty years old, to him they were still 'child.' 'Child,' he'd say, 'ain't fair to ask the Lord to reverse some process of Nature. Because He can't do that. Even when Joshua prayed to have the sun stay high in that sky at Gibeon so the Israelites could win that battle. Sure, the Lord could hold that sun up in the sky for a time. But sooner or later Nature said that sun had to set. And set it did. Not even the Lord could prevent that. So, child, don't ask me to pray for something that can't be. Ain't fair to the Lord to put that burden on Him. Ain't fair to you. Because if that thing don't happen you going to lose your faith.

All because you asked for something it was impossible for the Lord to grant you. Best leave natural things to Nature. And accept the outcome.'

"S'what he used to say," Marcy concluded as she also concluded her neurological procedures and put the instruments back into her black bag.

As she turned to leave, Lily said, "You heard me, didn't you?"

"Yes, Mrs. Young, I did. As I've heard so many mothers and wives and daughters before you. Prayer won't do it for Bud. Bud will do it. Together our efforts will do it. But if we fail, don't compound our failure by blaming God."

"Marcy . . . tell me . . . honestly . . . it's been more than five weeks. . . . What are Bud's chances?"

"That's really for Dr. Curtis to say."

"No, I want *your* opinion. I feel you know Bud better than anyone. You've been closer to him than anyone, even me. I want your sense of things."

"Mrs. Young . . . I can't explain why or how it happens. But there's a . . . a feeling . . . call it intuition . . . call it professional instinct . . . but I think he will come out of it."

"You really think so, honestly think so?" Lily pleaded.

"Yes, I do," Marcy said. "We just have to find the way . . . find the way. . . . "

She lifted up her bag and was on her way to the door.

"Marcy . . ." Marcy stopped and turned, "Marcy, would you do something for me . . . ?"

"If I can."

"From now on, I would like you to call me Lily."

"If you'd like."

"I would. I really would."

"All right, Lily."

"Marcy . . . what you told me . . . about your grandfather . . . "

"Yes?"

"Was he really that good a preacher?"

"He was indeed. The best and most moving preacher I ever heard. Things he said, things I heard him preach, have stayed with me all these years."

"No wonder you're the person you are," Lily Young said.

16

Marcia Ethridge entered Room 302 as usual, ready to say, "Good morning, Lily." But Lily Young was not there. One of the few times in all forty-seven days of Bud Young's coma that she was not.

A little late this morning, Marcy assumed as she went about her ministrations with the patient. *Hope there's no trouble. Probably just worn out. All those days and evenings spent here, waiting, watching, looking for signs that never appear.*

She had completed her physical exercises with the patient. His general tone was good and getting better. Breathing on his own quite well. Aside from the tube that fed him, he was independent of all other aids. That respirator had been banished to the corner of the room to be available only in the event of an emergency.

Now for the efforts to stimulate him to react. To demonstrate some sign that would give hope that he could emerge from his coma. Because the days were beginning to count heavily now. Marcy was aware that if he went beyond sixty days his chances of even partial recovery would slowly disappear.

As she had done every day since Mr. Young had brought that

football in, Marcy took Bud's right hand, his throwing hand, wrapped it around that football, pressing his fingers tightly against the pebbled leather. She held it there, very firmly. But as soon as she relaxed her pressure, Bud's hand went limp again.

She proceeded with the usual stimuli. Light into the eyes. Pressure on fingernails. Needles into the arms and thighs. There was no reaction.

She wafted the fragrances under his nose, pleasant to tempt him, obnoxious to provoke him. She elicited no response. As she was stowing away the instruments of her craft, on an impulse, either out of frustration or desperation, she suddenly pinched his thin cheek.

In a sudden move he turned his head away. It was a single jerk of the head, covering in all only a fraction of an inch in actual movement.

But it was a move! He had moved on his own. Not an affirmative move. A negative move intended to avoid, not to achieve. But at least it was a move!

She hovered over him, studying him. She pinched him once more. He jerked away. Another pinch. Another withdrawal.

It had not been a misperception on her part. Or a one-time phenomenon.

He *had* moved.

More, much more would be required before she could feel that a breakthrough had been achieved. She tried once more to wrap his hand around that football and make it hold. His hand went limp as before.

Of course, she realized, *expect no miracles. This war, if it is to be won, will be won step by step, day by day.*

But the elation she felt caused her to report the event to Dr. Curtis, who had come in to carry on her own neurological tests. She, too, pinched Bud's cheek. She evoked only the slightest turning away and felt that perhaps Marcy was unduly optimistic.

By the time Marcy returned to 302 for her afternoon therapy session she found Lily Young there.

"Sorry I wasn't here this morning. But I had to go for a checkup myself," she explained. Marcy's look of concern forced Lily to admit, "Last night . . . I . . . well, I was trying to have some supper . . . but you don't know how it's been these last few weeks. People call at all hours to ask how Bud is. And I have to keep saying the same things over and over again to each one of them. Mind you, Marcy, I appreciate their concern. But repeating and repeating, 'There's been no change. But thanks for calling,' does get to be a bit too much. Last night, with Gwen at her friend's house to study for a geometry exam and Pep late at A.A., I kept going from the kitchen table to the phone, then back to the table trying to eat my supper. . . . Marcy, please don't say a word to anyone, especially my husband . . . but last night when I got up suddenly to go to the phone . . . I . . . I guess I just blacked out. . . . Next I knew I was on the kitchen floor. So this morning I went to see Dr. Solomon."

"Low blood pressure," Marcy anticipated. "Loss of weight. General debility."

"Yes," Lily admitted. "He prescribed some vitamin injections. A better diet. And more sleep. I told him I do not want to get into the habit of taking sleeping pills. But he insisted that for right now, for a short time, I was to take one every night. I hate taking pills. I hate being dependent on anything. That's why I gave up smoking when I was carrying Bud."

Marcy debated the wisdom of her own impulse. Because worse than little hope is false hope. But her instinct told her it was worth the risk.

"Lily . . . I may have something that'll help."

"I know. Exercise. Dr. Solomon recommended that, too."

"No, not exercise. Something else. But you must promise not to get too excited. Or to start telling people," Marcy said.

The look on Lily Young's face was one of curiosity tempered by little lines of doubt around her eyes.

"Promise?" Marcy insisted.

"Promise," Lily agreed.

Marcy went to the head of Bud's bed. She leaned over to reach his cheek. She pinched, a single crisp pinch.

He jerked his head away.

Lily Young stared, then her breathing quickened. As if she dared not hope, she whispered, "Do that again. Please?"

Marcy pinched. Bud jerked his head away.

"Oh, my God," Lily said and started to cry. Through her tears, she said, "Pep. I've got to call Pep!"

"Not yet," Marcy cautioned. "Not yet."

She lifted Bud's right hand, massaged the fingers, flexed them, straightened them, flexed them again. She picked up the football to wrap his fingers around it. Then she loosened her pressure.

His hand fell away. Limp again.

The look of glee on Lily's face went limp as well.

"That's what I meant, Lily. We have to wait for affirmative signs. Actions of his own volition, not merely avoidance of things we do. That's the real test."

For the rest of the afternoon, while Marcy was engaged with her other patients, Lily Young stood beside her son's bed. She wrapped his hand around that football that he used to grip so strongly, used to throw for such long passes. But each time his hand refused to cooperate and ended up useless at his side.

She consoled herself with a single thought. *Today was better than yesterday. Tomorrow will be better than today. It will be. It must be!*

Whenever Pep Young's duties were to take him out of town he followed a procedure he had instituted since Bud's injury.

He sought out the best hospital in the city he was due to visit, contacted the Chief of Neurosurgery and arranged a consultation. Once his day's work with his salesperson was completed, he met with that surgeon.

He laid out before him all the facts of Bud's condition, even admitting the cause. Then he would implore, "Doctor, is there anything that the people at Mercy Hospital have left undone? Anything they failed to consider? Anything new that they might not have heard about? Doctor, please, is there anything you can suggest? Anything?"

Despite Pep's plea, which sometimes brought him to the verge of tears, the response was always the same. Based on Pep's description, everything that could be done for Bud was being done.

This evening, after another such disheartening consultation,

Pep Young drove to Mercy Hospital with an added burden. A burden he had carried with him ever since a brief early-in-the-morning phone call from Doctor Solomon.

"Pep, get your lady out of the hospital, out of the house. Make sure she eats a good hearty meal. And enjoys it. It would do no harm at all for her to have a drink or two. Understand?"

Pep had raced to the hospital with that intention. But when he arrived at 302 Lily was not there. He asked the floor nurses if anyone had seen her. Yes. But she had left. Said something about going home to prepare dinner for her family.

He called in great concern, "Lil? You all right?" '

"Oh, fine. Thought I'd have a nice hot meal for you when you came off the road. Where are you?"

"The hospital, of course."

Though aware of Marcy's cautioning, Lily was too tempted to resist.

"Pep, go to Bud's bed."

"I'm here now. On the phone."

"Pep . . . reach out . . . and pinch his cheek," she urged.

"Pinch his cheek . . ." Pep repeated. "Why?"

"Just do it," she insisted.

Pepper Young reached to his son's cool cheek. Gently, very gently, he pinched it. There was no response.

"Pep?" she asked with great expectation.

Puzzled, he did not know how to respond, or what was expected of him.

"Pep?" she insisted.

"Nothing, Lil . . . nothing . . ."

"But there must be! There was this afternoon. Try again."

He repeated his action, as gingerly as before. With the same lack of result.

"Still nothing," he was forced to report.

"You must be doing something wrong," she insisted, her fear that Bud had reverted to his earlier state causing her voice to become shrill.

"Lil . . . Lil . . . please," he entreated, since his mind had taken Dr. Solomon's advice and expanded its urgency and danger. *Is she having a breakdown?* he was forced to ask himself.

"Pep! Try again. This time pinch hard. Very hard!" she insisted.

Less because he had any conviction about it, more to please her, he reached for his son's cheek once more. This time he pinched harder.

This time his son jerked his head away. A slight move. But a move.

"Lil . . ." he said, "Lil . . . I saw it. He moved. Bud moved!"

"It's just the beginning, Pep. Marcy said, it's just the beginning. We mustn't expect too much too soon."

"No, no, we mustn't," he agreed. "But we do have something to celebrate, so let's celebrate. I'll be right home and maybe we'll open one of Beecham's bottles of . . ." He interrupted himself very abruptly. "I'll be right home and take my bride out for the best dinner in this town!"

Lily was relieved and delighted to reply, "If that's an invitation, I accept."

"I'm on my way, Lil, on my way."

Pep hung up the phone. He stared down at his son, at the football that lay alongside his body. He reached out for Bud's hand, wrapped it around the football, held it there. He would have continued to hold it there, hoping to transmit some of his own energy into his son's hand. But the door opened and the nurse entered to settle Bud for the night.

Feeling a bit self-conscious, if not foolish, Pepper Young released his son's hand and said, "I'll be out of your way. I was just going."

He kissed his son on the cheek and left.

Lily was standing at her son's bedside when Marcia Ethridge opened the door to Room 302. The position of Lily's body shielded Marcy's view until Lily greeted, "Have I got a good morning for you, Marcy!"

Lily stepped back from the bed to point at Bud's left hand resting on the football alongside.

"Just look! Look," Lily invited proudly.

Marcy approached the bed, stared at Bud's hand. It was firmly fixed in a grip on that ball. With an eager gesture Lily invited Marcy to feel for herself. When she tried to ease the ball from Bud's hand there was noticeable resistance. He was actually exhibiting an affirmative impulse for the first time since he had slipped into coma fifty-two days ago.

Marcy gently urged Lily back from the bed. Then she leaned in close to speak into Bud's ear in a full tone of voice.

"But . . . can you hear me? Bud!"

There was no response. Marcy tried once more. "Bud! I am talking to you, Willard Young. If you can hear me, open your eyes. Open them, Bud!"

There was still no response. But Marcy noted that his hand

resting on that football seemed to tighten. He was responding in some way.

Marcy beckoned Lily closer, then urged her to speak.

"Bud . . ." Lily began.

"Louder," Marcy urged.

"Bud, this is your mother. I'm here, Bud. I've been here from the beginning. If you can hear me, speak to me. Bud. Speak to me. Please? Bud? Bud!"

There being no response, Marcy opened her black bag. She took out a cowbell. She held it over Bud's head and rang it vigorously. As the clapper struck the bell and the sound reverberated, Bud stirred.

Marcy seized on that response and leaned close to command. "Bud, if you can hear me, speak to me. Bud! If you can hear me, and can't speak, open your eyes! Bud, open your eyes!"

His lids began to twitch, then tighten into small wrinkles.

"Open your eyes, Bud, open them! Now!"

Slowly, his eyes seemed to relax. Then, with a flutter of the eyelids, his eyes opened. Only for an instant, then closed once more.

Lily was about to speak but Marcy forbade it with a simple but commanding gesture of her hand. Both women waited. Then, after what seemed to Lily Young forever, her son opened his eyes and kept them open for a full second, until, as if exhausted from the effort, he closed them once more.

On the point of tears, Lily exclaimed in a reverent whisper, "He opened them . . . he opened them . . . he's going to be all right. I better call Pep!"

Marcy Ethridge had a split-second decision to make—allow Lily Young to cherish her moment of triumph or make her aware now that her expectations and assumptions far exceeded the realities of her son's condition.

Let her enjoy her first moment of relief since this all started, Marcy decided.

Lily was on the telephone insisting to Pep's secretary, "Sheila, no matter where he is or what he's doing . . . in with Mr. Beecham? I don't care. Get him! I said, get him!"

Within minutes Pep was on the phone, "Lil! What happened?

Bud . . . he didn't . . ." He stopped himself from expressing his first and worst fear.

"He did, Pep. He did!"

"Did? When?"

"Minutes ago, darling. And it was the most wonderful sight I've ever seen."

"Lil, what are you talking about?"

"He opened his eyes, Pep. He opened his eyes!" she exclaimed.

"Thank God . . ." Pepper Young said. That was all he could say, "Thank God. I'll be there the minute I can get away!"

When Lily Young returned to Room 302 she found Marcy no longer alone but accompanied now by Dr. Curtis, who observed as Marcy spoke slow commands to Bud and waited for his responses.

"Bud . . . open your eyes." Once he did, Marcy waited a second, then directed, "Close your eyes."

There was a moment of hesitation, as if it took Bud that long to comprehend the order and summon up the ability to obey it. Then he complied, closed his eyes, and lay at rest.

Marcy leaned in closer to him. "Bud, raise your hand." She repeated more slowly, "Bud . . . raise . . . your . . . hand."

The fingers of his left hand began to move slightly, one finger rising at a time though his wrist lay flat on the bed. Finally he was able to raise his middle three fingers slightly but could not manage his entire hand.

Slowly Lily's exuberance began to diminish. She looked to Marcy, then to Dr. Curtis, for some explanation, some reassurance. But they were too concentrated on the testing to pay heed to anyone but the patient.

At the doctor's silent urging Marcy continued, always slowly, to give other commands. If Bud did not follow, she proceeded to act out examples.

"Bud . . . put . . . your . . . hand . . . on . . . your . . . chest."

His eyes blinked in puzzlement.

Marcy repeated the command, even more slowly. Bud made a slight move with his right hand that seemed to be directed toward his chest, but it went no farther.

To Marcy and Dr. Curtis this small though unfulfilled action was encouraging. If he could not respond fully, he did at least exhibit some slight cognition of the words of the command.

Marcy proceeded, nodding her head as she spoke, "Bud . . . nod your head . . . yes."

This time, after a few moments, Bud Young managed two barely perceptible nods of his head.

"Very good, Bud . . . very very good. Now . . . shake . . . your . . . head . . . no."

Bud responded with a very slight movement of his head from center vaguely toward his right.

Marcy looked to Dr. Curtis for her opinion on continuing.

"Might as well try," Curtis said.

"Bud . . . open . . . your . . . mouth."

After some moments, and with Marcy repeating the command, then opening her own mouth as an example, his jaw quivered almost imperceptibly but he could not open his mouth.

Marcy and Curtis exchanged meaningful professional glances. But Lily was stunned.

"You mean . . . he couldn't do a simple thing like open his mouth . . . ?"

"He's tired, Mrs. Young," the doctor explained. "Patients with his kind of injury, coming out of coma, tire very quickly. We simply cannot rush them. Marcy, try later in the day."

"Yes, Doctor."

"Mrs. Young, don't feel too bad. This is a slow process and your son made great strides today. Great strides."

Dr. Curtis had left. Marcy followed with a soft "I'll be back at two, Lily."

Lily Young sat alongside her son, who seemed to be sleeping now. Somehow she could tell there was a difference between being in coma and sleeping peacefully. Whatever her shock at his failure to respond to some of the simplest commands, she was willing to accept the doctor's word: Her son had made great progress today.

Within an hour, the door to 302 opened briskly. Speaking as he entered, Pep Young demanded jovially, "Where is that son of mine?"

"Shhh," Lily warned.

His voice softening immediately, he asked, "What happened? Something go wrong again? Don't tell me he's back in coma?"

"He's sleeping . . . just sleeping . . . he's exhausted."

"Exhausted? From opening his eyes?" Pep demanded, all his expectations suddenly shattered.

"Shh, Pep. Just hold it down."

"Did he open his eyes or didn't he?"

"Yes, he opened his eyes. He even obeyed some commands. But very slowly."

"I've got to see this for myself," Pep declared.

"Pep, they said he was tired," Lily said, trying to dissuade him.

"Look, I know my son. That kid has more energy than anybody in this world. It can't be asking too much just to have him open his eyes," Pep said, moving to the head of the bed.

With a "just watch this" move of his hand to Lily, Pep leaned close to his son, "Bud. It's Dad. Hear me, boy? Dad! Now, son, you open your eyes and look at your old dad."

He waited confidently. Bud barely turned his head in Pep's direction. Pep beamed at Lily as if to say, See, I told you.

"Now, son, you open your eyes. You can do it. I know you can. You can do anything!"

For seconds that seemed much longer to Pepper Young, Bud hesitated, eyelids flickering, then finally opened his eyes.

"Oh, Lil . . . isn't that the most beautiful sight in the world? Hi, son!"

Bud responded only by closing his eyes once more. Discouraged at not being accorded more recognition, Pep continued nevertheless. He lifted the football, held it out to Bud. "Here, son, let's see you hold that ball. Grip it real good. Like you were going to throw one of those fifty-yard passes. Here, son. Take it. Hold it."

Bud's hand moved slowly, vaguely, in the direction of the ball. Pep lifted his hand, wrapped his fingers around it, and this time Bud's fingers remained somewhat firmly on the ball.

"See?" Pep said to Lily. "All he needs is a little help. But he can do it. He can!"

"Pep, please, they said not to tire him out."

" 'They said'! Nobody knows my son like I know my son.

Right, son? Look your old dad in the eye like you always did. And smile, son, smile! They can't beat you. Nobody can beat you. Did you know, Bud, I got a call from Turk Hingle . . . he's the coach of quarterbacks at Iowa. He heard about the accident. He wanted to know how you were. See, they got their eye on you, boy. All you have to do is get out of here, go into training again, and all this will be a bad dream."

Through Pep's excited recital of what he considered encouraging events, but which his son could not comprehend at all, Bud lay there, eyes closed. In his mind a confusion of ideas and events and questions, none of which seemed to make sense or have relevance to any other.

Words, words running together, words without meaning, sounds mostly.

"And another thing, son . . . son, are you listening to me? Son?" Pep pleaded, "Open your eyes. Son? Son?"

Wearily, very laboredly, Bud complied. But then closed them as slowly.

"Son," Pep begged. "Son, Dad is talking to you. Just look at me. Listen to me."

Lily tried to intercede. "Pep, no, they said not to force him."

"Lily, let me do this my way, please? Son. Look at your dad." He leaned closer to him, "Son, do you hear me?"

Slowly Bud Young turned slightly in the direction of his father, whose face was now only inches from his own.

Pep took heart and urged softly, "Bud . . . look at me . . . open your eyes and look at me. . . . "

Bud Young opened his eyes. Looked at the person hovering so close to him, pleading so desperately. But his eyes exhibited no glint or sign of recognition.

Shocked, terrified, Pep Young drew back from his son. He stared at his wife, seeking in her eyes confirmation of his shocking discovery.

"He doesn't know me," Pep realized in a whisper. "His own father and he doesn't know me. There's something wrong. Terribly wrong. Get the doctor. Get Marcy. They have to do something."

He raced to the door and in frantic fear cried out, "Dr. Curtis! Marcy Ethridge! Somebody!"

18

The outcry from Room 302 had summoned both Dr. Curtis and Marcy Ethridge from their other duties to converge on the source of the disturbance.

Quickly, Dr. Curtis ordered, "Mr. Young! You will come with me. And quietly!"

Once they had assembled in her office, Pepper Young refused to be seated but leaned across her desk to accuse, "Something is wrong! Terribly wrong! Now I'm not accusing anyone . . ."

Though to Marcy it was quite clear that by his declaration he was accusing her.

"I've learned in business that accusations and blame accomplish nothing. Fix what's wrong is the only answer. Now what is wrong is that my son, my own son, no longer recognizes me. He stares right into my eyes and I stare into his and I can see that he does not know me. I am a total stranger to him. Do something!"

Having allowed him to give vent to his fears, Dr. Curtis turned to Marcy Ethridge. "Bud Young is your patient. You handle this."

"Of course," Marcy said. "Mr. Young, if anyone is to blame,

blame me. Not because your son does not recognize you. But because you are surprised, even shocked by that. That *is* my fault."

Pep glanced at Lily, and she at him. What was this young woman trying to tell them?

"Mr. Young, perhaps I should have been more forthcoming with you. But I wanted to spare you, and especially your wife, any unnecessary pain.

"What I am about to say may sound cruel. But it is the truth and it is time you heard the whole truth. At the outset we didn't know if Bud was going to survive. We hoped he would. We did our best to make sure he would. But it was always very much in question. So I kept saying, if and when the time comes, I will tell them. Well, it seems that time has come."

Pepper reached for his wife's hand. To support her, he thought. But actually he needed support himself for what threatened to be grave if not terrifying news.

"Mr. Young . . . Lily . . . if you have been laboring under the belief that once Bud opened his eyes everything was going to be like it used to be—Bud would be the same bright, cheerful, terrific son and scholar and athlete he used to be—you have been living under a delusion."

"But," Pepper protested, "that was the whole purpose—get him to react, get him to open his eyes . . ."

"That was only the *first* step," Marcy corrected. "The step that would enable us to begin the real work, the long difficult day-to-day, week-to-week, month-to-month, maybe year-to-year work to bring him back."

The phrase struck Lily as strange. " 'Bring him back?' Back from where?"

Marcy looked to Dr. Curtis. "I think I can do this better in Bud's room."

"Of course," the doctor agreed. Then to the Youngs she said, "If after Marcy is done you have any further questions, I will be available and eager to answer them."

Marcy allowed Mr. and Mrs. Young to enter Room 302. She followed and closed the door to ensure privacy. They found Bud as they had left him, lying on his back, gastrostomy tube in place, eyes closed.

Marcy approached him to demonstrate to the Youngs the nature and extent of the problem that confronted all four of them.

She stood at the bedside and began to give instructions. "Bud, raise your hand."

After a moment to absorb her instruction, he lifted his hand almost imperceptibly, which proved too great an effort for he wearily allowed it to drop back once more.

"Bud, point to your nose," Marcy said.

He did not respond at once. Then, slowly and vaguely, he extended his forefinger in a direction far removed from his nose.

"Bud, point to the ceiling." When Bud did not respond, Marcy repeated, "The ceiling, Bud, point to the ceiling."

"Bud, open your mouth. Open it. Just a little."

She waited. Signs of struggle appeared around Bud's lips but he could not summon the ability or control to obey.

With each faltering response by her son, and each failure to respond at all, Lily Young became paler and more tense. Fearing she might collapse, Pepper edged closer to her, aiming to keep her upright with the closeness of his body.

"Bud, if you can hear me, open your eyes," Marcy said.

Bud slowly opened his eyes, stared at them all with no sign of recognition.

"Bud . . . it's Dad . . . look at me. If you can recognize me but you can't speak, at least blink your eyes. Bud? Bud! It's me. Dad! Blink your eyes!"

There was no response.

He turned to Marcy, his very look pleading, *This is what I was trying to tell you. Do something!*

"Bud," Marcy continued with her testing instructions, "Bud, open your mouth." When he failed to accomplish even that, Marcy reached out with both hands and opened his mouth for him. Then she ordered, "Stick out your tongue. Bud, stick out your tongue."

He appeared to be exerting some effort, indicating that he had understood the instruction but was unable to respond to it.

"You mean . . ." Pepper Young found it difficult to accept and ask, "You're telling me that he can't even stick out his tongue? He's that paralyzed?"

"Mr. Young, it isn't a matter of being paralyzed. It is a matter of relearning the use of his muscles. Relearning almost everything that you consider normal, usual, effortless conduct," Marcy said.

"But such a simple thing as sticking out his tongue . . ." Pepper protested. "Any child . . . any infant can do that."

Marcy beckoned the Youngs away from Bud's bed to the corner of the room. There she spoke in a low voice, which she explained by saying, "His tolerance and his ability to even hear is quite limited. And will be for some time. So the less input we give him at this time, the better.

"Now, as to simple things infants can do that Bud can't. What seems a simple thing to you involves the use of many different muscles working in coordination. The hyoglossus, the styloglossus, the genioglossus, the transverse muscle, and certain longitudinal muscles. Just opening his mouth or puckering relies on the orbicularis oris muscle. All that just to open his mouth and stick out his tongue.

"He will have to recover the control and the coordination of all those muscles to be able to do that simple thing. He must do all that and much more before he is able to speak."

"My God . . . I never realized . . ." Lily whispered in her growing fear.

"And the same will hold true for almost every other function that we take for granted. We have to think of him as a new person. With new needs and feelings. If he was warm and outgoing before, we can't expect that he will be like that again. He may show displays of anger that startle you. As to his cognitive skills, he may have difficulty studying. Or reasoning. He may read a page and not understand what he has read. He might tell you something one minute and not remember it ten minutes later. He will have to learn all over again how to sit up. How to stand. How to walk. How to write. How to read."

"He was always such a bright student . . . alert . . . quick to learn," Pepper protested.

"Mr. Young, what I am trying to tell you is that, as in almost all closed head injury cases, we have to take all these defective parts, try to retrain them and put them together to produce a new Bud Young, as healthy and functioning as possible," Marcy said in as straightforward a manner as she could.

"But it *can* be done," Pepper tried to exact a promise from her.

"How much can be done remains to be seen" was all Marcy could promise. "We try a little each day. We see if he responds. The only hope I can give you is that young brains recover more, and more quickly, than older ones. That's in Bud's favor."

"Marcy," Lily asked, "is there anything else you and Dr. Curtis have been holding back?"

"Lily . . . we haven't been 'holding back' as you phrase it. We have just refused to burden you with discouraging information until we were sure you needed to know it."

"And now we need to know it," Lily replied sadly.

"Which is good!" Marcy encouraged. "It means we've made progress. Bud's made progress. He's ready for the hard work we have to do together."

Pepper stared at his son lying motionless in his hospital bed, attached to his gastrostomy tube and two IV lines which, in the event of an emergency, would ensure his survival. Pepper turned back to Marcy. His eyes pleaded for an answer.

"Will he ever be like he was? The same terrific, loving, lovable young man he was?" Marcy asked Pep's question for him. "Dr. Curtis would want me to be honest with you. And I couldn't be any less than that. We do not know. No one knows yet."

Seeking even a shred of solace, Pepper persisted, "But you've had other cases, cases that have done well. Haven't you?"

"Yes. And I've had other cases that haven't," Marcy replied in complete honesty.

"Is there anything *we* can do?" Lily asked.

"Cooperate. Encourage. Conceal your fears. Applaud his progress. Do not let him read criticism or disappointment in your eyes when he fails. The rest is between Bud and me," Marcy stated. "And now, if you have no further questions, we must get started toward our first major goal."

"And that is?" Pepper asked.

"Teach him how to be responsive to commands, to speak and learn how to eat," Marcy said.

"Learn how to eat?" Pepper questioned.

"Yes. That simple, basic, and most complicated ability. He has to learn it all over again. Eating, chewing, swallowing, speaking, things you and I do without even thinking, he can't do now even if he concentrates all his limited abilities on it."

"Surely there must be something more we can do," Lily insisted.

"Bring me things that are familiar to him," Marcy said. "Pictures."

"Pictures?" Lily asked.

"Photographs . . . of family . . . school friends . . ."

"Team photos?" Pepper asked. "Like they took after the championship game?"

"That would be fine," Marcy said. "Anything familiar to stimulate him to remember, to get his brain working in some kind of proper order."

"What about that cup?" Pepper suggested. "Now would be the time . . ."

But Marcy shook her head firmly.

"No cup?" Pepper asked, his enthusiasm thwarted.

"Not *that* cup," Marcy said.

"What about a picture of Bud and Marylyn?"

"Who's Marylyn?" Marcy asked.

"Bud's girl. They've been dating the last year," Lily explained.

"Good. That could help. And with each photo, identification of who the people are," Marcy instructed.

"Identification?" Lily asked.

"Most likely he won't recognize them . . ." Marcy started to say.

"He won't know . . . his girl friend?" Pepper asked.

"He didn't know you, did he?" Marcy replied.

"True," Pepper had to admit.

"I need to know who each person is so I can tell him," Marcy explained. Adding, "It's a long slow process."

Both Pepper and Lily nodded grimly. Marcy's earlier words were beginning to take on an awesome meaning for them now.

Aware of their feelings, Marcy tried to sound as casual as possible as she added, "Of course, if you have tapes of family occasions, they help. And bring his radio. It's helpful to have the radio on from time to time. Auditory stimulation of any kind helps. We'll all talk to him as we work. Even the cleaning women and the porters will be talking to him. To keep him alert and engaged as much as possible."

As each suggestion was made Lily's look became more grim. The question was on her face, was in her eyes, yet she was afraid to ask.

But Marcy anticipated her, "How long will it take? And what will be the final outcome? Nobody knows. Not yet. But he will have every help we can give him."

Pepper Young stood at his son's bedside, silent and thoughtful.

All this . . . all this could have been avoided . . . if only . . . if only . . .

But that was past. This is present. Tonight's meeting at A.A. is present. My class with those South Side kids is present. My son lying here beyond my help is present.

And future.

The Youngs had gone. Marcy was left alone with her patient. She studied him as he lay there, immobile, eyes closed. He opened them but only for an instant. But long enough for Marcy to read his feelings.

Poor kid, she thought, *he's been out for almost sixty days. No thoughts, no feelings. Just darkness, total darkness. He wakes up not knowing where he is. Or how he got here. He can't use his arms or legs, this very active young man. Surely he must be trying to say something, do something. And can't.*

God, how must that feel.

But no time for sympathy now. If anything, from now on sympathy must not be allowed to play a part in the execution of her professional duties.

Time to start to reconstruct the body, mind, and skills of

Willard Young, Jr. Starting with the most basic. The ability to chew and swallow.

She went out to the kitchen to secure a bowl of ice chips. When she returned she spoke as she worked. Part of the therapy. Talk to the patient. Keep his mind engaged. Stimulate it.

"Now, Bud, we are going to try a little experiment. This won't hurt. You'll probably like it. Now, just open your mouth . . ."

She waited, hardly expecting that he would or could comply. She reached out, gently pried his mouth open to insert one of the chips as she said, "This is going to feel cold, real cold. But you just let it dissolve. Let that cold water trickle back in your mouth and down your throat."

She studied him closely, only to see the cool water dribble out of the corner of his flaccid mouth. She wiped his chin dry, saying. "Mustn't be discouraged, Bud. We're going to work on fixing that, starting right now."

Putting aside the bowl of ice, she slipped on a pair of plastic gloves, opened his mouth once more. She began to massage his lips, then reached in to manipulate his tongue and the muscles around it. Slowly, gently she worked, speaking all the while.

"Don't you worry about this, Bud. We're going to get those muscles working again. And you'll be able to swallow and chew like you used to."

This last may have been an exaggeration, since no one could predict now how much of his former skills he could recover. Or even how much of what Marcy was saying he could hear and understand. But she worked in hopes that some of it was getting through. That there was a contact and a confidence being established between them.

As for swallowing, even so little as melting ice water, that would have to wait for another day.

19

Since patient Bud Young was now physically stable and awake and could at least comprehend most orders if not respond to them, Marcy Ethridge felt encouraged to expand his treatment into three areas. She must help him develop his gross physical skills, rejuvenate his fine motor skills to learn the most rudimentary things such as dressing himself, caring for his intimate needs, relearning how to write—all the things he would need to live his life in the outside world. Especially he must learn to do two simple things everyone takes for granted: Eat and speak.

Two days after Bud Young had demonstrated his ability, diminished as it was, to comprehend and respond to commands, Marcy decided it was time to get him out of bed. Because of the uncertainty of the outcome, she had banished Lily from the room and at the same time had requested Dr. Curtis to assign two additional therapists to assist her.

Once they arrived, Marcy addressed the patient, "Bud, today we are going to stand you on your feet. All you have to do is cooperate."

She explained each step in detail. With a dual purpose. To keep him informed, thus instilling trust in her. Also because merely hearing a human voice was beneficial in stimulating his brain, which had even more learning to do than his body.

"Now," Marcy explained as she also performed each action, "I am going to turn you on your side. Very slowly. Like this. But don't worry, I'll be most careful of your feeding tube. Slowly, slowly we turn."

As she settled him on his right side at the edge of the bed, she said, "Ah, there we are. That wasn't so difficult, was it?

"And now, legs down. Slowly we bring your legs down like this. And the nice thing is, as I do that, we are automatically pivoting you and bringing you to a sitting position. Imagine that, Bud. You are now sitting up."

Behind him both of Marcy's helpers stood ready to catch him if he fell back. But she had him anchored by his legs, which kept him upright.

Now for the difficult part, she thought. *Once I get him on his feet and his blood pressure drops as it must . . .*

She signaled her helpers to be ready. She slipped her arms under Bud's armpits and raised him to his feet. At once both assistants came to his side to hold him in place. But after weeks in bed, the change was too much. He became too dizzy and collapsed in their arms.

It was obvious to all three of them that his sudden pressure drop was too great. The very orthostatic hypotension Marcy was seeking to overcome had won out this time. Yet it was vital to get him out of bed to prevent another attack of hypostatic pneumonia as well as to begin to reverse the low-blood-pressure syndrome resulting from lying in a supine position for so many weeks. Until his pressure could be raised to nearly normal limits, he would not be able to function in a standing position.

With patients like Bud Young one tried and, having failed, one tried again. As long as he was awake, aware, and out of coma, the opportunity always existed to try again.

Two more days went by. Bud Young was responding a bit better each time. He had not yet begun to verbalize or to exhibit the ability to chew and swallow. The muscles required demanded complicated coordination which would take time.

Standing, as the prelude to walking, could be helped along by other techniques. For two days Marcy helped Bud to his feet, twice each day. For two days, twice each day his dizziness overcame him. He collapsed into the arms of her helpers.

"After all," one of them said, "he's been in bed for almost six weeks."

"I know, I know," Marcy said. "I was hoping to avoid any mechanical aids. That idea seems to do something to young patients. They resist being dependent on anything. Especially in the presence of others. But I can see now it can't be avoided."

When Lily Young arrived for her midmorning visit she found that Bud was not in his room. She went at once to the nurses' station to discover that he had been taken out to the Rehabilitation Center. Without even asking permission she started down the corridor, following the arrows that led her to that department. She arrived in time to look through the glass insert in the door to see Bud being lifted off a gurney onto what looked like a padded leather exercise table. Except that this table had three wide, strong canvas straps. And the bottom of the table, instead of being rounded off in leather, ended in a flat metal bar some eighteen inches wide and more than a foot deep.

She did not know what those straps were intended for until she saw Marcy strap one tightly across Bud's hip area and the second across his chest. The third she placed firmly around his knees to prevent him from buckling and sliding down the board.

Once Marcy made sure Bud was securely belted to the table and that his feet were firmly planted on that metal section so that it formed a platform for him, Marcy operated the electronic controls. The entire table began to tilt, head rising and footrest lowering so that Bud lay at an angle of ten degrees from horizontal level.

At once Marcy affixed a blood-pressure cuff to Bud's right arm and took frequent readings as he lay in his tilted position.

When Marcy became aware of Lily staring through the glass insert in the door, she beckoned her into the room.

Before Lily could ask, Marcy informed in a whisper, "Tilt table. To get him used to normal sitting and standing attitudes."

She checked his pressure another time, and since the reading seemed satisfactory, she raised the table another ten degrees.

Though he could not express it in words, Bud began to exhibit resistance. He started to grunt in angry sounds.

"Take him down," Lily protested.

"Not yet," Marcy whispered. "Most patients don't like this. So it's not their reaction but their blood pressure that tells me how long they can take it."

She continued to read his pressure. He continued to protest with angry sounds. She tilted the table another ten degrees. This time the reading indicated his pressure had dropped. Slowly she brought him back down to the previous level, where she kept him despite his grimaces and his angry sounds.

After half an hour at a tilt of twenty degrees, she brought the table down flat.

He still grimaced at her. She leaned over him and said, "Go on, hate me. But this is only the beginning, Bud Young. Only the beginning. Before we're through you are going to want to kill me. In fact," she joked, "that may be the best incentive I can give you. You'll want to get to be strong enough so I can't boss you around anymore. Well, just you try it, young man, just you try it!"

With assistance, she slid Bud back onto his gurney and had him on his way back to 302.

As part of her plan for Bud's afternoon therapy session Marcy Ethridge decided that since he was young and in good physical condition, she would try him on the tilt board again. A boy of sixteen should be able to cope with that. And it would bring him along faster to the point where she could determine when, if ever, he was ready for walking.

Even as he was being transferred to the gurney and became vaguely aware of what that could mean, he had started to object. It was in his eyes when he looked at her. It was in his grimace as his face twisted into a hostile pose. But to Marcy, those were hopeful signs. The patient was aware, he was sensitive, he was fighting back.

The afternoon on the tilt board was a repetition of the morning session. She raised him ten degrees, which he tolerated well enough to be raised another ten degrees. She held him at that level for twenty minutes. His pressure readings were fairly stable. So much so that she raised him another ten degrees.

After five minutes at that angle, accompanied by his grunting sounds, his pressure began to drop. A cold sweat broke out on his face. His stomach began to convulse just before green vomit oozed from his mouth.

It was a disturbing reaction, but quite common when a patient had been extended to his limit on the tilt board.

He did not adapt as well as I had hoped, Marcy realized, *but unless I push him, how else can we make progress?*

She relied on the ultimate salvation of all therapists, without which they could not continue to work as hard and diligently as they did.

Tomorrow is another day.

Tomorrow would be another day for Bud Young as well.

20

The next day Marcy Ethridge entered Room 302 to find that Mr. Young had preceded her. He was just affixing a cork bulletin board to the wall opposite Bud's bed.

"I use this to illustrate for my sales staff," he explained as he began to mount photographs on the board, fixing them in place with varicolored pins. On each photograph hung a yellow sticker with names printed on it.

Pepper explained, "These are all family. Friends. This one here is our traditional New Year's dinner at my mother's. The whole family's in it. In fact, we were supposed to go to . . . well, doesn't matter," he concluded abruptly.

Once he had posted the last photograph he stood back and admired his handiwork.

"How's that?" he asked.

"It'll do," Marcy replied.

"Oh, there is one thing more," Pepper said as he reached for the plastic shopping bag that leaned against the night table. He drew out a red football jersey with a large number 11 on the back. Just over it in smaller letters the name YOUNG. "He'll like this. It'll be the first thing he remembers. You'll see."

He looked around for a proper place to hang it when Marcy said, "I'll take that."

"But . . ." Pepper began to protest.

"There'll be a right time to show it to him. But not now," Marcy said.

She took the jersey from him, folded it, and slipped it back into the plastic bag.

He was about to dispute her when he realized she had no wish to continue the conversation but had other plans that were inhibited by his presence.

"Well, I guess I better be going. . . . " He started for the door and then remembered, "Oh . . . the radio . . . I'll be bringing that tomorrow."

"Good," Marcy said. "Very good."

She waited until he left the room. She turned to her patient.

"Good morning, Bud," she greeted, loud and firm.

He opened his eyes slowly. This morning he seemed to have a fixed stare as he realized her presence.

"Today, Bud, we are going to have a big adventure. We are going to start you on the way to talking."

From his look she knew that he did not understand. In his eyes there was the reflection of his baffled, fearful state of mind.

"Now the first thing we are going to do is open your mouth. Did you hear me, Bud? Do you understand? Open . . . your . . . mouth!"

There was no sign of effort, no hint in his eyes that he understood.

She opened her therapist's bag, produced several flat wooden tongue depressors. She leaned over him. He tried to push her away but it was a vague defensive gesture that missed her completely.

She reached his lips, separated them, pressed down on his lower jaw to separate his teeth. She inserted the tongue depressor, not to press down on his tongue but to activate it into some degree of movement.

His jaws clamped shut in such a sudden fierce instinctive reaction that his teeth severed the wooden blade, leaving half of it inside his mouth and the rest clamped in Marcy's fingers.

"Bud! Open your mouth! Open it. I want that back! So open your mouth!"

More out of Bud's inability to respond to her command than stubbornness, his jaws remained locked. She tossed aside the broken blade. Quickly she slipped on a pair of thin rubber surgical gloves. She leaned over Bud. With her strong gloved hands she pried his jaws apart. She reached in with her forefinger. She extracted the broken blade carefully for fear that the ragged edge might inflict damage on his gum and the soft tissue inside.

Having retrieved it, she held his jaws apart. "Bud, stick out your tongue. Let me see your tongue. Bud, did you hear me? Stick . . . out . . . your . . . tongue."

When he did not, she reached into her bag for a gauze square, wrapped it around his tongue, and drew it out.

"Bud . . . that is what you do when I say, stick out your tongue." She relaxed her grip on it, watched it slide back into his mouth, watched his jaws close once more.

"Bud, open your mouth." When he did not comply, she repeated, "Open . . . your . . . mouth." She enunciated each word carefully and paused before the next one.

This time there appeared to be a flicker of understanding and reaction. Though his mouth did not open his jaws did move perceptibly.

"Stick . . . out . . . your . . . tongue," she ordered.

His lips twitched slightly. His lower jaw moved behind his closed lips. Then, with what seemed enormous effort, his jaws parted slightly.

"Good! Terrific, Bud! We're making headway now. Just try once more. Stick . . . out . . . your . . . tongue," she ordered expectantly.

His eyes appeared to respond but he could not manage to open his mouth wide enough. Marcy opened his jaws and said, "Now, stick . . . out . . . your . . . tongue."

She could see his tongue move but he could not yet obey her command.

She had to be content with the discovery that he was at least aware and marginally responsive. She would have to do most of the work today.

She held his jaws open with her left hand. With her right she reached into his mouth. She activated his tongue, moving it to the right, then to the left. She massaged the inside of his mouth to stimulate the muscles necessary for speech and eventually for eating.

When she had finished, she set about her physical therapy, exercising his arms and legs, his shoulder and back muscles, careful always to protect the gastrostomy tube that kept him nourished and alive until he would be able to eat on his own.

Under her strong brown hands, his muscles reacted well. His physical condition would prove a great help once his brain could be motivated and activated.

When she had completed exercising his body, she took hold of his hand.

"Squeeze . . . my . . . hand . . . Bud," she ordered. "Squeeze . . . my . . . hand."

His hand did no more than make contact with her soft skin.

"Bud . . . turn . . . your . . . head . . . to . . . your . . . right," Marcy suggested.

He appeared confused.

"Turn . . . your . . . head . . . to . . . the . . . right," she repeated.

Again no response.

"Turn . . . your . . . head . . . to . . . your . . . left," she said this time.

There was the slightest sign of movement, which seemed to require enormous effort. But finally he did make a small turn. And to his left, as she had asked.

It had been a long session. She was relieved that neither his mother nor father had been here to witness it. For what to her was a marked accomplishment would have appeared to them to be a dismal failure.

As yet there was no indication of his potential recovery. But he had made some advances. Some small advances.

As she began to close up her bag, she suggested, "Bud . . . look what Dad brought." She waited for him to open his eyes. She pointed to the photographs on the wall opposite.

He looked for a few seconds, then closed his eyes. He was not yet strong enough for prolonged exertion.

She took up her bag, and turning for the door, she called back, "See you after lunch."

As she reached the door she heard him make a sound. Not a distinct sound, surely not a word. A grunt. But still a voluntary sound. She raced back to his bedside.

"Bud . . . Bud . . . do . . . that . . . again. . . . Make . . . that . . . sound . . . again."

But he could not. She was disappointed but not surprised. No one could gauge or predict when such things would happen. But if it happened once, it could, and likely would, happen again. So she was encouraged.

Tomorrow would be better, she promised herself, until she realized, *Am I beginning to think and sound like the patient's mother? Better not. Tomorrow we will continue with oral stimulation as my protocol provides. And we will not become emotional or sentimental about the patient or his progress.*

In the afternoon, when Marcy Ethridge arrived at Room 302 for her second session, she found Lily Young standing at the foot of Bud's bed pointing to various photographs asking, "Bud . . . remember Gramma Young? The New Year's Day dinner? Uncle Bill . . . Aunt Tess . . . you remember Aunt Tess . . . the one who always . . ."

Interrupted by Marcy's arrival, Lily stopped and shook her head sadly. Obviously she had had no success evoking any memories in her son.

"How long have you been trying?" Marcy asked.

"Almost half an hour and nothing . . . no response . . ."

"Please, never half an hour. A few minutes. Five at most. At this stage he tires very easily. And will for quite some time."

Lily nodded. "Sorry . . . I didn't know."

Though Marcy would have preferred to work with a patient who was less tired, nevertheless, she proceeded to slip on a fresh pair of surgical gloves. She opened Bud's mouth and reached in to gently manipulate the muscles inside. She felt around carefully to see if his muscles were still in a resistant and defensive attitude. They seemed less resistant than they had in the morning. She massaged his gums gently. He seemed more aware than he had been and more compliant.

"Bud . . . stick out your tongue," Marcy ordered.

He needed a moment to comprehend. Once he did, he halt-ingly parted his lips, opened his mouth slightly.

"Good. Now, show me your tongue. Bud, stick out your tongue." When he did not seem able to comply, she illustrated by sticking out her own tongue, then saying, "Tongue . . . stick out your tongue."

He seemed to understand. He complied by barely edging his tongue between his teeth.

"Very good. Now, Bud, move your tongue from side to side. From one side . . . like this . . ." She illustrated once more, mov-ing her own tongue to the right. Then to the left. "See? Side to side. Do it, Bud. You can do it. Try!"

He stared at her. It was hard to tell if he understood or if he was taking the time to marshal the willpower and the coordi-nation necessary for what had become a complex task.

He finally tried, the tip of his tongue moving slowly right, then even more slowly to the left.

"Again, Bud, one more time. Come on now. Side to side."

The second time seemed only slightly more defined than the first.

Time, Marcy thought, to try him on fluids again. She brought in a bucket of fresh ice chips. Ordered him to open his mouth, which he was able to do. She slipped in an ice chip. She focused not on his mouth but on his neck and especially on his larynx to follow his swallowing activity, if any. Instead of what she had hoped to find, she was disappointed by a sound that was more a gargle than a swallow.

She poured some of the melted ice water into a cup, held it to his mouth. This time, without any suggestion, he opened his mouth. Marcy poured in a tiny bit of water to observe his re-action. She heard that gargling sound once more which, this time, ended in a cough.

As she had suspected, he could not yet control his muscles sufficiently. Some of the water must be dribbling down into his trachea. This could threaten his lungs, inducing not only pneu-monia but other complications.

There was only one way to make sure. She called down to

Radiology. Fortunately, they had an opening. So she eased Bud
onto a gurney and rushed him down.

In Radiology the technician assisted Marcy in moving Bud
from the stretcher into a chair. When he was strapped in, the
chair would keep him upright for a modified barium swallow,
which should reveal the cause of Bud's difficulty. At the same
time the procedure was being viewed on the screen, a tape would
be made on which Marcy could study, in a slow stop-and-go
motion, every detail of the process.

The technician mixed up a bowl of barium powder with water,
making a thin concoction which he fed into Bud's open mouth.

In the darkened room Marcy had her eyes glued to the video
screen. She watched as Bud's tongue struggled with the barium,
noting, *Defective bolus control. His tongue can't manage to get a sufficient amount of the stuff back into position to swallow. And what
little does get there is not handled too well by his epiglottis. It does not
perform its natural function. Does not close off his trachea from his
esophagus. It allows some of the stuff to leak into his airway.*

Work. This is going to take a great deal of work.

Automatic functions that every normal infant is born with
Bud Young would have to relearn.

Once she had returned him to 302 Marcy Ethridge assembled
the essentials for improving Bud's bolus control, that simple
function by which the tongue should automatically position
food for swallowing. She brought in a bowl of orange juice and
half a dozen strips of gauze. She raised Bud to a sitting position.
She dipped a strip of gauze into the juice.

"Open up, Bud."

Slowly he responded. She placed one end of the juice-soaked
gauze on his tongue. Gripping the other end, she instructed,
"Move it, Bud. Suck it back . . . to the back of your tongue.
Don't be afraid. I've got the other end in hand. See? All you
have to do is draw it in, on your tongue . . . right to the back.
And don't stop. You can't swallow it. So just suck it back, move
it back . . . that's right . . . better. Much better. Keep doing
that, Bud, keep doing that. Very good. Now, we'll rest a while."

Three times Marcy repeated the exercise. Each time, though
by his eyes, his attitude, and his grunts he resented it, each time

he improved slightly. Certainly enough to be encouraging to his
therapist if not to the patient himself.

His bolus control on the way to being trained, though it
would take days to make it fully effective, Marcy devoted her
afternoon session with Bud to working on his swallowing difficulty.

For that she adopted the Mendelson maneuver. This was more
complicated since it required the patient's understanding and
cooperation to a greater degree than bolus control.

The key to the Mendelson was allowing the muscles to process
a liquid through the specific details of swallowing. Clear water
or fruit juice was too thin. They move too swiftly for the muscles
to control. So Marcy thickened some orange juice with a modified food starch, which would allow the muscles time to remember how to function.

"Bud, this time I want you to hold your breath. Do you
understand me? Hold your breath."

She sucked in her breath, patted her flat stomach. She did not
exhale.

"Come now, inhale. Hold it!"

He followed instructions.

"Now I want you to tighten your throat muscles . . ."

She demonstrated once more by tensing the muscles of her
slender brown neck until they stood out.

"Let me see . . . tighten those muscles. . . . "

He made an effort but it turned out to be a vague imitation
of what he thought he had seen.

She persisted, "Once more! And this time, try!"

His second effort was somewhat better but not good enough
for her to feed him the thick juice.

"Once more," she insisted.

He tried again. This time she was satisfied.

"Now let's try it with a sip of orange juice."

She fed him a small sip. He struggled to tighten his throat
muscles, giving his epiglottis time to carry out its assigned function.

Several times they repeated the procedure.

Once she was satisfied, she arranged for a second visit to Radiology.

This time as she watched the screen, she saw the results of their work. His bolus control, still not perfect, not totally automatic, worked sufficiently well for his tongue to move the barium back into swallowing position. His epiglottis closed off the trachea, forcing the barium into his esophagus.

Having succeeded with fluids, Marcy asked the X-ray technician, "Do I have time?"

"Give you half an hour," he said.

"Then let's go for it," she said.

She reached into the pocket of her white lab coat to produce the materials necessary for her next medical experiment.

Two black-and-white Oreo cookies.

While the technician mixed some barium in a bowl, Marcy carefully separated the two layers of one Oreo. She then replaced the white icing with a layer of white barium. She broke off a small piece of the altered cookie and slipped it onto Bud's tongue.

"Chew, Bud . . . chew . . ."

Partly by vague chewing effort, partly by moving the cookie back by tongue action, he managed to maneuver the soft mashed substance to the back of his mouth. He tightened his throat muscles. His epiglottis had resumed its normal function.

The cookie, barium and all, had entered his esophagus.

He had swallowed his first bit of solid food. And she had followed the entire course of it through the barium which was picked up by the X ray and clearly shown on screen.

Bit by bit, she fed him the rest of the Oreo. She watched every step of the progress of each bit from tongue, to back of tongue, to epiglottis closing off the trachea, to the final entry of the mashed barium-laden cookie into and on the way down his esophagus.

A small journey, a simple natural process, but on this day in this radiology room, a great accomplishment for Bud Young.

Able to eat solid food, he would soon no longer be dependent on that gastrostomy tube.

If her patient did not appreciate the enormity of his accomplishment, his therapist surely did. One big hurdle overcome, with more, many more to follow.

Of which learning to feed himself was one.

21

Six days had gone by. Twelve sessions of work on improving Bud Young's various skills. He could move his arms and hands, though in limited fashion. But his cognitive skills lagged badly. He could make sounds, intentional sounds. But his inability to enunciate prevented him from cooperating in other areas of his rehabilitation.

In their morning session, on this day, Marcy Ethridge held out some common everyday articles, asking Bud to identify them. She held a fountain pen in her right hand, a pocket flashlight in the other.

"Bud . . . point . . . which one is the pen? The pen, Bud. Which one?"

He stirred to lift his right hand. It was not easy for him. She waited patiently. Patience seemed to be the key word in her profession. Patience and perseverance.

"The pen, Bud . . . point to the pen."

He managed to extend his forefinger slightly more than the others. He aimed it in the general direction of the fountain pen.

"Good man!" Marcy enthused because yesterday he had not been able to make a single identification. She held up a glass in her right hand, her notebook in her left.

"Bud, point to the glass." He did not respond. "The glass, Bud. Which one? Point to it."

He appeared confused. She waited for him to organize his thoughts. Finally, with his arm resting on the bed, he raised his hand far enough to point toward the glass.

"Terrific!" Marcy said, smiling encouragement.

He had not only progressed since yesterday, but he was bearing out what she had discovered yesterday afternoon after she left the hospital.

She had visited his high school, asked the principal if she could study Bud's academic record. Though at first he resisted, once she explained, he made all the facts available to her.

She was curious to discover how good a student he had been. What she could expect from him. What demands to make on him. And, as important, when not to demand what was beyond his capacity. She was encouraged to learn that he was actually a very good student. Though much of his out-of-class time was taken up with athletics, he scored well on his tests. His grades ranged from B to B plus and there were a number of As on his record.

He was excellent material for her skills. The danger, the real danger, was that he, and others, mostly his father, would be expecting too much from him.

The irony is, Marcy thought, *if he hadn't been so proficient in his scholastic work and his athletics they wouldn't be expecting so much from him now. Because even by the most optimistic of assessments, he can never be that again.*

Right now, even speaking and eating were beyond him.

She presented several more articles, some of which he could identify. Most of which he could not.

She proceeded to massage and gently manipulate his tongue and the muscles necessary for speech. After some minutes she inserted a wooden tongue depressor into his mouth and moved his tongue from side to side gently until it began to resist.

She sat on the bed facing him, and enunciating her own words slowly, exaggerating her own lip and tongue movements, she said, "*Bud* . . . your name is *Bud* . . . *Bud* . . . can you say *Bud?*"

She did not expect he could. But she wanted to see if his muscular movements could eventually lead to speaking.

His lips did move. Though they never parted, they twitched. His eyes reflected his effort.

She coaxed, *"Bud . . . say it, you can say it, Bud."*

He continued to make the effort but finally with a weary sigh he was forced to give up.

This afternoon . . . or tomorrow, Marcy thought as she proceeded with her physical therapy.

Since his muscle tone was good, having benefited from her previous work, today she introduced a new component into the therapy. She produced two small weights mounted on narrow canvas straps with Velcro fasteners. Light in weight, they would offer just enough resistance to build up the strength in his arms. Strength he would need for tests yet to come, now that he was reacting well to his daily stint on the tilt board.

She slipped the straps around his forearms, fastened them firmly into place. She raised his weighted arms several times. Then she said, "Now, you, you do it. By yourself. Lift. Lift, Bud!"

His arms lay on the blanket, palms up. He stared at them, at the weights. She could see in his eyes that he doubted he could do it. Nevertheless, she continued to urge, "Bud, *I* know you can do it. I want *you* to know you can do it. So try. Just try. For me."

He glanced into her brown eyes, which were encouraging yet demanding as well. He made an effort. He was able to raise his left arm not quite an inch off the blanket.

"Good! Excellent!" Marcy said. "Now, try the other one. The right one, Bud. Try the right one."

He made a determined effort but could not raise his right arm even that small distance. The more frustration he endured, the more intense his effort, until suddenly in an effort to rid himself of the weight he swung out, almost striking Marcy who had to rear back quickly to avoid him.

Well, she thought, *not exactly what he intended but a damn good move. Very encouraging.*

In her profession, anger, frustration, rebellion all served a purpose.

"Good work, Bud. You are becoming my prize pupil," she complimented, hoping that he understood her words and the praise she meant to convey.

She put her materials together, closed her bag, and said, "See you later." She enunciated the words once more, slowly so he could watch her lips. "See . . . you . . . later . . . Bud."

She left, allowing the door to slide quietly closed.

Bud Young lay in his bed, staring at the wall opposite. At the photographs mounted on the cork bulletin board. They were all strangers to him. He could not even recognize himself.

A few moments of staring exhausted him. He closed his eyes. He drifted into a troubled, disordered sleep that lasted only minutes.

He came awake. He tried to move his lips. Without knowing why or remembering, he knew there was something involving the movement of his lips that he wanted to do.

He wet them. He tried to move them once more. They began to respond. He took a breath. He expelled it, using his lips and, without knowing it, the other muscles Marcy had been exercising. A sound emerged.

Not the word *Bud* . . . but a sound that, had he been able to properly articulate it, *would* have been Bud.

He was unable to fully appreciate what he had done, but he felt somehow that it was good.

Lily Young had begun to integrate her visiting hours with Marcy's treatment sessions so that she would not impinge on them. Quite diplomatically, Dr. Curtis had explained that patients made more progress when not under the scrutiny of close family. Their presence created too much pressure, impeding the therapy.

Marcy had explained to Dr. Curtis that she did not think either of the Youngs could endure the slow and sometimes discouraging process involved.

So when Marcy returned to Room 302 for the afternoon session, Bud was alone once more.

To engage him in conversation, which was in itself part of the therapy, she observed lightly, "Have a good visit with Mom? What'd she have to say today? Nothing much, I guess. Otherwise you'd have told me."

As she talked, she began to unload her bag. So that she was not looking in his direction as he tried to speak.

Then she heard it.

"... uh ... uud ..."

She turned to him at once. Forming her own lips as a model she enunciated, "B ... ud ... B ... ud ... Bud."

His lips quivered. He seemed to gain control of them. He tried once more. "Uh.."

"Bud," Marcy enunciated

"... uuhd ..." he tried again.

"B ... B ... Bud ..."

"B ... uud," he finally spoke.

"Oh, that is just the greatest, Bud. Am I proud of you!"

She kissed him gently on the cheek. Then playfully pretended to punch him on the chin as men often do as a show of affection. The more physical contact, the more cutaneous stimulation, the better.

"Now for bigger and better things," Marcy declared with renewed enthusiasm. "Let's do a little work on our familiar faces."

She directed his attention to the family photographs, the team photograph, the photograph of himself and Marylyn at the Mall. He could not identify any of them. Referring to the list appended to the photos, she named each one. But before she was through, he had closed his eyes and drifted off to sleep.

My fault, she rebuked herself. *So excited at his progress that I did what I warn everyone else not to do. I overdid. Well, tomorrow is another day.*

But this was a good one, a very good one.

Before she left she turned on the radio to provide him with auditory stimulation since no one was there now to make conversation.

22

Four days had gone by. Eight sessions of therapy under the firm but diplomatic care of Marcy Ethridge. Bud had his periods of achievement when his eyes reflected his appreciation for what she was doing for him. He had his moments of resentment and rebellion when she insisted on keeping him on the tilt board for long stretches though she knew he had come to hate it.

He did not yet understand that it was only one step on the road to freedom. The other, which in his mind seemed unconnected, was an exercise that in his state of mind seemed more familiar.

Each morning and again each afternoon Marcy would strap those weighted cloths around his forearms, fasten them tightly with their Velcro closures and instruct Bud to raise his arms. The first time he could lift his right arm, which used to be his strong throwing arm, barely high enough to allow her to slip her own hand between his arm and the blanket.

The look in his eyes, the frown on his face, reflected his complete puzzlement and frustration at being unable to perform so simple a task. That his arm, which had been such a powerful part of his body, was now so weak and beyond his control tormented him. The harder he tried, the less able he seemed to make it respond.

All the while Marcy coaxed, "You can't do it all in one day. We take it a little at a time."

She did not burden his mind with an explanation that lifting his weighted-down arms was only one step in a larger plan that would eventually determine if he could ever walk again.

Small challenges, simple concepts, were difficult enough for him to cope with.

When he wearied of the weights, she put him through a regime of exercises that strengthened his biceps and his shoulder muscles.

Gradually she eased him into another phase of recovery. Perhaps the most difficult. Regaining the fine motor skills in his hands.

On this day she presented him with a tray of common, everyday articles which she asked him to identify.

"Bud, point to the glass. The glass, Bud. Point to which one is the glass."

She could practically read the steps through which his mind was working. First, to comprehend her instructions. Second, to formulate his identification. Finally, to execute the function of pointing to it.

But he did. And so he did with other objects on the tray. A safety pin. A rubber band. A paper clip. A spoon.

Her exercise in memory restoration continued, but with a special purpose in mind on this day.

For the last article on the tray waiting to be identified was an uncapped fountain pen.

"Bud, point to the pen," Marcy instructed.

His mind did not consider that it was the last and only unidentified item on the tray. He struggled to accept the word *pen,* then make his identification from that. Finally he pointed to it, extending his forefinger slightly more than the other fingers on his right hand.

"Very good, Bud. Excellent!" Marcy said, then paused a moment before she said, "Now, pick it up, Bud. Pick up the pen."

He glanced at the pen, glanced at Marcy, looked back at the pen. He dared to reach in its direction. She edged the tray closer so the pen was within his grasp. He rubbed his forefinger along it.

"Pick it up, Bud. Pick it up," she urged.

His forefinger resting on it, he tried to bring his thumb close to grip it. When he thought he had made contact with it, he tried to pick it up. He managed to lift it off the tray but at once it slipped from his faulty grip.

He glared at his deficient hand with anger and a look of betrayal. Slowly he started to reach out once more, but fear of failing again caused him to draw back his hand.

He appeared spent and sweaty from his effort.

To reward him for trying and to encourage him, Marcy produced from the upper left-hand pocket of her white lab coat another pen. This one quite different from any Bud had seen before. In all respects except one, it was a plain red plastic ballpoint pen.

But around its barrel she had wrapped layers of surgical tape which had been colored as red as the pen itself so as not to emphasize the difference.

The pen lying flat on her open pink palm, she invited, "Bud, pick this one up."

He stared at it, looked at her. Her bright eyes encouraged him.

"Go on, Bud. You can do it. Try."

He reached for it, while Marcy nodded to urge him on. He touched the padded pen with his forefinger to test it. With his forefinger pressed against it he brought his thumb up to form a pincer. He grasped it as firmly as his weakened hand permitted. He lifted it from Marcy's palm.

A look of triumph, even a slight smile came into his face, until the effort proved too much. Strive as he would to hold on to it, it fell from his fingers.

Triumph had turned to failure.

"You were terrific!" Marcy encouraged. "You did it. You lifted that pen right off my hand. And what's more, tomorrow you and I are going to do wonderful things with that same pen."

Whether she had completely succeeded in overcoming the sting of failure she did not know. But she had at least opened the door to the next phase of his treatment.

With the stroke victims she had treated, Marcia Ethridge usually had to contend only with their physical difficulties. But CHIs had the added deficit of having their very thought processes and their most simple skills impaired.

In the case of Bud Young she would have to help him not only regain the use of his right hand but reeducate it to write as if he were a student starting out in kindergarten. The place to begin, she knew, was at the beginning.

First, restore, as far as possible, his ability to move and control the movements of that right hand. Much as he would rebel, she would have to make him do it. But, she decided, perhaps she could introduce that as a counterirritant to that other aspect of his therapy that he had come to dislike.

That tilt board. Every time that gurney showed up, the hostile look on his face expressed all the feelings he could not verbalize. Even though he was now able to endure much longer periods of sustained tilting and at higher angles, so that he was now nearly vertical, he resented every moment of it.

He would resent as well the next phase of his treatment. Perhaps he might resent it even more. For it was not much different from what one would use to start a two-or three-year-old on the road to learning coordination and use of hands.

As had become usual in the past days, that afternoon the hated gurney appeared in 302. With the help of an attendant, Marcy coaxed and bullied Bud Young over to the edge of his bed and onto it. He was rolled down the corridor to the therapy room. There he was strapped onto the tilt table, raised up by degrees until he was in almost-standing position. He felt the initial dizziness and a slight nausea. But that subsided.

He appeared resigned, though he continued to scowl out of principle, for to do less would mean surrendering his one vestige of freedom.

Now, Marcy decided, now is the time to add that counterirritant. She brought out a tray not much different from the tray on a child's high chair. She attached it securely to the board at Bud's waist level. The look of suspicion in his eyes was rewarded only by Marcy's smile.

"Go ahead, scowl, make faces, curse me out if you'd like. But we are going to play a little game. Did you ever play marbles when you were just a little kid?"

She poured a cup full of marbles of different sizes onto the tray, then placed the empty cup beside them.

"Now, Bud, let's see how many of these marbles you can pick up and put back into the cup."

He answered her with a fierce look of disdain. He muttered a word which was not quite clear but which she chose to misunderstand.

"Witch, am I? Well, maybe. But that does not relieve you of the responsibility of putting each marble into that cup."

He glared at her, refusing to make an attempt. She said casually, "Okay with me. But you will stay up there until you do it. Even if it takes all day."

With that, she said to the attendant, "Tess, I've got other important things to do. So you just stay with him. And call me when he's finished."

She briskly turned and left Rehab. But once outside, she took up a position at the glass window in the door to observe.

Bud Young was still scowling. Still rebellious. His lips moved. If she could not hear what he said, she knew from the reaction of her assistant, who shook her head quite firmly in the negative. Evidently, in his halting fashion, Bud was insisting on being taken down. Evidently as well, the assistant was refusing to comply.

Suspended there, and with no other choice, Bud began to contemplate the challenge before him. Finally, slowly, he raised his right arm. He brought his right hand to the tray. He tried to flex his fingers. He managed a slight degree of control. But on his first attempt the marble he aimed for skittered away, rolling to the beveled edge of the tray. He considered trying to reach it but realized it was beyond his ability. He tried for one closer. He managed to grasp it between his thumb and forefinger but only for an instant. It slipped away. He stared at his hand as if it had betrayed him. He looked away from the tray and the small round objects that defied him. He would refuse to play this frustrating game.

None of which surprised Marcy Ethridge. She had been through these disheartening beginnings before. She waited. Minutes later Bud felt drawn back to the marbles. Staring at them, glaring at them. Until he tried once more. This time he held one of the large marbles long enough to carry it to the cup. But as he was about to drop it into the cup it popped out and skittered across the tray.

This time, instead of becoming discouraged and angry, he appeared more determined. His hand crept up on the next closest marble as if stalking its prey. He slowly enveloped it with his faulty thumb and forefinger, seized it, lifted it more carefully, and this time finally dropped it into the cup. There was a look of triumph on his youthful face.

Marcy went back into the room. She pretended surprise when she discovered the marble in the cup.

"Well, well, well, what have we here? And I left thinking you were a hopeless cause. You think you're pretty cute, don't you? What you won't do for me, you'll do behind my back. Or did you get Tess to do this for you?"

Bud protested. "I . . . no . . . no . . . I," he stammered.

"Then let me see you do it now," she challenged. "When I am standing right here watching."

In defiance, with the confidence of having achieved it once, Bud applied himself to the marbles. He carefully captured one, held it, transferred it to the cup. Then, with a look of defiance to Marcy, he performed that small miracle a second time. But on his third try, tired from his first two efforts, he lost the marble and ended up discouraged.

"Two out of three," Marcy pointed out. "That's batting six hundred. Good in any league. What you need, young man, is practice. Practice. Let's take these marbles back to your room so you can work on them there."

Regaining that neuromuscular skill was, like most advances in therapy, only a step toward greater goals. If he could master marbles, go on to other small objects like buttons and beans, then he could hold and manage that padded pen. And one day an ordinary pen.

But first the padded one. Hold it. Control it. Use it. So that in conjunction with other regained skills he would one day be able to write again. If not as easily as he had before, at least legibly enough to resume his life as a student.

But regaining even the simplest of such skills would be a slow, sometimes painful process.

The progress he had made in several days of picking up and transferring small objects from his tray into the cup encouraged Marcy to try him on the next step.

So, after he had been tilted to almost vertical position, this time, instead of the tray of buttons, marbles, and beans, which he had mastered and therefore no longer resented, she introduced two new objects.

The padded pen. And a pad of plain white paper.

He stared at them. He stared at her to demand, what do you want now?

"Bud, pick up that pen." She waited for him to comply. "I said, pick it up. Okay, don't pick it up. Just hang there for the rest of the day."

"B . . . itch . . ." he managed. Despite his struggle he endowed the word with all the anger he could summon.

"Pick it up. Or you'll learn how much of a bitch I can be!"

Since she had always managed to make good on her threats before, Bud realized he had better try. It turned out to be much simpler than his first encounter with that hated pen.

Once he held it between his thumb and his forefinger, Marcy wrapped his middle finger around the pen so that he now held it in writing position. She pushed the pad closer to him so that it was directly under the pen.

"Draw something, Bud. A line. Or a circle. Or even half a circle. Anything."

He found it impossible to translate her words into a concept. She took the pen. She began to draw wavy lines across the page, large lines widely spread as for a child to imitate. She held out the pen to him until he reached for it, slowly wrapping three fingers around it.

She surrendered it to him, saying, "Now you do it."

His eyes showed contempt for her order, since the task seemed so infantile. But when he tried to imitate her primitive scrawling he found he could not do it. He tried once more, only to give up in the middle of his futile effort.

He let the pen drop from his fingers. He tried to turn away from her to hide the tears of frustration in his eyes.

She shared his disappointment, his realization that even such childlike scrawling was beyond his present ability.

Marcy leaned her face against his cheek and whispered into his ear.

"Bud Young, I promise you, one day you are going to be able to write again. Words and sentences and whole paragraphs. You will."

Eight days had gone by. Bud's progress was noticeable but slow. He had not yet advanced to the point where he could manage a padded fork or spoon sufficiently to feed himself.

So Lily arranged her visiting hours to coincide with his lunch. She made sure to cut his solid foods into bits small enough for him to ingest and chew—slowly, almost mechanically, but chew nevertheless. She offered him his broth and milk from an infant's cup with a spout.

When he was done, she tried to interest him in drawing lines and circles like primitive Spencerian penmanship exercises. He tried, succeeded some of the time but tired too easily to make much progress.

Aware of her son's limitations, and desperately wanting to demonstrate some substantial improvement to his father, Lily tried to arrange to keep Pep away during feeding hours. She knew what it would do to him to watch his sixteen-year-old son be fed like a child of one.

During feeding, as instructed, Lily kept up a continuous monologue about familiar people, places, and events in an effort to stimulate Bud's memory.

As she fed him his applesauce, she continued to relate a family adventure.

"So there we were . . . Gramma's old Buick up to its hubcaps in the snowbank. And Dad . . . Dad," she repeated, "he is trying to budge it by rocking that old wreck back and forth by shifting from forward into reverse and back again . . . well . . ."

Bud had closed his eyes. She leaned over him carefully to determine if he had fallen asleep again. He tired so easily these days. While she hovered over him, he burst into an explosion of language. His enunciation was faulty, of course, but Lily could understand his words although they ran together as if a single long word.

Her first response was one of great relief and encouragement at his ability to speak so well and so fast. But her sense of relief was very brief. For as she listened and understood what he was saying she became terrified. His words ran together but totally disconnected in thought and without meaning.

". . . windowsgetthegameoverthehillyesterdaytwotimestwo-summerturntheleaveskillthepeoplewhereismarylynvanillachocolate-pistachioregulargaslegowhereislegoswingsledsdownthehillrounding-thirdcarrytheballdrawamaplet'sgolet'spicturesscooter . . ."

Lily drew back from her son's bed, came around to the other side to stare into his half-hidden face. His eyes were open but they appeared void of all feeling, all intelligence.

Yet he rambled on, "jacketarmpitspancakesthreefourfive . . ."

With a chill Lily Young recalled that her son used to say things like that when he was only six. He thought then he had an enormous appetite but never was able to finish even one pancake.

She was forced to ask herself, *Has his brain been so badly damaged that he is back to being six years old again? Oh, my God!*

She raced to the door, flung it open, and called out, "Marcy! Marcy Ethridge! Please! Please?"

Within moments Marcy came racing down the corridor. She took Lily by the arm to reassure her and at the same time ease her back into the room.

"Now, what happened?" Marcy started to ask.

Bud provided the explanation as he continued to erupt in his impeded speech, "Polishsausageraincoach'swhistlethirdandtwo-tricyclemashedpotatoesbaseballjacket . . ."

"He hasn't asked for a baseball jacket since he was nine years old. It's been football ever since. And he talked about pancakes . . . like he was six years old again. Marcy . . . Marcy, you never said, nobody ever said he was that badly hurt . . . to have the mind of a six-year-old again. He's got to stop . . . he's . . . do something . . . Marcy? Please?"

"Nothing to do. And no need for alarm, Lily," Marcy said in the calm reassuring manner she adopted to deal with agitated relatives and friends. "What Bud's doing is often a natural development in these cases. Confabulation. Suddenly a torrent of words comes out of them that makes no sense to us. But they serve a function for the patient. If you listen closely, you will hear that his diction is beginning to show some improvement. Perhaps confabulating helps him to improve."

"He still slurs his words," Lily protested.

"And he will, for quite some time," Marcy replied. "We simply have to work on it each day. But as for his confabulating, don't concern yourself."

Lily nodded, accepting Marcy's assurances. But Marcy could see the damp film of fear-sweat on Lily's upper lip. The woman was still terrified.

"What do I do now?" Lily asked.

"Exactly what you were doing before. When he comes out of this, feed him his lunch. And keep talking to him . . . about familiar people, familiar things."

Once alone with her son, Lily Young stood by his bedside and listened to his rambling, meaningless words, thankful for one thing. That Pepper had not been here to witness this. God knows how he would have reacted.

Once Bud had calmed, Lily fed him the rest of his lunch, then put him through his arm and leg exercises, which Marcy had stressed were so crucial in his future development.

At the same time she tried to revive Bud's memory about people and things by directing his attention to the photos on the bulletin board. Lily studied him as he studied the photos, hoping to find some glint of recognition in his eyes.

For an instant she thought she detected such a hint when she pointed out the one of him and Marylyn. Meticulously she pronounced the name, "Marylyn . . . Marylyn . . ." expecting that he might pick it up and repeat it. He did not.

But still, clinging to hope she insisted, *I'm sure I saw a glint of recognition in his eyes.*

It was almost four o'clock. Marcy Ethridge was returning Bud Young to 302 after his stint on the tilt board. She had expected that he would have advanced far enough on it to permit her to take him to the next level. But his blood pressure readings were not that encouraging. What advances he did make were in neuromuscular facilitation. He was able to control fine movement of his right hand much better. Soon he should be able to feed himself enough so that the gastrostomy tube could be removed, since it was now being maintained only as a safeguard.

But the emergence of his confabulating called for a somewhat different kind of therapy to end off this day. The way he ran his words together indicated progress in the use of the muscles involved in his speech. But on a thought level, something must be done to separate his words one from another so that he would speak more distinctly. Which by itself would also improve his use of language.

She had brought with her a small board which she rested at the foot of his bed. On it were all the letters of the alphabet, set up in large type, each standing alone, equidistant from the other.

"Sit up, Bud. You can do it without my help. Come on, now, don't be lazy. Up. Up you go!"

She sat alongside the bed and asked, "Bud, did you watch much television today?"

He did not respond.

"Bud, I turned the set on when I left earlier." She spoke very slowly to give him time to assimilate her meaning. "Did you see anything interesting? I had the movie channel on. Didn't you watch?"

"Watchjunkypicturestupidpictureyuck . . ."

She feared it might be a bit premature to try to remedy this particular problem but she decided to chance it.

"Okay, Bud, let's just stop for a moment. Let's play a game." Slowly she explained, "See the letters on that board? I want you to start all over again. Pick out the last letter of every word you say right after you say it. The last letter of each word. Understand?"

"Uhhuh," Bud responded in slightly more than a grunt.

"Now, let's start. What did you think of the film you saw on television?" Marcy asked.

"Junkymovie . . ."

"Hold it, Bud. Remember the game. You point out the last letter of *each* word you say."

He paused, tried to recall his first word, found it, then studied the letter board.

"Junky . . . las . . . letter . . ." He pointed to the large Y.

"Very good! Touchdown! Let's keep going!"

"Junky moviepretty . . ."

"Last letter, Bud, last letter."

He struggled to recall the word. Found it.

"Movie . . . las . . . letter . . ." Again he pointed to the Y.

"No, Bud, the last letter of movie is not Y."

He seemed confused, almost ready to dispute her. But on reconsideration he realized and corrected himself. "Movie . . . las . . . letter . . ." He pointed to the large E.

"Score ten more points for Bud!" Marcy announced.

So she led him through his reaction to a film he obviously hated but which served as the perfect exercise. By the time he reached the end of his critique he was separating his words, making his speech sound more normal than it had.

Not that Marcy deluded herself into thinking that once learned meant learned forever. She would have to repeat this exercise many times before she achieved the desired permanent effect.

She was just removing the alphabet board when the door swung open and Lily Young came into the room.

This time she was not alone. She was accompanied by a pretty blond girl of fifteen who, Marcy recognized at once, was the girl in the photograph with Bud.

"Oh, no," Marcy whispered to herself.

She moved quickly to block the young woman from Bud's view. Unfortunately, she was not quick enough. For Bud had already seen her. However slow he was to recognize and identify people and objects, somehow her appearance stirred some memory in him.

He uttered an indistinct sound, but clearly a sound of rage, accompanied by a sudden movement of his body which almost threatened to catapult him out of his bed.

Lily Young was speechless in surprise and terror.

Instantly Marcy ordered both women, "Out. Just get out!"

"I'm sorry . . . I only thought . . ." Lily started to apologize.

"I said, 'Out!' " Marcy repeated, physically pushing them to the door.

Once the door was closed, Marcy rushed to her patient, who was still raging in unintelligible sounds.

She embraced him to pin his arms against his body. She captured his right arm but his left eluded her. In his wild swing he caught her alongside her head just above her right eye.

Taken by surprise, she was deflected, but only momentarily. She grappled with him, finally capturing his left arm. She held him tightly until his rage subsided. Quivering, sweating, panting, he seemed resigned to surrender to her embrace. She allowed him to slip back into his half-sitting position.

They sat alongside each other, patient and therapist, both exhausted, physically and emotionally. They stared into each other's eyes.

Only then did Marcy become aware of the slow warm trickle from her forehead down her temple. Before she could touch it, Bud reached out his unsteady awkward right hand. His forefinger and thumb wiped the blood away. He rubbed it between his two fingers as if it were another exercise. But the look in his eyes, despite lack of verbal communication, expressed his guilt and told her how sorry he was.

He was aware enough to know he had hurt her and he was apologizing.

Once Bud was at ease again, Marcy went searching for Lily Young and Marylyn. She found them in a corner of the visitors' lounge. Marylyn, a badly shaken young woman, was trying to comfort Lily, who was in tears.

At Marcy's appearance, Lily broke away from Marylyn. She rushed to Marcy, asking, "Is Bud all right? What happened? Has he done himself any damage . . . that tube . . ."

Lily had a dozen questions and a hundred fears.

"He'll be fine, in time," Marcy said.

Lily noticed the slight cut over Marcy's eye.

"Did . . . did Bud do that?"

"Don't concern yourself about that," Marcy said. "But why did you ever bring this young woman here? Nothing against her. But he's not ready for such a confrontation. Not yet."

"This morning," Lily explained, "when I was going over the photographs with Bud, I thought . . . no, I felt sure, that he recognized Marylyn. I even thought he was on the verge of saying her name. So I figured if she actually came here, if she talked to him, it would help restore his memory."

"Lily, he's a young man. Still a boy, really."

"You told me that was good. That young brains recuperated faster, improved more than older brains," Lily replied.

"Yes. But young people are also far more sensitive. More conscious of their deficits. They don't want their peers to see them in that condition. Older people can adjust to the fact that they are never going to be perfect again. Young people refuse to accept that."

"Are you telling me that Bud knows . . . or thinks . . . he's not going to recover fully?" Lily asked.

"I mean he refuses to accept it. Even though it is very likely true."

"Poor Bud . . ." Lily whispered.

"Yes. Poor Bud."

"Please . . . whatever you do . . . don't tell his Dad," Lily begged.

"If his father can't accept it, then poor Dad," Marcy said. "That will make it our job, yours and mine, to get Bud to do the best he can with what he has."

24

Marcy Ethridge had just returned Bud Young from his session in Rehab, where he had been held in tilted position at an almost vertical angle.

She had him sitting up in a chair with his workboard before him and his padded pen in hand, drawing his approximation of a line of continuous E's across the page of his worksheet.

When he finished the E's she drew for him a small O and instructed, "Now, Bud, start here and just keep drawing O's across the page until you run out of space."

Pen in hand, he ventured his first O, which turned out to be two thin lines with scarcely any white space between them.

"Rounder, fatter, Bud . . . like the one I drew. Get a firmer grip on your pen and make a nice round motion like this."

She wrapped her fingers around his and traced a fat round O.

"There. You can do that. Just think of it and then do it."

He studied her sample, appeared to make up his mind, then began to write an O that was slightly rounder and fatter.

"Fine! Now just keep going. Clear across the page."

He started slowly but picked up his pace as he gained confidence and had just gone clear off the page when the door opened.

"Am I interrupting?" Lily Young asked, peeking in behind the slightly open door.

"No, you're just in time," Marcy said. "We're finishing up our writing exercises. Bud, Mom's here."

He did not look up but was determined to finish filling the page with O's. His newly acquired skill appeared to give him great satisfaction.

Lily took the moment to ask quietly, "How'd it go today?"

"Better."

Uncomfortable at having to question her son's therapist for fear it would be considered criticism, Lily prefaced her question with an explanation.

"I understand. But my husband, with all he's got on his mind, the office, that class he teaches youngsters on the South Side, and . . . well . . ." Lily hesitated, "well, he doesn't get home until late every evening . . . he goes to his A.A. meetings . . . then especially when he has to go out of town for a day or two, he depends on me for reports on how Bud's doing. And frankly, I . . . I can't just keep saying, 'Better.' He always asks me a thousand questions. Like, is he feeding himself yet? Is he sitting up by himself? Walking . . . when are they going to get him walking? You can understand, can't you, Marcy?"

"Mr. Young is not the first impatient father I've had to deal with," Marcy said. "Somehow fathers are more demanding than mothers. And more demanding of their sons than of their daughters. As if it's a reflection on them if their sons do not perform as they would like."

"How true," Lily agreed without mentioning the added pressure of her husband's guilt. "Now, he's going to call this evening—he always does when he's out of town—what shall I tell him?"

"The truth," Marcy said. "Bud's hand skills are coming along. He takes the tilt board well enough so that one day soon he'll be on the parallel bars, which is the first step toward walking, then . . ."

"How long will it take before he does walk?" Lily interrupted. "That's the first thing Pep asks, when are they going to get that boy on his feet?"

"Lily, it would be wrong to promise your husband anything at this stage. We work, we wait, we see. That's the most I can say for now."

"But when he asks . . ."

"Tell him what I told you. Bud is doing well. We look forward to getting him on the parallel bars. Then we can assess his capabilities and make our decisions," Marcy said.

She spoke with such finality that Lily knew she would not commit herself or the hospital any further.

Lily spent her time with Bud as she always did, talking of familiar places and people to stimulate his memory. At the same time she encouraged him to keep at his writing exercises.

She had just placed a fresh piece of scratch paper before him and urged, "Try making U's, darling. Like this."

She drew a continuous line of U's across the top of the page. As he studied them she continued talking.

"Well, you'll never guess who called again today. Mr. Venable."

She watched his eyes to see if he recognized the name. He did not appear to.

"Mr. Venable . . . from school . . . well, first thing I thought, Gwen's falling down in her grades. She's at that age now. Hairdos and boys are more exciting than French or trig. But, no, Mr. Venable said she was doing fine. It was *you* he was calling about. Wanted to know how you were doing. And went on for what seemed like hours about what a good student you were in his English class. He said, and these are his exact words, 'Bud's essays were always a pleasure to read. So neatly written and you could always expect something fresh and interesting.' That's what he said. He also said he hoped you'd be coming back to school in September."

Bud continued to draw U's without any indication that he had heard or understood anything his mother said. Lily would have been even more distressed than she was except for Marcy's warnings that one of the problems of recovering CHIs was difficulty in concentration. One problem at a time in these early stages.

He had finished his page of U's. Lily was about to suggest he go on to E's, but Bud himself began to draw crude geometric figures, lines that were meant to be straight, a sawtoothed figure with jagged edges, strokes that might have been intended to be representations of lightning.

If they had no purpose that Lily could identify, she realized that he took satisfaction from having control of the padded pen in his right hand.

All the while she kept rehearsing in her mind what she would tell Pep when he called from out of town this evening.

"His memory," Pepper Young asked on the telephone. "Did he show any improvement today?"

"Well," Lily began, trying to select the most encouraging words she could muster, "he's so wrapped up in his writing . . . he's like a kid with a new toy. Once he discovered he can handle that pen that's all he wants to do, write."

"Lil, his memory?" Pep asked again.

Lily had to admit, "It's not as good as it should be yet. But Marcy says that always takes time."

"Time," Pep considered, disheartened once again. Then he asked, "Lil, I'm not criticizing her. But is it possible that Marcy is being too soft with him? After all, it's not difficult to like Bud. Even in his present condition he's a likable young man. A kid anyone can feel sorry for. But sympathy may be the last thing he needs now."

"Pep, what are you getting at?"

"Marcy doesn't know Bud like I do. He doesn't take to babying. What he needs is a challenge. The old 'third and long.' That's when he's at his best. He needs incentive. Something to give him drive. A goal. Otherwise I'm afraid . . ." He trailed off, unwilling to voice his fears.

"Pep?" Lily asked anxiously.

"Well, during the war . . . during every war, there are some guys who, if you let them, shirk their duty by just lying in a hospital bed while the rest of the men do the fighting. Bud's not that kind. But he might become that way if he's not challenged. He needs something to make him fight. Hon, I'll be back tomorrow. I think I know exactly what will do it."

During late visiting hours the following evening, Pepper Young arrived on the third floor of Rehab Center of Mercy Hospital. In an innocuous-looking shopping bag with the supermarket logo printed boldly across it he carried a large object which was wrapped in sheets of plain brown paper.

Lily Young hurried alongside him as he strode the corridor with the gait of an angry, determined man.

"Pep, don't you think you should at least talk to Dr. Curtis?"

"He's been in the hands of Dr. Curtis and that Ethridge woman for months now. And what do they have to show for it? He can't even remember the simplest things you told him yesterday."

"He remembers some things," Lily pointed out.

"You said yourself he can't remember what you told him only yesterday. A bright young man like Bud and he can't remember? They must be doing something wrong."

"But, Pep . . ." Lily continued to protest.

"God knows, I've been willing to follow Newman's advice and Curtis's advice to let that Ethridge woman do it her way. But results! I don't see any results!"

"There have been some . . . so let's just go along a little while longer . . ." Lily pleaded.

"Lil! You stay out of this. In fact, I don't even want you in the room when I do it. Just let me handle this in my own way."

They were at the door of 302. Lily did not back off. Not until he glared at her. She knew that look. Not she, not anyone could change his mind now.

Very cautiously Pepper Young opened the door of 302. His son lay in bed, eyes closed. Resting or asleep, Pep did not know. He spoke a soft, "Hi, son . . ." Bud stirred suddenly as if wakened from sleep. He opened his eyes, turned in the direction of the door.

Pepper was not quite sure if, in the dim glow of the night light, Bud recognized him. He approached the bed. Reached out to pat his son gently on the cheek.

When Bud looked up at him, he said, "Brought you something, son. Something to help you remember."

Pepper put down the shopping bag, pulled up a chair alongside the bed to lean close to his son.

"Bud, remember the game? That big important game, when the league championship was on the line. And there we were five points behind and with only forty-seven seconds to play. And we were on our own fifteen. Remember that, son?"

He had failed to do more than bring a look of confusion into Bud's eyes. But Pepper Young was far from discouraged.

"You came to the sidelines. Coach gave you a series of plays. Three passes and a run. And you gained twenty-two yards. Then you worked the ball to the forty-nine with a carry of your own.

"But time was running. With only six seconds left, there you were on your own forty-nine. Everybody in the stands thought, sure as hell, there goes the championship. Everybody but you. Then you let fly that fifty-one-yard pass and it was a touchdown! Victory! Championship! Remember that, Bud?"

He searched his son's eyes. There was no sign of recognition.

"Well, I brought you something, son. Something to help you remember."

He reached for the shopping bag. He drew out the object wrapped in brown paper. Carefully, out of view of his son, he stripped away the paper like peeling a banana. Until he had exposed the badly damaged but still very recognizable silver trophy Bud had won as league Most Valuable Player of the year.

Keeping it below his son's eye level, Pepper began to make a speech very much like the one the coach had made at the victory banquet.

Using all his rhetorical gifts, Pepper proclaimed, "And now for the climax of the evening, the presentation of the trophy for Most Valuable Player. Without whose courage and skills this championship would not have been won. A young man who exemplifies the spirit and the determination this school has always stood for. I am proud and happy to present this trophy to Willard 'Bud' Young!"

Pep bent down and, in a dramatic gesture, presented the cup, holding it by both handles, though one was badly bent.

When his son did not react, Pepper asked, "Bud?" At the

same time he searched his eyes. "Bud . . . don't you remember? You have to remember that night. You must!"

Bud Young began to breathe in shallow spasmodic gasps. He tried to speak some words, which came forth only as angry sounds.

Then he screamed. A cry of agony and rebellion.

"Son . . . son . . . wait . . . no . . ."

Bud began to tear at the bedclothes. He managed to throw them off. He started from the bed. Pepper tried to catch him, hold him. But if Bud's muscles had been weak before, they appeared to have superhuman strength now.

Alarmed by the sounds of her son's outburst and her husband's pleading, Lily Young broke into the room to find them locked in a struggle, with Bud stumbling and flailing about.

She raced from the room toward the nurses' station, calling for help. The night nurse in charge summoned two orderlies, who arrived with a straitjacket and restraining sheets. Finally they were able to subdue Bud Young. They forced him back into bed. They tied him down with the restraining sheets, tucking them firmly under the mattress so that he lay there, seething, struggling, with his arms imprisoned at his sides.

Within half an hour, Dr. Curtis arrived to investigate the cause of this sudden and dangerous outbreak. She gave no special attention to the damaged cup for she had no knowledge of its history. But her observation of the patient convinced her to call Marcy Ethridge, who had to leave her young son in the care of neighbors to make a night visit to the hospital.

With her appearance the patient seemed to calm somewhat. He leaned toward her as she reached for his cheek. Once she had administered a sedative he finally went off to sleep.

Her patient in fairly good condition once more, Marcy Ethridge was free to give her attention to the cause of the episode.

"Dr. Curtis, something happened here that makes it impossible for me to continue on this case," Marcy announced.

"But you must," Curtis protested. "You have such rapport with the patient. He trusts you. You could see that. We could all see that."

"But I can't work with a patient when his family is working

against me. Everything I've tried to do these past few months has almost been undone by what happened tonight," Marcy said. "I think some other therapist . . . one who has the confidence of the family . . . would be much better for this patient."

As she started for the door, Curtis called, "Marcy, please . . ."

Marcy Ethridge stopped only long enough to point to the silver cup that lay where it had fallen during the struggle.

"The last and best thing I can do for this patient is to order, get that thing out of here!"

With that, she left.

A week and five days had elapsed. Physiatrist Curtis sat at her desk, phone in one hand and set of reports in the other. It was not unusual for her to have to carry on a conversation while at the same time studying the multiplicity of Functional Communication Profiles presented to her by the therapists on her staff.

With the proliferation of sports activities in recent years—riding, biking, Rollerblading—and the head injuries resulting from them, her Rehab Center at Mercy Hospital was overcrowded, her therapy staff overworked.

All of them had to record and submit each week, and sometimes more often, profiles reflecting progress every patient was making in the fields of speech, visual identification, physical coordination, and other aspects of recovery.

Curtis continued her telephone conversation. "Doctor, we cannot evaluate a patient merely from X rays and scans. We have to examine her. Here. Yes, yes, I will arrange . . ."

She interrupted herself to restudy the profile she had just opened.

In response to the doctor on the other end of the line, Curtis was forced to say, "Sorry, Doctor. I was distracted. If you can bring the patient in I will make room for her. Good. Monday morning? We'll be ready to evaluate her."

Curtis hung up the phone. She swung around to her file drawer and pulled the folder labeled *Young, Willard, Jr.*

She flipped through the various past reports and profiles on him. She found the one she thought she had remembered. She laid that down alongside the new one she had just examined.

She compared the various categories: *Ability to imitate oral movement. Attempt to communicate. Ability to indicate yes and no. Use of gestures. Awareness of gross environmental sounds. Awareness of emotional voice tone. Understanding of own name. Recognition of names of familiar objects.* Each marking progress from first awakening to the ability to use writing instead of speech and other abilities and skills that would enable the patient to resume a functional life-style.

What she thought she had detected was true. The report filed by therapist Stella Hanford indicated that rather than making progress, Willard Young had actually regressed in his speech and perception abilities.

At the end of the day Dr. Curtis sent for Hanford.

"Stell, what's going on with Bud Young? I thought he was doing well, coming along."

"I don't know the reason, but he's resisting me. I don't have that feeling of being in control, which is so essential. Frankly, I'm stumped. And you've never heard me say that before."

"Have you noticed things are worse when he's had visits from his family? Particularly his father?" Curtis asked.

"No. Those visits seem to cheer him up. But that does not change his attitude toward me. In fact, if you don't mind, I would like to report off his case. I'm not doing him any good. And, frankly, he's not doing my confidence any good either."

"According to these reports, no, you're not doing him any good. But it's not your fault. Give me a few days to work on this," Curtis said.

Aware by now of Pepper Young's evening visiting habits, Dr. Curtis stayed on past her usual hours to intercept him as he was about to enter Room 302.

"Mr. Young, I think you and I must have a talk."

"I agree. I've been meaning to talk to you, Doctor. Why isn't Bud doing more? He should be up and around. Walking. Doing things."

"I think you'd better come down to my office, Mr. Young."

"Before I even say hello to Bud?"

"Yes, before you even say hello," Curtis said.

Alerted by her husband's impatient voice outside 302, Lily Young came to the door.

"And you might come along as well, Mrs. Young," Dr. Curtis said.

Baffled as she was, Lily Young followed along.

Dr. Curtis gestured both Youngs to chairs at her conference table. She laid out before them the case history of Bud Young.

"Mr. Young, these are profiles we have on your son from his first day here. During his coma, his every reaction and lack of reaction. His emergence from coma and his subsequent progress.

"Now, I don't expect either of you, as nonprofessionals, to understand all of this. But I am sure you can read just these two profiles and see for yourselves that Bud has not only made no progress in speech and visual recognition but has actually lost ground. Even though he has been in the charge of a very capable and experienced therapist."

Pep and Lily Young studied both reports. The results were quite obvious. Bud's hard-won skills, imperfect as they had been, had diminished.

From the way the report he was holding started to flutter, Lily Young was aware that her husband's hand had begun to tremble. She suspected that he felt a sudden surge of thirst. A drink would help him now. But there was no drink. He had to face the issue.

"Doctor, what are you trying to tell us? That . . . that Bud's . . . that he's come to the end of the line? That from now on he's going . . . downhill . . . ?"

The possibilities were so alarming that he could not bring himself to put them into words.

"I'm not predicting anything. But I do think we are faced with the real possibility of his inability to make any further progress."

"No further progress . . ." Lily repeated in a whisper.

"Is that . . . I mean . . . does that happen in cases like Bud's?" Pepper dared to ask. "They only go so far, then they hit the wall?"

"We work like hell to make sure that doesn't happen. But there are times when it does," Curtis said. "However, in this case I think we are facing a different problem. I've gone over Bud's complete history. His progress at the outset was slow. But there was steady progress. Then at a certain point progress stops. Deterioration sets in. So I ask myself, what's happened to interrupt his progress? What's changed? Only one thing changed, Mr. Young."

This last she spoke as a challenge to him.

Pep Young stared across the table at the doctor. She was waiting for his response. He cleared his throat before he was able to admit, "Ms. Ethridge . . . is not on his case any longer."

"That's the only factor in his picture that has changed. You must understand, Mr. Young, that between patient and therapist a relationship develops which is crucial to the process. There has to be a feeling that the therapist is almost part of the patient in this endeavor. It takes a strong will on both sides to confront what seems like insurmountable obstacles. Because sometimes they prove to actually *be* insurmountable."

"Do you think . . . what I mean is . . . well, if Bud misses Marcy that much, you have my permission to ask her to come back on his case."

"I never took her off the case," Curtis pointed out.

"She quit. You were there, you saw it," Pep protested.

"Mr. Young, I think the only one who can ask her to come back is the person who made her quit," Curtis said pointedly.

Lily Young knew what a proud and sometimes stubborn man her husband could be, so she was silent all the way home from the hospital that night.

Gwen greeted them at the door to ask, "How's Bud doing?

Did he say anything? Maybe I should go back and see him again. Can I? This time I promise not to cry."

To ease her husband's burden, Lily said, "Maybe not right now, darling."

"Why?" Gwen asked. "He's all right, isn't he? I mean, nothing's happened, has it?"

"Nothing's happened," Lily insisted. "Bud's . . . Bud's doing fine. Now you go up, finish your homework, then get to bed."

Gwen kissed them both. She started up the stairs but stopped midway to look back and ask, "Are you sure Bud's okay?"

"He's fine," Lily reassured. "Doing as well as can be expected," she added, resorting to that oldest, lamest medical cliché.

Gwen continued up to her room. Lily asked, "Pep . . . did you have dinner before you got to the hospital?" When he did not reply she said, "I made some vegetable soup. I could warm it up."

He nodded as he began to untie his tie and unbutton his shirt collar which had been suffocating him ever since their meeting with Dr. Curtis.

When Lily announced that supper was on the kitchen table he came in, sat down, picked up his spoon, stirred the steaming soup, then slapped the spoon down noisily on the table.

"Okay, okay! Stop bugging me! I'll go see her. I'll . . . I'll see her tomorrow. Just don't keep harping on it!"

In the late afternoon of the next day, Pepper Young made it a point to arrive at the hospital before the end of Marcy Ethridge's scheduled workday.

He found her in her small office, writing up her reports on her day's patients. As he knocked lightly on the open door she looked up. Staring at him across her desk lamp she did not recognize him instantly. Then realized, "Oh, Mr. Young. What can I do for you?"

"May I . . . I would like to talk to you for a minute. . . . "

"Come in, come in," she said.

Her invitation was so cool and impersonal that he entered but did not presume to be seated.

"Marcy . . . Ms. Ethridge . . . I don't know if you have been following Bud's progress . . ."

"I . . . I ask from time to time . . . one never completely forgets a patient . . . any patient. And surely not a patient with Bud's potential."

"Then you know he's not doing too well," Pep said. "In fact, he's . . . he's doing less well than he was."

"I'd heard," Marcy admitted.

"Dr. Curtis thinks it would help if you came back on Bud's case," Pepper suggested gently.

"And what do *you* think, Mr. Young?"

"I never realized . . . I had no idea of the . . . attachment . . . the relationship that can grow between the patient and the therapist," Pep admitted.

"Yes, it can become quite strong," Marcy said. "There's a reliance, a trust . . . that takes time to develop. Then it not only grows but endures. And it is quite vital to our work. Because, you see, Mr. Young, there come times . . . and there will with Bud . . . when we have to get him to do things he may not like to do. May not have the *courage* to do, or the *will* to do. And we must by word, or example, or any means we can think of, challenge him to accomplish them."

"Bud likes a challenge," Pepper volunteered at once. "Just tell him it's third and long and you'll be amazed what he can do."

"Mr. Young, the reason it's so necessary for him to have faith in his therapist is that there will come a time, or even times, when it'll be 'third and long' and Bud *won't* be able to come up with something amazing."

"What are you trying to say?" Pepper asked, beginning to feel that same queasy feeling he'd had when confronted by Dr. Curtis.

"Nobody knows now the limits of Bud's recovery. Except that there *are* going to be limits," Marcy Ethridge said.

"Limits . . . what kind of limits . . . how much?"

"As I said, nobody knows," Marcy said.

She leaned across the desk so that her brown face, seeming even stronger now than usual, was bathed in the light of her desk lamp.

"Mr. Young, I have avoided talking to you about this before. But without meaning to, you have made it the issue. So I can't avoid it any longer."

"Don't try to spare me. Go easy on my wife but don't try to spare me. What's the worst you can see in Bud's condition?"

"I wasn't talking about Bud this time," she said very directly, her brown eyes fixed on him. "I was talking about *you*."

"Me? You can always talk freely *to* me and *about* me," he protested.

"All right. Let's talk freely. Mr. Young, unless there are special circumstances surrounding a patient's trauma, the manner in which he was injured is of no interest to the therapist. Whether he was thrown from a horse, or fell from some height, or ran his motorbike into a light pole, or cracked up his new sports car, what interests us are his X rays, his scans, his Glascow Coma readings, his ability to stabilize and survive. So I didn't inquire about Bud's injury. It was just the usual vague 'automobile accident.'

"But because Bud is so well known due to his athletic achievements I learned more about that 'automobile accident.' More than I cared to know. How it happened. Why it happened."

"It was my fault, if that's what you're trying to say," Pepper admitted openly. "But I'm doing something about that."

"Good," Marcy said. "But that does not solve *my* problem."

"*Your* problem?"

"Mr. Young, your guilt about what happened was interfering with my patient," Marcy accused.

"What do you mean, my guilt?" Pepper started to protest.

"I mean your outrageous intrusion with that trophy. I mean your need to rush his recovery, which cannot be rushed. I mean your feeling, whether you're aware of it or not, that if Bud gets all well, is once again the perfect son you had, then you don't have to feel guilty anymore."

He glared at her but she did not yield.

"What I am saying, Mr. Young, is that I will come back and work with Bud provided it is clearly understood that he is *my* patient. *My* duty, *my* job, is to bring him along to as full a recovery as I can, and as he can. I am treating Bud. Not you. I have no obligation to relieve your conscience. Any solace you derive from his recovery is not my concern. The thing *you* can do, is stay out of my way. Don't do anything or say anything, well intended though you may think it is, that will impede his progress."

"I only meant the best . . ."

"Of course," Marcy interrupted. "So what did you do? You brought in the very symbol of his problem. That cup, which meant he was the player of the year, the best. Now a bent and damaged thing, it means he's no longer going to be the best. Or maybe not even as good as the rest. You flaunted that in his face before he was ready to accept it.

"God, man, don't you realize the struggle that's going on inside your son? A torrent of thoughts and feelings. A whole missing memory of what happened. 'How did I get to be this way? Will I ever get over it? I want to be Bud Young again. I want to throw those long passes again. I want to outrun the defenders. I want to slip tackles. I want to know the feeling of victory. What am I doing in this place? Why can't I make myself understood? Why do I need someone to exercise my legs, my arms? Where did it all go so wrong so suddenly?'

"We can only guess what goes on in his mind. But it must be something like that. The appearance of that bent and damaged trophy evidently stirred some memory that caused him great emotional pain. Maybe *that* was the cause of his setback."

"Dr. Curtis thinks it was your leaving him," Pepper replied.

"Neither of us will ever know for sure. But we do know that his going out of control followed being shown that cup. Damaged. As he may be damaged for the rest of his life. Somehow inside his mind he made that connection. Too soon. Too soon," Marcy said.

"The question is, what can you do about it? And will you?"

"Give me your word that you will never again interfere and yes, I will come back," she said.

"You have my word," Pepper Young said.

"Good morning, Bud Young!" Marcy Ethridge called as she opened the door of 302.

Bud turned in her direction. Slowly. But with a faint smile on his face.

"I don't know what you're smiling about, young man," she warned. "Because from now on I am going to work your tail off."

She pulled back his blanket and ordered, "Let's see some action." She strapped the weights around his arms to help restore his upper-body strength. "Flex!" she commanded. "Let's build up those muscles."

As he slowly responded with great effort, to ease his task she kept up a running monologue, part jocular, part serious.

"What's this I hear about you goofing off, young man? Backsliding we used to call it in my church when I was just a child back in Georgia. Back then my old grandaddy . . . he was really my great-grandaddy . . . he used to preach up a storm about backsliding. He used to threaten those sinners with the fires of hell. The fires of hell'll be like a warm breeze alongside what I have in mind for you, Mr. Young. Backsliding! Why, when I saw those reports on you, I was shamed down to my roots.

"I taught you better than that. Words and things we long ago got over, you didn't even know. So I said, that young man, he is not going to spoil my record. I have a reputation around this hospital and I don't mean to let anyone . . . especially not you . . . do anything or *not* do anything to ruin it. So from now on, as they say, no more Mr. Nice Guy."

Bud Young strained as far as he could turn to catch a glimpse of Marcy's face. Especially her brown eyes. To see how serious she was.

She caught him at it and pretended to be angry. Though she was gratified to see that he was making conscious efforts to coordinate his thought processes with his actions.

"Don't you go spying on me," she warned. "I've got no secrets. I will tell you right now what I have in mind for you today. Today, you will start eating on your own.

"Yes, eating. I think you've been too lazy too long. Letting me, or your mom, or the nurse cut up and feed you your food. No more. Just you wait till we are done with our routine. Just you wait, young man."

She moved the weights from his arms to his legs and forced him to lift them. His effort was great, but the results were meager, indicating that he had indeed fallen behind in his development. And it was so essential that he have strong legs if ever he wanted to walk again. Though strong legs alone would not accomplish that particular task.

While he worked on his legs, she put him through his mouth exercises, to correct his enunciation, which was not yet acceptable. At the same time she was stimulating all the muscles required to chew and swallow, so that those responses would become more automatic when his concentration was required to cut his food and feed himself.

"And now, Bud Young, we are going to give you a little test. No more are you going to get away with simply pointing to a car when I say 'car.' Oh, no. Today we start putting two and two together and getting some fours. For instance . . ."

She presented a tray with familiar household items on it and asked, "Bud Young, how do you light a fire?"

He seemed puzzled, searched her eyes for some hint. But her eyes were as demanding as her voice had been.

"How do you light a fire?" she repeated slowly.

He struggled with the concept, mouthed the words, "Light . . . fire . . ." His eyes and his face slowly turned from perplexed to aware and understanding.

He pointed to the match on the tray.

"Hey, terrific! Let's try again. Write a letter, Bud. Write . . . a . . . letter."

He pondered a moment. This time he seemed to make the connection an instant faster. He pointed to the pen.

"Send a letter, seal, mail," Marcy suggested.

He thought, made the connection, half reached for the envelope.

"Wonderful. Let's keep going. To help me see and read. See . . . and . . . read, Bud," she coaxed.

He pointed to a pair of spectacles that were on the tray.

"See what time it is . . ." Marcy said. When he did not respond, she added, "Tell time, keep time, how much time to the end of the game?"

He smiled, he understood. He reached toward the watch.

She considered taking him a step further, was about to abandon the idea but decided that with time to make up, she should press on despite the risk of failure at this stage.

"Bud, what time is it?"

He appeared puzzled.

"Time . . . what time is it? What . . . is . . . the . . . hour?"

He pondered, shook his head ever so slightly. The thought process was too complicated for him. But she was satisfied with this phase of his accomplishment for today.

"Now, Bud, I want you to repeat what I say. Word for word."

She began to read from the prescribed comprehensive examination for aphasics still suffering loss of the ability to speak or understand fully.

" 'The day was very warm,' " she read from the list.

"The day . . . was . . . ver . . . very . . . warm," he repeated slowly, separating each word as she had insisted he do.

" 'Traffic was very heavy,' " Marcy read.

"Tra . . . traffic . . . was . . . ver . . . very . . . heav . . . y," he repeated.

"Good! Let's go on. 'The boy was late for school.' "

"The boy was . . . late . . . for . . . school," Bud repeated.

From the look in his eyes she could see that he had grown impatient with such simple lines. She decided to skip down the list to something more complex.

" 'The distance between here and Chicago is five hundred miles,' " she read.

"The . . . dist . . ." He made a special effort to say, "Dis . . . tance . . . be . . . tween . . . here . . . and . . . Chi . . . Chi . . . Chica . . ."

He could not encompass the word. Too many syllables perhaps. Marcy blamed herself for trying to move him along too fast.

Or was she experiencing a guilt of her own for having stayed away?

The look in his eyes was not only failure but puzzlement at not being able to pronounce the word.

To prevent his dwelling on that failure she said, "Now let's get back to this business of eating by yourself. When we eat, what's the first thing we do? We come to the table and sit down. So today, we start on step one. Sitting. You are going to sit up. Let's go!"

He lay there, expecting she would raise the bed electrically as she did each time she wanted him to sit up.

This time, she rebuked, "Oh, no! We are not going to be lazy today. We are going to do a little work. We are going to sit up. I mean really sit up. Thomas Edison did not invent electricity so Bud Young could become a lazy lout. When I was a child I used to hear grown-ups use that word. I asked, but no one seemed to know the exact meaning. So when I went to school I went to the library. I took down a dictionary so heavy it almost knocked me over. I looked up 'lout.' And you know what it said? 'A mean awkward fellow, a bumpkin, a clown.' That's how I discovered that most people use words they don't even know the meaning of. Just like now—you are not a mean awkward fellow, or a bumpkin or a clown. Oh, no. You are just lazy.

Because we have all been too easy with you. Well, as the song
goes, those were the days, my friend. But if you thought they
would never end, you were wrong."

She sat on the bed alongside him.

"Put your arms around my neck. Go on!" she ordered.

Slowly he raised his arms. She leaned forward to make it possible for him to reach around her neck.

"Lock your hands," she coaxed.

He made the effort. But his finger coordination was still not
secure enough to form a firm clasp. Aware of that, she encouraged him nevertheless, "Good! Very good!"

She slid her arms under his armpits to get a firm hold on his
back. Together they managed to raise his body into a sitting
position. She held him there for several moments and then relaxed her hold slowly. But she felt him tighten his hold around
her neck. He moved his head slightly to press his cheek against
hers.

Psychiatrists call it transference. Marcy had her own name for
it—patient-affection-syndrome. When the patient, accepting
the therapist as his means of recovery and eventual reentry into
the world, becomes dependent and turns that dependence into
love.

A good sign. But not without consequences as well. Depend-
ing on how the therapist used that affection.

Still holding to her, he whispered, "Mer . . . cy . . ."

"Marcy," she corrected gently, since this was the first time he
had tried to speak her name. "Mercy is the name of this hospital.
My name is Marcy. But if you are expecting any mercy from me
from now on you will be sadly mistaken. Now, as long as you
are sitting up, let's edge over to the side of the bed."

Making him assume most of the burden, she coaxed him into
a position where his legs dangled over the side of the bed. Yet
he was close enough to the bed frame to reach it if he felt insecure.

"Now you just sit there a moment while I . . ." As she
spoke she wheeled the movable table around so that he was
sitting as at a dining table. "Now we just serve a little late
breakfast. . . ."

She produced a knife and fork from her bag. Bud stared at them with suspicion since they were different from the padded pen he had become accustomed to.

"Pick up the fork, Bud. Pick it up. You can do it. Just stretch your fingers a little. Remember all those exercises with the marbles, the buttons, and the coins that became smaller and smaller. You started with quarters and worked your way to nickles, then pennies, then dimes. Well, with a little effort you can do this. Go on, Bud. Go on!"

She considered that maybe she had overtaxed him, until he began to make an effort to slowly wrap his fingers around the handle of the fork. She felt herself straining with him and experienced great relief when he finally had a grip on it. He lifted it some inches off the table. Then he lost control. It fell to the table, then onto the floor.

Quickly, she retrieved it and placed it on the table once more, not giving him time to dwell too long on his failure.

"Let's try again, Bud. Come on now, we try again."

More tentatively he began the process once more. Reaching, slowly forming his fingers around the fork handle, and finally lifting it.

This time he held it. Though his hand trembled slightly, he continued to hold that fork.

"There we are," Marcy encouraged. "We'll have you eating on your own in no time."

He was sweating, as after a workout in the gym, but he had the satisfaction of having achieved a very important step in his recovery.

Then, without her coaxing, he reached for the knife. Slowly, but with conscious effort and control, he wrapped his fingers around it. With all the pressure he was able to exert, he clamped his fingers into a grip and lifted it. With great pride he held it out to Marcy, but as she reached to take it he could no longer sustain his grip, and it fell into her outstretched hand instead of being placed there.

"Do it again, Bud, do it again."

He repeated the procedure. This time he was able to hold it long enough to place it in her hand.

"There we are! You did it, Bud, did it all by yourself!"

His abilities, damaged as they were, far from perfect as they were, were coming into place.

His ultimate goal, walking—even the decision to try—was still beyond him, she knew. But in her profession the rule was one goal at a time, at times half a goal at a time, and sometimes, unfortunately, that ultimate goal was never achieved.

She must be content today with having accomplished two objectives. She and Bud were back on track again. He was trying, trying on his own, even in the face of failure.

In their afternoon session she would put him back on the tilt board and hold him at an almost vertical angle while at the same time making him practice his lettering. Soon, if things worked right, he should be able to start writing simple two- and three-letter words.

Yes, she decided, he could hate that tilt board, but as long as his blood pressure indicated he was able to take it, she would keep him up there.

Because without being able to endure that, he could never walk.

"Good morning, Bud Young!" Marcy greeted with unusual exuberance as she opened the door of 302.

By this time Bud Young had sufficient cognition to suspect that she had some new and special activity in mind for his exercises on this day.

"Damn . . ." he tried to say, then said it. "Damn . . . tilt . . . board."

"No, Bud, no more tilt board," she promised. "Today, after our usual routine, I have a special treat for you. Very special."

He took a moment to absorb that thought before his eyes revealed his resistance. His lips twitched a bit as they had become accustomed to doing before he would make a determined effort to speak.

"Yes, Bud?" she coaxed.

"Not . . . not . . . Ma . . . Mary . . . lyn . . ." he rejected.

Marcy never ceased to wonder at the manner in which thoughts came back to aphasics in the strangest way and at the strangest times.

What had brought Marylyn to his mind at this moment, she wondered. Until he said, "She . . . came . . . be . . . be . . . fore."

Good God, she realized, was he somehow, even in his then diminished state, aware that she had been here? Someday someone will figure out a method, or invent some marvelous electronic work of genius, to read the minds of aphasics.

"Yes, Bud . . . she was here. She wanted to see you, talk to you. But you wouldn't let her."

He shook his head grimly, indicating that neither would he allow it now. If ever.

"All right, Bud, how about a little arm exercise? And today we are going to add a little more weight. Just a pound more," she said as she strapped the canvas belt around his right forearm. "Now, raise it up. Up we go. There. Now stretch out. Good. And now, far as we can."

Thus she began the morning's routine. She had him do both arms, both legs. Then she produced a small red rubber handball. She made him grip it as tightly as he could as many times as he could. First in his right hand, then in his left.

All the while she watched the muscles in his arms and shoulders tense and ease, tense and ease, evaluating how they would respond under added physical stress. That was an important key to her next move.

She put him through his hand facilitation exercises, with a regular pen, a normal fork and knife. Today she had brought in a slice of soft melon with the rind already trimmed off. She placed it before him.

"Cut. Cut it into small pieces and eat it."

Bud devoted himself to the task with the diligence and purpose of a scientist working on a highly important experiment. He cut off a piece of melon. Stared at it. Considered it too large to ingest in a single bite. He cut it in half. This time he brought it to his open mouth, started to chew, then swallowed it without any difficulty. Encouraged, he proceeded to carefully slice and eat the rest of the piece.

"Very good, Bud! You deserve your adventure," Marcy said. "So, lie back. Rest a bit while I go out for a minute."

He lay back, breathing in a far easier manner than usual after so much activity. He felt a sense of accomplishment. He felt it not so much from what Marcy had said as from the look in her eyes. She had, he thought, the most friendly and wonderful eyes he had ever seen. And he had pleased her today. He was sure of that.

In the midst of his reverie, the door opened once more. Marcy entered carrying a flat board that seemed too large for her to manage.

It took him a moment to assemble his thoughts, but once he had, he said, "Damn . . . board . . . No!"

"Bud, this isn't a tilt board," she said as she slipped the edge of the board under his buttocks to secure it in place. "This is to get you accustomed to getting out of bed by yourself. And onto this . . ."

She was out the door, this time only for an instant. She returned with a wheelchair. At the sight of it, Bud stared. Then turned to challenge Marcy who was ready with the explanation.

"This is just to get you to the Rehab room. So let's get going. Edge your way over to this board. That's right. Move on your own. You can do it. Unless you decide to goof off or screw up in some way. Because I know you can do it and so do you. Now, move!"

"Mer . . . cy . . ." he mocked.

"Not mercy. Marcy, the one without mercy," she reprimanded. But secretly she was pleased. He was able to make a joke. Not very usual with patients in his condition who had lost their sense of humor even if they had been blessed with one before their trauma. "Move!" she ordered.

He glared at her.

"Bud Young, you move, or I will move you!" she threatened. "And if I do that, maybe I will put you back on that tilt board!"

He studied her eyes. They corroborated that she was quite serious.

Slowly he marshaled his strength. With the combined effort of his arms and legs he managed to move himself to the side of the bed. Marcy pushed the edge of the board farther under him so it held in place. Then she brought the wheelchair up to the board.

"Now, Bud, you are going to slide over onto the board. Go on. I won't let you fall. Come on now, slide slowly, slowly. Attaboy. There. You can rest on the board for a moment."

She allowed him time to catch his breath.

"And now we slide across the board and into this chair."

He studied the chair. He glanced at her, a hostile glance. Then he glared at the chair again.

Aware that at his age, with his athletic background, even the idea of a wheelchair was anathema, she assured, "Bud, it's just to get you into Rehab. I've got a big surprise for you there . . . Bud? Don't you believe me?"

He could not resist her plea, for she had never lied to him before. He started to slide himself across the board toward the wheelchair. With more assistance from her than he realized, he made the transfer from board to wheelchair.

Having done that, he sat back expecting that she would wheel him out the door as had happened those times he had made the journey on a wheeled stretcher. She did not move behind the chair to grip its handles. He half looked around at her.

"Bud, put your hands on those wheels. Get moving! Why do you think we've been exercising those arms, those hands? So you can begin to do for yourself. Your lazy days are over, young man. Get moving!"

For the first time in his entire life, sixteen-year-old Bud Young had to reach out to the guide wheels of a wheelchair, grip them, try to roll himself forward. He felt the rubber rims of the wheels. He was able to get his fingers around them, his left hand more easily than his right. But now he had a grip on both wheels. Using all his effort he moved them forward.

Marcy was quick enough and nimble enough to get to the door before he did. She opened it. He tried to go through but could not manage it. He collided with the doorjamb on his right side. He was not yet able to coordinate the actions of both hands and arms. Nor could he judge distances too well.

She eased the chair through the door, then guided it down the corridor to protect others who were walking through.

They arrived at the door of the Rehab room. Dr. Curtis had been watching through the glass insert in the door, evaluating the performance of a patient who was up for release to outpatient status.

At the approach of Bud's wheelchair, Curtis turned, "Bud! How good to see you up and out. Ready for the big adventure?"

The doctor had used the same elliptical expression as Marcy, but Bud was too confused to ask exactly what this mysterious adventure was.

The doctor held the door open while Marcy guided the chair through. Once inside the large room, in which a number of patients were exercising under the guidance of their therapists, Marcy headed the wheelchair in the direction of a set of parallel bars different from any Bud had seen and worked out on in gym class.

These were shiny stainless steel. Instead of being high, they were at about hip height for someone his size.

Bud noticed that standing to the side of the bars, waiting, were the same two assistants who had worked with Marcy to get him up on the tilt board and keep him there. Against his will most times.

He could not resist trying to turn and accuse Marcy. She wheeled him to the bars. There she locked the chair in place in a fixed position.

"Okay, Claire," she said.

The taller of the two assistants, a blond-haired young woman who seemed almost as tall as Bud himself, produced a canvas belt not unlike the ones attached to the tilt board.

When she slipped the belt around Bud and tried to fasten it he did not resist. Neither did he make her job any easier.

"Now," Marcy ordered.

Both assistants came behind the chair; each slipped a hand under one of Bud's arms ready to help him up, as Marcy urged, "Take hold of the arms of your chair, Bud. A good strong grip."

He felt awkward and incapable. He wished he did not need two women to help him.

"Get a good grip on those arms, Bud!" Marcy ordered.

He overcame his resistance, which was as much fear as resentment. He lowered his hands, gripped the arms as firmly as he could.

"Now raise yourself to your feet, then grip these parallel bars!"

With considerable assistance from both women, Bud raised himself until he was on his feet. Subtly Marcy gestured the women back. She wanted to see how long, if at all, Bud could maintain himself on his feet with his hands clutching the parallel bars.

It was an important clue to both his stability and his equilibrium, vital to his being able to ever walk.

To Bud it seemed a long time. But it was only a fraction of a second before he felt weak and dizzy. He feared he would collapse, but both assistants seized the protective belt to save him from falling to the matted floor.

He was in their grasp and breathing hard. He could feel the perspiration oozing down his chest and his cheeks. Weak as he had been, he had no inkling that he could not sustain himself on his feet, especially with the aid of the bars.

He sat in his wheelchair trying to catch his breath as he slowly regained his control.

"Bud?" Marcy asked.

He stared down at his hands. He clenched them, opened them, clenched them, opened them. As if he could develop in them the strength they did not have only moments ago.

"Bud?"

He stared past the bars, past everything and all the other patients within his sight. He was fighting a battle within himself. When he spoke, it was a single word.

"Again," he said.

"You've had enough for one day," Marcy tried to dissuade.

"Again," he repeated.

He gripped the arms of his chair and tried to lift himself. Marcy signaled her assistants to help him. Together they raised him up so he could grip the bars once more. This time they hovered even closer than before to seize that belt if it became necessary.

He closed his hands around the bars. He exerted all the strength he had developed in his arms. But almost at once he became dizzy again and lost his grip. They caught him just in time and settled him back in his wheelchair.

Once he was returned to Room 302 he lay in bed staring up at the ceiling, deliberately ignoring Marcy. For he felt that she had betrayed him, promising him a great adventure which turned into utter failure.

"Ad . . . ven . . ." he was trying to say.

"Say it, Bud. You can. Adventure."

He enunciated it a syllable at a time. "Ad . . . ven . . . ture." Then he added, "Crap!"

"No, Bud, not crap at all. It *was* an adventure. Your first time on your feet. Your first time in more than four months. You shouldn't have expected to do it all at once. I know you felt dizzy. You felt weak. Everyone does. You have to regain your sense of balance, of equilibrium. Then the dizziness will disappear. You have to strengthen all your muscles and joints, ankles, knees, hips. They have to work together to bear your weight. All that has to happen if you want to walk again. Bud, this is the only way we know. The only way."

She could not tell from his attitude or his eyes how he had reacted to her explanation. But she knew that tomorrow they would try again. And keep trying. And trying.

She slipped out quietly to leave him alone with his agitated and confused thoughts.

In minutes, tears formed in his eyes and began to trace down his cheeks.

28

Bud Young lay in bed, his hand gripping his football, then relaxing; gripping, then relaxing. He could feel the strain in his fingers and also up his arm to his elbow. But the greater the pain, the more he persevered.

Meantime, his disordered mind imagined all sorts of possibilities. That afternoon stint on the parallels, discouraging as it had seemed at the time, was really the promise of great things to come. Though his reasoning was still faulty and incomplete, he had conjured up a series of events that eventually led to walking.

Then running. He could remember, vaguely, running across grass on sunny afternoons. As he concentrated on that image, that feeling of swift flight, he had a slight but imperfect memory of being pursued. What he was trying to remember were events from his football days. But it did not fit together as well as he would have liked. He abandoned the vague parts and concentrated only on running. Running.

The football—he knew what that was for. Marcy had said so. Exercise. Use those fingers. Strengthen those hand and arm muscles. And one day . . . one day he would be able to pick it up and throw it.

He had grown tired from all his activity as well as from the emotional stress involved in those parallel bars. Mom had been here, even watched him feed himself lunch. Slow as he was, he refused her help. After school Gwen had come by.

She mentioned something about Marylyn, who had asked about him again. But he did not feel ready to see her. Or any of his classmates.

"Not even the band?" Gwen asked.

"Not . . . the . . . band. No," he said, as firmly as he could say anything in his present condition. "Don' want them . . . to . . . see me . . . like this," he was able to say.

"They already did . . ." Gwen started to say.

"They . . . saw . . . me . . . no," he protested.

"When you were in coma. They came here, they played. Very loud," Gwen said.

"They . . . and . . . and I didn' hear them?"

"You were in coma. That's why they were here. Familiar loud sounds to try to get you out of it," Gwen said.

"They . . . saw . . . me . . . they . . . saw . . ."

"Gee, Bud . . . I'm sorry. I thought you knew," Gwen apologized.

"S'okay . . . okay . . ." he said, before confessing, "I . . . don . . . wan' . . . any . . . anybody . . . to . . . see . . ."

When he began to grope for the word and could not find it, Gwen recalled Marcy's warnings about overtaxing him.

"I better go, Bud. I got piles of homework. Ever since the school dropped out of first place in scholastic standings, they've been working us to death. So got to get going."

She kissed him. While they were close she whispered, "Everybody . . . everyone at school is rooting for you, Bud. And everyone at home. Gramma calls. Sometimes twice a day. The whole family. They all want to come. But Mom says no. Not yet."

"Yeah. Not . . . not . . . yet . . ." he managed.

Evening.

He had his hand on that football, was drifting off when there was a very light, guarded knock on the door. He turned his head in that direction. The door eased open, admitting the brighter light from the corridor.

He heard his dad ask softly, "Son . . . you still awake?"

"Yeah," he replied.

With that, Pepper Young started into the room with great energy and excitement.

"Mom told me! It's true, isn't it? True? Bud?"

"True . . . what . . . ?

"On your feet. You were standing up. On your feet today. You were, weren't you? Bud?" He was pleading for confirmation.

"Yeah . . . on . . . my . . . feet," Bud conceded with not nearly as much pride of accomplishment as his dad had expected.

"Okay, then, tell me. What was it like? How'd it feel to be able to get up and around finally?"

"Dad . . . I . . . I . . . didn' . . . get . . . around . . ." Bud began to stammer.

"What do you mean, you didn't get around?" Pepper asked. Then immediately realized, "Of course, I didn't mean you ran the hundred-yard dash or anything. I mean, you were up on your feet, weren't you?"

"Yeah," Bud admitted.

"Well, that's terrific. That's progress. Big progress. You know what they say, the Chinese . . . or somebody, they always say the longest journey begins with a single step. So today you made your first step." Pep tried to be as enthusiastic as he could, considering that he had taken Lily's modest report and enlarged it into his own desperate fantasy.

"Dad . . . I . . . didn' . . . take a . . . a . . . single . . . step. . . ." Bud felt forced to admit.

"But you were on your feet, weren't you?"

"Yeah."

"Okay. That's great. That's what I meant when I said a single step. I was using . . . it was . . . what do they call it? A simile . . . no, no, a metaphor. You know, when you say 'the first step is' . . . when you don't mean step at all. . . . What you mean is the beginning. The first . . . the first . . ." Then out of sheer embarrassment he smiled and said, "The first step. But not this kind of step . . ." And he took a step toward the bed. "You mean the beginning. Today you got up on your feet and you made a beginning. Which is pretty damn terrific, son. Pretty damn terrific."

They continued to talk, mainly chatter by Pep because Bud was growing more tired. He closed his eyes.

Pep interrupted the story he was telling about some inconsequential event at the office.

"Bud . . . you still awake?" he asked softly.

Bud heard, but since his father appeared to be under great strain merely to carry on a boring conversation, he did not respond, thereby releasing him.

Pepper Young opened the door to 302 with extreme caution so as not to wake his son. He held the handle until the door closed without making a sound.

Bud lay in the dimly lit room, eyes closed, trying to find answers to many questions that had begun to puzzle him in recent days—now that his thoughts came to him in somewhat more orderly fashion and he had become more aware of other people and their reactions.

Why . . . why does Dad . . . why does he have trouble talking . . . trouble talking . . . to me? . . . He never had trouble talking. I can't remember some things Mom talks about . . . like what I did yesterday or two days ago . . . but I . . . I remember kid things . . . going to Gramma's lake house . . . when I was so small they wouldn't let me go out to the end of the dock alone . . . and Grampa was still alive . . . I remember that . . . and I remember everyone always used to say . . . Pep Young, he can talk a blue . . . what did they say? . . . talk a blue . . . blue something . . . and the time Mr. Beecham came to dinner at the house . . . I couldn'a been more than eight or nine and he said to me, "Son, just you watch your dad. Listen to him. Learn to talk like he talks and you'll make a great salesman one day." Like being a great salesman was the most wonderful thing in the world. But now when he comes here Dad can't seem to talk at all.

I mean, he talks, but he doesn't say anything. What's he so nervous about? Is it he doesn't have confidence in me, in my getting better? Is that what's making him so . . . so . . . uptight? I'll get better. I know

I'll get better. It'll take time. Marcy always says we make progress one day at a time. Well, we are . . . we are . . . today was just one of those days . . . days when we take the first step. Tomorrow I'll ask her about not just standing at the parallels but actually taking a step.

And why can I think so much better than I can say what I mean? It's confusing . . . it's all so confusing. . . .

Now I remember what that blue thing was. They always said Dad could talk a blue streak. Streak, that's what it was.

Pepper Young pulled slowly out of the parking lot at Mercy Hospital. He reached the exit gate and turned left, heading for the church and his A.A. meeting. He had come to accept that church basement as a refuge. Though he had resisted the idea at the outset, and had even asked Larry Burke, his attorney, to find some way around Judge Bruce's sentence, he had found peace there. The assurance that when troubled he could avoid that need for a drink by merely being in the company of men and women with whom he shared a common bond.

He had advanced sufficiently so that Hector had asked him if he felt ready to assist others in their time of weakness. Though he felt stronger now than many weeks ago, he did not yet feel able to take on that burden.

In fact, on such a night as this he felt himself in need of support. His session with Bud had unsettled him completely. As he drove toward the church, feeling the need to get there quickly, he kept reviewing in his mind the events of this day.

Exactly what did Lily say to me when she called? She said, I swear I heard her say, and she was excited when she said it, "He did it. Today. Today he did it. Was on his feet." And I asked, "Hon, did you say on his feet?" I know I asked her that . . . at least I think I asked her that. And then she said, "Marcy said he's taken his first step on the road to becoming independent."

Ah, I can see now where the idea of his taking steps came from. She was really using it as a metaphor. First step on the road to being independent is not exactly the same as taking his first step. No, not the same at all. I have to remember not to expect too much too soon. No pressure. I must remember not to put too much pressure on Bud.

Or, he realized, *on myself either. When I expect too much and I'm disappointed, that damn itch comes back. That thirst. That need for a drink. It's what they used to call back in Psych One a conditioned reflex. Pepper Young gets frustrated, Pepper Young needs that drink. Does it ever stop? Do I have to be on guard for the rest of my life?*

Is that why the rule is, one day at a time? Stay dry one day at a time?

Thank God for Hector, and all those other people. It's as if in pooling our troubles we find solutions.

Especially for me tonight, he thought as he pulled up across the street from the church.

The next morning after Marcy had put Bud through his basic exercises—hand coordination, speech, word and sentence structure—she introduced a new aspect of his treatment. What at first appeared to him to be another form of neuromuscular facilitation was actually the beginning of preparation for eventually returning him to homelife.

She had had Lily bring in a shirt. A plain everyday shirt of the type that Bud would wear to school or to go shopping at the mall.

This day Marcy introduced that shirt. She presented it to Bud in its neatly ironed and folded form.

"Bud, today we start to learn all about buttons. Not picking them up and putting them into a cup. But how to handle buttons when they are attached to a shirt. Now you take this . . . go on . . . take it . . . and open it up."

He took the shirt. Had trouble trying to unfold it. But once he stopped, thought about it long enough to remember how he used to unfold shirts his mother left folded in his closet drawer, he unfolded it at the middle, opened out the sleeves, and turned it faceup.

"Now, Bud, unbutton it," Marcy said.

He stared at her, then at the shirt.

"Go on, Bud. You handle buttons very well when they're loose. These are the same size, the same kind. Just start slowly."

He studied the shirt. But made no move.

"Bud . . ." Marcy coaxed.

"Steps . . ." he said.

"Steps?" Marcy was confused.

"I . . . want . . . to . . . take . . . steps," he said.

She realized finally what he meant. Had he come up with this idea on his own? If so, it might be a good sign. If not, who had put the thought in his mind so prematurely? He was days away from taking his first steps. And with no positive outcome at that.

"All right, Bud. First we'll do the shirt buttons. Then we'll go back to Rehab and try some steps," she agreed.

With that promise he started on the shirt, taking on the top button first. He started too quickly, realized that error, stopped, rethought the process, then very slowly, very carefully he undid the first button.

"Terrific, Bud. Now the next one."

So he went from button to button, carefully and with great concentration undoing each.

"Now we are going to put this on and button it up."

She held the shirt open for him and subtly helped him slip his arms into it.

"Pull it around you. Take both sides and draw them together. That's it. That's fine. Now, start to button it."

He looked down at the open shirt which seemed to present an imponderable challenge.

"Top . . . or . . . or bottom?" he asked, more to put off having to do it than asking instruction.

"How do you always do it, Bud? Top or bottom?"

He thought a while and then admitted, "I don't remember."

"Then let's start at the top," Marcy suggested.

He stared down at the top button, then at her. When she smiled he started on the button first below the collar. Buttoning proved far more difficult than unbuttoning. But he managed three buttons before he tired so obviously that Marcy said, "That's great for a first time. Super. Bud Young, you are turning out to be my best patient."

Instead of smiling, he replied, "Steps . . ."

"Yes, yes, of course, steps," Marcy agreed, controlling her impulse to forbid it since he was far from ready to take any steps. But she would let nature handle that once they got to Rehab.

She held the door open at Rehab to see if he could wheel himself in. But he was still lacking visual perception and judgment sufficient to allow him to guide the wheelchair into Rehab without colliding with the doorjamb.

She helped him through. He discovered that at the parallel bars awaiting his arrival stood the same two assistants who had aided him yesterday. They carried that same wide belt. When they moved to strap it around him he said, "No."

The assistants looked to Marcy, whose eyes insisted, put that belt on him. For she knew what he intended and what the outcome would be.

Against his protest, they strapped the belt around him. They helped him up. He reached out, took as firm a grasp on the bars as he could. Using the strength of his upper body he maintained himself on leg muscles that were too weak, too disorganized to sustain him. He refused to accept that. He made an effort to move his legs.

The assistants were about to forbid it, when Marcy said, "No. Let him."

He struggled, refusing to believe that his legs would not respond to his demand. He persisted, trying desperately to make them obey, but they were still too weak. In his struggle he ignored his hands, thus loosening his grip. He started to fall forward. Both assistants moved more quickly. They caught the belt in time to keep him from falling to the mat, which was there for just such emergencies.

Once they had assisted him back into the wheelchair, Marcy knelt beside him.

"Bud, you are not ready for steps. You have to stand there, holding the bars, getting used to being erect, being on your feet. After a few days of that you will be ready to try taking steps. Now, let's start again. And this time just hold on. Get the feel of it. Get comfortable with it. And that will be enough for the day."

Though he hated the idea, he could only agree, for he had learned the limits of his abilities as of this day.

Closely guarded by two attendants and carefully observed by Marcy Ethridge, Bud Young was ready to try to lift himself from his wheelchair to the parallel bars. He pressed down on the arms of his chair and with subtle assistance raised himself high enough to grasp the parallel bars at his hips. He was standing. He held that position until he felt secure.

Once Marcy was sure of that, she said, "Now, Bud, slide your right leg forward as if you were going to take a step."

He hesitated, summoning up the nerves and muscles involved in the process required to take his first step in more than four months. He started to slide his right foot forward but it crumpled beneath him.

"I can do . . . I can . . . my left leg . . ."

Marcy was prepared for that. Patients always resorted to the strongest of their limbs when it was the other, the damaged one, that needed to be tested.

"No, Bud, your *right* leg," she corrected. "Let's move that right one."

He made another effort with his right leg. Again it gave way under his weight. He looked to Marcy, half in anger, half in a plea.

"The left . . . I can . . . do . . . the . . . left," he said, laying out each word to indicate his insistence.

"No. The right. Let's try it," she ordered.

Though he resented her, he made a halfhearted effort, as if intending to fail just to prove his point. But despite himself, that right leg did slide forward—slowly, haltingly, but it did move.

"Now . . . now the left, follow with the left," Marcy urged.

Bud complied. The left moved somewhat more easily, though not nearly as smoothly as he had expected.

"Right one!" Marcy ordered.

Again Bud barely dragged his right leg forward.

"Left!" Marcy called out.

Bud complied.

Thus it went, slowly, agonizingly. Marcy ordering the sequence, Bud trying to comply. Step by step he made his way from one end of the parallel bars to the other. It took minutes and enormous effort. When he was done he was in a sweat, exhausted. He was frustrated as well. He had undergone hours of football regime with less effort, less exhaustion. His disoriented mind found it difficult to accept.

Finally the effort to maintain his grip on the bars proved too great. But both attendants, expecting that, were right there ready to grasp his belt and sustain him.

Marcy wheeled up the chair. They settled him into it. He sat there, breathing in quick shallow gasps. But he was enjoying a sense of accomplishment. He had succeeded today at what he had failed before.

But Marcy Ethridge had other and more serious concerns. For in her eyes, far from succeeding, he had only confirmed one of her worst fears. True, his legs were too weak, but he also betrayed a tendency, not unusual in cases of this kind, for his head to turn up. Which would present more problems later. For the body followed the head and if he could not control his head, his sense of balance, so necessary to walking, would be off, dangerously so.

Suddenly in place of his look of achievement a frown clouded his handsome young face.

"I . . . I . . . once . . . ran . . . ran . . ." he said, "ran . . . hundred yards in . . . in . . ." He was even more frustrated at not being able to remember what his time had been. Weakly he ended up, "Ran . . . hundred . . . yards . . ."

With a slight shake of her head, Marcy dismissed both attendants. She knelt at Bud's side.

"Bud . . . Bud . . . you mustn't take this so hard. We are just beginning. We have a long way to go. A long way. Day by day we're going to work at it. Day by day you're going to improve. Each day doing a little more than the day before."

"How . . . long . . . ?" he asked.

"How long what?"

"Before . . . I . . . run . . . again?"

Since there was no honest answer to that question, and since it would be devastating at this stage of his recovery to tell him it was possible he might never run again, Marcy said, "We don't know. We just go from day to day. Doing the best we can each day."

She had no way of knowing how his troubled mind interpreted or accepted what she had said. But it was the only answer she could give him that, should later developments prove disappointing, would not undermine his trust in her.

"How . . . long?" he asked once more.

"I told you, Bud," Marcy replied.

"I . . . I . . . mean . . . how long . . . to go from one end . . . to the . . . other?"

"Bud, it doesn't matter how long. The important thing is, you did it."

"How . . . long . . . got . . . to see . . ."

He gripped the wheels of the chair and started to roll himself back to the start of the parallel bars. Marcy realized that he would not be satisfied until he was timed in accomplishing that stint once more.

She mobilized her assistants with a brisk signal. They assumed their positions. Bud wheeled himself into place at the head of the bars. He gestured for help. They aided him to his feet. He gripped the bars, steadied himself, then appeared to gather his full strength for the challenge.

He started to slide his left leg, then remembered Marcy's instructions. Unsteadily, slowly, he advanced his reluctant but braced right leg first. He followed with his left leg, then the agonizing right once more. Then the left, then with greater effort the right once more and then the left.

All the while Marcy timed him with her stopwatch as he proceeded leg by leg, slowly, very slowly. Hands ahead of his legs, he dragged right leg . . . left leg . . . right leg . . . left leg . . . The more determined he appeared, the more labored his progress.

When he reached the end of the long metal bars he was bathed in sweat. He held on, trying to catch his breath and at the same time ask, "How long?"

Because it would be a good comprehension exercise for him, instead of telling him how much time had elapsed, Marcy showed him the watch. It had stopped at two minutes twenty-six seconds.

"Ten . . . point . . . seventeen . . ." he said.

Now it was her turn to be puzzled. Had he misread the time? By now his visual perception and his ability to tell time by looking at a clock had fairly well returned.

"Ten point seventeen?" Marcy questioned. "Ten point seventeen, Bud?"

"I . . . once . . . ran . . . a hundred . . . in . . . ten . . . point . . . seventeen seconds," he said.

Oh, God, Marcy thought, *I hope he has no such ambitions now. I would consider it a triumph if he could just walk on his own two legs. And he wants to run again. A hundred-yard dash in ten-plus seconds. He'll never know how relieved and delighted I was that he could go twelve feet in two minutes twenty-six seconds.*

His stability is still very much in doubt. And we haven't yet had a good chance to test his equilibrium. Running? Walking would be a triumph if even that is possible.

Each day for the rest of the week, after his other exercises had been completed, Bud Young was assisted into a wheelchair and ordered to roll himself into Rehab. There he was helped to the parallel bars. Each day he insisted on dragging himself the length of the bars, holding on with both hands, slowly moving one leg at a time.

Each day he insisted on Marcy timing him. Each time she did, he insisted on trying again to see if he could reduce the time.

By the end of the week he had reduced his time for going the twelve feet to two minutes nine seconds.

He felt a sense of achievement. But Marcy experienced a growing concern. For no matter how he managed on the parallel bars, the really important tests still lay ahead.

Lily Young was delighted with Bud's new attitude. She began to share in it. It was reflected in the way she spoke to relatives and friends who called almost daily for reports on Bud's progress. It was reflected, too, in the way she confided to Marcy, telling her of the plans she and Pep were making for this summer. At the rate Bud was progressing, they should be able to spend a whole month at the family's lake house. Swimming would be great exercise for Bud's legs and arms. By the end of summer he should be his old self again.

"And Pep thought, this year, he would take a whole week off at the end of Gwen's school. So he is planning on our going to visit his sister. She has this place in Colorado. Up in the mountains. Terrific country. Bud always loved it there. And they have horses. He'll be able to ride by then. Won't he? At the rate he's going now?"

"It's too early to be making plans," Marcy said. "Any plans. We have to see how he does day by day and week by week."

By the end of his second week on the parallel bars Bud Young had cut down on the time he took to reach from one end to the other by almost half a minute.

His upper body was improving almost daily, his arms growing stronger, the muscles in his shoulders resuming some of their former power.

Marcy knew he was ready for the next step in his recovery.

The following morning she worked with him on his writing skills, which served a double function. It helped to improve the control his right hand exercised over the pen. But it also stimulated his thought processes, enabling him to write two- and three-syllable words. He took great pride in his newly regained skill, causing him to add a flourish to some of his letters.

"Showing off today, are we?" she chided him with a smile. "One day soon you'll be writing a whole book."

"I . . . I can write . . . sentences," he said in his still halting style. Though it, too, was improving daily.

"Oh, can you?" she teased, to see if he had the confidence to try.

"Yes," he said.

He leaned forward on the table so that she could not see what he was doing. He worked laboriously until he was satisfied with his handiwork. Finally he turned the pad around for her to read.

Written in his imperfect script was the sentence: *I love Marcy.*

She stared at the words. She felt her face flush. She recovered sufficiently to comment, "What a nice thing to say, Bud. And I love you too."

To put things into perspective at once, she added, "You are my favorite patient." Briskly she directed the conversation into other channels, "Now, today, young man, no more parallel bars."

"But I have to break my record," he protested.

"You're way beyond that, Bud. You are going to try some real walking."

"Walking . . . without the . . . bars?"

It was obvious he did not feel quite ready for that.

"Without the bars," she affirmed. "But we have something new for you. A device we call a walker. It allows you to really get around. You won't be limited to the bars. You'll be able to go from one end of Rehab to the other. On your own. How about that?"

"Gee . . . that'll be . . . be . . . great," he agreed, though unsure.

"Then let's get into that wheelchair and go!" she said.

Since she had to assist him as he slid across his board into the waiting wheelchair, they were close. He pressed his face against her bosom and whispered, "I . . . I really . . . really . . . do . . . love . . . you."

It was not the first time she had heard such declarations from dependent patients. She knew it served a purpose in their recovery.

But she also knew that when the final outcome was not as favorable as they hoped, there could be a sense of betrayal that would damage, if not destroy, that trust.

"Bud, this is what we call a walker," Marcy Ethridge said as she displayed the three-sided wheeled framework of stainless steel. "It's a temporary device. We use it to get the patient up on his feet and . . . and doing what its name implies, walking."

Bud Young stared at the waist-high structure. He had seen an elderly stroke victim use one of them at the mall. Marcy could detect the resistance in his eyes.

Young patients, Marcy thought, *though they have the greatest potential for recovery, are also the most resistant to admitting they need the help of such devices. They refuse to accept that they are no longer the free, independent human beings they once were. Unfortunately, if they cannot bring themselves to endure these first indignities to their youthful sense of independence, they will likely never make any progress at all.*

Yet, the honesty she demanded of herself forced her to admit, *I can give this fine young man no guarantee that even if he follows my every instruction, cooperates in every way I suggest, he will ever walk on his own again.*

Nevertheless, she smiled as she encouraged, "Come on, Bud. Give it a try. Hands on your chair arms. Lift yourself! Then reach for this walker. Up and then reach!"

He hesitated, not only to summon up the muscular coordination necessary to perform that act but to overcome his inner resistance. The part of him that warned, *If you accept this now, are you going to be saddled with this damned thing for the rest of your life?*

"Bud!" Marcy insisted.

He stared at her, stared at the metal object that now seemed to taunt him. He looked to her again. Her warm brown eyes both challenged and encouraged him. He finally yielded.

He slowly lifted himself, then reached out both his hands, his left more aggressive than his right. His fingers slowly wrapped around the uppermost hollow steel rod of the walker. He tightened his grip as securely as he could.

"Good . . . good . . ." Marcy encouraged. "Now start to slide your leg forward." At the same time Marcy signaled her two assistants, who had deliberately lingered in the background until they were needed.

As Bud rested there, hands clutching the walker, Marcy encouraged, "Come on, Bud . . . make the effort . . . start forward . . . start."

With every intention of complying, Bud leaned forward, strained with all the ability his body possessed to move himself forward. But the effort proved too much. His hands lost their grip on the walker. He dropped back into his wheelchair, exhausted.

Refusing to accept defeat, even before Marcy could urge or encourage him, he protested, "I can do it . . . Just . . . just . . . give . . ." He still had difficulty speaking when his emotions came to the fore.

"Take it easy . . . think of what you want to say . . . then say it. Slowly," Marcy coached.

"I . . . want . . . to . . . say . . . just . . . give . . . me . . . time. I can . . . do . . . it," he insisted.

Where he had been reluctant before, he was determined now, Marcy observed. But not without mixed feelings. Determination was most useful when it succeeded. But it was also a severe emotional hazard when it failed.

Bud pushed down on the arms of his wheelchair with more

determination than before. Now he had what he considered a secure hold on the walker. Encouraged, he started to slide his leg forward. But he could not quite manage it.

Unable to fully succeed, unwilling to surrender and fall back into the chair, he hung there precariously. Marcy signaled for help. The assistants quickly came to Bud's side to aid him to complete his intended action.

He was on his feet. His hands gripping the steel frame as firmly as he was able. He was standing. Cold, sweaty, he was standing. Until he felt himself grow dizzy. His legs went wobbly under him. He began to waver. He could feel his hands grow damp, now loosen their grip. But he had not the power to reverse it.

Suddenly everything went black for him. He had no way of knowing that he had begun to fall. Or that only the intervention of Marcy and her assistants prevented his hitting the mat.

He was unconscious for only moments. When he came to he was aware first of Marcy's closeness through the fragrance of her pleasant light perfume. He opened his eyes to find himself looking up into her eyes.

"You blacked out, for only a moment. Dizziness," Marcy explained.

He looked down at where he lay. He was on a leather-covered exercise table large as a king-size bed. He had noticed it before but never knew its uses. He would learn them now.

"Now, Bud, you and I are going to do a little two-step," Marcy began. "Not the old-fashioned dance two-step, but a sort of double exercise. While we work I will explain why we are doing the things we do. Okay?"

"Yeah . . . sure . . . okay," he agreed, curious as to her intentions. Yet, in view of his most recent failure, apprehensive as well.

She could read it in his frank young eyes.

"Bud . . . all the physical exercises we do have a double purpose. We've always been accustomed to having our brains educate our bodies. What to do. How to do it. The brain controls the body. But in cases like yours, the body can help educate the brain."

"The body educates the brain?"

"Yes, by actually performing certain movements, your body educates or wakes up your brain to recapture old habits, old functions. So right now we are going to start that process. Now, first roll over. That's right. It won't be easy, but try. Roll off your back and onto your belly."

With every command she assisted him so that he could not resist.

"Now, up on your hands and knees. Come on, you can do it. Here we go—get that left hand forward. Now the right. Lean on them, go on," she both bullied and assisted.

"Your legs! Bring that left leg up to kneeling position. Come, now, Bud. No stalling. Move that leg! There . . . there we are," she said as she brought the leg forward and bent it into place. "And now, now for the right one. The right's a little more difficult, but do it anyhow. Come on now. Let's move that leg. Move it, I said!"

Sweating, panting, resenting, he was finally on all fours.

"Like . . ." he tried to talk but had to overcome the demands of his exertions first. "Like . . . like . . . wrest . . ."

When he could not complete the thought, and though she knew what he wanted to say, Marcy did not assist him but waited.

"Like . . . wrestling . . ." he said. "Greco-Roman style."

"Were you on the wrestling team, Bud?"

"No . . . just . . . liked it . . . sometimes."

"Okay now," Marcy resumed in her usual brisk style, "we are going to have a little workout. First, raise your left arm. Up and wide. Up . . . come on now, Bud . . . up. Good. Now swing it as far out to your side as you can. Way out, way way out . . ."

She knew it was beyond his power to swing it far out, but if he extended himself even a little it was an achievement. She followed with similar instructions for his right arm. Then she had him raise his left leg. And then his right.

Though her concentration appeared to Bud to be on forcing him to perform his exercises, actually Marcy Ethridge was much more concerned with observing the *manner* in which he carried out her instructions.

She was seeking to determine the degree of his stability. Stability in her profession meant his ability to control his muscles so that they functioned in coordination. For no single set of muscles performs even the simplest of functions without the automatic, unconscious cooperation of many other sets of muscles.

The mere act of rising from a sitting position to standing brought into play muscles in the trunk of the body, the arms, the legs, the back, all working in unison.

Soon she would have to make a crucial determination. Could Bud Young ever recapture that simple ability?

But first, work on strengthening the trunk of his body. It would take hours of exercise, days. And as always, with no guarantees.

By the tenth day of work on the exercise table, Marcy thought he had advanced far enough to test him. To attempt to have him progress to the next step. He was in his kneeling position on the table.

"Today, Bud, we are going to go from all fours to sitting up in a kneeling position."

He looked around at her, unsure once more.

"You can do it. Just exert some pressure on those arms. Push up from the table. Come on, now. Push! There we go. Now, get into sitting position. Your back straight as you can. Gradually draw your arms in. Go on. I won't let you fall. Even if you do, you can't hurt yourself on this table. It's padded. So don't be afraid. Arms straight, raise your body. Lean back. Sit up. Good. Good!"

She made him hold that position for a few moments.

"Now you can relax, Bud. Slowly, slowly down on all fours again. Good."

Once he was relaxed in the more familiar quadruped position, she said, "Now, that wasn't so bad, was it?"

"No," he granted.

"We'll do that every day from now on. And we'll also do this."

She moved closer to him. She placed her strong hand on his arm and ordered, "Press, Bud, press against my hand. Try to move my hand. Come on, resist me. Press against my hand with all your strength. Don't be afraid that you'll hurt me. Come on, give me all you've got. Push against me. Hard!"

He exerted himself to the fullness of his present diminished strength. She did not remark on her disappointment but proceeded to exert pressure on his other arm, and on both his legs, insisting each time that he resist and push back.

Several days of sitting up in kneeling position, of resistance applied to his arms, to his legs, and Marcy had him sitting up and reaching out with one arm, then both arms.

She was ready now to push against his body while he was sitting up. Always ordering him to push back, to resist with his entire body. She pushed him from one side and then the other. She pushed him forward, then back.

All with one purpose—to build stability in the core of his body.

Exerting pressure against his shoulders, she had him leaning forward as she coaxed, "Come on, Bud, you can push harder than that. I know you can. Push! Push!"

When he had reached the limit of his exertions for the day, Marcy paused for a moment to consider, *Do I test him now? Or is he too exhausted for a test so crucial it can determine not only his treatment but his future life as well?*

If he's going to make it, he should be ready to prove it now. But let's give him every chance. Tomorrow will be the day!

On the following morning, Marcy Ethridge appeared in Room 302, her attitude deliberately even brighter and more encouraging than usual. She wished to conceal from Bud Young the important nature of what would happen today. To know would only increase his state of tension. That would work against him at a time when he needed all his mental and physical resources.

"Okay, Bud, off we go into the wild blue yonder. Except that in our case that means the Rehab room."

"No writing today?" he asked. "I was . . . getting . . . ready . . . to write a . . . a"—he searched for some outlandish ambition—"a . . . a sonnet . . . yeah, a sonnet."

He laughed, a free, easy laugh.

She laughed along with him, but cautioned herself, *Let's hope there's still cause for laughter when this day is over.*

Once inside Rehab, by habit of recent weeks Bud wheeled himself toward the exercise table until Marcy said, "Not today, Bud. Back to the bars."

"The parallel . . . bars?"

"Yes, Bud, the parallel bars. All those days, all those exercises, were only preparation for going back on the bars. So let's go."

He wheeled himself toward the long shiny metal bars. He maneuvered his wheelchair into place so he could use the chair's arms for support to lift himself to the bars and assume walking position.

"About time . . . I got . . . out . . . of this . . . damn . . . chair," he said.

"Okay, then, Bud, take a good grip and let's go."

He extended his arms. The bars were slightly too high. Marcy pressed the controls to lower them several inches to slightly below his hip level, making them more supportive once he was on his feet.

"Now!"

He pressed down on the arms of his chair to lift himself so he could wrap his hands around the steel bars. He seemed to falter but Marcy lent him a hand. For that part of the test was not as important as what happened once he was on his feet.

He was standing, both hands on the bars.

"Now try walking, Bud . . . try . . ."

She stood back from the bars to observe, to make a professional appraisal of what would happen now.

Bud started to move his left leg, then remembering what had happened previously, he paused, slid his right leg forward. Encouraged that he was able to manage that more easily than in the past, he followed with his left leg. Whether concentrating on his legs made him neglect exerting sufficient pressure with his hands, or whether he could not control his head and it slowly rose from level position, he began to feel dizzy. Suddenly he lost control. He slumped forward with a cry of great fear.

But for Marcy's swift intervention he would have fallen forward on the mat. She seized him, urging, "Lean on me, Bud. Lean on me."

She assumed the full weight of his body, gradually, slowly, assisting him back into the wheelchair.

"What happened, Bud?"

"I . . . I don't . . . know," he stammered.

"What did you feel . . . what made you let go?" Marcy pressed.

"I . . . I guess . . . I got dizzy . . . again . . ." he confessed.

"Dizzy . . . yes, that can happen," Marcy said.

To give him the benefit of every doubt, to afford him every chance to overcome her professional reservations, she repeated the exercise on the parallel bars the next day. And the day after. Each time with two assistants close at hand. Both times they were forced to come to Bud's aid.

She considered giving him another opportunity to prove his development by testing him on the big ball. A ball large enough and strong enough to support the weight of a full-grown man. Being round and easily moved, it was a good test of a patient's balance. Though she doubted Bud's ability to succeed at it, in desperation she tried it.

"Sit on it, Bud. That's right. Sit on it. And keep your eyes fixed on that doorknob. Don't let your eyes wander, or your head lift. And while you're concentrating on that, I will try to push you off that ball. But you resist."

He lowered himself from his chair onto the ball. When he had grown accustomed to sitting on it, and had his eyes fixed on the target, Marcy pushed him from the side. Though he strained against her, he toppled off the ball and fell to the mat more quickly than she had expected.

She encouraged, "Come on, you can fight back better than that. Pretend I'm an opposing tackle on a pass rush and about to hit you. Fight back. Let's go!"

He tried . . . desperately. She knew that. But once more he slid off the big ball. She tested him again. And again. Each time he was pushed off the ball and fell to the mat.

Reluctantly, she had to conclude it had been a mistake to extend him this far or expect more from him.

This was the moment, Marcy knew. This was the time she had warned his father about. When it would be "third and long" and Bud had not been able to perform that miracle. Even if it was only demonstrating stability and equilibrium sufficient to maintain himself atop a big round ball against pressure.

The unfortunate results dictated her conclusion.

Marcy Ethridge stayed late on the evening of that third day. She knew her young son was waiting to be picked up at hospital day care. And waiting anxiously, as usual. Their time together, limited, was therefore more precious to both of them.

But on this evening Ezra would have to wait just a little longer as his mother pondered the phraseology she would write into the record of patient *Young, Willard, Jr.*

She had to admit that over the months they had worked together she had formed an affection for this patient. He was a fine young man. With good attitude. Though, like all brain-injured patients, he had his moments of sudden impatient anger and rebellion.

But in this decision she could not allow personal regard for the patient to interfere or influence her professional judgment. For, in the long run, to do so would cause him more harm than good.

Looking at his case in cold professional terms, she saw that after months of rehabilitation he had not achieved the two requisites for becoming ambulatory. Neither stability—control of his muscles, particularly his legs. Nor equilibrium—his balance and the ability to stand on his own. Any patient who still needed the support of other people, in this case of two assistants, could not qualify as functionally ambulatory.

Not functionally ambulatory.

Those three very scientific-sounding words meant, in the language that patients and their families understood, "This young man is not, and will not, be able to walk on his own again."

For a long time Marcy Ethridge had her pen poised over the space allotted for her prognosis before she could bring herself to write those words on the chart of Bud Young.

Then, in his own best interests, she proceeded to write them.

Not functionally ambulatory.

31

"Not functionally ambulatory," Dr. Phyllis Curtis read from the chart of patient *Young, Willard, Jr.* She stared beyond the file at Marcia Ethridge, who sat on the opposite side of the desk. "Marcy?"

"I hated to come to that conclusion," Marcy admitted. "But I had to assess the patient based on his total lifetime assets. He has recovered his cognitive skills to a good degree, which promises he will continue to do so. He was an intelligent young man before and I believe he will be so again. Therefore, I asked myself, what can we do with the best of his abilities in face of his disabilities?"

"You believe, then, that he would become adjusted to living the rest of his life in a wheelchair," Curtis concluded soberly.

"He can finish high school. Go on to college. Then to professional school if he determines to do that. He can marry, even have children. In other words, he can have a fairly full and satisfying life."

"All in a wheelchair," Curtis commented grimly. She felt forced to explain her nonprofessional interest in this particular case. "You know I've never reversed your decision in any case before. But this time . . . this young man, I would like to examine and test this patient myself."

"I expected you would. He will be available to you any morning," Marcy replied.

"Tomorrow. First thing."

Bud Young lay in bed, flexing his hands. First the left. Then the right. He applied twice as many flexes to his right since that was the one that was least stable.

But I'm gaining. Gaining. I've almost got it working as well as my left. One day, one day soon . . . soon . . .

He wrapped his right hand around that football and raised his arm almost to the point from which he used to fire those passes. Even the long, long Hail Mary pass that famous day.

I'll do it again, I'll do it again.

There was a soft knock on the door of 302. Expecting Marcy he called out, "Nobody here . . . except us . . . chickens."

Instead of the expected smiling face he had grown accustomed to, waited for, when the door opened, he saw Dr. Curtis peering in to make sure she wasn't intruding.

"Doctor . . ." Bud said, his puzzlement obvious.

"Marcy'll be by in a little while. I wanted to see you myself first."

"Yes, ma'am," he replied, still puzzled and somewhat alert at this change in the routine he had become accustomed to over the last months.

"I won't take you away from your exercises for very long, Bud. I'd just like to see you get out of bed and on your feet. Can you do that?"

"Yes, ma'am," Bud said.

Without taking his eyes off her, he pushed back his light blanket. Slowly he moved his legs toward the edge of the bed. He lowered his legs as Marcy had taught him, so that by the compensating movement his body pivoted into sitting position. But now his slow movements came to a halt. To Curtis he appeared to be organizing his thoughts before he was ready to make his next move.

"Need help?" she asked.

He appeared relieved that she had offered. Her hand under his arm, together they brought him to his feet. She stood back to study him.

Between the time she released her hold on him and the instant it took to stand back, he wavered. He tried to shake his head to clear away the dizziness. Then he pitched forward. Curtis moved even more swiftly to catch him.

She supported him back to the edge of the bed, where she assisted him to a sitting position. But even there he could not hold himself erect and fell back to lie gasping, his legs still hanging over the edge of the bed. Curtis lifted his legs so he could lie flat.

She could take him into Rehab, put him through the routines on the parallel bars, on the exercise bed. But that would only confirm what she had just witnessed. His stability had not progressed to the point where he could be ambulatory at any time in the future. His equilibrium was far from sufficient to give promise of improvement.

Reluctantly, she had to confirm Marcy Ethridge's conclusion. *Not functionally ambulatory.*

"How will we tell him?" Curtis asked.

"He's my patient. I'll tell him," Marcy replied.

"That would be best," Curtis agreed.

It was never a responsibility easily carried out. Especially when so young a patient was the subject. In her time, Curtis had done her share of such shattering interviews.

"Will you do it alone? Or do you want his parents present?" Curtis asked.

"Alone," Marcy decided.

When Marcy arrived at 302 later that morning, Bud greeted her with the football in his right hand, the hand back close to his ear as if ready to throw a pass.

"Don't stand . . . there . . . run . . . wide and . . . to the . . . the sidelines," he instructed, joking.

"Not today," Marcy said.

He brought his hand down, but still clutched the football.

"I know. Today more writing. Then . . . then . . . can . . . we go back . . . to Rehab? I think . . . I know . . . I can . . . I can do it . . . today."

"We won't be going to Rehab today, Bud. We're going to do some exercises right here. First, we're going to get you out of bed and into that wheelchair. Let's go," she said, while moving his sliding board from the wall where it leaned. She slipped it partway under his buttocks. She wheeled the chair into place parallel with the board. "Let's go, Bud, let's go."

He began to edge himself to the side of the bed and onto the board.

Instead of helping him, Marcy stood back, asking, "Bud, do you think you can make it the rest of the way yourself?"

"All the way into the . . . the chair?"

"All the way into the chair," Marcy replied.

He hesitated, marshaling the moves that would be involved in that simple yet complicated maneuver. Having prepared, he slowly worked his way across from the bed onto the board. Across the board to the edge. There he stopped. He had to consider his next move and how to make it. Once he thought he had the problem solved he edged toward the chair. At the crucial moment of transfer midway between board and chair he lost control and gasped in terror.

Marcy caught him to assist him into the chair.

He took a minute, a long minute, to regain his breath, then whispered, "Thanks."

"Bud," Marcy began to instruct in a methodical manner, "up to now I've been doing all the little things about this chair that needed doing. Like . . ."

She bent down on one knee, "Like these footrests. They're up when your chair is not in use. But I lower them into place so your feet have a place to rest. Well, that's something you must learn to do for yourself."

She proceeded to illustrate. "Like this. Left footrest down. Right footrest down. The arms. They are up now. But once you're in place, we put them down. Can you put them down, Bud?"

"Yeah . . . I . . . I think so . . ." he replied, curious.

He tried, did not succeed the first time. But after considerable effort he managed in a loose and awkward way.

"Very good," Marcy approved. "We'll practice each day. You'll get so used to it, it'll be easy. Now, as you know, this chair has brakes. So it won't move accidentally when you don't want it to. These are the brakes. You can reach them easily. Try it and see."

Bud felt for the brake with his left hand.

Always that tendency to use the good left hand first, never the right as he should, Marcy observed. *But he did lock the left-hand brake in place.*

He had trouble with the right brake. Finally he gave up from sheer exhaustion.

"Don't worry. A day or two at it and you'll learn," Marcy assured.

"Now, can . . . can we . . . go to Rehab?" he asked. "I can . . . can do . . . it . . . today."

Marcy sat down on the visitor's chair so that they were both at eye level, her soft brown eyes staring into his blue eyes. Hers as warm and sympathetic as she could be. His curious, yet tense, aware that something of importance was about to happen here.

"Starting today, Bud, we are going to do much of our training in this wheelchair. You're going to learn how to use the wheels on level surfaces. On carpeted surfaces. Over bumps and depressions. How to get through doors without my help. How to get around obstacles. How to get up and down curbs . . ."

"Curbs?" he asked, "Why curbs? Curbs are . . ." He pointed toward the window indicating the world outside, from which he had been shielded for many months now.

"Yes, the curbs are out there. Let me explain, Bud. When one has the kind of injury you've had, they can slowly recover their former abilities. As you have. But they don't always recover them perfectly, or recover all their abilities. Sometimes including the ability to walk."

On hearing the word *walk,* Bud's eyes turned away from hers, refusing to hear any more. But she persevered.

"You're an intelligent young man. You have a right to know the facts of your case. In order for a person to walk, any person, two things have to happen. That person has to develop stability—the control, coordination, and management of all the muscles necessary to stand erect and move his legs. And also equilibrium. The ability to maintain upright posture and avoid dizziness. To most people equilibrium is so simple, so natural, we never think of it. But it's a complicated process. It takes the cranial nerve, the inner ear, the eyes, and the part of your brain called the cerebellum all functioning together to achieve equilibrium."

Marcy took a slight pause before she said, "In your case that hasn't happened."

"Not . . . not yet . . ." Bud protested.

"Bud, we've tried. Tried for months now. It hasn't happened. Yesterday you couldn't stand erect. This morning you couldn't."

"So that's . . . that's why . . . Dr. Curtis . . ." Bud realized.

"Yes, Bud, that's why Dr. Curtis was here this morning."

He sat there staring, not at her but through her. He was deep in his own muddled thoughts.

Every day, every day, we went to Rehab. I was doing better. I know I was doing better. I felt better. Each time. Sure there . . . were times . . . when I . . . didn't feel so . . . when I . . . I was getting the hang of those . . . what do they call them? . . . oh, yeah, bars . . . like in school gym . . . para . . . para something . . . those bars . . . but . . . I was able to hold on . . . hold on. I did . . . did hold on . . . I did, his troubled mind protested.

The first flush of denial spent, he had to admit, *Sure, times I get a little dizzy . . . anyone could . . . get dizzy . . . so many months in bed . . . that's . . . nat . . . nat . . . natural . . . yeah, that's natural . . . to get dizzy . . . sometimes . . . even all the time . . . natural . . . almost fell, yeah, two times . . . three . . . this morning . . . but I . . . I . . .*

He fixed his eyes on Marcy, who had had enough experience with patients at such critical junctures to be fully aware and sympathetic with them.

"Take me . . . to Rehab. I . . . want . . . to . . . go to Rehab!" he said, more firmly than he had said anything since he had regained consciousness.

"Bud . . . it won't . . ." Marcy protested.

Without another word from her, he placed his hands on the rubber-tired wheels of the chair. He started to move himself along the bed, then toward the door.

Her first impulse was to block his way, but she decided, *No, let him go. Let him find out for himself.*

In his rebellion he was even less adept at steering the chair through the door. Twice he collided with the doorjamb. On his third try he barely made it through. He swung the chair to his left and started along the corridor.

Marcy followed close behind to prevent him from getting into serious harm. He headed for Rehab on an erratic course, causing nurses and other hospital personnel to jump out of his way.

The door to Rehab being on an automatic catch, Bud's chair collided with it, was forced to stop abruptly. Marcy intervened only enough to turn the knob and allow Bud to push the door open by propelling his chair forward.

He made for the parallel bars in an uneven manner. He drew up at the same end from which she always made him start. He glared at her to demand her close attention as he demonstrated that he was quite capable of standing on his own, walking on his own.

As he started to move, the chair slid back. He wheeled it up to the bars once more. He reached down, felt around until he located the brake on his left side. He set it. He started once more to lift himself out of the chair.

The muscles of his upper body, exercised during all the days of his coma and thereafter in Rehab, responded. Applying his hands to the arms of the chair, he struggled to lift himself. He was barely up when he slumped back down. He took a fresh breath. With new determination he tried once more. Once more he had to stop and wait. He realized he had ignored an important step.

He bent down, groped for the footrests. He found the left one and lifted it. He used his left hand to find the right step but had more difficulty raising that one. But he finally managed to accomplish that.

With the solid floor beneath his feet, he let his legs down one at a time. Now he struggled once more to try to lift himself.

With a single desperate effort he raised himself. Groping for the bars he attempted to gain his feet.

Marcy watched, silently urging him on, as his hands reached the bars, his left securing a firm hold on one bar. He held himself up by sheer determination until he could find the other bar with his right hand. While Marcy watched, straining with him.

Gripping both bars he was determined to demonstrate that he could walk, that he would walk. For just an instant Marcy was ready to believe that he could. Then he began to waver. Dizziness overcame him. Her original conclusion was, unfortunately, confirmed. A patient at this stage, with months of rehabilitation behind him, who could not walk would never be able to walk.

Bud Young could remember wavering, but not falling forward.

When he regained consciousness he was flat on his back, breathing hard, cold with sweat. Marcy was leaning over him.

"Bud . . . Bud . . . are you all right?" she asked.

"I . . . I was . . . was walking . . . and . . . something . . . something . . . what happened?"

"You lost your equilibrium, Bud," Marcy explained.

"No, I . . . it just . . . everything started to . . . started to go . . . go black . . . black," he protested.

Despite his protest, he finally accepted the facts of his condition by starting to weep. Silently, without gasping, he wept.

Marcy put her arms around him, lifted him into her lap. She leaned close so she could whisper to him.

"Bud . . . Bud, listen to me. Because we have a great deal of work to do."

"Walk . . . I'll walk?"

"No," she said at once. "From now on we concentrate on all the things you *can* do and make the best of them. You are young, bright, with great abilities that will grow as we work on them. And you will be able to get around. Go back to school . . ."

"Not in that chair," he insisted.

"Yes, in that chair. You will go back to school. Then to college."

"I was all set for a football scholarship. Four big universities. Two in the Big Ten," Bud protested.

"Bud, I saw your school grades. You can get an academic scholarship if you work hard," Marcy declared. "Then after college you can become anything you want. Except a quarterback in the NFL. We don't have any guarantee that you could have made it in the NFL. But we do know that you can be a good student. A good productive citizen. A success at any number of professions and jobs. We have to focus on that.

"Our goal is to make sure that you are the best Bud Young it is possible for you to be. Remember that. The best Bud Young you can be."

He did not refute her; neither did he share her determination. He only continued to weep, silently.

32

"Wheelchair . . ." Lily Young gasped in a whisper. "For how long?"

"The rest of his life," Marcia Ethridge replied as gently as one could speak those words.

"The rest of . . . no, no, that can't be . . . can't . . . not Bud," Lily protested.

Marcy expected the shocked mother would begin to cry. Instead Lily asked, "Bud? Have you told . . . does he know yet?"

"Yes."

"What did he say, what did he do?"

"Exactly what you would expect," Marcy said. "That's why I wanted to talk to you alone."

"Yes, of course. Pep . . . he wouldn't . . . wouldn't understand. Wouldn't be much help at such a time," Lily realized.

"It'll be up to us to help Bud through this adjustment."

Lily Young stifled her need to cry. That could wait until later. Until she was alone. "Tell me what to do, I'll do it," she said with great determination.

"First, I have to visit your home. See that it is prepared to receive a wheelchair occupant," Marcy informed.

"Yes . . . yes, of course," Lily agreed, her mind in turmoil. Trying to balance the needs of her son with the reaction she feared from her husband. "Anytime this afternoon. Before six. Pep'll be home by then."

"Mrs. Young, you can't protect him forever," Marcy warned.

"I know. But let me tell him in my own way," Lily pleaded.

"Yes, of course. I'll be at your house at four-thirty this afternoon," Marcy said.

Promptly at four-thirty, Marcia drove her car into the driveway of the Young home. On her way down that street she had already observed that the curbs on the corners, in conformity with federal regulations, were already graded to accommodate wheelchairs, baby carriages, and other such conveyances. That solved one of Bud's problems. It would permit him convenient mobility, freeing him from being confined to his own block, giving him not only greater independence but, just as crucial, a strong sense of self-reliance.

She rang the doorbell. Lily answered so quickly it betrayed both her state of anxiety and how carefully she had been counting the minutes until Marcy's arrival.

"Come in, come in," Lily said, so hastily that it seemed she felt this was a covert operation, to be kept secret from the neighbors as long as possible.

Lily led the way toward the living room, where she had set up coffee and cookies. But Marcy had no time for such amenities. Instead she stood in the foyer and looked around. Then she asked, "Is there a spare room on this floor?"

"Spare room?" Lily asked.

"We want to give Bud as much freedom as possible. He couldn't cope with these stairs to the second floor. So, if there's a spare room . . ."

"Aside from the kitchen and dining and living rooms, the only other one is the library. Which is really Pep's workroom. He does lots of work there at night and over weekends."

"Why couldn't he work in Bud's old room?" Marcy asked, starting to walk through the hall into the kitchen, making her own private assessment of conditions that would affect her patient, adding, "Unless, of course, you'd rather install one of those wallside elevators to haul him up and down each time."

"No, a room on this floor would be better," Lily realized.

Marcy looked around the kitchen. Refrigerator handles a good height for a wheelchair occupant. She opened the doors, looking in.

"I could arrange to have the things he likes closer at hand for him," Lily volunteered.

Marcy turned to her, "Lily, believe me, I appreciate the shock this is for you. But always remember we have to tread a fine line. Make things possible for Bud. Without babying him. *Make* him reach. *Make* him do as many things for himself as he can. The more he does, the better, physically and mentally. He is not an invalid. He is a young man who can't walk. He has to accept that. We have to accept that. We have to adjust to it. But always remember, he can do everything but walk."

"Would it help if we got him one of those powered wheel-chairs?"

"Definitely not! He needs the exercise. The upper-body strength he'll get from pushing that chair himself. Good for his body tone, good for his heart and his vascular system," Marcy explained.

She assessed the accessibility of the water taps at the kitchen sink. The reach for the stove controls. She would have to suggest a device to allow Bud to heat up things when he was alone and hungry.

"And now that den," she said.

As Lily led the way they passed one door that had not been explained.

"What's this?" Marcy asked.

"The guest powder room," Lily informed.

Marcy opened the door to find a small tiled and wallpa-pered room decorated in colors harmonious with the rest of the house. Under the mirror was a shelf with neatly laid-out hand towels. Marcy surveyed the room, then said, "You'll have to make a number of changes here. Handrails so Bud can han-dle the commode by himself. Nothing distresses wheelchair occupants more than lack of privacy. So, handrails around the commode. Then enlarge this room so he has his own tub and shower."

She opened the mirrored door to reveal an empty medicine cabinet.

"This'll have to be lowered, of course. Perhaps put it to the side of the sink," Marcy said.

"I had no idea . . . all the things . . ." Lily said.

"Another person is coming to live here. A different person from the young man who left. If this house is going to be his home, it has to be made functional for him."

"Of course," Lily agreed, already contemplating the moment when she would have to confront her husband with what their future lives would be like.

"You'll have to have a ramp built outside. A good architect can design it so that it's harmonious with your front steps. And another ramp from the garage into the house."

"Yes, yes, of course," Lily agreed. "It just seems so overwhelming."

"Lily, from my experience, after the first period of getting used to things, people do adjust. Families adjust. It's only at the beginning that it seems overwhelming. The important thing is to tell Mr. Young. As soon as possible."

"Yes. As soon as possible."

"I'd do it myself. But you know how he feels about me," Marcy explained.

If there was any solace for Lily in this grim situation it was that after she would have to tell Pep, he would be going to his regular A.A. meeting. The shock of this news, devastating as it would be, could be mollified somewhat by the considerable strength and support he derived from his faithful attendance at those meetings and his adherence to the principles and steps he absorbed there and practiced.

In preparation for her confrontation with Pep, Lily explained things first to Gwen, who was stunned and could only whisper, "For the rest of his life?"

"Yes, darling, for the rest of his life. We have to accept that. We have to do more than accept it. We have to help Bud accept that," Lily declared.

"We will, Mom, we will!" Gwen said, doing her best to appear steadfast. But she could not succeed. She broke down and started to cry.

In moments, mother and daughter were embracing and crying together. Finally Lily wiped her tears away with the palms of her hands. She brushed aside Gwen's tears and straightened her red hair.

"We don't want Dad seeing us looking like this. Not tonight of all nights," Lily said. "Maybe you'd rather have dinner early so you don't have to be here when I tell him?"

"Mom, we're a family, we're all in this together. I better be here."

"Good, darling. I'll need all the support I can get."

Determined to handle the matter with the least upset to Pepper, who had been highly tense these days, Lily decided not to mention Bud's condition as soon as Pepper arrived. First, she had resolved, a relaxed, uneventful dinner. Then before he went off to his A.A. meeting she would broach the subject as calmly as possible. Sometimes the manner in which bad news is presented can determine the spirit in which it is received.

Through dinner she asked Pep about his day and how it had gone. Wasn't this one of the afternoons he was supposed to give a class at Martin Luther King High School? He liked to talk about that because he felt he was having a good effect on those young students there.

But her resolve to control the situation was suddenly undermined when in the middle of her queries, Pepper asked, "Lil . . . Bud. You haven't said a word about Bud. How'd it go today? Is he up on his feet? Is he walking yet?"

Gwen stared down at her plate, yet she could not control her eyes which instinctively glanced to her mother.

Lily took a moment to regain her poise before she said, "Bud's fine. But there *is* something we have to discuss . . ." she started to say.

"Then by all means let's discuss it," he invited.

"Pep, it's not exactly dinner-table talk," Lily said. "The den might be a better place."

Puzzled by her strange approach, Pep agreed. "Okay. Fine. We'll talk in there."

He settled into his favorite club chair, the one in which he always watched football and baseball with Bud when he had a free Sunday afternoon.

"Okay, Hon. We are in the den. What's this mysterious thing we have to discuss?"

Lily began with considerable hesitation, "Pepper . . . I got some bad news today."

"Bad . . . what kind of bad news?" Then immediately arrived at his own conclusion. "Don't tell me. You had another checkup and Solomon found something. Well, don't worry. I'll see him first thing in the morning. I'll ask him for the best specialist there is and we'll . . ."

"Pep . . . Pep . . ." she tried to interrupt.

"Chicago . . . New York . . . Rochester . . . we'll find the best specialists in women's diseases . . ."

"Pep!" she interrupted firmly, so strongly that he stared at her. "Lily?"

"Pep, darling, this hasn't to do with me."

"No? Then who?"

Lily took an instant to draw a deep breath and maintain control of herself. Then she felt ready.

"Willard, today I was told that Bud will have to be in a wheelchair."

"I know. I've seen him in that damn thing often enough."

"Permanently," Lily informed.

"Perman . . ." His mind refused to accept the concept. "Not permanently . . . that's impossible."

"No, Pep. It's true. From now on this whole family has to adapt to the fact that Bud is going to come home in a wheelchair. Live here in a wheelchair. Go to school in a wheelchair."

"No! There must be a mistake. That young woman . . . I knew all along she was too easy on him. We've got to find him a new therapist. And he'll do okay. You'll see!" he insisted.

"Pep, please . . ."

Pepper Young was up out of his chair, pacing, talking. Unaware that it was his fears and his guilts coming to the fore.

"We shouldn't have let it go on this long. If Newman didn't want to remove that young woman we should have taken Bud out of that hospital!"

"Pep, listen to me!" Lily insisted.

He turned on her, "Lily, I've listened to you and everybody else long enough. Tomorrow I am putting that boy on the company plane and flying him to the best sports medicine specialists in New York. I should have done that months ago!"

"Pep, you don't understand . . ."

"Oh, don't I? Because I've been so busy all these months I've allowed you to take charge of Bud. And every time I've complained about his treatment you've said I don't understand. Well, we can see now what all your 'understanding' has done for my son. Yes, *my son!*"

"Pep, please. I talked with Dr. Solomon. He checked with Newman, with Dr. Curtis . . ."

"I don't care who you checked with. When it comes to my son *I* do all the checking. Lily, from now on I forbid you to go near that hospital!"

"He's my son, too, you can't forbid me!" Lily protested.

"*Was* your son. I am taking charge of that boy and his treatment. Wheelchair! I will take him to the best doctors, the best. And he will walk. He *will* walk!"

"Pep, please, listen to me . . ."

"I am through listening. Through being patient. And reasonable. Through trusting that woman. Trusting you. Because if you want the truth, if I have to choose between you and my son I will choose my son! You can have this house. You can have everything. Except my son!"

Without listening to another word from her Pep Young turned sharply and strode out.

Lily and Gwen sat in silence even after they heard the door to the garage slam shut. Gwen crossed the room to embrace her mother, as much to find comfort as to offer it.

"I've never seen him like this before. Never," Lily said softly.

"We'll go right on being a family, Mom. We will!"

"Of course, darling, we will," Lily agreed.

But she felt far less conviction than her daughter. For this was the first time in the eighteen years of her marriage that it had been so severely threatened.

By sheer habit Pepper Young pulled up at the church where his A.A. group met every night. He turned off the ignition. But instead of getting out and starting for the church doors he sat there staring at them.

After a shock like the one he had experienced less than an hour ago he knew what he needed. Not another session with his group. He felt too dry and thirsty for that. He needed a drink.

Just one, he promised himself. *Yes, after a shock like this a man needs—no, deserves—a drink. And I can handle it now. I've proved that. Of course, Hector would say I should go in there. Talk to him. Ask for his help. But what the hell does Hector have to do with this? This is my son. My problem. I am going to that hospital.*

One drink and I am going to that hospital.

Careful . . . careful . . . Pepper Young cautioned himself as he kept both hands tightly on the steering wheel.

He had had that one drink. And four more. Or was it five or six? No matter. He might be a touch under the weather but he knew the consequences if he was caught driving in that condition again.

He was not merely careful, he was overly careful. He stayed to the right, kept under thirty-five miles an hour all the way to the hospital.

He parked in one of the spaces reserved for DOCTORS ONLY, feeling that the gravity of his mission justified it. He entered the hospital. The woman in command of the front desk was about to challenge him until she recognized him.

Accustomed to the fact that his demanding business had permitted him late visitor's privileges over the past months, she greeted him, "Hi, Mr. Young. Go right on up."

Pep headed for the elevators, had to wait only briefly. He stepped into the car. It was occupied by two women and a man, each in a white lab coat, each with a plastic identifying name card pinned to the upper left-hand pocket. Two doctors and a lab technician. Pepper forced himself to stand erect and in as dignified a posture as he could manage.

He was relieved that the car went directly to the third floor so he could get out without incident. He started down the corridor. He was acknowledged by several of the night staff. He returned their greetings with what he thought was a warm smile.

At 302 he paused. He reached into his pocket for a mint, sucked on it long enough to believe that it had concealed any hint of liquor on his breath.

Bourbon was a mistake, he realized. *Vodka, I should have stayed with vodka. No telltale odor. This is the one time I don't want him to know I've been drinking. Got to be calm. Got to be . . . got to be . . . fatherly. Yes, fatherly. This is the time to be fatherly.*

So determined, he reached for the door, pushed it open slowly, peered in, in the direction of Bud's bed. The bed was empty. He felt betrayed. He had imagined the scene. Bud in bed. He himself pacing up and down, delivering one of the most convincing speeches he had ever given. Inspirational. Inspiring enough to make his son get out of that damn chair and walk!

But his son was not there. Pep went out to the nurses' station to discover that Bud was in Rehab. Pepper Young started down the corridor in that direction. When he reached it, he peered in through the small glass insert in the door to discover that the large room, with all its equipment, parallel bars, exercise tables, exercise machines, was unoccupied. He was about to turn away when into his limited view rolled Bud's wheelchair.

As Pepper watched he saw Bud execute sudden sharp turns. Forward and back he maneuvered that wheelchair, making stops and turns. He wheeled it about in tight circles. He speeded up, aiming directly at one of the exercise tables, only to stop just inches short of hitting it.

He's practicing to use that damn thing, Pepper realized. *He's not resisting it, not fighting it. He's trying to master it. He's accepting it. I can't let him do that. I won't!*

Pepper Young pushed open the door.

"Son!" he greeted.

"Dad . . ." Bud replied, not surprised to see his father at this odd hour but feeling compelled to explain. "Just practicing . . . I . . . I think I'm . . . getting better at it . . . won't ever like it, but I'll . . . I'll . . . do the best I can."

"The best you can . . . or the best *they* tell you you can?" Pepper demanded.

Puzzled, his mind not yet attuned to picking up all the nuances in other people's conversation, Bud asked, "Dad?"

"Come here, son." Pepper gestured him closer.

Bud wheeled up closer. Pepper bent down on one knee.

"Son, you know doctors aren't always right about everything. I can tell you about cases . . . well, like that one time . . . this was years ago. You were only a little shaver at the time. But I'll never forget it. Lucas Peterson. Assistant to old Beecham himself. He came by the house to drop off some papers. He took a liking to you. Played ball with you while we were discussing business. I didn't like the way he looked. And I mentioned it to him. He laughed. Said he'd been checked out in his annual physical by BCI's own doctors. Fit as a fiddle, they said. Four days later he was dead. Heart attack. So doctors don't know everything.

"Take your mother's aunt Sylvia . . . doctors gave up on her years ago. But that old lady is still alive and kicking. So as I said . . ."

"Dad . . . what are you . . . *not* . . . saying?" Bud asked.

Pep leaned closer to Bud so they were face to face, eye to eye. So close that Bud realized, *Drinking, he's been drinking. He's never come here before like that.*

Pepper Young placed his hands over Bud's hands, which rested on the arms of the wheelchair.

"Son, what I am saying is this. These doctors, your therapist . . . Marcy . . . they're wrong. You can walk. All you have to do is believe you can do it and you will. Look at you. You're young. You're strong. Here . . . grip my hand!"

Bud took his father's outstretched hand.

"Grip it! Hard! Harder! Hard as you can! Go on!!" Once Bud had complied to the limit of his capacity, Pepper said, "There, you see. You've got the strength. You can do it. What you have to do is forget all that nonsense they've been giving you."

"Dad, it isn't nonsense. It's . . ." Under pressure to respond to his father who, he suspected, was not in his most rational state of mind, Bud began to falter. "It's . . . Marcy says . . ."

"Forget her and everything she told you!" Pepper insisted.

"But I . . . Dad, it's a matter of . . . of . . ." He was stammering again. He hated that he could not speak up more strongly in Marcy's defense. He stopped, took a moment to regain control, then started again, this time with labored precision, "Dad, it is a matter of . . . of stability . . . and . . . equilibrium. . . ."

"Words, words, words!" Pepper disposed of them, "Christ, son, words are my business. I can twist them. I can use them to make them mean anything I want. I'm not talking words. I'm talking actions. I'm talking get up out of that chair and walk!"

"But, Dad . . . I tried . . . and I . . . I can't . . ."

"Yes, you can. All you have to do is want to enough. Right now, if you wanted to, you could get out of that chair. Look, I'll lock the wheels." He bent as he talked and fixed the brakes in place. "There. Steady as a rock. Now, get a grip on those arms and lift yourself. You can do it! I know you can. Son! Come on! Try!"

"Dad . . . yes . . . I can lift myself, but it's after that . . ."

"Do it!" Pepper ordered, frustration causing his concern to turn to anger. "Son! I said, do it!"

When Bud did not respond or move, Pepper exploded, "God damn it, I said stand up!"

"Dad, it . . . it won't . . . I can't . . ."

"Bud Young, I do not want to hear the words 'I can't' from your lips now or ever again! So, stand up! Stand up!"

When Bud shook his head, Pepper, in his drunken rage, seized his son by the shoulders to lift him from that chair to his feet.

"Dad! No!" Bud resisted.

But Pepper would not relent. Using every ounce of his own strength he lifted his son out of the wheelchair. He held him up until his feet touched the floor. Then Pepper moved back unsteadily, convinced that, if forced to, Bud would stand on his own two feet.

For an instant Bud stood there, wavering. Then his dizziness, his muscle weakness, overcame him. He lost control. He fell forward.

Pepper Young caught his son in his arms. He set him down on the hard wood.

In a voice tinged with both anger and guilt, with the bourbon speaking, Pepper accused, "I know why you're doing this to me!"

Recovering from his fall, Bud asked, "Doing . . . what . . . to you, Dad?"

"You *can* walk. But you *won't,* just to punish me!"

"Punish . . ." Bud repeated in confusion. He had grown accustomed to being confused and uncertain about things that people said. Ever since he had wakened from his coma and had to contend with mental processes that did not function as easily and quickly as they used to, he had had moments of confusion. But that had been getting better over the last few months. Yet now, the word *punish* coming at him so suddenly, with no connection to the previous conversation, baffled him completely. "Punish?" he repeated.

"Don't deny it!" Pepper accused.

"Dad . . . I don't . . . don't know . . . what you're . . ." Bud stammered.

"This is your way . . . maybe it's even your mother's way . . . of getting even with me. Well, if it makes you feel any better, I have been living with this guilt since the moment it happened. I don't need anybody to remind me. I don't need to see you in a wheelchair to feel accused. I feel accused every waking moment. And I can't tell you how many times I wake up in the middle of the night trying to recapture that moment so I can change it. So I can undo it. God, son, what kind of man do you think I am?"

"Dad . . . what are you . . . talking about?"

Pepper Young knelt over his prostrate son. He looked into his eyes.

"Bud . . . are you telling me . . . do you want me to believe . . . that you don't know?" Pepper asked.

"What?"

"They never told you . . . your mother never told you . . ."

"Told me what?" Bud asked.

"The accident . . . how you got to be this way."

"They said it was a car crash."

"That's all they said?" Pepper asked. "All your mother said?"

"Why? Is there more?" Bud asked.

"Is there more . . . ?" Pepper echoed. "They never did tell you. Well then, I have to. Bud, that car crash . . . which you can't remember, like so many other recent things that you can't remember . . . it was New Year's Day. I was driving. I was drunk."

"Drunk . . . " Bud repeated in a whisper. "The accident . . . everything that's happened to me . . . was because you were driving drunk . . . "

"Yes, son."

Instead of replying in words, Bud Young responded to Pep's shocking revelation with a loud anguished cry followed by "No . . . no . . . no . . . no . . . " before he began to weep.

Bud's outcry had penetrated the walls of Rehab and echoed down the third-floor corridor, summoning one of the night nurses and an attendant to his aid.

Confronted by the sight of the patient on the floor and his father kneeling over him, the nurse took command. With the help of the attendant she lifted Bud back into his wheelchair.

"Back to your room," she ordered.

Once he had wheeled himself out, she turned to Pepper Young.

"Mr. Young, I don't know what happened in here. But I will have to report what I found."

By the manner in which she sniffed she made it clear that she was aware of Pepper's condition. "Under the circumstances, I must insist that you leave this hospital. At once."

Without a word of protest, Pepper Young left Rehab. He stared down the long corridor to see his son disappear into his room. He had to stifle the impulse to follow him. But the events of the last few minutes had sobered him sufficiently to realize he should not.

Bud Young wheeled himself back into room 302. Aside from the blue night-light the room was dark. He rolled to the side of the bed. Instead of trying to lift himself he sat there motionless, still stunned by what he had learned so suddenly and without warning.

Dad . . . I'm the way I am because of Dad . . . the moment he mentioned it, it all came back . . . warning him . . . my wanting to drive . . . his insisting . . . then the brake . . . he hit the brake . . . the car began to skid . . . hit the overpass . . . hit the overpass. . . . I think I remember something after that . . . but I'm not sure. . . . I think I remember . . . sirens . . . somebody . . . police maybe . . . Am I remembering or am I making this up . . . ? But the part about Dad . . . I remember that now . . . I remember that. . . . He's been carrying that around with him all this time . . . all this time. . . .

And nobody told me . . . nobody told me . . . not even Mom.

Pepper Young drove down their street slowly as if he dared not pull into his own driveway. When he finally did, he sat behind the wheel, the motor running, the drive lever in neutral.

Vaguely the thought crossed his mind. All he had to do was activate the garage door, drive in, allow the motor to continue running, and it would all be over. Quietly. Painlessly.

The sight of his son captive in a wheelchair had scarred his mind forever. Worse was the look in his son's eyes when he discovered who was responsible for his crippled condition. His outcry of anguish would follow Pepper Young forever.

Forever need only be a matter of minutes if he raised the door, drove into that garage. He had destroyed his son's life, his own life. Lily and Gwen would both be better off without him.

He had promised himself more than once, *If only I could hear Bud say, "Dad, I forgive you," it would solve all my problems. That can never happen now. And why should it? What have I done to be worthy of his forgiveness? Get drunk again? Shock him with the terrible truth?*

He reached for the garage door control above his sun visor. Found it. Pressed it. The door rose slowly. He was about to put the car into drive when, from habit, he glanced up at Gwen's window above the garage. Always, when he came home later than expected, he would glance up to see if there was still a light on in her room. If there was, he would stop in to kiss her good night.

He never knew or else couldn't remember what happened in cases where someone committed suicide by carbon monoxide. Could those fumes rise and penetrate the rooms above, endangering anyone up there?

He drove into the garage, turned off the motor. He was just getting out of his car when he heard Lily from inside the house.

"Willard . . . is that you?"

He slipped out of the car, straightened his coat to achieve some semblance of neatness and dignity, started for the kitchen door. It opened before he reached it.

In her eyes he could tell that she knew he was drunk. She had that way of looking. Without a word, she could render a verdict that was more condemnatory than any jury.

As he passed her, he could swear that though he kept his lips pressed tight she could smell the bourbon on his breath.

"They called," she said.

"They? Who?" he asked, turning to confront her.

"The hospital. Bud."

She chose not to discuss it in the kitchen. She headed directly to the living room. He followed, wondering, *What did they tell her? What did Bud say?*

She waited for him to be seated in his favorite chair, his watching-football-and-basketball-with-Bud chair.

"They said you were drunk. But they didn't have to tell me that."

"Now, Lil . . ." he started to explain.

"Willard Young, shut up! This is one time *I* am going to do the talking. You showed up drunk. You tried to force Bud to do the one thing he cannot do. And then . . . then . . . you *told* him. God, how could you do that?"

"I didn't know that he didn't know. I thought that you would have told him . . ."

"Did you? Did you really think that?" Lily demanded.

"I assumed . . . I . . ."

"Then I think you're right. I've been thinking about it all night."

"Thinking about what?" he asked.

"All the things you said before you left here. About ending this family. Until I heard that you'd told Bud how it all happened I was unsure. But that settled things for me. I realized then, you don't understand me. Probably never did.

"How could you think that I would tell our son . . . your son . . . that he'll be crippled for the rest of his life because of what his father did? How I could be so cruel? To confront him with that at a time when he is struggling to recover his ability to speak, to use his hands, to use his legs, even his ability to think? Above all, why would I want to drive a wedge between my husband and my son? I've been trying to hold this family together. Bud's knowing should have come a long time from now. When he would be able to handle it. When he's made as full a recovery as he can. Not when he has to grapple with living his life in a wheelchair.

"So, no, I didn't tell him. I wish to God you hadn't either. I don't know what this will do to him. I'll have to talk to Marcy."

"I'd talk to Dr. Curtis if I were you," he countered.

"I already have," Lily informed.

"You already . . . when . . . now . . . tonight?" he asked.

"The hospital called her. She called me."

"And . . ." Because he feared the response, he had difficulty asking, "And what did Curtis say?"

"First, that you are never to visit Bud in the hospital again."

"They can't do that," he protested.

"Yes, they can," Lily replied firmly. "And if you try I will report to Judge Bruce what happened tonight. And you know what that would mean."

"Lily, you wouldn't do that . . ."

"To protect my son I will do anything. And he's never needed my protection more than when he's facing the most difficult time of his life."

Pepper stared at her. She had spoken with a conviction and strength he had never seen in her before.

"Lily . . ." he started to say.

She cut him off abruptly. "This family can never be the same. Not after tonight."

"It was just one night . . . I was . . . I don't know . . . call it deranged. I said things I didn't mean . . . did things I didn't mean to do. . . ." he tried to explain.

"Some things said leave a long memory. And some things done cannot be undone. From now on, until you find other quarters, you will sleep down here."

"Lily . . ." he called to her as she started from the room.

She turned back only long enough to say, "And don't try to go around me by talking to Gwen. She's even more shaken by this than I am."

He heard her climb the steps to their bedroom. Now that she was gone he knew what he had wanted to say. Maybe it would have mattered. Although from the firmness in her voice, from her strong words, he knew that nothing would change her mind.

But he should have said, had wanted to say, *You had no right to tell me about Bud the way you did earlier tonight. . . . To tell a man his son is going to live the rest of his life in a wheelchair . . . that should be said differently . . . there must be some way to handle that that's not so painful . . . maybe it's the doctor's duty to tell a father something like that.*

Maybe there should be some . . . some . . . preamble . . . some preface . . . some introduction that eases the shock . . . that makes it not so . . . oh, God, Lily, how do you think I felt when you told me? Sure, you could take it like a strong woman, a good mother . . . but you don't bear the guilt . . . you didn't do it, I did! Don't you see the difference?

He heard the bedroom door close, as firmly as her words had been spoken.

Lily . . . Lil . . . I've destroyed everything . . . Bud . . . this family . . . everything. But the worst thing of all—even before Bud said a word—was the sight of him in that wheelchair. I wanted to tear my eyes out to erase that image from my mind. My son . . . my Bud . . . that terrific young kid . . . with all that potential . . . with his whole life ahead of him . . . sitting there in that wheelchair. I want to see him . . . I want to apologize to him . . . I want to make it up to him . . . as if anyone can . . . that's what did it, Lil. The sight of him in that chair. Once I saw that I went out of my mind . . . out of my mind.

———

The next morning after sleeping it off on the living-room couch, he woke to find that Gwen had left for school. At the archway that led from the living room to the entry hall he found his suitcase packed, with a note attached.

> *Pepper: Here's everything I think you'll need. If you want any-thing else call and leave a message. I expect to be spending more time than usual at the hospital now. Lily.*

When Lily Young arrived at Mercy Hospital that morning she found Marcy already at work in Bud's room. She had him practicing his writing and had introduced a new stimulus.

She was instructing Bud when Lily slipped into the room.

"This diary is going to be part of your life from now on."

"Girls keep diaries," Bud said with a degree of chauvinistic superiority.

"Girls," Marcy agreed, but corrected, "And *my* patients. You are to note in there everything you do during the course of the day. And not just write, 'Went to store.' Oh, no. I want a full account. Where you went and why. What you found. What you thought."

"I don't have to write that, I can tell you that," Bud protested.

"Not after you leave here, you can't," Marcy countered.

"I'm leaving here . . . when?"

"Soon as all the changes are made at home. We have to get you settled in so you'll be ready for the fall term at school," Marcy explained, then turned to Lily. "Have you and Mr. Young contracted for those changes at the house? How long will it take?"

Lily's failure to respond at once was a signal Marcy was quick to detect. She refrained from pressing the issue by turning her attention back to Bud.

"Now, you take this diary and as of today start to write in it everything. Events, even the most minor. Opinions. Even of me, especially when you think I'm pushing you too hard, too fast. Use all the nasty words you can think of. Just spell them cor-rectly and write them clearly so I can read them. Got it?"

"Got it," Bud agreed.

"You can start right now. You have half an hour before we go to Rehab for a new kind of torture I've devised," Marcy threatened with a smile.

As she started out, she said to Lily, "I think he needs to be alone with that diary for a while."

Once they were outside the room, Marcy said, "Let's go have a cup of coffee."

They were seated at a quiet corner table of the hospital cafeteria. In her usual manner, more given to directness than diplomacy, Marcy began by saying, "I know everything. Everything that happened here last night. And I can guess the rest."

Lily's look of skepticism urged Marcy to explain.

"Lily, this isn't my first case. Or my fiftieth. I've seen this happen before. CHI injuries and the consequences can and do break up families. There are always one or two members who can't take it. Who can't face a lifetime of what this means."

"You should have warned me, someone should have," Lily protested.

"How could I?" Marcy responded. "What if *you* proved to be the one who couldn't face it?"

Lily nodded, accepting her reasoning.

"Of course," Marcy continued, "under the circumstances, why in the world did your husband ever expose Bud to the cause of the accident now, of all times? When Bud has his own serious problem to deal with."

"Guilt," Lily said simply. "Has Bud said anything to you about it?"

"No. But I could see he's greatly upset. That's why I introduced that diary. Since he can't talk about it, I want him to write about it. I don't usually give my patient a diary until he leaves the hospital. It gives us a continuing relationship while he's an outpatient."

"Is there anything any of us can do to help him get over last night?" Lily asked. "Anything I can do?"

"This will take time, Lily, time."

Lily accepted Marcy's advice with a forlorn nod.

In a voice that made her remark seem a very sobering after-thought Marcy admitted, "Of course, I've never had a case like this before."

In response to Lily's puzzled reaction, Marcy explained, "Where the patient's own father was the cause of such a devastating injury."

Three days had passed. On the morning of the fourth day Marcy Ethridge entered Room 302 to find Bud sitting in his wheelchair, staring out the window, diary in his lap, pen in hand.

"Bud," she said softly, intruding on his reverie.

He turned his head in her direction. She noticed the signs of dried tears on his handsome young face.

"Bud?"

"I . . . I . . . am . . . all . . . right," he replied precisely, as if practicing his speech skills.

His reply was too studied to please Marcy. Since he had never spoken about, or written in his diary any reference to, his father's drunken night visit she knew he was still concealing his feelings about it.

"Well, let's get started," Marcy said. "And first . . ." She reached for his diary. The page was blank. No thoughts this morning. No reference to anything that had happened since she left him yesterday afternoon.

He was aware of her disappointment.

"Looking out the window I have been thinking . . . how soon?"

"Within several weeks," Marcy said. "If you keep improving as you have been."

"What's it like out there?"

"The same as it was the last time you were out there. Except then it was January, cold and snowy. Now it's June and kind of warm. In fact, if you'd like, we could go out today. You could practice the wheelchair on the hospital grounds. Moving on grass, going up and down ramps. Would you like to try that?"

"What'll happen when I see people for the first time . . . they see me for the first time?"

"Not as bad as you imagine," Marcy said.

"Dad, he couldn't take it."

"Your father was in an upset condition before he ever arrived here that night," Marcy pointed out diplomatically.

"You can say it. It's the truth. He was drunk," Bud said. "He is so terrific all the other times. Why does he do that?"

"Come on, Bud, we have our work to do," Marcy urged.

He started to go through his upper-body exercises, exerting his strength against Marcy's strong pressure. During the exercise he tried to speak, though in breathy fashion.

"Never came back . . ."

"Who?" Marcy asked, pressing down hard on his forearms that rested on the wheelchair. "Lift, lift, Bud."

As if reminded, he replied, "Oh. Yeah." He lifted his arms, fully clearing the armrests. He seemed more intent on speaking than exercising.

Good, Marcy thought, *now that he can manage his words and phrases, let him start putting thoughts together and by fall he'll be in shape to resume his place in school. So let him talk, encourage him to talk.*

"You were saying about Dad . . ." she prodded.

"He didn't come back," Bud said, his tone and attitude revealing his puzzlement.

"Didn't Mom tell you? Because of the havoc he caused the last time when he showed up drunk, he's been barred from the hospital," Marcy explained. "But he calls every day to ask about you."

"And what do they tell him? That I'm still in a wheelchair. That's the real reason he doesn't come. He can't stand to look at me like this."

Because she could not truthfully deny that, Marcy did not reply but applied herself to his physical routines.

"I . . . I know how he feels. I can't stand to look at myself," Bud revealed. "When I move to here . . ."

He broke away from Marcy. He wheeled himself to the wall opposite his bed. He jockeyed himself into a position that allowed him to see himself in the mirror over the washbasin to the side of his bed.

"I can look in there. I see myself the way others will see me. Jody and Chuck and Chris . . . and . . . and Marylyn . . . oh, sure, they'll all smile, even try to make jokes. They'll say how terrific I look . . . because they've been coached to do that . . . but inside they'll all feel sorry for me. I don't want anyone feeling sorry for me!" he shouted, then at once he broke into tears.

She said not a word.

Let him cry himself out. Let him experience all these feelings now. It's proof that he's been getting ready, mentally ready, to leave the hospital. Which will happen soon, since we've done all we can for him here.

He was wiping his eyes on the sleeve of his pajama top.

"Sorry," he said.

"No need. You were only living up to our agreement. I'll be honest with you. You'll be honest with me."

He swung his chair around to confront her.

"Then tell me, is there any chance . . . any chance at all . . . that I'll ever get out of this chair and walk?"

"Bud, we've been through that before. Many times. Stability. And equilibrium. Without those two abilities no one, not me, not you, no one can walk," Marcy replied, not without great regret.

He nodded. He accepted her word. If only for the moment. There would be many times, as there had been since he was first told, times during the night when he was alone, and during the day when the outside world beckoned to him, that he would fight this battle, rebel against it, and eventually have to yield to the fact that his life would be lived in this chair from now on.

He had a million questions he asked himself and hid from everyone, including Marcy, whom he trusted and loved.

What would it be like in school? Moving from room to room every time the bell rang to announce the end of one class and the beginning of another? How would he be able to maneuver in that flood of traffic when the guys came pouring out of those rooms? When the corridors were crowded with everybody going every which way?

He would hate for them to make a path just for him. And if anyone tried to help him by putting a hand on his chair to steer him he'd curse the sonofabitch out.

I don't want to depend on anyone. And I don't want anyone to feel sorry for me!

Marcy could almost read the defiance on his young face. But she did not pry. It would come out. One day it would come out.

He had been to Rehab, worked his wheelchair exercises. He was getting pretty good at that. He worked the weights to exercise his upper body and his stomach muscles.

His lunch was on his table when he returned to 302. He pulled himself up. It was one achievement in which he took pride. He had gone from being fed by Marcy, or a nurse or Mom, to being able to handle a spoon, fork, and knife so that he could feed himself.

He opened his napkin, tucked it into the collar of his pajama top. He picked up the cup of orange juice. He could hold it in his right hand now. Still a touch shaky but he could bring it to his mouth, drink it, all without spilling a drop.

Big deal, he silently derided his achievement, *I can drink orange juice. Kids of two can do that. Throwing a football. Running for daylight. That's an achievement.*

He applied himself now to the salad, noticing that the greens had already been cut into small pieces for him. He resented it. He could have done that for himself. He was good with a knife when it came to buttering his roll. Maybe not quite as good as he would be one day. But he could surely cut up his salad if he had to.

"And with my right hand!" he defied.

He was halfway through his salad when his phone rang. He swung his chair about, quickly, precisely. He was getting better at that every day. He reached the phone on his bedside table. It must be Mom explaining why she would be a little late today.

"Hi."

"Bud?" It was Gwen. She sounded very tense, very disturbed.

"Gwen? What's up?"

"You all right?" she asked.

"Yes. I'm all right. Why?"

She's very upset, he realized. *She'd have to be to call me in the middle of the school day. Even if she's on lunch hour, what's she doing calling me now?*

"Gwennie . . . what's wrong?"

"What are we going to do?" she asked. "Bud, what are we going to do?"

"Do? About what?" he asked, mystified. "Gwennie, what are you talking about?"

"Bud, I hate to bother you when you have troubles enough but you're the only one I can talk to . . . the only one who can do anything."

"Do anything about *what?* Hey, you're not in trouble, are you?"

"No, it's not me . . . it's Dad . . . and Mom."

"Dad and Mom? What do you mean?"

"Mom didn't tell you?"

"No, what?"

"They're . . . they've split . . . he's gone. She put him out," Gwen said. She could not contain her anxiety, which spilled over in tears. "What are we going to do, Bud, what are we going to do?"

"God, I never thought . . . that's the kind of thing happens to other families. Not to us. What happened?"

"I don't know exactly. It was the morning after Dad did his drunk bit at the hospital. You know how Mom's always felt about that. Well, this time she'd had it."

"Did you talk to her about it? Or to Dad?"

"I never had a chance to talk to him."

"I'll . . . I'll talk to Mom when she gets here," Bud promised. "So don't you worry. Just go back to class. Okay?"

"All right, okay, Bud." Then she added, "I love you."

She must be upset. Really upset, he realized. *Even though we feel that way about each other, she's never had to say she loves me. She must be scared, poor kid.*

He had no appetite for the rest of his lunch. The more he dwelt on Gwennie's call, the more he himself felt shaken. All his thoughts about leaving here were centered on going home. In his fantasies everything he did always included Dad. Mom, for sure. Gwen, of course. But Dad, too. Dad would always be there. To talk men's talk to. To watch ballgames with. It wasn't home without Dad. It wasn't family without Dad.

He must talk to Mom the minute she got there.

Lily Young had her own plan for informing her son about the new family situation.

She laid the foundation for it in her apology for being late today.

"Sorry, son," she said as she kissed him, "but I was delayed at Harry Helgeson's office."

"Helgeson," Bud commented. "The lawyer? He was at the Jansers' on New Year's Day. What are you seeing him about?"

"Bud," she began to report to him all the events of four nights ago.

When she had finished, Bud said softly, "My fault . . . it's really my fault."

"Your fault? It isn't your fault you can't walk. It's his!"

"Mom . . . if I could walk none of this would have happened."

"I will not let you blame yourself. If he isn't man enough to face something he's responsible for, that's his fault, not yours!" Lily declared. "I am through protecting him from his own mistakes. His own weakness. We can't live our lives in constant fear that tonight or tomorrow he will turn up drunk again. From now on it'll be just the three of us. And, by God, we are going to be a family. You will leave here soon. Go back to school in the fall. Go on to college. You've got a great life ahead of you, Bud Young!"

"Yeah, but Dad . . ." Bud tried to protest.

"He couldn't face it, Bud. It happens to families like ours."

"You mean families who are burdened with someone like me."

"Don't you dare to say that about yourself, you hear?"

"Mom, there's no use denying . . ."

"I won't listen to such talk!"

He realized there was no use protesting. Not in the mood Mom was in now.

Silently, Bud continued to protest, *But, Dad . . . Dad . . .*

36

Bud Young lay in his hospital bed staring at the window. He had a game he played on nights when he could not sleep. He tried to guess the time from the darkness or dawn that leaked in from around the drawn shade.

On this night, he decided it must be very early. For if it was five o'clock or later, there would be a border of light around the shade. If it was going to be a sunny day, that border would be a rosy color.

He had been having a restless night. He would fall asleep, then wake suddenly. Fall asleep, then wake suddenly. Each time he woke his first thought was . . . *Gwen . . . I never heard her sound so frightened. But if she's scared, what did she think I was? I broke out in a sweat when she told me. No more family? Can't be. Can't. And Mom, sure, she tried to sound as if this was the right thing, the only thing. But I could see in her eyes how painful this is for her. This family just can't break up . . . can't.*

Sure Dad's to blame for driving while he was drunk. But that's past. Right now what brought this on is my not being able to walk. It's that damn wheelchair. That's what scared him. The idea that he is going to have to see me in that damn wheelchair for the rest of his life.

If I could walk, this whole thing would be over. Dad would come home. We'd be the Youngs again. People always talked about us that way. The Youngs. Dad, Mom, Bud, and Gwen. The Youngs.

If I could walk . . . I have times when I feel sure I can. I can walk. I can! But then when I get out to Rehab and those damn parallel bars, that three-sided walker, something goes wrong. Something . . . Marcy talks about equilibrium and stability, but doesn't determination have anything to do with it?

Wanting to. Wanting to so the family stays together. I've seen movies where people who couldn't do something were able to do it in a time of emergency. They didn't stop to think of all the reasons why they couldn't walk. Like equilibrium and stability. They just did what they needed to do to survive or to save someone else. Mothers who single-handed rescued their children from burning buildings or lifted cars to free their kids from danger.

Wanting to is important. Well, who has a better reason for wanting to walk than I do? I bet right now if I wanted to hard enough, I could walk. I could.

He lay still, arms straight alongside and pressed against his body. His fingers, strong once more from all his exercises, pressed into his thighs. He was trying to infuse some of the strength of his hands into those resistant, uncontrollable legs of his. He breathed determinedly, taking a deep breath, then exhaling. Another deep breath, then exhaling. With each breath his determination increased.

He felt ready. He lifted himself from the pillow, sat up. First he moved his right leg to the edge of the bed, then his left one. Recalling the manner in which Marcy had first made him sit up, he compressed it into a single impulsive action. He dropped his legs over the side of the bed, pivoting and bringing himself to a sitting position at once.

He sat there for a time, breathing regularly, with purpose. Deep breaths. Preparation. He felt ready now.

Do this like a man who can walk, not like an invalid. Do this for Dad, for Mom, for Gwen, for our whole family.

Now. Do it!

He pushed down on the bed, rising at the same time. He was on his feet! Standing! Alone! No bars! No walker! Nothing! What a feeling!

Until suddenly he lost all control. He plunged forward. His head struck the visitor's chair. He blacked out.

The nurse who came in to assist him with his morning duties found him. He had a slight cut along his right cheek. But the blood had crusted over and he was in no danger. She summoned help to put him back to bed.

Within twenty minutes Dr. Curtis came in to see him. Her examination, detailed as it was, did not reveal any need for further X-ray or MRI procedures.

During her examination, she tried to ferret out the reason behind his foolish if bold attempt. He proved completely uncommunicative.

Marcy, Dr. Curtis decided. *Marcy is the person to handle this. He trusts her.*

Briefed by Dr. Curtis, Marcy entered 302 that morning in her usual breezy and impertinent way.

"Good morning, one and all," she greeted. Then, focusing on the bandage on his right cheekbone, "Cut yourself shaving, did you? I thought we'd progressed your neuromuscular facilitation to the point where you could shave without cutting yourself. Or did something else happen here?"

"You know damn well what happened here," Bud replied. "They must have told you. Dr. Curtis surely told you."

As she began to manipulate his arms she replied, "Yes, Bud, yes, she did tell me. Not a very wise thing to do. You could have damaged that brain of yours again. And it's a very good brain. You should take better care of it. So never try that again. I know you'll be tempted. Patients in your condition always harbor the thought that if they try, really try, they can walk. If they could, would we confine them to wheelchairs? Would I confine you to a wheelchair?"

He did not reply but continued to grip and relax his hold on the rubber handballs that were part of his therapy.

Having delivered her reprimand Marcy said, "And now let's have a look at that diary. You've been working on that, I hope."

He did not respond, indicating his resentment of her brusk lecture.

She picked up the diary from the night table alongside his

bed. She opened to the first page. She studied it less for content than for the style of his handwriting. Fair. But with promise of improvement. Most of the letters were contained within the printed lines on the page.

She read the text to discover his progress in the thought process and in his correct understanding and use of words. Good. Very good. He had delivered an accurate account of the day's activities. Also some comments that indicated that his mind was indeed regaining its earlier cognitive abilities.

She turned the page to find printed there in large letters, controlled letters, BREAKING UP. EVERYTHING BREAKING UP. POOR GWEN.

His head being deliberately turned away to express his resistance, Marcy walked around the foot of the bed, stood over him with his diary in hand.

"Bud . . . 'Breaking up? Everything breaking up'?"

He tried to turn on his left side to avoid her but she pinned him with her strong hand.

"Bud . . . was this why?"

He did not respond at once.

"Was it?"

He avoided her eyes, even though she forced him to face in her direction.

"Bud?"

"Yes," he finally admitted.

"Don't ever do anything like that again. You really could hurt yourself," she said softly. "Now, let's continue with our work."

He carried out his day's routine but with such lack of enthusiasm and purpose that Marcy Ethridge was greatly concerned. The patient's intention and desire to progress was essential to make her therapy effective. Stroke victims and other brain-damaged patients needed that drive to recover or else they gave up hope and settled not for their least damaged condition but for their most damaged condition.

Was Bud Young slipping into that swamp of despair, of self-destruction? With all the abilities he still possessed, and which would increase, it would be a terrible waste of a very promising human being.

Marcy had treated patients who in their wheelchairs had

gone on to become lawyers, one a doctor, two teachers, another a designer of clothes. But it took drive, desire, and courage.

If Bud lost that, she could foresee a long discouraging life ahead for him.

She had fed her own little Ezra his supper. Together they had read through his newest book until he fell asleep in her arms. She settled him into his bed. She arranged for her neighbor to keep watch over him. Despite the hour she went back to Mercy Hospital.

Her assumption proved correct. Bud Young still lay awake. She could see the whites of his open eyes in the unlit room.

"Bud," she said softly.

With darkness as his shield he was able to speak more freely than he had earlier.

"My fault . . . all my fault . . . Dad . . . the family . . . it's breaking up . . . there is not going to be any Young family anymore. I've seen it with friends of mine. Dad takes off for some reason. The mother, the kids, they still live in the same house. But it's not the same. It's not a family anymore. It's Mrs. Wilson and her kids. Or Mrs. Young and her two kids. But not a family. Gwen and me, we used to talk all the time about how sorry we felt for kids whose families broke up.

"Never in my life did I ever think that would happen to us. Not to us. Never. Any family in the world but not the Young family. But it did happen . . . it did . . . all because of me. I failed."

"Bud, you didn't fail. It isn't your fault. Isn't something in your control," Marcy tried to console.

"No?" he defied. "Tell me—tell me the truth—you've had other patients with my kind of brain damage."

"Yes, of course, that's what I do. What every therapist does."

"Then tell me, have you had other patients like me who *did* walk?" Bud demanded. "The truth!"

"Bud, no two patients are exactly the same. You can't lay down their MRIs and their scans and say these cases are identical. They never are."

"I didn't ask for identical," Bud protested. "All I'm asking, have you ever had patients like me . . . with my kind of brain damage . . . who *did* walk? The truth!"

Aware of what he was driving at, still Marcy was forced to admit, "Yes, yes, I've had patients . . . like you . . . who succeeded in walking. Some with canes. But yes, they ended up walking."

"I want to walk!" Bud declared.

"Bud, we've been through all the steps . . . gone as far as the therapy provides . . ."

"I want to walk!" he persisted.

"Bud, it takes more than wanting."

"Then I'll do more!" he replied.

"It isn't that simple," Marcy tried to explain.

He didn't give her a chance to explain. "What is happening to my family, to Gwen, is my fault!"

"Bud, you can't blame yourself for an accident you had no part in."

"I don't care about that. All I know, if I could walk my father wouldn't have to see me in that wheelchair for the rest of my life. This family would be together. We would still be the Youngs. Except for me, we'd be . . . we'd be family again. So, it is my fault. Marcy, please, I want to walk. I have to walk. Don't you understand that?"

"Bud, you know by now that no one can walk without first achieving stability."

"Teach me stability!" he insisted.

"Even if I could, there's always the problem of equilibrium," she pointed out. "Far more complicated. And that's beyond teaching. It involves interaction between the cranial nerve, the inner ear, the eye, parts of the brain. You can't 'teach' anyone that."

"No, no, no, wait now," Bud replied. "I've been thinking about that. Didn't you once tell me that during this kind of therapy sometimes the brain teaches the body how to regain ability?"

"Yes," Marcy conceded.

"But didn't you also say that other times the *body,* just by doing, can teach the *brain*? Remind it of abilities it used to have? Didn't you say that, Marcy?"

He was pleading with her for confirmation of his theory.

"Yes. I did say that . . . but in a case like yours . . ."

"Marcy, please, I must walk out of this hospital. Else I never want to leave here. Help me. Promise you'll help me."

Worthy as his purpose was, he was still a desperate young man, with a desperate ambition.

But because he was, because he wanted it so much, Marcy Ethridge said, "I can give you only one promise. I *will* help you. But you have to give *me* one promise."

"Anything," he replied at once.

"If we fail, you won't blame me. But especially you won't blame yourself."

"I won't blame you," he promised at once.

"The other part," Marcy insisted.

"I . . . I won't blame myself," he conceded.

Aware of the enormity of the challenge he had set for himself and the odds against success, Marcy said, "Okay. Today we start."

She could only justify her decision by thinking, *What is it we strive to instill in all our patients? What's the most vital ingredient in the recovery process? The will to recover. The persistence it takes to labor day after day after day at boring exercises and frustrating tasks to achieve even a little progress. This young man has that will, that determination. I've never seen a patient who had more. Maybe . . . just maybe this can work.*

Or am I beginning to think and sound like the patient now?

"Once more!" Marcy Ethridge said, kneeling before Bud Young, who was seated on the edge of the exercise table. "You push forward. I will push against you. And this time, let me feel it."

She raised her hands, placed them firmly against his shoulders, and ordered, "Push!"

His face already bathed in sweat from effort that had extended him to his ultimate, he nodded. He pressed forward. She pushed against him. He summoned up all his power and tried to lunge forward.

"Better," she said, "but not good enough. Now, let's see some real effort. This time, all you've got! Let's go!"

Once more he tried to push against her strong hands. Once more she prevailed until he slumped in exhaustion.

She held out a handkerchief to him to wipe his damp face. He stared at it.

"If you think I'm going to do that for you, think again, Mr. Young. Take this. Wipe that ugly face of yours so we can carry on."

He glared at her, took the handkerchief, mopped his face,

which felt like it would never be dry again. When he had regained his breath, he dropped the handkerchief onto the table, then confronted her, daring her to do her worst.

"Okay, if that's the way you feel," she said. "Now, in addition to pushing against me, reach out with your arms at the same time."

She placed her hands on his shoulders and waited. He gathered his strength. He leaned forward at the same time, vaguely reaching out with his arms.

"Push harder. Reach farther."

With great determination he tried to perform both chores at the same time but finally failed, collapsing onto the table, his sweaty body staining the black leather. He lay there breathing in quick shallow gasps.

Marcy rose to her feet just in time to notice that Dr. Curtis had been watching the entire procedure through the glass insert in the Rehab door. From the look on Curtis's face, Marcy knew that an explanation was in order.

"Take five, Bud. I'll be back."

Once she stepped outside the door Marcy was confronted by a very disapproving Dr. Curtis.

"Marcy, what in the world do you think you're doing?"

"Giving him his chance."

"Chance to do what? Break his heart? He'll have problems enough as it is. I think the most constructive thing we can do for him is determine his remaining skills and reconcile him to making the most of them."

"He is determined to walk. He thinks that will bring his family together."

"And you consider that a good enough motive to drive him this way?" Curtis demanded.

"Dr. Curtis, whatever motive gives the patient the persistence to drive himself to achieve is good enough for me. All I need is a patient with the will to recover. And Bud Young has it."

"Marcy, we are not in the business of performing miracles. You know as well as I what his chances are of ever walking on his own."

"He's determined to try."

"And, it seems, you're determined to help him," Curtis remarked tartly.

"Doctor, even if he never takes a step on his own, it's crucial to him for the rest of his life to know that he tried."

"Marcy, never forget, you're a physical therapist, not a psychiatrist."

"I'm well aware of that, Doctor," Marcy said with great formality. But added, "So if there are any residual psychiatric benefits, I'm sorry."

With that she turned and started back into Rehab, leaving Dr. Curtis to think, *If she weren't such a terrific therapist I wouldn't put up with her insolence for a minute.*

"Okay, Bud, enough goofing off," Marcy said. "On your knees!"

He drew himself up to assume the kneeling position.

"Now, no matter what I do, you hold firm. I push, you don't budge. You just hold that position."

Bud nodded. He took a firm, almost belligerent, position on the leather surface. Marcy stood behind him. She reached out with both hands, placed them against his right shoulder. She tried to push him to his left. He fought back, holding firm. But after a count of nine he keeled over to fall onto his left side.

"Come on, we can do better than that," Marcy taunted as if she were his drill instructor. "Up! Let's have another go at it."

"You're . . ." he started to say, but since his concentration was focused on his physical challenges, his verbal skills had deserted him for the moment. He caught his breath and started again, "You're doing this on . . . on purpose."

"Doing what? For which purpose?" Marcy demanded.

"Days . . . days . . . you been doing this . . . to make me . . . quit . . ." he accused.

"*Do* you feel like quitting?" she demanded.

"No!" he spat back in defiance.

"Then obviously I'm not doing a very good job of it, am I?" Marcy asked, that twinkle in her eyes that let him know she was doing her best so that he would do his best. "Now, come on, let's make believe this is Friday afternoon. We have a big football game tomorrow. We're running that one last drill before the coach says, 'That's it.' Okay?"

"Okay," he replied.

"Then up on your knees. Hands on the mat. Brace yourself!"

Once he was set, she placed both hands on his left shoulder and pushed. He fought back. This time he could not resist as long as he had before. But she expected that. His right side was now, and possibly would always be, somewhat weaker than his left. But she was encouraged that he held fast as long as he did.

"Once more," she insisted.

They repeated the exercise, she pushing hard, he resisting until finally he keeled over on his right side. He lay there, breathing hard, in a cold sweat.

"Tomorrow . . ." he said, repeating, "Tomorrow . . . tomorrow . . ."

"I'll be even tougher tomorrow. Now into your wheelchair, back to 302, and work on your diary," she ordered.

He dragged himself to the edge of the exercise bed, where his wheelchair stood locked in place. He shimmied to the edge of the bed, leaving a damp trail of sweat on the black shiny leather. He grasped the arms of the chair, lifted himself up and into it, where he seemed to collapse. But only for an instant, for with Marcy staring at him, he defied her by unlocking the wheels of his chair and propelling himself toward the door.

She watched him open the door and hold it while at the same time trying to maneuver his chair through it and out. It was difficult for him, and she felt a strong urge to help him. But she refrained, thinking, *Let him come to hate that chair even more. It may be just the incentive he needs for what's ahead.*

Bud Young propelled his chair down the corridor toward Room 302. Once inside he gave way to the total exhaustion he had felt but was too proud to let Marcy notice. If she was tough, he'd prove he was tougher.

He fell immediately into a deep sleep. He woke when he sensed the presence of someone in the room.

Without looking around he asked, "Mom?"

"Yes, darling," Lily answered, interrupting her knitting. "Did I wake you . . . the sound of my knitting needles?"

"What time is it?" he asked.

"Marcy always insists you answer those questions for yourself," she reminded.

"Oh. Yeah. I keep forgetting. So many things I keep forgetting," he said as he looked at his wristwatch.

To make him exercise his mental faculties Marcy had insisted that Lily bring him an old-fashioned watch to replace the digital watch he wore at the time of the accident. The mental exercise of reading time was more constructive than having it presented to him in numbers. He resented this watch every time he had to resort to it.

"Quarter after four. Have I been asleep that long?"

"Evidently needed it," Lily replied. "From the way you sounded. Were you dreaming?"

"I think . . . I think maybe . . . I don't quite remember but I think it had to do with . . . it was a trophy of some kind. . . . Before this all happened, did I get a trophy?"

Lily hesitated, wondering, *Do I tell him? Marcy didn't like it when Pep showed it to him. And when he finally saw it he went into a tantrum. Is this the right time?*

"Mom?" he asked again.

"Yes, dear, there was a trophy."

"A cup?"

"Yes, a silver cup. With your name on it. MOST VALUABLE PLAYER OF THE YEAR WILLARD 'BUD' YOUNG."

"Where is it?"

"Home. In your room," she said.

"Could you . . . could you bring it . . . maybe not tomorrow . . . but some day?" he asked.

"Yes . . . yes, if you like . . ." Lily replied, wondering if she was doing the right thing.

"I think I would like. I think I want to get back to old things."

"Old friends?" Lily asked, somewhat hopeful. "Guys on the team have been wanting to visit. They call almost every day."

"No, no, not that. I don't want them to see me like this."

"Bud . . . some day they'll have to," Lily said.

"No!" he insisted. "They'll never see me this way."

Lily did not press the issue. But before she left she found Marcy, "Marcy, now he's got himself convinced that he's going to leave here on his feet. Can he do it?"

"I don't know. He doesn't know. But I am going to break his butt, and mine, finding out," Marcy said.

"And when he fails?"

"I'd rather break his butt than his heart. If he fails, and I grant you the odds say he will, I don't want him to reproach himself years from now, saying, 'What if I'd tried, would I be able to walk? Would my family have stayed together?' It might make living in that chair a little less difficult."

"Marcy, he dreamed about the cup. Asked for it, wants to see it. What do I do?"

"Not yet, not yet," Marcy advised.

When Marcy Ethridge entered Room 302 for their late afternoon session she discovered Bud at work on his diary. At the sound of her he snapped the book shut.

Aware that he regarded this particular entry as highly confidential, she avoided making an issue of it by saying, "Well, not a bad morning, was it? You held up better than I expected. Of course, this afternoon will be tougher. But first for some of what we call by the fancy term cognitive skills. Which among other things mostly means just plain old readin', writin', and 'rithmetic. Let's see some of those handwriting samples."

She reached for the diary. Reluctant to surrender it, he tightened his grip. Nevertheless she took it, opened it. Studied the last page he had written.

"Very good, Bud. Every letter within the lines. Clean, clear. Come fall, you'll be ready to go to class and make notes with the best of them."

She did not comment on what he had written. For the words read, *Today was toughest day yet. Is Marcy trying to tell me I can't make it?*

On the line below he had written, *Is she right?*

38

Marcy Ethridge was briskly proceeding down the corridor on the way from one of her stroke patients to Room 302 when she was alerted by her beeper.

She stopped at the nurses' station to pick up the call.

"Ethridge," she announced.

"Miss Ethridge . . ." She heard a familiar voice but could not readily identify it. "Marcy . . . this is Mr. Young . . . Bud Young's father."

"Yes?"

In a voice both humble and contrite, Pepper Young continued, "Look, I don't want you to break any hospital rules. But tell me whatever you can. How is Bud? How's he doing? How's he reacting to being in that . . ." He had difficulty even saying the word. "In a . . . wheelchair?"

"He's resisting it," Marcy informed. "But that's only natural."

"Yes, yes, natural. Especially for him. He's a fighter. Never gives up. Did he ever tell you about that last-minute touchdown he threw?"

"No, he didn't."

"That's what I mean about him . . . modest . . . a really great kid. And because of me . . ." He began to falter. "Because of . . . of me . . ." He could not continue.

Though he backed away from the phone Marcy could hear him sobbing. She waited, then due to the urgency of her duties she was about to hang up when she heard him once more.

"Sorry. I . . . lately I . . . never mind. Just, would you tell Bud that I called? Can you do that?"

"Yes, I can. And I will."

"Thanks. Thanks a lot," he said, sounding greatly relieved.

Poor man, Marcy thought, *what happens to him if we fail? Hey, wait one minute. Suddenly it's not Bud, it's "we." Do I want this as much as Bud does? More?* Then she protested, *I'm only doing my job. Let's get on with it.*

She entered 302 in unusually businesslike fashion this morning. That call had stimulated added incentive.

"Okay, Bud Young, first we do our handiwork," she ordered crisply, employing the term she used to cover those daily chores Bud must learn to do for himself in order to be released from the hospital.

The simplest everyday things, washing himself, dressing himself, going to the toilet, doing all those things from a wheelchair. The ultimate aim of the therapist was to make her patient as self-sufficient as possible under those limiting circumstances.

"First, move up to the sink . . . reach for the extended faucets. . . . Your mother will have those installed at the house as soon as we give her the word."

She stopped, interrupted by Bud's refusal to roll his chair up to the sink.

"Bud . . ."

"It doesn't make sense," he protested, "to learn how to do all those things from a wheelchair when I am not going to *be* in a wheelchair."

"Bud . . . I promised you I'd help you as much as I could. But I never promised you that you'd walk. Remember that!" Marcy pointed out.

"I know . . . that's why you're trying so hard to make me fail."

Suddenly the words in his diary came back to Marcy. *Was he beginning to lose faith in her? Or was he losing faith in himself and trying to place the blame on her? Unfortunate. Especially today. I was going to test him today.*

Neither of them said anything while Bud went through his routine of turning on the faucets, washing his hands and face, drying them. He selected his clothes from the low rail in the closet and struggled to slip out of his pajamas. Marcy watched closely, critically, from time to time making a suggestion or a correction, which Bud accepted in desultory fashion. But he complied nevertheless.

He was washed and dressed and presented himself to Marcy for inspection. She had to point out, "Your shirt . . ."

"What about it?" he asked, prepared to dispute anything she said.

"You started out wrong. So all the buttons are one buttonhole off. Now unbutton them all and start over."

"What the hell's wrong with you today?" he shouted suddenly.

Marcy was neither surprised nor did she take it personally. Patients with closed head injuries were often given to sudden explosions of temper, sometimes from frustration, sometimes for reasons unknown even to themselves.

"Bud Young, you unbutton that shirt. Then button it correctly. I do not want you going out in public looking like a slob."

He glared at her. She stared back, unrelenting.

He looked away, but he did begin to unbutton his shirt to start over again. While he struggled with that, though she could see the improvement since his early exercises with buttons, she said, "I had a phone call today."

He glanced up at her.

"From your dad."

"Yeah?" Bud asked, interrupting his progress to hear more.

"Keep buttoning," she ordered. "He's very concerned. Very sorry for what happened the last time he was here. He wanted you to know how much he cares."

"How did he sound?" Bud asked.

"As I said, greatly concerned."

"I mean . . . he wasn't . . ."

"Drunk?" Marcy interpreted. "No. He was apologetic . . . contrite actually, Bud. He was crying."

"Oh, God," Bud said softly. "Dad . . . Marcy, we've got to make it work, got to!"

"Okay. Change into your sweats. Let's go!"

They had worked on the exercise table. She exerting more pressure against him than the day before, he resisting to the utmost of his strength. She had pushed from his right side until, despite his resistance, he toppled over. She had worked on his left side. Again until he finally toppled over. But at all times she evaluated that his resistance was stronger today than yesterday. And much stronger now than a week ago.

She decided, yes, put him to the test today. Perhaps the word about his father would give him that added stimulus to make a big step forward.

"Okay, Bud, back into your chair. Then, what do you say we have a go at the parallels?"

He looked up from where he was resting on the table.

"You think . . ." He did not dare ask.

"We're going to find out," she said.

He wheeled himself to the shiny metal bars. When Marcy reached for the controls to lower the bars to just below his hip, he anticipated her. He reached out himself, pressed the controls, adjusted the bars to the right height.

Showing off, Marcy thought. *Good. Unless it's pure bravado because he still feels so insecure. We'll see soon enough.*

The bars set, Bud wiped his perspiring hands on his sweatpants. Hands on his chair arms, he raised himself, grasped the cold metal bars. Slowly he lifted himself to his feet. He paused until he felt more secure. With his arms bearing his weight, he started to move, sliding his feet along the matted floor, left leg first, then right. Until he remembered, Marcy always liked to have him move his weaker right leg first. He stopped. He started again, this time right leg first.

To prove to her that he had remembered and was following

her instructions, he turned his head to look at her. His loss of concentration caused him to falter. With a half-suppressed outcry of fright, he started to fall forward. Even before Marcy could reach him, he clutched the bars again to remain standing. His legs, out of control, wobbled under him. But he was still on his feet, though his hands and arms actually supported him.

Badly shaken by this near disaster, he was covered in a sudden sweat. His legs could not seem to stop trembling despite all his efforts to control them.

Marcy's most discouraging observation, *He still doesn't have sufficient control of his legs. And his equilibrium is not nearly developed enough. But,* she decided, *one problem at a time.*

Determined not to allow him to dwell on his failure, Marcy ordered, "Bud! We've got work to do, lots of work. Come on, back into that chair!"

He struggled back to the beginning of the bars, settled himself into his chair, started to roll himself to the exercise table, but Marcy ordered with a crisp, "Follow me."

Bud turned to her ready to disagree but her stern look overrode his protest.

She started out of Rehab. He rolled after her. He followed her around a corner and down a short corridor to another door. There she stopped, held the door open for him to roll through.

He found himself in a small room not much larger than his own room. The floor was covered with one large exercise mat. In one corner of the room was a small three-step set of stairs. In another corner that instrument he had come to hate. A large inflated ball. And alongside it, a smaller blue and white one of soccer-ball size.

He turned to look back at Marcy, awaiting her instructions but ready to dispute them at the same time.

"Bud! We've got to work on your stability. And on your control of your legs. So, first, stability. Roll up to that ball. Get out of your chair. Sit down on that ball."

"You know I can't do that. I failed at that before."

"Try it now. If you need help, just ask."

In defiance of her offer, he glared at her, rolled up to the big ball which reached to the level of the armrests of his chair. He surveyed the problem. Made his decision. He locked his chair in place, fixed his hands on the sides of his chair, and lifted himself slowly from a sitting position to his feet. He started to transfer his weight from the chair to the ball, but it rolled out from under him. He fell forward to the matted floor.

Marcy started toward him but he called out, "No! Damn it, no! I'll do this my way."

She backed off, watching as he gathered his strength, wrapped his arms around that huge ball, and as if climbing a mountain, crawled up to finally mount it, sitting there as if he had climbed Everest.

He glared at her. She wanted to smile but suppressed the impulse. For what she had to do now might deflate his sense of victory.

"Now, Bud, remember all the things we've been saying about equilibrium. Eyes level. Concentrate on keeping your head level. As soon as you feel it rising, or even a tendency to rise, keep your eyes fixed on some object in this room. Like those stairs. Remember, if you can see the ceiling you've lost the game. Except this isn't a game. This is for all the marbles."

Bud listened, nodding, a look of determination forming on his handsome face.

"Now, for the hard part. I am going to try to dislodge you from that ball. I am going to push you left, then right. Forward, then back. And you have to resist me. I will knock you off. You will climb back on. And I will knock you off again. But all the while, remember equilibrium. Eyes level. Head level. Are you ready?"

He nodded with determination.

The contest began. Marcy pushed him from his left side. He resisted, pushing back from his uncertain perch. Another push and he lost balance. The ball rolled from under him, sending him to the mat. He looked up at Marcy, resenting her. She glared down at him.

"If you can't take risks, if you can't come back from a fall, you'll never make it," she declared. "What do you say?"

He gathered his strength, crawled back to the ball, and mounted it again. Once he felt secure he invited her attack with a defiant glare. This time she pushed from his right side. He pushed back. She increased her effort. He increased his, at the same time keeping his eyes fixed on those stairs, determined not to allow his head to raise up. But soon, too soon, he thought, the ball seemed to roll from under him and he fell to the mat again.

Before she could say a word, he called out, "Again!"

So it went for more than half an hour. Bud sitting on that ball, Marcy pushing from either side, from the back and then from the front. Each time she dislodged him and he ended up on the mat.

The last time he was breathless and his sweatsuit was black with his perspiration.

She started to kneel to help him up but he said, "Never mind!"

He lifted himself to his knees, made his way to his wheelchair, and climbed in.

As he started to wheel himself toward the door, Marcy called after him, "Bud! For a first drill this has been pretty good!"

But the look in his eyes flashed the message, *Don't baby me. I don't want to be babied. Or lied to.*

As she watched him wheel himself down the corridor back to his room, she asked herself, *Have I been too tough on him? Driven him too hard? Was it that phone call from his dad? Or am I becoming too involved in this case? Is my judgment being affected? Is that why I rushed him too fast? If Bud weren't so dependent on me I'd resign this case. No, no, I wouldn't. This is now a personal challenge for me, too. And I am not backing off.*

At four o'clock, when she had finished with her other patients, Marcy Ethridge returned to Room 302. Bud was not there. His wheelchair was not there. She went out to the nurses' station. One nurse had seen him on his way to Rehab.

Marcy hurried down the corridor. The mood Bud was in when she left him this morning, there was no telling what foolish thing he might do. The wrong activity could be counterproductive, if not dangerous. Falling, even on a mat, could result in injury.

She did not find him in Rehab. She went searching in the smaller rooms. She found him in the same room they had worked in this morning. She peered through the small glass triangle in the door.

She saw him. Wheelchair to one side, he was climbing back on the huge ball. From the damp condition of his sweatshirt he had been at this for quite some time. He sat astride the ball and began to rock back and forth, seeing how far he could extend his weight before falling off. He hit the mat, seemed to be more determined because of his failure, and started all over again, this time rocking back and forth until he fell backward to the mat.

She noted one thing about him—he was keeping his head level, his eyes fixed. But he was overdoing. She had to put a stop to that. She opened the door.

"Bud . . ."

He looked up from the floor. Her presence spurred him to brush aside exhaustion and challenge. "Try me! Now, try me!"

"Bud, you're exhausted . . ." she tried to point out.

But he insisted, "Try me!"

"Okay," she agreed.

He climbed back onto the ball, set himself, fixed his eyes on the step stairs. He was ready.

She started to push from his left side. He pushed back. She increased her pressure. He increased his resistance. But eventually, as was inevitable, he rolled off the ball and onto the mat.

He lay there breathing hard, but worse, feeling that he had failed.

Marcy knelt down beside him, "Better, Bud. Tired as you are, it *was* better."

"No . . . not till I can stay there no matter what you do," he protested.

"We'll work at it, Bud, every day. We'll work at it," she encouraged. "But I had another exercise planned for this afternoon."

"Another . . ."

"This won't take the same kind of effort. But it's just as necessary."

"You're not just . . ." Bud started to question.

She anticipated him, "No, Bud, I'm not saying this to cover up what happened. But think back to this morning. When you were hung up on the parallel bars and your legs were wobbling out of control."

He nodded. That feeling of weakness had stayed with him.

"We are going to work on that. Right now. Get back in that chair."

He climbed back up into his chair. Once he was seated, Marcy rolled the blue and white soccer ball over to him.

"Raise your footrests, Bud."

Once he had, she rolled the ball between his feet.

"Place your right foot on this," she ordered. "Roll this ball around, back and forth, in all directions, without losing control of it."

He stared down at the ball, glared at her, expressing his disdain for an exercise so simple.

"Go on. Try it," she ordered.

He raised his right foot, carefully planted it on the ball, started to roll it back and forth. He lost control of his foot and of the ball and it rolled out of his reach.

She brought the ball back. "Do it again," she ordered.

What he had considered so simple turned out to demand far more control and skill than he imagined. But he could see the purpose of it. To regain control of his legs.

He applied himself more diligently this time. But again the ball escaped him.

Eight times he tried, eight times he failed. But the ninth time that Marcy placed that ball between his feet he was able to control it with his right foot. He actually began to enjoy the exercise, finally smiling at her. Until he lost concentration and the ball eluded him again.

They both laughed, enjoying his embarrassment.

"We will do that every day for days," Marcy promised. "Until we get it right."

As she watched him start down the corridor, she felt, *Today has been a tough day, but a good one. Maybe, just maybe this is going to work.* It was the first time she had dared to be so optimistic. But time, she would need time, much time, if this were to work.

A distressed, tense Lily Young sat in the office of Dr. Phyllis Curtis, nervously playing with the plain gold wedding band on her left hand.

"You understand, Doctor, I'm not complaining. I think that Marcia Ethridge has done wonders with Bud. But lately, the last few weeks, something's happened to him."

"Exactly what's 'happened,' Mrs. Young?"

"Well, she's got him doing things . . . *overdoing*. For instance, the last few days, during all the time I visited he's been working with that ball. Just rolling it around, rolling it around with his right foot, then with his left . . . all through my conversation, that's all he does . . . like he's a man possessed."

"It's an exercise, Mrs. Young. To help him regain control of his legs. In order to stand, eventually to walk, the patient must be able to control his ankles, knees, hips, all working in unison. So they can bear his weight, which is the key to standing and walking," Dr. Curtis explained.

"But she's got him thinking he actually might walk again."

"What's wrong with that?" Dr. Curtis asked.

"There's nothing wrong with *wanting* to walk . . . but to get him thinking that he *will* walk again . . . that's something else. Because if it doesn't happen . . . and so far there's no sign that it will . . . I'm afraid of what it will do to him."

"What it'll 'do to him'?"

"Doctor, you don't know my son. I do. He's the most determined young man you'll ever meet. Has been since he was just a kid. When he sets a goal for himself he makes it."

"That's good, isn't it?"

"Not in this case. Not when Marcy and you, yourself, said he's a wheelchair case."

"He refuses to accept that and he's willing to work on it. I wish more of our patients showed such determination. One of our problems is that exercise is so repetitious and boring many patients just give up. I think you should be encouraged that he keeps trying," the doctor advised.

"And what happens, Doctor, when he fails?" Lily asked. "He's never before failed at anything he's worked on this hard. What's it going to do to him then?"

"He'd be no worse off than before," the doctor replied. "He's adapted well to his wheelchair, uses it very skillfully."

"But his spirit . . . it will crush his spirit. I have these terrible visions of his turning into a bitter young man who has no ambition to go on, no desire for life. So unless you can promise me that he has a chance, a very good chance, of walking, I want you to put a stop to this."

"I can't make such a promise. No responsible doctor or therapist could. But I'll talk to Marcy."

Dr. Curtis had reviewed the entire case history of patient *Young, Willard, Jr.* from the night he had been admitted to the hospital, through surgery, succeeding treatments and tests, including his lengthy coma, and all reports on his progress through physical and cognitive skills therapy.

There was also appended to his file a note from the Accounting Office which she chose to disregard for the moment.

With the file still before her she summoned Marcy Ethridge to her office.

The doctor quickly summed up the pertinent medical and

therapeutic facts in the Young file, and stated Lily Young's concerns before she asked, "Marcy, in view of his case history and your experience with similar cases, can you honestly tell me that Bud Young has a good—or even a reasonable—chance to walk on his own again?"

"Doctor, I admit that if you fed all this material into a computer the answer would come back, no, he cannot walk."

"Then how can you justify driving him the way you do?"

"I'm not driving him. He's driving himself," Marcy replied.

"Don't you think it's your job to reconcile him to the facts and help him to accept them?"

"Doctor, when I was a little girl we had a teacher in school who wanted to inspire us to work hard, to aspire and to achieve . . . we were a class of black children . . . so she posted a sign on the bulletin board where we could see it every day.

"And the sign said, 'According to the laws of aerodynamics the bee, being fat and round, cannot fly. But the bee, not knowing that, continues to fly.' I know what it did for me, and for most of us. We just kept on trying. And a lot of us made it."

"The point, Marcy?"

"As long as Bud Young, not knowing what is in this file, is determined to walk, I am going to help him."

Spoken softly, but with grim determination, it was as close to insubordination as Marcy Ethridge had ever come.

"Marcy, may I point out to you that medically speaking I can discharge Bud Young today?"

"Yes, I realize that. But I am asking you to withhold judgment. Give him a chance. I promise you the minute I think he can't make it I'll tell you. But until then . . ."

"Marcy," Curtis interrupted, "I'm not in position to make deals. Not with this staring me in the face."

She handed across the desk a single official-looking letter. Marcy scanned it, then looked up at Curtis.

"Yes, Marcy, from Mr. Young's medical plan. They don't like the idea of Bud staying in this hospital any longer than absolutely necessary. He's been here six months. Admitted on January first. It is now June twenty-sixth."

"I can't worry about medical plans," Marcy said.

Curtis interrupted, "Marcy! Mrs. Young was in this morning. She's afraid."

"Afraid of what? That he's overworking? Sixteen years old. Aside from his residual neurological deficits he's in very good physical shape."

"She's afraid of what it will do to him if he fails. What it'll do to his spirit, his future."

"She said that? I never detected anything but determination in him. He feels such an obligation to bring his family together again."

"A mother knows her own son," Curtis pointed out.

"Of course," Marcy admitted. "Still . . ."

Before Marcy could continue to plead Bud's cause, Dr. Curtis ruled, "Two more weeks, Marcy. Then I must discharge him to outpatient status. Prepare him."

"Only two more weeks?"

"Two weeks," Curtis stated flatly.

Marcy Ethridge left Dr. Curtis's office, started down the corridor thinking, *Two weeks . . . only two weeks . . . even working every day that's only fourteen days, twenty-eight sessions. Instead of getting him to slow down I have to work him even more and accelerate his routines. Get him up on his feet. Faster than I planned. But too fast can lead to a setback and destroy all the good work he's done so far.*

Two weeks . . . two weeks.

When she joined Bud in the small Rehab room she found him working the soccer ball with considerable skill. As soon as she appeared, he switched from using his left foot to his right to indicate his skill with what had been his weaker leg and foot.

Showing off, she thought, *he's showing off. And so he should. He's mastered that exercise. But we've no time for showing off now.*

"Very good, young man. But that's only the beginning. It's going to take a lot more than that."

She went to the small locker in the corner and rooted around, coming up with a smaller ball, this one a soft ball about the size of a grapefruit. She threw it to him. He caught it and bounced it in his hand.

"Go on. On the floor. Roll it around. Let's see how good you really are," she challenged.

Bud dropped the ball to the floor, lifted his right foot to place it atop the ball. He started to roll it back and forth and around and around. It proved to be more difficult than he had expected. He felt as if he were starting all over again.

He glared at her. She fixed him with her own stare that commanded he continue. His legs began to ache, his feet seemed lead heavy. But he persevered.

She hoped that in her necessary haste she had not discouraged him.

When he had gained a semblance of control over the smaller ball, she ordered him to sit on the big ball again. He considered it a reprieve. This was an exercise he had mastered during his time working with her and working on his own. He had begun to feel at home and in control there.

He wheeled himself over to the big ball, used his strong arms and back muscles to slip out of the chair and onto the big ball.

"Okay, let's go!" he defied.

Marcy worked him from side to side, back and forth. He resisted and this time she could not dislodge him. He kept his eyes fixed on the spot on the wall he had used as his focal point to keep his head from gradually turning upward, depriving him of his equilibrium.

He was feeling triumphant and vindicated when the exercise was over. Until Marcy said, "Now. Eyes closed."

He turned to look back at her.

"Eyes closed," she repeated. "You haven't regained your equilibrium until you can maintain it with your eyes closed. So, let's go!"

Though he resented this sudden change in routine, he closed his eyes, sat there, and realized that it indeed made a difference. A great difference. Suddenly he felt removed from the world around him. The space around him. But after a time he felt he had adjusted to it. Until Marcy began pushing from the side. He tried to resist but slipped off. He climbed back on, determined to resist her. A number of times she pushed, each time he eventually fell off. Each time he climbed up more determined than ever, since he sensed something about Marcy that was different today.

They had worked on the exercise table. Bud straining harder than ever. Marcy pushing harder than before. When they finished, they were both sweating freely.

As Bud lay there breathing hard, dark areas of sweat across his chest and under his armpits, black damp hair pasted to his forehead, he said, "Marcy . . ."

"Yes, Bud?"

"What's wrong?"

"Wrong? Nothing. You've done terrific work today."

"Not me. You," Bud said softly. "Ezra? He sick or something?"

"No, he's fine. Right this minute he's down in day care. He loves it there. Sometimes when I come to pick him up at the end of the day he wants to stay on."

"Then what's wrong?" Bud persisted.

"What's wrong with what?"

"You. You're different today," he pointed out.

"I warned you I wasn't going to go easy with you. The tougher I am, the better it is for you."

"Marcy, you've never lied to me before . . ." Bud said softly.

"Lied to you . . . you think I've lied to you? I told you from the start there are no guarantees that you'd walk."

"I know. But today something *is* wrong. I can see it in your eyes. I can hear it. It's like a secret you're keeping from me."

Preferring to keep Dr. Curtis's ultimatum from him, she hesitated before responding.

"Okay," he said. "Don't tell me. I know. You've given up. You don't think I can make it. Be honest with me," he pleaded.

"Bud," she confessed, "we have two weeks . . . just two weeks. After that, Dr. Curtis will discharge you in a wheelchair."

He was stunned and silent for a time before he pondered softly, "Two weeks . . . is that all . . . two weeks? Marcy, can we . . . ?"

She avoided answering by saying, "Enough talk. Back to work."

She won't lie to me, but she didn't answer me either, Bud realized. *Has she given up? I've got to do something today to change her mind.*

He worked his way to the edge of the table, eased his legs over the side so his feet hung inches from the floor. Marcy took her usual kneeling position before him. She planted her hands against his shoulders.

He pressed against her hands with all his strength. She remained planted in her kneeling position.

"Once more," she insisted.

He pushed harder.

"More!" she insisted.

He tried harder, breathing more deeply.

"Harder," she persisted. "Harder! Two weeks, Bud, two weeks. Harder. Push harder."

He pressed forward with even greater effort and strength. Slowly, bit by bit, he pushed Marcy back from her kneeling position.

"Ah, that's better. Now we're making progress," she said with a finality that indicated the exercise was over.

Instead of relaxing, Bud said, "I want . . . I want to stand up."

"Bud, you've done enough for one day. More than enough."

"I want to stand up. I feel I can do it. I want to try. Please, Marcy?"

She considered his request, his insistence, realizing that on the heels of his accomplishments today his confidence exceeded his abilities. But he was so eager, the look in his eyes so importunate, she decided to risk it.

"Okay," she finally agreed.

She started across Rehab to roll a three-sided walker over to the table.

"Now, Bud, rock back and forth a little. Build up a momentum. Get a good grip on the top rail of this walker. Then get it all together and get up. Remember, ankles, knees, hips, all in control, all working together. Now, try!"

He reached out, felt the cold aluminum of the top rail, gripped it. He rocked back and forth slowly, more to energize his will than his legs. When he felt in control, and ready, he started to lift himself from the table.

Marcy watched, straining with him.

He felt his feet on the floor. Felt his body start forward and lift off the table. Marcy watched with growing hope.

Until his feet escaped his control, his hands relinquished their grip. He slumped forward, out of control, hanging over the walker as he called out, "Marcy!"

She rushed to his side to embrace him and assist him back onto the table, where he lay panting and weeping.

Marcy realized, *It was a mistake to have let him try so soon. He needs much more control over his legs.*

She would have to find a way.

Meantime, he whispered, "Two weeks . . . two weeks . . ."

At the end of her day, Marcy Ethridge picked up her son, Ezra, at the hospital's day care center. He ran to greet her. He threw his arms around her. He showed her the little basket he had made, of red, white, and blue papers pasted together to help at the Fourth of July picnic. It was a hand-skill activity that also allowed the teacher to include an explanation of the holiday and its meaning.

"We goin'?" five-year-old Ezra asked.

"Going?" Marcy pronounced meticulously.

"Picnic. We goin-g on a picnic?"

"If you want, honey," she promised, but her mind was elsewhere. She was thinking, *Two weeks, two weeks. I shouldn't have let him fail again today. I must admit there was a moment there when I thought he would get up on his feet. Would be ready to walk. He seemed on the verge. Just a little bit more . . . just a little bit more.*

"Ice cream, Mama?"

"What?" she asked, taken by surprise.

"Got to have ice cream."

"We have ice cream in the freezer at home, darling."

"The picnic . . . ice cream for the picnic," her little son insisted as they got into her car.

"Before that," Marcy said, "we have to pick up some things for supper tonight."

She was wheeling the shopping cart down the vegetable aisle, picking up the makings of a good healthy salad, when she realized that Ezra had wandered off. She turned to look for him, calling, "Ezra! Ezra . . . where in the world . . . ?"

She turned the cart around quickly and, with the panic of parents in these dangerous times, she went frantically searching for him. Back up the vegetable aisle she sped, calling, "Ezra! Ez!"

She looked down the condiments-and-salad-dressing aisle. But no sign of little Ezra.

"Ezra!" she called again, even more anxious now.

As she passed the canned-fruits-and-juices aisle without any sign of him, she began to rebuke herself for having been so distracted with professional matters as to put her son at risk.

An elderly man with a sparsely loaded cart signaled to her, asking, "Lady, you looking for a cute little boy who's going on a picnic?"

"Picnic? How did you know?" Marcy asked.

"He invited me. And darn near everyone else at the ice cream case. He's got his nose pressed up against that glass so hard I thought he was frozen there," the old man said. "Please, please, take him on that picnic. I never saw a kid with his heart so set."

"Oh, he'll go on that picnic. But first, that young man is going to get a lesson in obedience."

Now that she was reassured she could afford to be angry.

She found Ezra at the ice cream section. He was already pointing to the flavor he wanted. She tossed it into her cart, saying, "Ezra Ethridge, put your hands on the handle of this cart!" Once he complied, she said, "And *keep* them there until we get to the checkout counter! Understand?"

His ice cream needs attended to, he could afford to be obedient. "Yes, ma'am,"

He grasped the handle of the shopping cart with both hands. Dutifully he clung to it as ordered.

Marcy resumed her shopping, picking up a carton here, a jar there. She would dart away to select a certain food, allowing little Ezra to push the cart, sometimes alongside her, sometimes ahead of her. She had piled up quite a quantity of food, half-gallon-size skimmed milk, large orange juice, two. Ezra drank juice instead of water, though she wished he didn't.

The cart was loaded now with enough to see them through the week and the holiday beyond. With Ezra still clutching the handle, pushing the cart along, Marcy remembered something. Relish for the burgers. She retraced her steps along the aisle, picked up a jar, started back to rejoin Ezra.

She looked down the aisle to see him struggling with the overloaded cart, now so heavy he could hardly budge it. But there was something about the movement of his young body that intrigued her. She watched as he kept thrusting his little body forward against the cart. Until finally it moved. But once it moved it seemed to carry him along with it.

She could not tell if he pushed the cart or the cart pulled him. Or was it all one integrated motion, so fluid that it seemed natural and easy.

The image troubled her all night. Twice she dreamed about it.

40

"Lady, if you will excuse the expression, we are in the business of selling *groceries,* not shopping carts!" the harried manager of the supermarket exclaimed, then shouted over Marcy's head, "Angelo! The beer display! The Fourth of July beer display!"

"Look, mister, if you will excuse the expression," Marcy replied in kind, "I do not want to *buy* a shopping cart. I want to borrow it."

"Borrow? I have people stealing carts every day and when we catch them they say they're only borrowing it. Sorry. No!"

He was about to turn away when Marcy seized him by the lapels of his maroon manager's jacket. She held him long enough to say, "I need that cart. I need it at Mercy Hospital. For therapy. All I want to know is how much of a deposit you require for me to borrow it!"

"Therapy? Lady . . . are you crazy?" the man asked.

"Maybe. But that does not change things. Deposit. How much?"

"How much . . . How . . . twenty dollars, how's that?"

Marcia dug into her purse, drew out two ten-dollar bills. Handing them to the man, she wheeled the cart toward the exit.

He called after her, "Well, at least you didn't steal it!"

By that time the automatic door slid open and Marcy Ethridge was on her way.

Bud Young was brushing the sweat back from his forehead. His gray sweatshirt exhibited its familiar dark areas in the usual places. He had to admit to himself that he was glad this morning's therapy was over. Marcy had driven him even harder today than before. She seemed almost more determined than he was.

He was breathing easily, enjoying the privilege of just sitting on the edge of the table watching other patients in other areas of the room beginning to go through the early training he had already mastered.

Old women and men, stroke victims, young women and men, victims of accidents of one kind or another, even a ten-year-old girl who had been thrown from a horse, all working under the care and instruction of their therapists.

His view of the scene was interrupted when, through the far door, appeared a shopping cart with Marcy right behind pushing it. His curiosity increased when it became obvious that she was heading the anomalous if familiar vehicle in his direction.

"This, Bud, is a shopping cart," she announced.

"I know that," he replied. "I identified a picture of one along with a thousand other things during my early therapy."

"Good!" Marcy announced, as she lined up the cart so the handlebar faced him. "Now, Bud, we are going to try something different. Instead of working with a walker, we are going to use this. *You* are going to use this. Sit up!"

He complied.

"Reach out!"

Bud extended both his arms. Wrapped his hands around the handle of the cart. He was poised and ready.

"Now, Bud, before you move. Think. The objective is to start up and forward so that you rise pushing the cart. Understand?"

"Up, forward, push," Bud repeated. He nodded. He rehearsed the procedure in his mind.

"Now, Bud! Now!"

In a single determined effort he started up and forward. He had reached a standing position and was beginning to feel great exhilaration when suddenly he lost control of his legs. At the same time his hands lost their grip. Marcy intervened before he could fall to the floor.

She held him tightly, edging him back to the exercise table, where he was relieved to relax once more into his sitting position.

He looked up at her. He said nothing. But in his eyes was a look of failure and also of rebuke.

What had seemed so natural and promising to Marcy in the early hours of the morning when she first awoke had turned into another disappointment.

Two things were apparent to her now. Even if her plan for the cart were to succeed, he still needed more work for better control of his legs. Also there was something wrong, something lacking in her cart strategy.

"Okay, Bud, that's it for this morning. We work out again this afternoon," she promised.

She wheeled up his chair and locked it in place. He worked his way into it. Unlocked the chair. As he turned to propel himself toward the door, Marcy saw the look of discouragement in his eyes.

The rest of the morning, as she worked with her other patients, her failure with Bud continued to plague her. She kept analyzing her past experience for some hint as to how to accelerate his therapy to a successful conclusion within the time limit set by Dr. Curtis.

Her morning schedule of patients completed, Marcy started for the day care facility. No matter the press or urgency of her daily routine, she always set aside her lunch hour as a time for Ezra. Together, while they ate lunch she reviewed with him the events of his morning. What he had been taught, the games he had played, the songs he had sung.

In that way, she had an hour with her son, shared in his enjoyment, his education. At the same time she was able to supervise his diet, making sure that his sweet tooth was balanced by a goodly share of vegetables and carbohydrates.

Lunch was over. The director of day care announced, "Rest hour!"

In the late afternoon during his mother's visit Bud continued to practice while they conversed. Whenever the soft ball escaped too far from him Lily would recapture it, without interrupting their conversation.

At one point he was rotating the ball slowly, with what he considered good control, when he said, "He called again."

"I know," Lily said. "He calls home almost every day. Talks to Gwen. He's given up talking to me."

"He doesn't talk to me either. Marcy. He talks to Marcy," Bud said. "I guess me in a wheelchair is still too much for him."

"Don't blame him, Bud. Just feel sorry for him. Every dream he didn't fulfill in his own life he found in you. He lived his whole life in you. If you're confined to a wheelchair, so is he." Lily paused to find the proper words before she asked, "What . . . what does Marcy say . . . about . . . about how it's going?"

"She's still not making any promises. And we're down to days now. Days."

He continued to work on the ball, using first his right leg, then his left. When his supper was brought in, Lily left. She knew by now that her son did not like to be watched while he ate. For even at this stage in his recovery he sometimes lost control of his fork or his spoon.

Two days had elapsed. Two days during which Bud had practiced with that smaller ball until both his legs ached when he lay in bed. At night he also wondered what would have happened if he had not failed so badly in that experiment with the shopping cart. If he had a second chance . . . He would ask Marcy in the morning.

The following morning during their time in Rehab for their usual workout, in which Marcy had him reaching even farther than before with both his arms and his legs, he asked, "That cart . . . I would . . . like to try that . . . again."

"We'll see," Marcy said in a noncommittal way.

But he noticed that when she studied him working with the

ball she was more intense than before. He sensed the challenge. He determined to meet it. He worked the ball with his left foot. Back and forth, round and round. A number of times. Never losing control of the ball. Then he switched to his right foot. This was more difficult. It took greater concentration, more control. Back and forth, round and round he worked the ball. Once he almost lost control but before it could elude him he recaptured it.

He had completed the exercise without a fault.

"Now," Marcy said. "Now, I think we're ready for another try."

She was gone. Some minutes later she was back with the shopping cart. She lined it up so that the handlebar faced him. He extended his arms, his fingers wrapped around the bar. He mobilized his strength, summoned up the muscles of his back, his stomach, his biceps, his shoulders. He was ready for the most important effort of his life.

When he felt secure, he started to rise, feet planted on the floor. Body moving forward, he pushed the cart. The cart eased forward but did not pull him with it, causing him to falter, lose his grip and fall back onto the table.

Marcy watched, as disappointed as Bud. The cart had not done for him what it had done for Ezra that evening in the supermarket. Bud's control of his legs proved that the exercise with the soft ball had done its work. But when he pushed the cart it did not respond, nor did he, in the way she had expected. Getting up, pushing the cart, the cart pulling him forward to walk should have had that same smooth continuous fluid movement that occurred with Ezra.

The last half of her plan had failed. Why?

"We'll try again this afternoon, Bud," she said, hoping that she had been able to conceal her disappointment from him. For she knew how deeply he had suffered this failure.

It was during lunch while she was listening to Ezra's report of his morning activities that she suddenly stared at him in such a way as to make him look up and ask, "Mommy? I do somethin'?"

"No, honey, no, you didn't do anything wrong. But I think maybe Mommy did."

Throughout her afternoon session with Bud, Marcy Ethridge kept repeating to herself, *When Ezra started that cart and it continued to pull him, it was loaded. Full. Could it be the weight that did it? Why not? We use weights in therapy all the time. Why not with that shopping cart?*

Bud had finished his exercises on the big ball. His days of diligent work had paid off. His equilibrium now was infinitely better than it had been.

Marcy slipped out, leaving Bud sitting on the edge of the exercise table. She reappeared, pushing the shopping cart.

Bud sat up more erectly. He would have his second chance. But his enthusiasm for the challenge was suddenly deflated. He saw that Marcy had placed a stack of large telephone books in the cart.

He had to ask himself, now that his days here at the hospital had about run out was this her subtle way of telling him she had decided that he couldn't make it, could never stand on his own? Never walk on his own? Had she piled up the odds against him so that he would accept failure and be content to leave in this wheelchair?

Silently he defied her. Dared her.

Once she had lined up the loaded cart for him to reach, she stepped back and ordered, "Bud! Hands on that bar. Up on your feet and push. All in one move! I know it's heavy. But give it everything you've got. So get ready. Now, push!!"

He glared at her. She glared back. He gathered his strength, summoned up the results of all the months of grueling training he had endured. He reached out, wrapped his hands around the handlebar. In a determined effort he rose, at the same instant pushing the heavy cart forward. Once it began to move, as if taking on a life of its own, the cart continued. And moving, pulled Bud along with it in that continuous and fluid movement Marcy hoped for.

Bud was on his feet. He was standing.

"Keep going, Bud, keep going!" Marcy encouraged.

He glanced at her. She urged him on with a smile. He nodded. Gripping the handlebar even more tightly, he began to slide his feet along the floor. Left foot, right foot, left foot. He pushing the cart, it pulling him along, slowly they moved forward together. They were like a team.

He pushed on. He had gone nine steps in all. He stopped to catch his breath. Refreshed, enthused, he started again, sliding right foot, left foot, right foot, left foot . . .

He was walking! Far from the way he used to. But on his own two feet.

"Walk . . ." he tried to call out. But in his excitement he had lost control of the speech skills he had relearned. As Marcy had taught him to do, he paused, thought carefully what he wanted to say, then for everyone in Rehab to hear, he called out, "Walking! I . . . am . . . walking!"

He smiled at Marcy, and was still smiling when tears started down his cheeks.

But by that time Marcy's eyes were so misted over that she could not see.

It was early evening. Bud Young, exhausted but happy, sat in his wheelchair staring out the window at the parking lot below. Visitors were arriving. Nurses, orderlies, doctors going off duty were leaving. For the first time he felt a connection with the world outside. Wanted to be part of that world. He had not permitted himself to think of it until today. Until this afternoon when he took those first uncertain sliding steps.

He heard a knock on his open door.

"Yeah?" he called back.

"Bud . . ."

It was Marcy's voice. She entered behind him, leaned forward so they were cheek to cheek.

"It's been a great day," she said, "a breakthrough day. But only the beginning. We've got a long way yet to go. You'll have to master the three-step stairs. Tomorrow we start on that."

"But I can walk. I just proved that," Bud protested.

"Bud, listen to me," Marcy said gently but purposefully. "We can't let you leave here until I can certify you as functionally ambulatory. And I can't do that until you prove that you can climb a whole flight of stairs. On your own. And that you can walk without help on terrain far less easy and flat than the floor of Rehab."

"A whole flight of stairs . . ." he considered as if he were being asked to climb a mountain. "And walk on terrain not flat . . ."

As if victory had been stolen from him at the last instant, he cried out, "Damn it, Marcy, every time you tell me I've got to learn to do something I do it! And every time you always come up with another exercise! Another challenge! When will it finally happen, Marcy, when?"

She could understand his frustration, his anger. But she could not allow sympathy to interfere with therapy.

Very firmly she said, "Tomorrow the three-step exercise."

Two days of practice with the loaded shopping cart and Bud Young had advanced to the point where he could rise, stand, and walk without it.

He still slid his feet along the floor, slowly, and with concentration, but he was walking.

He practiced in Rehab. He practiced along the corridor. He practiced alone in his room. He practiced until his mother was forced to seek Marcy's intervention to make him rest.

"Let him go," Marcy advised. "Fatigue will tell him when to stop. Besides, I want him ready for tomorrow."

Tomorrow had arrived. Bud Young stood before the three-step set of stairs in Rehab. In the middle of the large room, resting on a thick mat, with no supports close by, it was a vastly different challenge from merely walking on a level floor.

Bud studied the steps, looked to Marcy, who deliberately stood far enough away so he could not depend on her. He looked back at the steps, trying to summon up the will to start.

To Marcy, ability was part of the test. But an equal part was courage. To try, to face the risk of failing, of falling, of suffering defeat.

He edged closer. His feet were lined up at the base of the stairs. He was about to lift his left foot but he hesitated. Would Marcy approve if he started with his left foot? He decided to start with his right.

He raised it slowly. Bearing in mind, *Ankles, knees, hips, head level, eyes fixed,* he set his right foot down on the first step. Shifting his weight to it, he raised his left foot until he was standing on the first step. Both feet firmly planted, he had surmounted the first challenge.

He worked his way to the second step. Feeling more secure, he looked to Marcy seeking approval, at the same time raising his right foot to the third step, a bit too quickly and with less caution.

His right foot sought that third step but was uncertain and failed to find it, causing him to waver, then topple to the side before Marcy could reach him. Fortunately the mat was there to ease his fall and prevent any injury.

Marcy was leaning over him, reaching to help him up. He avoided her hand. He raised himself to a sitting position. He rolled over. Using his hands and arms for support he raised himself to his standing position. He paused to rehearse in his mind, *Ankles, knees, hips, eyes, head.* He approached the stairs again.

This time he concentrated on each step, blocking out all other things. He started once more. Right foot . . . up. Left foot . . . up. He was on step one. Following the same tedious process he mounted to step two. Again right foot, left foot and he was on step three atop the apparatus.

He stood there, enjoying the moment. Now he started slowly down the other side. Step three to step two. Step two to step one. Step one back onto the mat.

He had made it. And having made it, he slowly turned around to begin to repeat the procedure. Four times he executed the exercise. The fifth time, from fatigue and overconfidence, his left foot caught the second step instead of landing on it. He fell forward onto the top step and lay there.

But when Marcy came to his side, he protested, "I'm all right. I'm fine. I'm . . . I'm . . . just . . . just let me do it . . . do it on my own. . . ."

Slowly, he lifted himself. He started again.

So he went through his entire morning session. Doggedly, sweating freely, he continued to climb up the three steps on one side, and down on the other. Slowly, with great effort and control, he persisted until finally Marcy had to insist he stop.

Even before the time for his afternoon session he had started down the corridor to Rehab to take command of the stairs before any other patient could reach them. Sliding along, step by step, he deliberately shunned the safety railing along the corridor wall. He insisted on making it on his own.

By the end of the afternoon, sweaty and tired as he was, he confronted Marcy, "Am I ready?"

"Ready?"

"To walk that flight of stairs. To make it across that uneven ground," he said.

"Another day on these steps, until you can do them with your eyes closed," she said.

"I can do that now!" he insisted.

"Don't push it, Bud. You're tired, too tired."

"No, I can. Watch me!"

He turned from her, slowly made his way to the three steps. He looked to her, then closed his eyes. He started to raise his right foot to the first step. He made the first step with both feet but in reaching for the second he lost balance and started to fall backward. Marcy was there to catch him.

"I . . . I can . . . do it. . . . I know I can. . . . " he insisted.

"Tomorrow, Bud . . . tomorrow."

"If I do it tomorrow, then can I do that flight of stairs? That uneven surface?"

"Yes, Bud . . . yes," she finally agreed.

All morning in Room 302 Bud Young practiced walking with his eyes closed. By the time Marcy was ready for him in Rehab, he was ready for her.

Eight times he had climbed those three steps. Eight times descended the other side. Eight times, slowly, deliberately, but without faltering or falling. The ninth time he closed his eyes and started up, first step, second step, third step. Second step, first step, then he felt the mat under his feet. He opened his eyes. He looked to Marcy.

She smiled and nodded.

"Tomorrow?" he called to her.

"Tomorrow," she agreed as she joined him to wipe his face dry. "There's a staircase at the end of the floor that isn't used much. I always have my patients try that one. If you do that, we can drive over to the small square at the end of the street. The lawn there is a good test for uneven surfaces."

"Does it have to be there?" Bud interrupted.

"No. Any lawn will do. Why?"

"I . . . I've been . . . thinking . . ." Bud started to say, then fearing his desire too sentimental he shook his head.

"Bud?" Marcy asked. When he did not respond, she coaxed, "Secrets? From me, Bud? After all this time?"

He half looked away when he said, "Ever since you mentioned a flight of stairs, an uneven surface . . . I've been thinking . . . I would like to try this at the stadium."

"Stadium?" Marcy was totally puzzled.

"The school. There are flights of stairs up to the seats. There's the football field for an uneven surface. It gets pretty chewed up," Bud explained.

"I've never had a patient try that before," Marcy said.

"Please . . . somehow, it would be . . . would mean so much if I could prove it there. . . . "

"I don't see why not," Marcy finally conceded.

Lily Young cornered Marcy Ethridge in her office at the end of the day.

"Marcy, Bud told me. Do you think it's wise . . . out there in the stadium? Where there might be other people to see?"

"To witness his failure, you mean," Marcy pinned the issue down.

"Yes," Lily was forced to admit. "Such a blow could be a terrible setback, could shatter his confidence."

"Lily, your son is more resilient than you know. So stop trying to protect him. If he fails, I want to see how he handles it. That's as much part of his treatment as trying. Right now I'm encouraged that he's willing to take the risk."

The next morning, in place of Bud Young's regular eleven o'clock morning therapy session, a small red car pulled up at the open end of the modest horseshoe-shaped stadium of Central High School.

The door on the passenger side opened. Bud Young, attired in a fresh set of gray sweats, eased out, one cautious leg at a time. Marcy emerged from the driver's side.

They started toward the open area but were taken aback on discovering that, at the other end of the field, the football coach was holding preseason tryouts to select his squad for the fall term. Most of the candidates were members of Bud's championship team.

"That's my team," Bud said softly.

Marcy deliberately refrained from saying a word. The decision must be solely Bud's. For, just as the physical was part of Rehab for CHIs, so also was the cognitive ability to resolve conflict, to make decisions.

Bud stared at the activity down the field. Two quarterback candidates aiming to become his replacement were throwing passes to receivers running downfield. Two pickup teams were running formations from scrimmage under the watchful eye of the coach and his assistant.

"Bud?"

Only a moment of hesitation before he said, "Let's go."

They started along the running track that circled the field. When they reached the flight of stairs climbing the first section of bleachers, Bud stopped.

"Here. I'd like to try it here," he said.

He approached the concrete steps. He studied them. Each step seemed a little higher than the familiar steps in Rehab. Mentally he made the adjustment. He wet his lips, which had gone dry. He stole a quick sideways glance at Marcy. He felt ready.

He rubbed his hands together. Cold. They felt cold for a day in early July. He rubbed them against his thighs. He lifted his right foot. He set it down on the first step. Using it for stability and balance he raised his left foot. He had managed the first step. Relieved, encouraged, he continued. Right foot . . . left foot. Slowly, carefully. Right foot, left foot.

He had climbed the first six steps. He looked up to count. Fourteen rows of seats meant eight more steps. He reached seven, eight, nine, ten. Short of breath, more tired than he had expected, he realized now why it was necessary to prove he could climb a whole flight. He pushed on. Eleven . . . twelve . . . thirteen . . . fourteen.

He was at the top concrete step. He turned to look down. It seemed a far shorter distance than it had felt when he climbed up. But there below was Marcy at the foot of the stairs looking up, a big smile on her encouraging brown face.

Now for the long climb down. Conscious and careful of each movement of each foot, he started. Fourteen, thirteen, twelve. He was about to start down to eleven when he was shaken by a shout from down on the field.

"Bud! Hey, guys! That's Bud!"

Startled, his concentration broken, Bud froze. His right foot down on step eleven, his left still on twelve, he teetered there.

Below, Marcy had to suppress the urge to race up the stairs to try to prevent his fall. She waited. She watched. Behind her a whole squad of forty young players gathered to watch their friend and idol try to make his way down the stairs.

Bud Young looked down into their faces. He saw love there, admiration there, encouragement there. He lowered his left foot to stair eleven. Then slowly, gaining strength and security, he continued.

Step four, step three, step two, step one. He was back on the ground once more.

The entire squad applauded, calling, "Way to go, Bud!" Jody Hines brushed by Marcy intending to embrace Bud but she called out, "Not yet! He's not finished!"

Jody stepped back. Bud faced Marcy, who said, "Across the field, Bud. And I'll be watching."

He crossed the running track onto the turf of the playing field. At once he could feel the difference. He realized why it was important to be able to manage such a surface to be considered ambulatory. Unlike solid wood or concrete, the grass was not only soft to his step, but no two steps felt quite the same. Some sloped slightly. Others had hidden depressions or up-grades.

Meantime the squad broke into two and lined up across the field so that Bud had an escort every slow step of the way. When he reached the other side they broke out in a cheer.

Bud Young turned and waved to Marcy Ethridge on the far side of the field. She waved back, smiling broadly.

Of all his achievements on this field, this was Bud Young's most satisfying.

"And here, Bud, is a new diary, your outpatient diary," Marcy said, handing him the black book. "Each week when you come back for evaluation and for new exercises, I want to find in here not only your experiences but any problems. And I want to see progress in your handwriting. Your sentence structure. Your use of words."

"Yes, ma'am!" Bud replied, in mock military response.

"Don't you 'Yes, ma'am,' me, Bud Young," Marcy said, but could not suppress a smile. "Think you're pretty smart, don't you?"

"Yes, ma'am!"

They were both smiling now.

As she handed him his diary, he asked, "Is this graduation day?"

"In a way," Marcy replied, then turned more sober. "Bud, I think you know now there are certain things you used to do that you can no longer do. Football, baseball—your reactions will be too slow for that. But there are other sports. Golf. Bowling. Walking. Eventually running. You can do all those and learn to do them well. Soon you won't have to be conscious of every step you take. Walking will be easier, more natural.

"Though for a time you will have trouble making decisions. If you're not quick enough to become a trial lawyer, you will be studious enough to become a research scientist. Your purpose from now on is to use the abilities you have to their utmost. God knows you've got enough abilities to make a great and satisfying life. And, we discovered, you've one thing more. The will to do it.

"Your dad once said to me, 'Just tell Bud it's third and long and he'll perform miracles.' I thought that was just a proud father speaking. After your recovery I know what he means."

"Dad . . . yes . . ." Bud said, and saying that, had said a great deal more.

"I can't tell you how to settle that. No one can. Now Mom's waiting to drive you home. See you next week, Bud."

Marcy held out her strong brown hand. As they shook hands he said, "Marcy, this one time . . . may I?"

She was puzzled but for only an instant, then she nodded.

He kissed her on the cheek.

He had walked up the carpeted stairs without needing to rely on the banister. He approached the door of his old room. He looked in, trying to recall if anything had changed since he last saw it seven months ago. It appeared larger than he remembered. Everything seemed to be in place. Neater than when he left it last. That's Mom. Everything in place. His eyes fell on the silver trophy.

He approached it, rubbed his fingers over it. The last time he had held it, it had been perfect. It never would be again. Nor would he. In its present condition it seemed more appropriate to the way things were. He had other victories he could point to now. They may not give trophies for them, but in the end they are the most gratifying.

He started down again. Mom and Gwen were both waiting at the foot of the stairs, eager to respond to his every wish.

"Son, it's been a big day. You must be tired. You should rest a bit before dinner."

"Dinner . . . the first time I won't be eating alone. A family dinner. That'll be a treat."

"But rest now. I'll call you in plenty of time, dear," Lily said.

Bud smiled, "Mom, I'm okay now. I don't need an afternoon nap. In fact, I need to do a little catching up. Call the guys . . ."

He was interrupted by the sound of the phone. Instinctively all three of them started for it. But Bud said, "No. Let me. That'll startle whoever it is."

He reached the hall phone, lifted it. "Bud Young speaking," he said with a grin, which turned to so serious and startled a look that Lily asked, "Bud?"

He explained by saying into the phone, "Yes, Dad. Home. I'm home. And I feel great. Great."

"Bud, I can't tell you what it means to me to hear your voice, and so strong," Pepper said. "Son, is . . . is your mom there? I'd like to talk to her."

Bud held out the phone to Lily. She resisted.

"He sounds . . . sounds . . . fine. Honest," Bud pleaded on his father's behalf.

Lily took the phone, "Pepper . . ."

"Thanks, Lil, for even coming to the phone. Before you say anything I want you to know that I haven't had a drink since that terrible night. I swear. And I haven't missed an A.A. meeting."

"That's good to hear, Pepper, good to hear," Lily replied.

"I've been living like the rest of the world. And I discovered that I like it. I like it, Lil."

She smiled in a way that puzzled Bud, who asked, "Mom? What's he saying?"

"It isn't so much what he's saying, as the way he's saying it." Then she spoke into the phone. "Pepper, if you happen to be free for dinner tonight . . ."

"I'll be there, I'll be there. What time?" he asked anxiously.

"Seven o' clock, Pep."

At precisely seven o' clock the doorbell at the Young household rang. Three times. Three long rings.

To Bud that was a signal. When he was just a little boy Dad used to announce his arrival that way. Three long rings. And Bud would go racing to open the door.

Now he rose from his chair in the living room. Slowly but very steadily he walked to the front door. He opened it to face his father.

"Dad . . ."

"Bud . . . son . . . you're on your feet, you're . . . you're walking on your own . . . walking . . ." There were tears in his eyes. Pepper Young embraced his son. "Welcome home, son, welcome home."

"That goes two ways, Dad, two ways."

The following week Bud Young appeared in the Rehab wing of Mercy Hospital. Diary in hand, he was ready for his first outpatient appointment with therapist Marcia Ethridge.

"Come in, Bud, come in," she invited.

He sat down alongside her desk, handing her his diary. She opened it.

Inscribed on the front page were only four words.

To Marcy, with love

To conceal how touched she was, she reverted to her professional tone and attitude as she said, "Bud Young, I thought I taught you to make rounder fatter O's than these."

"Yes, ma'am!" Bud responded in military fashion.

They both smiled and she turned to the next page.